THE DARK SIDE

The Wild Side - Book 2

M.J. SCOTT

emscott enterprises

 Formatted with Vellum

Praise for M.J. Scott

The Shattered Court
Nominated for Best Paranormal Romance in the 2016
RITA® Awards.

"Scott (the Half-Light City series) opens her Four Arts fantasy
series with the portrait of a young woman who's thrust into
the center of dangerous political machinations... Romance
fans will enjoy the growing relationship between Cameron and
Sophie, but the story's real strength lies in the web of intrigue
Scott creates around her characters."
—*Publishers Weekly*

"Fans of high fantasy and court politics will enjoy The Shattered Court. Sophie is such a great heroine..."
—*RT Book Reviews*

The Forbidden Heir
"This story was packed with action, political intrigue, schem-
ing, and high stakes."
—*Alyssa - Goodreads reviewer*

"This is a marvelous book. The world building is unique and complex. The characters are well developed and likable and there is intrigue for days. If you've read the first book in the series it only gets better in this one."
—*Lissa - Goodreads reviewer*

"'Forbidden Heir' is a great rarity: a sequel that I liked better than the original book."
—*Margaret - Amazon reviewer*

Fire Kin
"Entertaining...Scott's dramatic story will satisfy both fans and new readers."
—*Publishers Weekly*

"This is one urban fantasy series that I will continue to come back to...Fans of authors Christina Henry of the Madeline Black series and Keri Arthur of the Dark Angels series will love the Half-Light City series."
—*Seeing Night Book Reviews*

Iron Kin
"Strong and complex world building, emotionally layered relationships, and enough action to keep me up long past my bedtime. I want to know what's going to happen next to the DuCaines and their chosen partners, and I want to know now."
—*Vampire Book Club*

"Iron Kin was jam-packed with action, juicy politics, and a lot of loose ends left over for the next book to resolve that it's still a good read for series fans."
—*All Things Urban Fantasy*

"Scott's writing is rather superb."

Blood Kin

"Not only was this book just as entertaining and immensely readable as Shadow Kin—it sang in harmony with it and spun its own story all the while continuing the grander symphony that is slowly becoming the Half-Light City story. . . . Smart, funny, dangerous, addictive, and seductive in its languorous sexuality, I can think of no better book to recommend to anyone to read this summer. I loved every single page except the last one, and that's only because it meant the story was done. For now, at least."

—*seattlepi.com*

"Blood Kin was one of those books that I really didn't want to put down, as it hit all of my buttons for an entertaining story. It had the intrigue and danger of a spy novel, intense action scenes, and a romance that evolved organically over the course of the story. . . . Whether this is your first visit to Half-Light City or you're already a fan, Blood Kin expertly weaves the events from Shadow Kin throughout this sequel in a way that entices new readers without boring old ones. I am really looking forward to continuing this enthralling ride."

—*All Things Urban Fantasy*

"Blood Kin had everything I love about urban fantasies: kick-butt action, fantastic characters, romance that makes the heart beat fast, and a plot that was fast-paced all the way through. Even more so the villains are meaner, stronger, and downright fantastic—I never knew what they were going to do next. You don't want to miss out on this series."

—*Seeing Night Book Reviews*

"An exciting thriller . . . fast-paced and well written."
—*Genre Go Round Reviews*

Shadow Kin

"M. J. Scott's Shadow Kin is a steampunky romantic fantasy with vampires that doesn't miss its mark."
—*#1 New York Times bestselling author Patricia Briggs*

"Shadow Kin is an entertaining novel. Lily and Simon are sympathetic characters who feel the weight of past actions and secrets as they respond to their attraction for each other."
—*New York Times bestselling author Anne Bishop*

"M. J. Scott weaves a fantastic tale of love, betrayal, hope, and sacrifice against a world broken by darkness and light, where the only chance for survival rests within the strength of a woman made of shadow and the faith of a man made of light."
—*National bestselling author Devon Monk*

"Had me hooked from the very first page."
—*New York Times bestselling author Keri Arthur*

"Exciting and rife with political intrigue and magic, Shadow Kin is hard to put down right from the start. Magic, faeries, vampires, werewolves, and Templar knights all come together to create an intriguing story with a unique take on all these fantasy tropes. . . . The lore and history of Scott's world is well fleshed out and the action scenes are exhilarating and fast."
—*Romantic Times*

For everyone who occasionally feels the urge to howl at the moon.

Chapter 1

"EVER HEARD the phrase 'out of the frying pan into the fire'?" Dan muttered as we stared at the huge, black-mirrored doors.

"You know, that's what I love about you, always the optimist," I said, trying to convince myself there was no reason for my reflection to look so nervous. Beyond the doors subterranean bass pounded, vibrating through my chest like a warning. A warning I had to ignore.

"We can still leave," Dan said, sounding calm but looking grim.

"This will get me off the hook with Lord Marco," I reminded him. And, frankly, repaying a debt to the oldest vampire in Seattle was the only reason good enough to get me to walk through these particular doors. Into Maelstrom—darkest of the city's dark clubs—and, even worse, into a meeting with Lord Esteban, the vamp who owned the place.

Dan frowned, rubbing the fading scar on his right wrist. "It will get you off one hook."

Like I needed the reminder that this favor wasn't all I owed Lord Marco. After all, Dan and I had been fighting about my other debt for six weeks now. The fact that I owed blood to an Old One wasn't exactly easy to forget. Talk about making a deal with the devil.

Though I'd done it to save Dan's life. And some would argue that, for an Old One, and the ruler of Seattle's vampires, Marco was hardly devilish. From what I'd seen of him, he ruled more with the velvet glove and less with the iron fist. But velvet glove or not, I was certain that welching on a debt to him would be a bad idea.

So I was trying to tough it out even though Marco was sending me into the lion's den, so to speak. I still hadn't figured out why he'd asked me to assist Lord Esteban—probably his biggest rival for power—to clear my debt. Strange are the ways of vampires.

I shot Dan a reassuring smile. "Let's focus on right now, huh? We see what Lord Esteban's problem is. It can't be that bad. Marco can't ask me to do something that could hurt me. That was part of our agreement."

I sounded certain. I doubted Dan would buy it but I had to at least try to sound more optimistic than I felt. I tugged at the leather halter I wore, trying to make the pointed edges meet the waist of the matching pants.

It didn't work. It hadn't worked any of the hundred or so times I tried to do the same thing since my assistant, Jase, had kitted me out in the latest in dark club chic. Which equated to sleek black leather and not that much of it.

I'd wanted to wear body armor.

Jase said that'd only flag me as fresh meat. In a dark club, that could have an all too literal meaning.

Hence the dominatrix Barbie look I was sporting. Leather, chains, too much black eyeliner, and wine-red lipstick. Not me at all. Clients tend to like their accountants to wear suits, not spikes and skin. And, speaking as their accountant, I prefer it too.

Dan had been subjected to Jase's fashion direction as well. But I liked *his* outfit. Black leather pants hugged his long legs, outlining every hard-earned muscle, and a thin black T-shirt that was exactly the right degree of tight did the same for his chest.

I let all that hard male flesh distract me from Esteban for a moment and stepped a little closer, breathing in his scent. "You know, I think you should keep these clothes."

One side of his mouth lifted. "Really? What did you have in mind?"

"How about I tell you later?" I pressed closer to him, felt his heart speed up and saw the smile widen, just a fraction. I was happy to see the smile, even if it was only half an expression. Things between us were kind of strained. Six weeks ago, I'd kind of proposed. And he'd kind of accepted. But that was before he'd found out about Marco and the deals I'd made.

Before we'd had the mother of all arguments.

"You should tell me now," Dan said, smile still lingering. I wished it would stay in place just a bit longer. Since the argument we'd been circling each other warily. He hadn't produced a ring and there'd been no talk of weddings, despite some not so subtle hints from our pack's Alphas. What there had been were some spectacular fights and some even more spectacular make-up sex.

There hadn't been many smiles. There had been lots of me feeling like I was walking on eggshells and failing miserably to not crush them. Especially since Marco had called in his favor two nights ago.

I was hoping getting at least one of my debts settled might ease things between us. Get us moving forward again. Maybe give me back some semblance of a normal life.

"More fun in private," I said.

Dan's smile disappeared. His head turned back to the door. "Private? Ash, inside those doors most people wouldn't blink an eye if we did it in the middle of the dance floor." His voice gave no hint of the growling rumble it held when he was happy. Or horny.

Talk about a mood killer. I stepped back, as the reality of where we were returned. A dark club. Where the crowd played rough in more than one sense of the word.

BDSM, vampires feeding on willing—and maybe not so willing—victims and other things I didn't really want to know about. And that was just the public areas.

The rumors of what went on in the private rooms were nasty. Though they were just rumors. No one had ever successfully prosecuted an owner of a dark club.

And Lord Esteban was the biggest, baddest owner of them all.

Maybe Dan was right. Maybe I should just go back to Marco and tell him no deal. But then I might just have two pissed off Old Ones on my case. While there was a chance that Marco might be willing to let me off, everything I'd heard about Esteban suggested the concept of letting it slide wasn't one he was familiar with.

Marco had always treated me with courtesy. But I'd never met Esteban and I couldn't assume he'd do the same. The one vampire of his lineage I had met hadn't seemed that friendly. Therefore, backing out was not an option. Even though, not for the first time since Dan had reentered my life, I wished desperately that I could go back to being boring old Ashley Keenan, forensic accountant.

Not Ashley the werewolf, killer of psychopathic vampires and debtor to Old Ones.

Sadly that was about as likely to happen as me enjoying the next thirty minutes.

"We're going to do this like we agreed, right?" I said, watching Dan's face. He'd flat out refused to let me come alone. I was happy to have backup but had insisted that he let me do the talking. Cue yet another fight. He'd finally accepted my argument that looking weak in front of Esteban was hardly going to keep me safe. "Dan?"

I got one short nod and a growled "Fine." I suddenly felt

more eggshells crumbling beneath my feet but there wasn't anything I could do to fix things right now. So I turned back to the doors, resisting the urge to turn tail and bolt. Instead, instincts screaming at me, I stepped forward and pushed them open.

Time to ride the whirlwind.

As we stepped through the doors, the music crashed over us like thunder. I fought the urge to wince. I needed to look tough. Jase had drilled that into me. No backing down or I'd just be inviting trouble. Cringing at the screeching industrial metal assaulting my senses was definitely not tough.

I squared my shoulders, relying on the nearness of Dan's scent to know he had my back and moved farther into the club. The darkened space smelled of heat and sweat and too many people in a place that never saw sunshine. The odors of wolf and vampire and human mingled in dizzying jumble of scent that made my nose itch. Underneath it all I smelled fear. And blood. Old and new.

My throat tightened. The smell was too familiar. I still smelled it in my nightmares—the ones I tried to forget and mostly succeeded—except when something triggered the memories all over again. Like the scent of blood.

No freaking out allowed. I tried to breathe through my mouth and slow my heartbeat. No point acting tough when most of the people around you can hear your heart pounding with fear.

As my eyes adjusted to the lack of the light—one advantage of being a werewolf—I tried to get the lay of the vast room. Bodies packed a huge central dance floor, twisting and writhing to the relentless music. Ultraviolet lights shone down from weird angles, turning skin unnatural shades of gray and purple, making it difficult to make out individual features. In the middle of the dance floor was a raised square platform. Empty. Thank God for small mercies. I had no desire to take in the sort of floorshow a dark club might offer.

Spiky-looking metal tables of various heights formed an uneven square around the dancers. To our left a steep metal staircase led up to the metal-railed balcony ringing the room. According to Marco, we'd find Esteban's office upstairs. Apparently the entrance to the private areas of the club was up there too. The areas I *really* didn't want to see.

Any more than I wanted to meet Lord Esteban. The thought of climbing those stairs suddenly felt as inviting as walking the plank. I was all too aware that there were many, many sharks circling.

The music tore at my ears, full of weird dissonances my brain translated as screams. Steeling myself, I started forward then stopped as a man and a woman stepped into my path. They looked at me and smiled with a nasty sort of anticipation that made my spine stiffen. I didn't smile back.

Dan moved up behind me and I let myself relax a little. I wasn't here alone.

The guy cocked his bald head at me, one hand tucked into the waistband of his way too tight jeans. The jeans were the only thing he was wearing. Which meant I had an eyeful of unnaturally smooth chest. His nipple ring looked almost neon purple in the lights. The barely-there top the too-thin too-bleached blonde at his side wore revealed a matching piercing.

"Want to play?" Baldy's voice was as unattractive as the rest of him, squeaky and grating all at once.

Ugh. "Not really." I tried to move past and he grabbed my arm. I snarled, heard an echoing growl from Dan, but the guy's hand remained clamped around my bicep. I sucked in a breath. He smelled human—old sweat, cheap vodka and cheaper aftershave. I could deal with him. "You might want to reconsider."

His fingers tightened. "Am I hurting you?"

He was, a little. Probably not as much as he wanted to. I narrowed my eyes at him, hoping he'd get the message. I didn't have time for this. His girlfriend scowled at me and I almost laughed. She wasn't even close to the most intimidating thing I'd seen recently. "You should pick your targets a little more carefully," I said, and then yanked my arm out of his grip.

His eyes widened. Obviously he hadn't picked up that I was a shifter. "Bitch."

Dan rumbled again behind me and I held up a hand, smiling at Baldy. "You got that right," I said and shoved him aside with enough force to send him and his lady skank tumbling backward.

"Let's go," I said to Dan, moving toward the stairs, trying to avoid body contact with any more patrons. I half-heard a commotion behind me and turned just in time to see idiot boy launch himself at Dan who promptly backhanded him, sending him crashing to the floor. This time he had the sense to stay down. No one moved to help him up, not even Blondie who'd staggered to her feet and was ruining her makeup with shocked sobs.

Dan and I moved on through the mass of clubbers. A lot of them wore a lot less than either of us. Chains and spikes featured heavily, as did piercings in places that hurt to think about. I paused to let a woman leading a half-naked guy by a heavy chain attached to a collar move past me. Both of them turned their heads to look at me, the woman blowing me a kiss through blackened lips.

But it was the guy who had my attention. The lower half of his face was covered by a—well, you could only call it a muzzle, the leather fastening behind his head, hiding his mouth. Silvery mesh left a small breathing hole and elaborate silver designs mimicked fangs around the space. On the face of things, it wasn't any creepier than half the outfits in the place but something about him made my stomach twist uneasily. I froze, watching them until they disappeared into the crowd.

It took an effort to move forward again and almost immediately a tall black man stepped into my path. "Where you going, pretty?" His head was shaved and his clothes were a dark, dark red, if my eyes were translating the weird light correctly.

I suppressed a shiver. I hated being called pretty. When I'd been held prisoner by McCallister Tate—the psychopathic vampire who'd killed my family—his henchmen had called me that. "To see Lord Esteban."

He put his hands on his hips, effectively blocking the stairs. I stared at him, not sure if he was vamp or human. The crowd was thicker here and there were too many scents hitting my nose, too many bodies close by, for me to know which one was his.

He smiled unpleasantly, revealing fangs. Mystery solved. "You expected?"

"Yes. I have an appointment." I waited, praying I wasn't about to have confrontation number two. I still had Esteban ahead of me. Another fight might just use up all the acting tough I could muster. But hopefully, if this guy worked for Esteban then he had to treat Esteban's guests courteously.

Finally he stepped aside. "Enjoy." His tone suggested this was unlikely.

So did my brain.

I put my hand on the banister. Then snatched it back as my palm started to burn.

"Silver chips in the paint," the vampire said from behind me. Amusement laced his voice.

What kind of idiot put silver chips in the paint when some of the clientele were shifters?

"Just keep climbing."

Dan's voice was right in my ear. I did what he suggested, ignoring the fading pain in my hand.

"Silver in the paint?" I whispered to him as we climbed, both avoiding contact with the banisters. It wasn't that easy.

The stairs were steep with large gaps between the treads, making it very tempting to cling to something for support.

"Some people like pain."

Dan's tone was matter of fact. I felt like an idiot. I knew what went on in the dark clubs. I knew what BDSM was. And Dan and I had put his handcuffs to nonofficial uses from time to time when he'd been a cop. But the stuff that went on here was way, way beyond. I'd never understand someone *wanting* to be hurt.

Pain was bad. And I'd had enough of it to last more than a lifetime.

So what the hell was I doing here?

Trying to get things back to normal. Right. Wearing leather and surrounded by freaks. I bit my lip. No point panicking. This should be simple. It was probably an accounting problem—I couldn't think of anything else Marco would think I could help Esteban with—and I ate accounting problems for breakfast. So easy. Deal with the big bad vamp's finances, repay my debt to the other big bad vamp in the process and everything would be fine.

Just fine.

The door to Esteban's office, like those leading into Maelstrom, was a black mirror. My reflection still looked nervous. The music had faded to a dull roar but that only meant I could pick up other sounds. Groans. Screams. And dull thwacks that had to be the sound of leather hitting flesh. I swallowed, hard.

"We can still leave. I can handle Marco," Dan said. His reflection didn't look any happier than mine.

Any sorting out Dan did with Marco was likely to get ugly. A werewolf-vampire political blow-up, if not actual violence, was not my idea of returning to normality. "If it's not this, it could be something worse." I wasn't sure what worse might be. But I was sure that I wanted to deal with at least one of my obligations to Marco.

Just like any other business meeting, I told myself as I pasted on my polite and professional face, lifted my hand, and rapped on the glass.

The door swung open silently, revealing a woman in the doorway. One I knew. A vampire named Leah who was high up in Esteban's organization. She'd been at Marco's when I'd made my deal.

She hadn't liked me then and her expression suggested her opinion hadn't changed. "Ms. Keenan."

"Hello, Leah." I nodded at her, trying to be polite. The long dark green dress snaking around her body made her skin look very pale, and her lips very red. Like she'd just fed.

She didn't acknowledge the greeting.Instead she looked past me to Dan. "Who is this?"

"Daniel Gibson," I said.

Her dark eyebrows shot up. "The FBI agent? From the Supernatural Taskforce?" The last words were a sneer.

"Yes. But he's not here in an official capacity."

"We do not let the FBI come sniffing around." She put one hand on the doorframe, blocking our way.

Well, no. Not if half the stuff said about dark clubs was true. But I didn't want to get into a pissing match with Leah. So I played my trump card. "I said, not in an official capacity. Lord Marco said I could bring him." Marco was the oldest Old One in the city. Esteban had to do what he said.

"Let them in, Leah." The words came in a low golden rumble that brushed up my spine and somehow reminded me how little clothing I was wearing, as though a warm breeze had blown past me.

I didn't like my reaction. Leah blocked my view of the speaker, so I couldn't see who it was but the voice was very much used to being in command. When Leah melted out of our way without protest I knew it could only be one person.

Esteban.

Curiosity warred with caution as I walked into the office,

Dan on my heels. Marco had been nothing like I'd expected an Old One to be—less of the pain and terror and more of the charm and honor. I wondered whether Esteban would surprise me as well.

When I saw the man—vampire behind the desk, surprise wasn't quite the word. A lot of vampires are good-looking. Whether it's because they like to pick pretty prey or because they can use some of their abilities to make you think they're attractive, I've never been quite sure.

Lord Marco was gorgeous, in a suave, Italian, charming male model sort of way.

No one would call this man gorgeous or even handsome, really. No. He was something far more primal than that.

He wore black. Black shirt, black tie, black suit. Which only made the golden tones of his skin and hair gleam brighter. His eyes were a blaze of blue and his face was chiseled. It should've added up to All American boy. But, what it actually added up to was sex. Sensuality rolled off him like a wave.

My stomach tightened in response then heat flared through me. Dan growled low in his throat. Apparently I wasn't the only one affected.

Which meant the sex scenting the air was some sort of vampire power. My throat clamped closed and I had to remind myself to breathe as I tried to see the reality of a nice-looking guy rather than the silky steam and seduction he projected.

"Ms. Keenan." He rose from his chair with a nod. Ornate, heavy chased silver rings glinted from each finger breaking up all that gold and black. "Why don't you take a seat?"

It wasn't a suggestion. More like an invitation wrapped around a command. Now that I was close to him, the voice sounded even better. The deep rumbles seemed to promise all sorts of rewards if you just did what it asked. And you wanted to do what it asked. I took a step toward him before I knew it.

Which made me want to get the hell out of there. I'd had a vampire seduce my mind once and he'd had to thrall me to do it. I wasn't so sure Esteban would need to go that far.

Sweat broke out on my back, nerves shrilling at me to run. My mouth dried as I tried to back up a little.

My logical side told me to stay put.

Damn. I didn't need any more complications. I stayed still for a few seconds, debating once again whether I should leave even though I knew I couldn't. All the time, feeling a pull toward Esteban like a tide.

Esteban watched me, and the amusement in his eyes told me he knew exactly what I was fighting. Luckily I'd had a fair bit of practice in controlling my instincts and urges the last few months. I stood my ground, just long enough to make it clear I was moving under my own free will, and then took another step.

Dan's hand pressed into the small of my back possessively as I moved toward the chairs arrayed in front of the desk. His touch didn't help me suppress the heat curling through me but he wouldn't take it well if I shrugged him off. I tried to remind myself that it wasn't a sexy guy in front of me, it was a *vampire*.

One with a nasty reputation.

Esteban still looked amused.

The closer we got, the stronger the pull to move closer still. No wonder his clubs were successful. You'd just need Esteban to walk through the room and people would be panting.

As I neared the chair, another vampire appeared beside me, pulling it back for me. I jumped then did a double take when I got a look at his face. If Marco was all charm and Esteban was pure sex then this guy was sheer beauty.

The kind to make painters weep and women sigh.

Like Leah, he was dark. Deep brown hair, skin a deeper olive gold than Esteban's and eyes darker than the hair. None of which conveyed the utter perfection of his face.

He smiled while I gaped at him. I sank into the deep

leather seat and his gaze sharpened as he turned his attention to Dan. He walked around me, smooth vamp gait making it look like he almost floated, and pulled a chair out for Dan as well.

"Why don't you sit?" he asked in a tone close to a purr. The voice was almost as sleek as his gray suit. Dan stared at him, face unreadable.

"Niko, don't play with our guests," Esteban said.

The vamp slanted a glance at Dan then shrugged a shoulder and backed away. Dan's shoulders relaxed a little and he sat. Though he stayed perched on the edge of the chair, eyes scanning the room.

Ready for action.

I straightened as well, trying to watch where Niko had gone out of the corner of my eye.

"He will behave." Esteban's voice implied 'or else.' "Niko, go with your sister." He gestured toward the door and Leah.

Wait a minute, *sister*? Were they actually related or did Esteban mean related by lineage? I hoped it was the latter. I'd never heard of siblings being turned together before. Though they did look alike and also looked to be close in age—frozen in their early twenties. It was possible but I couldn't imagine wanting to follow a brother or sister into vampirism unless the relationship was way closer than usual.

Leah looked like she wanted to object.

Esteban lifted one golden eyebrow and his hands flattened on the desk, rings clicking flatly against the wood. Just that small movement was enough to make it feel like the temperature in the room had dropped. The fog of arousal vanished like I'd been doused in cold water.

Thank God.

From the look on Leah's face, she felt chilly herself. She headed for the door, waited there for Niko to join her.

A few seconds later the door closed behind them. Silence filled the room. Esteban watched us while we watched him.

Finally I decided to break the stalemate. "Lord Marco asked me to come see you." Couldn't hurt to remind Esteban I was under Marco's protection. "He said you might have a job for me?"

Esteban leaned back in his chair. "For you, not the FBI agent."

"Dan's just here to escort me," I replied carefully. "He'll keep his mouth shut." Or so he'd promised.

The assessing expression in Esteban's blue eyes didn't change. He was very still. "You two are bonded?"

I glanced at Dan, waiting to see if he would reply. The answer wasn't entirely straightforward. Werewolves mate for life. And marriage vows are only part of the reason.

The other part is chemical, a physical change within each partner. Bonded mates started to smell the same. Their pheromones change. But there are also similarities in scent that run in pack lines. Dan had been the one who turned me. I had the same strain of lycanthropy as him. Our scents were similar, I knew that. Whether it was due to a true bond hadn't yet been decided. Or at least, neither of us had exactly pushed to find out from our Alphas what our real status was. At the moment, the emotional connection we shared seemed shaky. I knew I loved Dan but that didn't mean we could make it work.

"To be determined," I said, trying to sound like I didn't particularly care while my stomach twisted.

I didn't know if it was possible for a werewolf to deny the chemical bond once it occurred. Because of the pheromones, a bonded wolf isn't attractive to other werewolves. Which makes for good harmony within the pack but also limited possibility of divorce.

Unless you decided to date people other than werewolves. People who wouldn't be affected by your altered scent. It wasn't an appealing option. Humans were at risk of infection and I wasn't willing to do that to anyone. And vampires were just not dating material in my book.

Though apparently my hormones weren't so convinced of that, at least not while under the influence of whatever mojo Esteban had going on. Up until now I hadn't been sure whether I could still be attracted to other males who weren't wolves if I was bonded—not that I wanted to be but I had wondered, in the aftermath of one of our fights, what happened to bonded wolves if the relationship crumbled? Were they doomed to celibacy, unable to replace the mate they couldn't be with? Now I had an answer. Or did I? For all I knew, this could be an exception caused by vamp powers or, maybe, an indication that our bond really was tenuous.

Esteban pursed his lips. "And yet he wants to protect you from the big bad vampire."

Yes. He did. For which I was very grateful. The state of the bond between Dan and me was something I definitely needed to discuss with Ani. A little girl talk with my Alpha who was tiny and red-headed but could also kick my butt six ways from Sunday if she decided I needed it. Oh goody. But bond or no bond, I knew Dan wouldn't leave me unprotected.

"Pack protects pack," I quipped.

Dan was silent beside me. Too silent. I bit my lip again. Sure, I'd asked him to let me do the talking but this was one subject I'd be happy to hear his opinion on. But his silence—and the tension roiling around him—meant I had no idea whether he was keeping his promise or had nothing to say on the subject. Part of me couldn't help thinking that maybe it would be easier if we weren't bonded. Sometimes I got the feeling Dan wished there were other options. Particularly when I did things like make bargains with vampires or risk my life.

Which seemed to be happening a lot lately.

Esteban's eyes darkened. "Loyalty. It isn't only the were-wolves who understand loyalty."

"No, of course not." His sharp tone puzzled me. I hadn't said anything disparaging about vampire loyalty. There was no reason to. Vampires were generally fanatically loyal to their lineage, obeying the Old Ones of their bloodline and their sires. Though, whether obedience won by the threat of having your head ripped from your body was necessarily loyalty was an interesting philosophical point.

Wider vamp interactions are more Darwinian. Lineages rise and fall with the strength of the Old Ones. Marco currently ruled Seattle and had done so for over a century. But that didn't mean that one day a younger, more powerful vamp couldn't take him down.

Vamp eats vamp.

I'd rather be a werewolf. Of course, I'd have preferred being human but Dan had taken that choice away from me when he'd bitten me in an attempt to stop me being turned into a vampire after I'd been given McCallister Tate's blood. From Dan's point of view, the gamble had paid off. Lycanthropy had proved more infectious. I was a werewolf now.

I still had issues with that fact but faced with choosing between a rock and a hard place, I'd choose werewolf over vampire any day. Pack politics have the potential to get messy but they were something I still hadn't experienced a lot of. And, as far as I knew, nobody got killed.

"Does loyalty have something to do with me being here?" It was a guess but at the rate we were going, this conversation was going to take hours.

"The matter is more to do with your area of expertise."

I frowned. I'd been expecting an accounting problem. But a general accounting problem. I specialized in forensic accounting but I could do the everyday stuff too. Needing my expertise—if he meant forensics—would mean...holy shit, was someone ripping off Esteban? Talk about having a death wish. "You have a financial issue?" Hopefully that was diplomatic.

"There have been...discrepancies." He looked from me to Dan then back as if wondering how much to say.

I knew that look. I'd sat in countless client meetings where that look had passed between partners or board members or whoever had hired me. Someone *was* ripping him off. Crap. I schooled my face into my 'trust me, I'm an accountant' look. There were two ways this conversation could go. He'd spill the beans or I'd have to gently dig out the facts.

Esteban didn't speak. Option two it was then. Great. Getting people to talk about fraud was dicey at the best of times. When the client was a vampire who wasn't known for his scruples, it would be more like trying to tap-dance through a minefield. "And?" I prompted.

"I have need of your services, that is all." He inclined his head slightly toward Dan and then settled back into vampire stillness.

Whatever the problem was, he clearly wasn't going to talk in front of Dan. I tried not to let my dismay show. Investigating the finances of vampires was familiar ground for me but my clients weren't usually as scary as Esteban. I made sure of that. Nor did they dabble in the kind of murky areas he did. I'd been counting on Dan having my back but apparently I was going to have to do this part solo. And frankly, trying to find out who was dumb enough—or, worse, considered themselves invulnerable enough—to try and embezzle from someone like Esteban just wasn't appealing.

After all, it was poking into Tate's finances for Dan that had led to me, my aunt and Dan being kidnapped. Not to mention resulting in me being turned into a werewolf, committing murder—though the police had been happy to call it self-defense—and Dan almost dying.

I glanced at Dan. He had his Special Agent face firmly in place but I could smell his unhappiness with the whole situation.

Which meant he was thinking all the same things I was.

That this visit, rather than solving a problem, was creating more. Esteban wouldn't involve a forensic accountant for a small problem. This had to be big.

Dan had been right. Goodbye frying pan, hello fire.

"Dan, would you wait outside?" I couldn't believe I was asking him to leave me alone with Esteban. The sudden flare of fury on Dan's face told me he couldn't believe it either. But I didn't see another option. I had to get Esteban to talk.

"No," Dan said flatly.

I leaned over toward him, put my hand on his leg. Contact always seemed to make things easier. "Please. Just for a few minutes. I'll be fine."

I felt rather than heard the growl rumble through him. "Please," I said again, trying for conciliatory. "Trust me. I've done this before."

"Not with someone like him." His voice was low, tinged with the wolf.

"I have a lot of vampire clients," I reminded him. "This is my job. I promise, I'll yell if I need you."

I just wanted to get this conversation over and done with. It was after 2 a.m., my pants were starting to cut off the circulation to sensitive parts of my body, and I had a tension headache that there wasn't enough ibuprofen in the world to cure. I wanted to go home.

Which meant I had to find out exactly what Esteban needed.

"She'll be perfectly safe," Esteban said. He smiled at me and, once again, sexual heat seemed to flavor the air.

"You'll have to forgive me if I don't find that confidence inspiring," Dan said. His shoulders were rigid and the smoky tinge of true anger was rising in his scent. "Your ideas of safe are a little different from mine."

"Shut up." I hissed. I didn't need Esteban to get all insulted. *Neither* of us would be safe if that happened.

Esteban smirked. "I won't do anything to her she doesn't want me to."

This time Dan's growl was plainly audible. I stood and

stepped in front of him to block his view of Esteban. He glared at me.

Touch wasn't going to help at this point. I could only try and talk him down a little. "Daniel. Please. Wait outside. This will only take a few minutes."

His lips pressed together. I knew that look. He was going to get stubborn. "You promised," I mouthed. "Don't make this worse."

Fury burned in his eyes but then he got up, pushing past me to stalk to the door. It slammed behind him with a rattling thud that made me fear for the mirrors.

My heart sank. So much for getting rid of my debt making things better between us. But I'd have to worry about that later. Right now, I had to deal with Esteban.

Chapter 2

I TURNED and sat back down. "I apologize, Lord Esteban. He's just being protective."

Esteban tilted his head at me, still smiling. "I understand protecting one's belongings. After all, that's why you're here."

I forced a polite smile. I wasn't anyone's 'belonging' and sending Dan out didn't mean I liked doing it. "Why don't you tell me what the problem is? We've taken up enough of your time already."

He shrugged. "I always have time for pretty wolves." Another wave of temptation rolled over me.

A shiver ran down my spine even as my body reacted. His voice was sexy but the stories I'd heard about him and what he liked to do to his playmates weren't. The combination of lust and revulsion made my head throb harder. "Try to think of me as an accountant, then. I bill by the hour."

"Touché. Though, your rates are quite reasonable." His smile widened. One long finger traced circles on the dark wood desk. It was hard to look away. Or remember what we were talking about. It was almost as if he was tracing the circles on my skin. Small shivers skimmed up my arms.

Focus. Accounting. Right. I wasn't cheap but he was

getting me for free. That was about as reasonable as it got. "The problem?" I asked again, trying to keep things on familiar ground.

The finger stopped circling. "Certain financial discrepancies have been brought to my attention."

I nodded, wishing he'd get to the point. But clients rarely do. Not straight away. "Here at Maelstrom?"

"No." A decisive headshake. "I am here too frequently. But some of my smaller clubs are not so closely watched. Things have been let slide."

Spread yourself too thin and employees started to stick their hand in the cash register. That was common enough. Though you'd think the threat of having a vengeful Old One after you would be enough of a deterrent. "How many clubs have discrepancies?"

"Maybe fifteen."

Fifteen? How many dark clubs were there in Seattle if Esteban owned fifteen 'smaller' clubs? "All in the city?"

"No. Some are here, some in other parts of Washington and some in California."

Great, diversification. He had to be working with another vampire lineage to have any sort of presence in California while he was based here. He'd need an Old One there to enforce things for him. Whether he was running things or they were wasn't clear. Which meant I didn't know who was really running the show. This was just getting better and better. But I'd get to the really sticky questions after I knew the extent of the problem. "How much are we talking about?"

"At least ten million in the last six months."

"Dollars?" I blurted. Very unprofessional. I dealt with big numbers all the time. But I'd never imagined the clubs were such big business. Mainly because I'd avoided thinking about them at all.

"Yes."

"And you've only just noticed?" How big was his cash flow if a ten million drop didn't cause a blip on the radar?

"It wasn't all at one club or all at one time. Business fluctuates. But I've been thinking of selling a few properties. That's how we found this problem."

"Do you think it's an employee or your accountant?"

"I have not yet decided one way or the other. But my accountant has been my accountant for fifty years. He is a wealthy man."

Didn't mean much. In my experience, wealthy men could —and did—commit fraud just as easily as poor ones. Sometimes more easily. So far, the situation sounded fairly straightforward if you ignored the vampire element. Lucky me. "So you want me to investigate the fraud for you?"

"Yes. You find the culprit and I will deal with them."

I didn't think he meant going to the police. But I could deal with that issue once I'd found the perpetrator. "It sounds doable."

"You'll have to work at the clubs. I don't want the financial information being taken off the premises."

I'd half expected that but my stomach still churned. I didn't want to hang out in dark clubs. "I'll need to take some data for analysis."

"Can't that be done on site?"

"Some of the programs and routines I run take a long time. I'm sure you don't want us in the way any longer than necessary." Truth but not the whole truth. I could do the analysis at the clubs if I had to. Hopefully Esteban wouldn't know that much about how forensic accountants actually worked.

Esteban frowned. "Anything you need to copy, you will run past me."

That much I could live with. "I'll also need to work during the day, outside operating hours is easiest."

He shook his head. "Some clubs operate twenty-four

hours, but most don't. I don't want anyone getting curious about why there's an accountant poking around out of hours."

Crap. "Won't sending in an accountant raise suspicions anyway?"

"There have already been accountants doing due diligence for the sales. You can be one of them. Or we'll come up with some other story. But you will have to work during the hours of operation, just like the others do."

Luckily I was good at juggling. My schedule was starting to approach seriously crowded territory but I would make it work. I had to make it work. And hope none of the balls in the air were chainsaws in disguise. "I'll need staff. At least one assistant. Someone I choose." Backup was not negotiable.

"Anyone but the FBI agent. Or any other FBI agent."

I wanted Dan. And I didn't want Esteban to think I was a pushover. "My employees are my business."

He straightened. "And this is *my* business."

I gripped the arms of the chair. "I can't help you if I don't have the necessary resources."

"Ms. Keenan, do not make the mistake of thinking I am Lord Marco. I am not so...lenient." He stared at me and the wolf bristled at the challenge.

Wolves don't always have great survival instincts. But my human side knew a threat when it heard one. Both sides of me knew better than to show weakness to a predator so I had to say something. "I—"

I didn't finish the sentence. Esteban lifted one finger and lust engulfed me. Fire blazed along my nerve endings, branding them with need. My heartbeat sped and I moaned as quivers started to roll through me—the first tremors of an orgasm.

"Quite frankly, I could make you do whatever I wanted," Esteban continued. His finger lifted again and the sensations doubled, leaving me panting and writhing. I wanted the pleasure, wanted completion, but he left me hanging, unfulfilled, to the point of pain. But underneath the physical delight, my mind twisted, knowing this was wrong. That I was helpless. I bit my lip, trying not to scream.

Esteban cocked his head. "I could leave you like this. Send you back out to your wolf so needy that you'd fuck him in front of me if I asked. I wonder what he would think of that?" He bared his fangs. "Would he be pleased?"

I managed to shake my head.

"Then do you understand me? In my domain, you will do things my way?"

I bit my lip harder, hard enough I tasted blood. Blood that suddenly tasted way too good. I fought to still my body and nodded.

"Good." He smiled and there wasn't the slightest hint of anything human or kind in the expression. "What a pity Marco found you first. We could have fun, you and I."

Not any sort of fun I wanted to have. I dropped my eyes, still fighting the need screaming at me to go to him and do whatever he wanted if it meant satisfaction.

Then just as suddenly as it had started, the sensations died. My heart still pounded and it took me a minute to unscramble my brain as my nerves tried to figure out what the hell had happened to all those very pleasurable feelings.

I lifted my head, reluctantly. "No FBI, got it." My voice was steady. Just.

Esteban laughed. "Very good, Ms. Keenan. I begin to see what Marco likes about you. When can you start?" He leaned back in his chair like he hadn't done anything wrong.

I dug my fingers harder into the leather as my wolf raged with the need to strike back. If I wanted to, I could rip the arms clean off the chair and take a swing at him. But that wouldn't end happily for anyone. I was under Marco's protection, yes, but Marco was a long way away and there were probably any number of vamps of Esteban's lineage in the club tonight.

None of whom would hesitate to hurt me or Dan if Esteban ordered them to do so. So I had to be sane about this. Play things his way. Besides, Esteban's little display of power—and the fact he hadn't had to thrall me to make me feel what I'd felt—had awakened a healthy dose of fear. I'd had a vampire take over my mind and make me feel things against my will before but I'd never expected to have one do that to me when I was still in control.

I wanted out of there.

Fast.

So I had to do the job. I reached for my best locked down auto-pilot professional mode and kept my face neutral. The icy sour smell of my fear hung in the air around me but I couldn't let fear rule me. Esteban's pleased smile told me he smelled it too.

Do the job. Get out of there. Get him out of my life for good.

I ignored his smile and thought about what he'd told me. If he was like most clients, now that he'd admitted his problem, he'd want the problem solved. Immediately.

The accountant part of my brain understood the urgency. I'd be pretty unhappy to discover someone had waltzed off with ten million dollars of mine. And, quite frankly, all parts of my brain were pretty keen to get Esteban out of my life ASAP. "I'll check my schedule tomorrow and then set up some initial meetings. Is there someone I should deal with?"

"No. This goes through me." He leaned across the desk, opened a heavily engraved silver box, and withdrew a business card. "You can reach me with these."

He held the card out. I reluctantly leaned forward to take it, not sure what would happen if he actually touched me. Thankfully, the cool brush of his skin didn't ignite another firestorm.

All the same, I pulled back quickly, pretending to study the card. It was heavy white stock, slick and cool to the touch. There was no name, just a single dark red E in the right hand corner along with a single cell phone number and an e-mail address. I slipped it into the back pocket of my pants. There were probably lots of people in Seattle who'd love to have Esteban's card but I was wondering just how soon I'd be able to burn it and forget I'd ever had it in the first place.

"I'll call tomorrow," I said, and rose before I could dig myself any deeper.

* * *

I closed the door to Esteban's office behind me, tempted to lean back against it and sigh with relief. Or cry. Or maybe both, I wasn't sure. One thing I did know was that I wanted to go home and sleep. Tomorrow—or rather later today—could only be an improvement over the last few hours.

Dan stood sentry a couple of feet from the door. He still smelled mad and his 'just try me' vibe made the hairs on my arms stand to attention. Niko was nowhere to be seen but Leah lounged against the wall a little away from Dan, just close enough to be pushing the boundaries of his personal space, looking amused. I wondered what she'd been doing to him while I was inside with Esteban.

Asking would be pretty dumb. I didn't need Dan exploding on top of everything else. His control was very good but everyone has limits and he'd been at the edge of his the last few weeks. So I ignored the satisfied smirk on Leah's face, and focused on Dan.

For a moment we just stared at each other, me trying to let him see I was sorry, him looking even more tightly wound than I felt. His eyes scanned my body as if reassuring himself that all my limbs were still attached. I couldn't think of anything clever to say, so I stayed quiet and let him look and hoped he wouldn't be able to smell the lust Esteban had aroused.

Maybe he could. His hand snaked out, closing around my neck and pulling me close while his mouth found mine. His kiss burned through me, igniting the fire all over again. Heady. Wild. Intense. I moved closer, wanting more, but Dan slowed the pace, gentling the kiss, before he eased me back from him completely with a tiny shake of his head.

Current mood assessment: worried, glad I was okay but still pissed off. There was nothing I could do about that with Leah as an audience.

"What a touching reunion," Leah said into the silence.

I turned. "What's wrong? No one waiting to kiss you hello at home?" She bared her fangs. I ignored it. If her boss needed me, she couldn't actually do anything to me.

"Shall we go?" I said to Dan.

Leah's muttered, "Don't hurry back," floated to my ears. I kept walking. Behind me, I felt Dan start to follow. Since I'd become a werewolf, I no longer felt a buzz around shifters but I could tell when Dan was close. It wasn't a tingle on my skin like shifter buzz but rather an awareness, like a distant hum inside my head. I wasn't sure if the connection was part of being bonded. Something else to put on my growing list of questions to ask Ani.

Knowing Dan had my back made me feel a little better. After letting Esteban kick him out, I'd half wondered whether he'd be waiting or whether he'd leave me to wade back through the crowd alone. But apparently he wasn't mad enough to completely abandon his good guy instincts.

The screeching music grew louder as we descended, sharpening my headache until the throbs in my temples synchronized with the pulse of the bass. Wincing, I dodged through the throng, making a beeline for the doors.

A slow beeline. More people were packed into the club than before and the atmosphere had sharpened—more anticipatory, more focused. Expectation saturated the air, sliding over my skin like the gleaming edge of a razor and making me shiver.

All that hungering energy seemed to be focused toward the middle of the dance floor. Toward the stage. Toward whatever it was that Esteban considered suitable entertainment for this crowd. I didn't want to know. Instead, I kept my head down and pushed my way past one person after another, breathing deeply to try and ease the pain in my head.

Bad idea.

Mingled with the sweat of too many bodies was the faint metal-salt trace of fresh blood. Faint enough that a human wouldn't notice but the wolf did. The instinct to find the source flared strongly. I pushed it away. I'd accepted hunting animals in wolf form. I wouldn't go any further than that. I might be a werewolf but I didn't have to be a monster.

And I didn't want to be around anyone who held a different view.

I shook my head, trying to clear the scent from my nose and almost walked straight into the vampire who'd been guarding the stairs. I managed to avoid a collision at the last second but only by rocking back on my heels. Fortunately my boots weren't the stilettos Jase had pushed for or I would've ended up on my ass. Instead, I just wobbled like an idiot for a couple of seconds.

"What's the rush?" The vamp grinned down at me. "The show's just starting." He jerked his head toward the stage and my eyes followed the movement automatically.

Mistake.

Big mistake.

The stage wasn't empty anymore. Instead, a silver whipping post spiked up from its far end, complete with mostly naked blond girl chained in place. Welts streaked her back, some of them a deep enough red to make it clear she was the source of the blood I smelled.

The man wielding the whip wore a black leather mask but I saw short light brown hair and the bulge of muscle as he drew back his arm. The rattle of chains as the woman shuddered and cried under the blow made the stage seem to blur and shiver. I was suddenly back in Tate's room with him standing over me, my blood staining his mouth. Icy fingers of dread clawed my stomach and my hand clutched my throat reflexively.

"Ash?"

Dan's voice brought me back and I sucked in one unsteady breath then another, fighting nausea as I tried to believe I was okay.

Tate was dead. I'd killed him. He couldn't hurt me anymore.

At least not physically. But the emotional aftershocks of the events he'd set into motion were doing a pretty damn good job at fucking up my life.

The faint scars on my throat seemed to throb and I closed my eyes, struggling to breathe. I couldn't afford to do this. Not here. Not now. Tate was dead and I was damn well going to stay in control.

The blonde on stage was there voluntarily. Her choice. And not illegal. Nothing I had any right to interfere with.

The rational approach worked for a few seconds until the whip cracked again, making me flinch as though it were my skin seared by leather. My head started spinning as panic sucked all the air from the room.

The crowd surged toward the stage, their eagerness and excitement tainting the air around me with sex and bloodlust. To my horror, the same sensations flared in me. Pulse pounding, head reeling, I looked back the way we'd come.

Esteban stood at the top of the stairs. His eyes locked with mine then he smiled and made a sweeping gesture over the crowd. The bloodlust grew fiercer around me. The room reeked of violence and hunger. Hunger that called to me.

I swayed, fighting Esteban and the fear tearing at my
control as bodies seemed to press in on me—bodies that
suddenly smelled very tempting. The scent of blood pulled at
me, rich and thick, making my mouth water as the wolf
hungered.

I had to get out of there before I became like everyone
around me. Enjoying the pain and fear. Wanting it. Before
Esteban's power unraveled the control I'd fought so hard for
and dragged me under. But I couldn't move.

Frozen to the spot by the pull of the blood and my
inability to fight the twin hungers Esteban invoked. My
stomach wanted to heave even as my body ached.

Dan's hand clamped around my arm, his shifter-warm
skin burning like a brand. "Ash."

Esteban's smile widened and I took a step toward him.
Dan's grip tightened.

"Ash, look at me." He stepped between me and Esteban.
"Look at me. Don't think about him. Think about me."

Him? Blood roared in my ears and a growl rose in my
throat. I wanted blood or sex or—

"Okay, we're leaving." Dan spun me around and yanked
me forward.

Motion broke the spell and as the lust for blood drained
away, panic flooded in to take its place.

With a sob, I dodged around the vamp and plunged into
the crowd, redoubling my efforts to get through the bodies,
shoving at people blindly, almost running through the doors
once I got clear of the worst of it. The sudden volume drop as
I hit the street was like going deaf.

Thankfully the bloodlust vanished too, leaving me feeling
battered and suddenly exhausted like the downside of an
adrenaline surge. Worse than the exhaustion was the lingering
sense of fear and disgust. God.

Esteban had done this to me. Controlled me and the
whole club without breaking a sweat. And I'd agreed to work

for him. I was going to have to face him again. Return to his world again. Put myself within his grasp. What if I couldn't handle it, couldn't stay in control under his influence?

Dizziness swept over me. I bent down, bracing my hands on my knees and trying not to throw up as I breathed in traffic fumes and the smell of wet tarmac, the drizzling rain forming a cold film over my heated skin.

Behind me, I heard Dan push his way through the line of people waiting to be let into the club. I straightened as he stopped next to me. His eyes, usually silver, were a flat stormy color in the glow of the streetlights.

"Are you okay?" he said.

"I'm fine," I said between breaths. My heart still pounded furiously, and the pain in my head bit in unison with each pulse. I knew Dan could smell the fear rising from my skin but I needed the lie to convince myself not to have a total meltdown.

"I told you this was a bad idea." His voice was as flat as his eyes.

"I know you did." My knees wobbled. I looked around for something to lean on, but there was nothing unless I wanted to sit in the gutter. Not a good plan if the whiff of rotting food and dirt rising up from the puddles at my feet was anything to go by. What I really wanted was for Dan to put his arms around me and tell me everything would be all right.

Which was about as likely as me growing wings and flying through the darkness. My head throbbed again as he glared at me. "It's just a job." Maybe if I said it enough I'd convince myself.

"You still think you can handle this?"

I forced myself to stand up straight, ignoring the rapidly increasing wobbly feeling in my legs. "He needs a forensic accountant. He can get me for free thanks to Marco. End of story."

Talking made the pain spike deeper into my head. I dug

my fingers into the back of my neck where the muscles were doing a pretty good imitation of granite. "I'm under Marco's protection, Esteban can't hurt me."

"He just did." Dan lifted my arm. My hand trembled. I snatched it back, hugging myself to try and get warm.

"It's not Esteban, it was that place. The whip...." I trailed off before my brain could start showing images of Tate. "I'm fine now."

"Until the next time you go near him. Why do you think I didn't want you to come? He's dangerous," Dan said, the words half snarled. "Christ, Ash. Do you think I can't smell what he did to you? That isn't safety. Marco can't help you if you agree to do whatever Esteban wants."

"I wouldn't," I whispered.

"Really? How can you be so sure? I could smell you while I was outside his office. You wanted him. You weren't thralled and he got you wet. If he tried harder, he could've had you." His voice was spiked with anger and fear, roughened and hard. He grabbed my shoulders, his grip hard enough to bruise and I started shivering. He was usually so careful with his strength.

Silver eyes burned into mine. "Don't you understand? He's strong. He could make you do anything. And he'd enjoy doing it. I've heard the stories. And a lot of them aren't just stories. He likes to hurt people. He'd cut off your clothes and play you like a goddamned violin. Make you get down on your hands and knees and let him fuck you in front of whoever he wanted. Make you beg him." Dan's voice grew rougher still. Darker. Like steel spiked velvet scraping my nerves. "That would be just the beginning. He likes whips and knives and blood. You want to be the one sucking him off while he carves his initials into your skin?"

I couldn't breathe. I just stared at him. I'd never told Dan exactly what Tate had done to me. How the vampire had done almost exactly what Dan was describing. Tate hadn't raped me but he'd made me like everything else he did to me.

"You wanted that girl's blood back there," Dan continued. "You could taste it, couldn't you? He could make you lose control of the wolf. Let the beast out until all you think about is hot blood and soft flesh tearing under your teeth. Is that what you want to be? A rogue? A killer?"

My teeth chattered as my gut twisted. "He w-wouldn't. Marco—"

Dan growled, a real growl. The sound a human throat shouldn't make. His scent was drowning in smoke and electricity. "You think he gives a fuck about Marco? They're Old Ones. One day one of them will probably kill the other. You want to be a casualty of that war?"

I shook my head, tears stinging my eyes.

"Then listen to me. You're not doing it. Whatever he asked, forget it." His fingers tightened again. "Understand?"

I tore myself free, stumbling backward. Christ, how did everything get so screwed up? I couldn't let Dan get in the middle of my problems again. The last time he'd done that, he'd almost died. "And how am I supposed to explain that to Marco? Or Esteban?"

A muscle ticked in his jaw. "I said I'd deal with Marco."

And there was a statement that scared me even more than Esteban ever could. I swallowed hard. "You can't start a fight with an Old One. Ani and Sam would kill you if Marco didn't."

"Screw that," he said. "Just look at you." He ran his hand down my arm and I leaned into the warmth before I could help it. "An hour with Esteban and you're a wreck."

Clear concern threaded under the anger. He was right to be concerned. He was right about Esteban. But I had to do what I'd agreed anyway. "This is my mess to clean up. I went to Marco."

He dropped his hand, anger tightening his face into a

nearly unrecognizable mask. "Why are you being so goddamn stubborn?"

"Because Marco helped me save your *life*. I owe him. I *promised*." I clenched my teeth together before I could say something I'd regret. Like admitting that I was doing it to get Dan to forgive me, to let us move forward. I couldn't handle that conversation right now. Tears rose in my eyes again and a half sob caught in my throat.

The fury on his face evaporated and he looked like Dan again. "I'm taking you home. We can talk about this later."

"I—"

He put an arm around me, drawing me close and I leaned against him, needing to feel something solid. "Don't argue. We're going home. You need to get warm. My place."

It wasn't a question. I nodded, glad of the reprieve. This wasn't an argument we could solve tonight. I wasn't sure it was an argument that we could ever solve. But I didn't want to fight with Dan anymore.

* * *

We didn't talk on the way back to Ravenna. The silent ride gave me plenty of time to discover damp leather is cold, uncomfortable, and in no way a distraction from the fact I'd just agreed to take on an Old One as a client.

Or from the fact the Old One in question had nearly given me a meltdown. It wasn't just the leather that was causing the shivers I couldn't quite control. I've worked for vamps before but my clientele tend to be those vamps who prefer acting mostly human. Not the big, scary, mojo-you-into-orgasms powerful ones.

If I was going to go through with this, I needed to find out if there was a way to protect myself from whatever power it was Esteban wielded. Otherwise, everything Dan had said might just turn out to be true.

Jase was the obvious person to ask but he was going to be as mad at me as Dan was once he found out we'd be working for Esteban. Adding an admission that Esteban could voodoo me wasn't going to improve the situation.

But I had to ask someone. Every time I thought of Esteban, part of me burned even as the rest of me chilled. I hoped like hell the former was going to wear off soon.

If I wasn't going to ask Jase or Dan, I needed to ask Ani. I made a mental note to call her as soon as possible.

Dan's Jeep bumped its way into his front drive and I came back to myself with another shiver.

"Are you feeling better?" Dan asked as he climbed out of the car.

I shut the passenger side door, stood for a moment while my legs decided whether or not they wanted to keep me upright. Then I walked over to him, hoping not falling down was proof of my statement. Cold warred with exhaustion and a desperate need to sleep. But I wasn't as freaked out as I had been. "I'm okay."

Dan's gaze sharpened. "You're lying again." Anger smoked through his scent. He pulled me against him. Heat ripped through my body.

Too hot. Too fierce.

Esteban's voodoo still riding me. I pulled free.

Dan frowned. "What are you doing? You're freezing."

I realized the leather vest wasn't hiding the fact my nipples were hard and crossed my arms. Damp leather rubbing across sensitized flesh only made heat spike again and I trembled. The good kind of tremble. Problem was I couldn't be sure if it was Dan or Esteban causing it. "I'll be fine." Despite my efforts to quell the heat, my voice quivered.

Dan's nostrils flared. "Still lying," he said.

Damned werewolf senses.

I looked at him, eyes silvered in the moonlight, tall and strong, leather and cotton clinging to all those muscles, and felt the heat bite again. Maybe I shouldn't fight the feeling. After all, sex was better than fighting. Surely I deserved one good thing out of this mess of a day, Esteban or no Esteban?

I stepped closer, breathing in the edge of wildness that was pure Dan. Familiar. Soothing, even as it swirled across my nerves and drove warmth through my body. Warmth that didn't burn and bite like the feelings Esteban had evoked. Warmth that felt right. Natural.

Maybe hot sex with Dan could drive away all the demons nipping at my heels.

I smiled, tilting my head back to look at him. "You could warm me up."

"Is that so?" His voice deepened a few notes.

A nod. "Yep. All this wet leather is...cold." I backed toward the house, tugging the vest away from my skin slightly. Dan moved forward as I moved back, all male intent and grace as he stalked toward me.

Desire licked my nerves as warmth turned to heat and heat loosened the tension in my muscles. It felt wonderful. We reached the porch and Dan reached for the door. I didn't want to wait. Needed what he could give me now. Needed skin and heat and us to drive away everything else. I ducked under his arm, blocking the door by leaning back against it and arched toward him. "Where're you going in such a hurry?"

His eye widened. "Inside?"

I tugged at the laces holding my vest together. "What's wrong with right here?" The porch was shadowed, the moonlight flickering through the clouds unevenly. The darkness seemed to kiss my skin with more heat.

"Isn't this a little public?" Dan sounded confused.

I worked the lace free of the first few holes, baring my cleavage. "Don't tell me the big bad wolf is shy?"

"Ash, let's just—"

I made a frustrated noise. Too much talking. I'd had enough of voices. Of arguments. Of shoulds and shouldn'ts. I wanted hands and lips and skin. Wanted to feel instead of think. I reached for his neck, pulled myself up on tiptoes and nipped his lip. "*Here.*"

He growled low in his throat. "I hope you're sure."

The rumble in his voice made me even needier. I bit his lip again. "Less talking. More fucking."

This time the growl vibrated against my lips as he kissed me with all the hunger I could desire. My back hit the door with a thump that rattled through me as he surged forward, pressing us close.

Need to need.

Skin to skin.

His hands tangled in my hair as the taste of him filled my mouth. I rocked my hips forward, feeling the length of him through two layers of leather. Warm. Hard. All mine. I pressed harder.

"Not so fast." His voice rumbled in my ear—his tone husky with need and edged with anger—as his lips brushed my lobe and I sucked in a breath.

"Dan—"

He growled softly and the sound vibrated all the way down to my toes. "My way. You're going to do everything I say."

Oh God. Heat rushed to my face even as it curled through my stomach. "I—"

"Don't talk." His hand slid up from my waist, brushed my nipple through the leather and something about the combination of hot male fingers and damp leather short-circuited my brain, making me whimper.

"You like that, don't you?"

I nodded, breathless.

"Lift up your arms," he said, pinching slightly harder. Pleasure spiked through me. I did as he asked, feeling the carved wood of his door bite the back of my wrists as I waited, pulse speeding.

He smiled at me, a long lazy smile edged with hunger. "Good girl." One hand reached out and, with a yank, the laces parted completely, baring me to his gaze. Heat streaked through me, pinning me where I was as effectively as shackles.

His eyes darkened as he watched me. "I'm going to make you scream, Ash," he said. "You're going to wake up the neighborhood." His fingers returned to my breasts, not gentle. It should've hurt. Instead it made me moan.

"Not yet. Not until I tell you to." He pressed a finger to my lips then traced their curves. When he pushed, I obeyed, taking his fingers into my mouth and sucking them. Hard.

His free hand curled around my wrists, holding them where they were as he slid his fingers free. Moisture brushed my skin as he trailed his hand down my throat and slicked those damp fingers back to my nipple.

Obviously Maelstrom had given him some ideas.

Ideas I shouldn't like. I shouldn't want to let him call the shots, take me how he wanted. But I did.

Heat flowed through me as he teased me. He took his time, setting each nerve on fire with tantalizing pressure. All the time his eyes never left mine.

I wanted to close my eyes, to look away but all that focused heat was irresistible. He had me trapped.

His hand drifted down, flicked open the buttons at my waistband then stroked the skin at the top of my panties. My hips arched helplessly toward him as need roared in my ears.

"Dan—"

"I said no talking." He took his hand away and I whimpered.

"Guess I'll have to find you something else to do with your mouth," he whispered. Then he leaned in and kissed me. If it could be called a kiss. There was nothing gentle about it. Our mouths met like the clash of armies, need and possession and hunger smoking between us.

I groaned under the assault and Dan's hand slid back

between my legs, tearing leather and fabric like it was tissue to find bare flesh. The heel of his hand pressed down, sending lightning streaking behind my eyes as I widened my legs. The slide of his skin against mine was heaven and hell.

I tried to free my wrists so I could touch and play Dan the same way he was playing me but his fingers didn't budge, one hand pinning me effortlessly. It wasn't often he used his true strength but he was now. I moaned and he pulled his mouth away. His eyes were fierce as he stared at me.

I knew what he wanted. Submission. Control. Something to soothe the alpha wolf who'd been so tightly leashed all night. He wanted to stamp my very skin with possession and know that I'd do whatever he wanted.

And I wanted to give that to him. Loved the dizzying mix of lust and anxiety and safety that being pinioned against the door while he did whatever he wanted sent boiling through my veins. I tilted my head slightly, just the slightest baring of my throat. Let him win this round.

His mouth met mine again, sweeping me away, pleasure screaming through me as his fingers played me and I swayed against him with another groan. This time it was met with another growling rumble and suddenly my hands were free. Dan sank to his knees and my legs started to tremble. I put my hands on his head for balance. His hair was soft under my palms. Dan.

His tongue flicked against me just as I heard the rumble of a car engine. Then lights swept down the road, briefly illuminating us and making me feel like a rabbit in headlights. I squealed, pushed Dan away and dropped to the tiles.

Dan fell back, chest heaving. "What?"

"Car," I managed.

He blinked, looking as lust-fogged as I'd felt until the headlights. "It's gone now."

"So am I." I hauled myself to my feet, pressed my hand to Dan's whiz-bang palm reader front door lock and ducked inside as soon as it opened. I'd barely gotten six feet down the hall when Dan strode through the door, his hair sticking up every which way.

I tried to draw some of the tattered shreds of leather around me. "Someone could've seen us."

"You started it," he said, his voice dangerously low.

"Yes, I did. I changed my mind." The headlights seemed to have acted like a bucket of cold water to my libido. My headache had returned with a vengeance and suddenly all I wanted to do was crawl into bed and sleep for a week or two.

He moved closer. There was enough light for me to see he was still ready for action. I shook my head. "I think we've lost the moment."

"Christ, Ash, I'm not some toy you can switch on and off when you're in the mood." He moved closer and I backed against the wall. "You started it," he repeated. "You liked it."

"Yes," I admitted. "That doesn't change—"

"Did you even know it was me?" he snarled.

"What?"

"Admit it, you were riding whatever wave Esteban set off. I was just handy." His eyes burned. "Whose face did you see?"

"Whose face did you see?" I shot back. "You were in that room too. I know he got to you."

"Not like he did you. I've been a wolf longer. My control is better." He lifted my chin. "So who was it, Ash? Who got you all hot back there?"

Did he really think I was thinking of Esteban? I stared at him, not knowing what to say as guilt suddenly twisted at the back of my mind.

He stepped back with a snort. "You don't even know, do you? Jesus, you're a mess."

The scorn in his tone made my temper snap. "How do I know you weren't thinking of Leah?" I shot back.

His face twisted. "Because it's never been anyone but you. No matter what they do to me, all I see is you."

Shame boiled in my stomach. He loved me. I loved him. So why was it so goddamn hard right now? "I didn't mean to—"

"Admit it. You're out of your depth. You need to turn down this job. You're not ready for something like this."

I squared my shoulders. "I know that. But I don't have any choice."

"There's always a choice."

Not if I wanted us to have a chance, there wasn't. "You can't have it both ways," I snapped. "You can't hate me owing Marco and then hate me trying to stop owing Marco."

He shook his head. "Yes, I can."

Every muscle in my body tightened with frustration. "You want to explain why that's okay?"

"Because I can't protect you," he roared. "Don't you get it? You go somewhere like that and I can't protect you."

"I'm not made of glass, Dan. I don't need to be wrapped in cotton wool," I yelled back. I'd kind of proven I could take care of myself. Hell, I'd beaten Tate and survived.

Dan made a chopping motion with one hand. "Yes, you do."

My hands curled against the urge to snatch something up and fling it at him. "If you're so keen on protecting me, why didn't you warn me about Esteban? Did you know he could do that?"

"I'd heard rumors."

"Then why didn't you tell me?"

"Because I figured Ani was teaching you about shielding," he snapped.

"Shielding?" I had no idea what he was talking about.

"Guarding against vampire mind powers. You mean she isn't?"

"No. Why aren't you?"

"You have to learn it from an Alpha."

Great. Something else I was being kept in the dark about.

Of course, I hadn't exactly given Ani many chances to tell me anything lately. I'd been avoiding her because I didn't want to have to tell her about my problems. "You didn't tell me that either."

"I figured she would've." He studied my face for a moment. "Let me guess, you haven't been talking to her?"

I dropped my gaze.

"Christ. And you wonder why I need to protect you when you won't even learn how to be a werewolf."

"I didn't ask to be a goddamn werewolf," I yelled.

He went still. Too still and I wished I could take the words back. "I—"

He closed the gap between us in one too-fast move-ment. We were body to body, face to face, temper to temper.

"Too bad." He snarled. "Because you are one. You can deny reality all you want but it's not going to change the situation."

"I'm perfectly aware of the reality of my situation."

"Are you? Because you don't act like it. The reality of your situation, Ashley, is that they'll try and take you again," he said in a tone that made me wince. "Don't you understand? Tate was supposed to kill you. He didn't but we haven't caught the people pulling his strings. They still want you dead. They're coming for you *again*."

His voice cracked a little and I wondered what it cost him to admit his fears.

"Jesus, Dan. Do you think I don't know that?" I couldn't let his fears rule my life. Rule *our* lives. I had to make him understand.

He blinked. "What?"

I blew out a breath as I took advantage and ducked around him, gaining some space. "I know they'll try again. But I can't put my life on hold and let you lock me away to keep me safe."

"Why not?" He swiveled as he spoke, eyes like silvered glass as they locked with mine again.

So much for understanding.

I stared at him, feeling like there was a double-reinforced plate glass wall between us. We could see each other easily but neither of us could make ourselves heard. He wanted to protect me. I got that. But I couldn't seem to make him see that I wanted to protect *him*. Him and everyone else in my life. And I couldn't do that, couldn't help solve the case, couldn't do anything if I was under twenty-four hour lockdown. Besides, if I lived my life in fear, if everyone I cared about had to live their lives in fear, then Tate and Doctor Smith and whoever the hell was behind all of this had already won.

"This is my life now, Dan. The life you and Tate gave me. It's not the one I wanted. It's probably not the one you wanted. But I have to deal with it."

He shook his head. "Dealing with it doesn't mean risking your life."

"I'm not. And I don't intend to. But I will do whatever I can to make it a good life."

"Hanging out with Old Ones is hardly a good life."

"I'm not 'hanging out', I'm clearing my debts so they'll leave me alone. Leave us alone. Why can't you see that? You want the picket fence and the happy family. We can't have that while an Old One has a hold over me."

"We can't have that if you get yourself hurt." The unspoken 'or killed' hung in the air between us.

My teeth ground together. He was scared, I knew that. I was scared too. But I wasn't going to let it rule me. I'd worked too hard to build a life for myself after Tate killed my family, to not let fear and grief destroy me, to give into it now.

"We can't have it if you want me to do everything you tell me to all the time. That's not how we work."

"This doesn't feel much like a 'we' right now."

"Then goddamn bend a little for once."

He didn't speak. But I could tell what he was thinking. I was the one who should bend. Trouble was my whole life had been bent almost out of recognition since Dan had reappeared. I didn't know how much more I could give without breaking.

And he just stood there, looking like everything was my fault. It was all too much. I had to get away. I turned and ran moving blindly through the house until I reached the back door.

Chapter 3

I slammed the screen door behind me, not caring who heard. The wood vibrated and for a moment I was tempted to pull the whole damn door loose from its hinges. Instead I raced down the backstairs and into the yard, trying to wipe tears away.

The moon—blooming toward full—shone down and silvery light washed over me. It should've been calming but instead, it made the wolf snarl. Too much anger, too much stress, too many people pulling me in too many directions.

I wanted just to be. The peace of the wolf mind seemed irresistible and I just changed before I had time to think too hard and talk myself out of it.

The world blurred. Suddenly I was several feet shorter and the night air was alive with sounds and smells my human senses—even the improved by lycanthropy versions—just never noticed.

My headache had vanished.

I shook myself and stretched. Front legs and then back, drinking the night in. I wanted to run, to explore but I knew that this wasn't the Retreat and the sight of a Great Dane sized wolf sprinting down the streets of Ravenna—while not completely unusual in a city with a reasonable sized werewolf population like Seattle had—would be enough to cause a commotion. I paced around the yard instead, winding my way around the various bushes and garden beds and pieces of patio furniture, trying to work off some energy.

Problem was, in this form, I was more aware than ever that this was Dan's house. His scent was everywhere, both his human scent and the muskier wild version of his wolf form. It was both enticing and infuriating. I shook my head, whining softly. I wanted to get away from him, from everyone.

Then I remembered Dan had bought this house because the yard backed onto Ravenna Park, which had all the space a gal could want. A six foot fence is no big issue to a werewolf. I cleared it easily and landed in the soft grass, pausing to scent the air and check whether anyone else was using the park for a very early morning stroll.

Nothing. I smelled people and dogs and other small furry things but the scents were faded, nothing was fresh and immediate in the way that would mean someone was in the park with me. The only sounds were leaves rustling and the creak of a distant swing set moving in the night breeze.

Much better.

I eased forward from the fence, letting my eyes double-check what ears and nose were telling me. Deserted. So I just let go and ran. Ran with the effortless ground-eating stride that drove all thought from my head and let the wolf take charge.

When my lungs started to burn, I sat on my haunches beneath a tree and half-closed my eyes.

"Having fun?"

The mental voice startled me and I twisted, a snarl rising as I realized I'd zoned out enough to let someone sneak up on me.

Dan. In wolf form, fur darker than the shadows. He moved forward out of the shelter of a neighboring tree.

Downwind. Which made me feel slightly better about being startled. But only slightly as I wondered how long had he been there and what had he seen me doing?

"*What if I was?*" The fur on the back of my neck and shoulders lifted, ready for round fifty-seven of our argument.

Dan stopped and sat just out of reach. He tilted his head, showed his teeth in a wolf grin. "*I'd say good.*"

I blinked. Good?

"*You need to change more. It will make you stronger. Besides, it's good to let off steam.*"

"*Then why come find me?*"

"*I wanted to know if you were okay.*"

I whined. God. I'd pushed him all night, had made him go to Maelstrom with me, had let Esteban come between us when I'd given into the lust and he was worried about me. I didn't deserve it. I dropped to the grass, whining softly.

"*Ash?*" He padded forward, nose touching my ear.

I closed my eyes.

"Ash, what's wrong?" The voice was human this time and I opened my eyes to see him kneeling next to me, naked in the moonlight.

He reached down and ran his hand over my head softly. He'd never touched me like that before, me in wolf form and him human. It felt weird but good and I leaned into the caress, suddenly understanding why dogs liked being petted so much. His touch soothed me, made the guilt fall away. The smooth flesh of his palm moving over my fur felt sensual, like someone rubbing velvet across my skin.

"Why don't you change and we can go back inside?" he coaxed.

I whined again and nuzzled his hand.

"Sssssh, everything's going to be okay," he said softly.

I wanted to believe him. I wanted him to hold me until I did believe him.

I shifted in a rush and held out my arms. "I'm sorry."

"Nothing to be sorry about." He pushed me back into the grass, covered my body with his. I knew I should object. This wasn't really any different to the front porch. But the park was deserted and no one could see us. The trees cast dark shadows, the night air felt good and Dan felt even better. As his mouth descended on mine I suddenly forgot there was anything to object to.

I drank his scent in as we kissed, letting the wild male tang surround me and arouse me. He tasted even better than he smelled and I abandoned myself to his mouth, wrapping my arms and legs around him, suddenly wild to get as close as possible.

This was what I was working so hard for. This. These moments when it was just Dan and me and nothing mattered except the fact we were alone with each other. Not just sex but togetherness. Dan-and-Ashley. The place where the world made sense.

He moved against me then changed the angle of our hips slightly and slid inside. The world went away in a blur of pleasure. There was only the dark and Dan and the incredible feeling of moving with him. Of loving him. We spoke in touch and sigh, in movement. Languages we could understand.

Languages that united us in the chase of sensation instead of pushing us apart. Languages that urged us closer, faster, wilder until there was nothing except the other and the sheer power of the orgasm that took me.

* * *

"Wake up." Dan shook me awake far too soon after we'd gone to sleep.

"Whuh?" I blinked up at him, trying to make my brain work as my body protested the thought of moving from the nice warm bed. His bedside clock insisted it was just after seven a.m. Given I usually work midday to midnight to accommodate my vampire clients, seven was early, early, early. Particularly when it had been close to five when we'd crawled into bed.

He tugged the covers from my grasp. "Get up. There's been a vamp suicide." He was already dressed.

How had he managed to avoid waking me? We'd gone to sleep curled around each other, not really talking after we'd come back from the park, neither of us wanting to shatter our temporary truce. I rubbed my eyes, trying to wake up. "Why do you need me?"

"It was right outside your building. Do you know where Jase is?"

Jase? They thought it might be Jase? I froze, pulse pounding, mind flooded with fear.

Jase.

Shoving the fear away, I scrambled upright, looking around for clothes. "He wouldn't." I looked at Dan, wanting to see reassurance in his face.

It wasn't there. His eyes were the mirrored shade they turn when he doesn't want anyone to see inside. "Witness reports say it was a guy. I don't want to take any chances."

I hadn't reached Jase by the time we got downtown, and every time his phone went through to voicemail the knot of fear in my stomach pulled tighter. The uniforms waved us through when Dan flashed his badge. I tried not to let myself think for one second it might be Jase who'd gone up in flames. He was fine. He had no reason to commit suicide—choosing the sunrise the vamps called it—he was *fine.*

Despite what I was telling myself, my fingernails were cutting into my palms as we approached the car. It was blocking the street, parked at a wonky angle across the middle of the road.

From the rear it looked pretty new. Recent tags and lovingly polished metallic red paintwork. But after the cops let us through the crowd and past the yellow and black tape cordoning off the car, we got close enough to see the driver's side. The door was open, window shattered, the leather of the seat and lining the door smoking and charred black. Vamps burn hot. And they don't leave much behind. The paint on this side had scorched and blistered, like a giant had smeared something black and acidic along the panels. The road was scorched too, bubbled with heat and covered with fine gray ash. The air smelled like burned tarmac and oil and a greasy throat clogging acrid smell.

"It's not Jase's car," I said, speaking a little too loudly so I could hear myself over the pounding of my heart. My throat tightened, making me cough. Mistake. I just breathed in more of the stinking air with each splutter.

"Does it look familiar at all?" Dan asked.

I studied the car, then the plates. Nothing jogged in my memory. The windows shone with the bluish purple gleam that said they'd been UV treated and were therefore safe for a vamp to drive but I didn't think I'd seen the car before. But it was hard to think between the fumes and the fear. "No."

"Have you run the plates?" Dan asked the bored-looking uniformed cop nearest us.

The cop nodded. "It was reported stolen two days ago. The owner's from Bellevue, but he's in D.C. for a business trip. Reported the car missing right before he left. He sounded pretty pissed."

"You ask if he knew any vampires?"

The cop shook his head.

A muscle tightened in Dan's jaw. "Then I suggest you contact him and ask. Is anyone else from the Taskforce here?"

That got a headshake. The cop pulled out his phone and walked away, leaving us alone with the ruined car. Dan started circling the car, skirting the burned areas of pavement, studying the vehicle intently.

I didn't know what he was looking for. I wasn't an FBI agent or an ex-cop. I wasn't used to standing next to the spot where someone had burned alive. Or had been burned. The unwelcome thought popped into my head. It seemed stupid; how would you force a vampire to climb out of a car into daylight but I had to ask. "How do you know it was a suicide?"

"Witness saw the vamp get out of the car. And didn't see anyone else nearby."

So much for that.

Feeling helpless, if somewhat relieved, I reached for my cell to dial Jase again. I willed him to answer. Where the hell was he? I stared at the car and the ash coating everything, trying to tell myself the tears stinging my eyes were from the fumes as I listened to the sound of nobody picking up. Jase was fine, I told myself firmly.

But looking at the wreckage I couldn't dispel my fear. I'd never seen the aftermath of a vamp hitting the sunlight before; I'd killed Tate under moonlight using good old-fashioned teeth and claws. The burned acid stench in the air suddenly reminded me of the taste of Tate's blood and I realized that was what I smelled.

Incinerated vamp blood.

Bile rose in my throat and I stepped backward automatically, not wanting any of the ash to touch me. I didn't need any more death. Didn't want to know the scent of torched vampire. Hopefully this would be the last time I'd have to smell it. My stomach swirled uneasily as a breeze stirred the ashes.

"Can you identify anything from that?" I said, hoping conversation would distract me and stop me disgracing myself by puking at Dan's crime scene. If a suicide was considered a crime scene.

Dan shook his head. "Unless there's something in the car, it's pretty unlikely. No one's ever been able to extract DNA from vamp ash. Burns too hot to leave any bone fragments."

He stared at the car, face twisted in a frown. He smelled nervous. "Anything from Jase?"

I shook my head and walked to him, wanting to breathe Dan-scent instead of dead vampire. I moved slowly, peering at the car, hoping that maybe there'd be something useful like a 'hey, I'm not Jase' sign left behind by the mystery vamp. Nothing. Just various degrees of heat damage and stink. I took another step and a glint of silver by the front tire caught my eye.

"I think there's something down there." I pointed.

"Where?"

Dan crouched down to look. I squatted beside him to stay close, filling my nose with his comforting smell.

"What the hell is that?" Dan straightened and yelled for some gloves and an evidence bag. Guess it was treated like a crime scene after all. One of the cops jogged over with the stuff Dan had asked for.

When Dan straightened the second time, he held a charred brownish lump. The top of it was partially covered with twisted silver. The whole thing stank like the burned remains of God knows what.

Dan's nose flared with disgust and he held it away from his body. "I have no idea what this is but maybe it will help."

The partially melted silver had formed the sort of angles that could give Escher a headache but something about them tugged at my memory. I leaned closer.

"Ash? Do you know what this is?"

I studied it, trying to make sense of the silver, trying to undo the damage done by the fire and imagine the thing whole and untwisted. Angles. Points. *Teeth.* An image of the muzzled vamp from the club flashed in my mind and I jerked backward.

"Ash?" Dan repeated, waving the burned lump near my face.

"There was a vamp at Maelstrom," I said as the returning

memories sped my pulse. "He wore a mask, like a muzzle almost. Brown leather with silver fangs over the mouth."

"You think this could be that?" His voice went deep.

I looked up to meet his gaze. There were shadows under the silver eyes. Shadows in their depths too. Worry. Fear. My fault. Guilt added another thread to the knotted emotions riding my gut. "Honestly? I don't know. Maybe." It could be but the damage was pretty extensive and I'd only seen the muzzled vamp for thirty seconds or so.

Dan frowned. "You saw this vamp last night? At Maelstrom? When?"

"When we first came in, just after that bald guy got in my face."

"Was he alone?"

I closed my eyes, searched for the memory again. "There was a woman with him. Holding his leash." Dark hair. Dark eyes. Black painted lips blowing me a kiss. The image in my head made my spine crawl.

"Did you know her?"

"I don't know anyone who hangs out in dark clubs."

The frown lines between his eyebrows deepened as he stared down at the muzzle—if that was what it was. "I don't like it. It's too much of a damn coincidence. First you see a vamp in the club wearing something like this, then there's a vamp suicide right outside your office."

"There must be close to two hundred people who work in my building," I pointed out. "And thousands more in all the buildings round here. What makes you think this has anything to do with me?"

"Instinct," he said shortly. "I'm going to get the security tapes from the club."

Esteban was going to love that. But Dan's expression suggested he wasn't going to be dissuaded. A legitimate excuse to rattle Esteban's chains added to the suspicion that this suicide had something to do with me would make him pretty damned determined. I didn't want another argument. Plus, a small part of me couldn't shake off the feeling that maybe, just maybe, Dan was right.

I was trying to work out how to say 'please try not to piss off my new client too badly' without starting an argument when my cell rang. Jase. Finally. A smile of relief spread across my face as I answered. "Where were you?"

"I could tell you but then I'd have to kill you," he said with a laugh. "What's up?"

The sound of his voice made me feel like I could breathe again. *Safe.* "I'll tell you when you get here."

By the time Dan's team arrived, so had Jase. He called me from the office.

"I'm here. What's all the commotion down there?"

"I'll be up in a minute." I didn't want to tell Jase about a vamp suicide over the phone. Most vamps didn't like to talk about even the possibility of dying.

"I've checked the messages. Your aunt called already."

Aunt Bug? Crap, had she seen something on TV about the suicide? I scanned the crowd and sure enough, there were several pairs of microphone-toting reporters and cameramen. Crap. No doubt there'd be some sensational story on the news already. Or a video on YouTube. There were always people willing to stir up tension between humans and supernaturals. "Did she say what it was about?"

He sighed. "The memorial, what else?"

Oh God. The memorial. I'd forgotten. Next week was the thirteenth anniversary of the Caldwell massacre. The night McCallister Tate had slaughtered thirty people in my hometown.

Including my family. And my best friend.

Damn.

"Give me two minutes." I hung up and told Dan where I was going. Then walked across the street, trying not to think about the memorial. Which was about as successful as you'd expect.

Every year Caldwell held a service for the victims and my aunt insisted I go, even though I hated it. This year was going to be worse. This year, they were trying to make me into some sort of hero because I'd killed Tate.

If they'd known the details, they wouldn't be so impressed. Biting someone's head off—literally—is not so heroic for your average person. But the FBI had kept the specifics of the death quiet and just released pictures of Tate's coffin being delivered to the crematorium for incineration.

Better safe than sorry, even with no head.

To the general populace of Caldwell, I was the one who'd finally brought some closure to a lot of shattered lives.

Someone to be admired.

But given that most of them had an aversion to supernaturals close-up, I wasn't sure I wanted them to know all the gory details. Particularly the fact that I was a werewolf now. I wasn't sure how far that little piece of news had traveled.

Or what my reception would be like once the town knew the truth.

Which was why I didn't want to go.

And why I'd been avoiding my aunt.

Jase was waiting for me with coffee and a lot of rapid-fire questions about what was going on downstairs.

I took the coffee and drained half the cup, trying to kick-start my brain. The thirty seconds or so didn't really reveal a brilliant way to avoid telling Jase the truth so I just said "Vampire suicide."

Jase went pale. On him pale is *very* pale.

"Hey." I reached out to grab his hand. His skin was cool under my fingers and I wanted to warm him up. But you can't warm a vampire. "It's okay."

He nodded but his color didn't come back and his eyes turned toward the window. "Sunrise?"

I nodded, wondering what he was thinking. Jase had chosen to become a vampire when he'd been diagnosed with terminal cancer at twenty-three. Suicide wasn't a concept that sat well with him. All life was good. "Seems that way."

"Do they know who it was?"

"No, there's no ID. The Taskforce will look into it." I had no idea how you tracked down a missing vampire. I sipped more coffee, waited for the next question.

His gaze came back to me. "You thought it was me," he said, sounding hurt. "That's why you've been calling. Ash, you know I would never..."

"I know," I said, gripping his hand tighter. I knew. Jase wouldn't leave me that way. We'd been friends before he turned and I hadn't been able to push him out of my life afterward. I was the one who'd flirted with suicide after I'd been infected.

I shivered. Too much death. Jase was right. Life was something to cling to. Fighting Tate—knowing I might die at his hands—had taught me that. "I know. But Dan was worried because of the location." No need to tell Jase just yet that Dan was maybe a little spooked because of Esteban. One set of bad news at a time. "And then I couldn't get hold of you."

Gray-green eyes studied me for a moment and then he smiled. "Next time have a little faith."

"Let's hope there isn't a next time," I said with another shiver. If random vampires wanted to start frying themselves in Seattle, they could do it far away from me. The lingering cold feeling stroking my spine reminded me that maybe it wasn't so random. Maybe Dan was right.

God. When was my life going to get back to normal?

We sat in silence a little longer while I finished my coffee. But procrastination wasn't going to help anything. I couldn't help investigate vampire suicides but I could do my job. "If we're here, we might as well get to work."

"Call Bug," Jase called after me as I headed into my office.

I stashed my bag and turned on my computer, ignoring the red message light on my phone.

After everything that had happened at Maelstrom and afterward, I wasn't sure I was up to Bug right now. Not when I was going to have to tell Jase we'd acquired Lord Esteban as a client and ask him about how I might fend off vampire sex mojo. I needed more coffee before I faced any of it.

Coffee rebooted, I fired up my email. More messages. Including one from Rhianna Anders. Bug I could ignore for a little while but Rhi? Tate had killed my family and her big sister, Julie. My best friend. Rhi and I had bonded in grief. She was, after Bug, the closest thing to a relative I had.

And I hadn't talked to her since before Dan had turned up in my office a few months back.

Great. More guilt. Plus, no doubt, she was emailing to nag about the memorial too.

I opened the message. Yep. She wanted to know if I'd be there. So I fired off a quick 'sure, can't wait, see you then, how's life?' response then stared at the phone. The red 'message waiting' light shone accusingly.

I sighed. Might as well get it over with. If I didn't call back, Bug would just keep calling. So deal with her, then with telling Jase about our new client. "No time like the present," I muttered and dialed her number.

"Hello, Aunt B," I said after she answered with a crisp "Good afternoon."

"I need to know when you're arriving on Friday."

Bug didn't believe in beating around the bush. "I'm not sure," I hedged. Mainly because I was actually planning to go down Saturday morning, attend the memorial service and then get the hell back to Seattle before anything could go wrong.

"It makes it hard for me to plan, if you don't tell me."

She sounded tired and I pulled a face as guilt pinged. I wasn't the only one who'd lost someone in the massacre. My family was her family after all. And she'd lived in Caldwell all her life. She'd known every single victim. Half of them had been her students at Caldwell High.

But that was another part of the reason why attending the service was so hard—I hated seeing Bug sad instead of fiery.

"I'll try," I said. "But I've picked up a couple of new clients recently, so I might not be able to finish early enough to make it on Friday." No way was I telling her that one of those clients was Lord Esteban. She already gave me enough grief about the fact I was still working on the Tate case. She figured Tate being dead was good enough, problem solved.

"Try hard, dear." She hung up leaving me feeling even guiltier. I knew she worried that something else might happen to me if I kept working on the investigation and didn't understand why I couldn't go back to being just an accountant.

She didn't know what kept me working with the Taskforce.

She didn't know about the anti-vaccines that Tate had been involved with, the ones designed to not only reverse immunity to the vamp virus, but ensure that victims would turn if bitten without having to drink the vamp's blood. And also ensure that anyone they bit would turn as well. She didn't know because I couldn't tell her. The existence of the anti-vaccines was pretty tightly wrapped up in layers of government classification.

Tate had tried to use the vaccine on me. Dan had saved me by biting me, gambling on the fact that lycanthropy was more contagious than vampirism.

We still didn't know whether he'd succeeded because that was true or whether he'd just gotten lucky or whether Tate's drug had also reversed my were vaccinations. The doctors had been unable to tell once the lycanthropy had taken hold and started working on my DNA.

But no matter why I'd changed, the implications for the vamp population were pretty scary if the anti-vaccines worked. The truce between the races held at the moment because humans had some faith in the vaccines to protect them and because they far outnumbered vamps and weres. If the vamp population suddenly exploded and humans realized one bite could result in them developing a hankering for O positive fresh from the jugular, then everything would change.

And I doubted it would be for the better.

Vampires weren't my favorite people in the world but I didn't want fear of vamps to extend to fear of weres. After all, I was one now. As was Dan. If Dan and I actually did walk down the aisle, it was almost certain our kids would be weres too.

I didn't want my children to grow up being feared and hunted.

We had to track down Tate's finances and hope the trail would lead us to Dr. Smith and whoever the hell else was behind this lunacy.

All while keeping my aunt happy, not annoying Esteban, and making it through another memorial service.

Simple.

The thought made me laugh. I wasn't even sure I knew what simple was anymore.

Sighing, I buzzed Jase. If I was going to have any chance of making it to Caldwell and back into Aunt Bug's good books by Friday evening, then I needed to do some schedule reshuffling.

"What's up?" Jase slid into the chair on the far side of my desk.

I jumped. Pens and paper went flying. I hadn't noticed him come in. That was happening more and more lately. Whatever Jase was doing with Marco, it seemed to be strengthening his vamp talents. Or maybe just making him more relaxed about using them.

I told myself it made no difference but it still freaked me out occasionally when he did something really vampy like suddenly appear in a room.

"I need to move some things around. I have to leave early on Friday." I concentrated on picking up the pens I'd scattered and trying to remember exactly what meetings and client deadlines were in my schedule.

"And?" Jase leaned back in the chair, blue eyes nailing me. He never had to take notes. He had an annoyingly good memory.

"And what? This is the part where you tell me what appointments I can move." I didn't look at him. His question had nothing to do with the schedule. He wanted to know what had happened at Maelstrom.

"There's something you're not telling me."

I looked up. He was frowning. I debated not telling him about Esteban for a moment. It would be nice to have one person in my life who wasn't mad at me.

But I had to tell him. Firstly, because with Dan *persona non grata* as far as access to Esteban's records were concerned, I'd need help and secondly, because Jase's psychic abilities were getting stronger. For all I knew he might just be able to pluck the truth out of my mind.

"I need you to open a new client file," I said reluctantly. "High level security."

Chapter 4

J{\small ASE} {\small SHOOK} {\small HIS} {\small HEAD.} "Please tell me it's not who I think it is?"

"It's not who you think it is," I quipped.

"You're lying," he retorted. "Damn it, Ash. You're taking Esteban on as a client? I'm beginning to think Dan is right about you."

"Right about me?"

"You have the self-preservation instincts of Bambi."

I bristled. "Hey, it's not like I have a choice here. I owed Marco. I do this and we're clear."

That earned me another eye roll. "Apart from the blood debt."

I hunched my shoulders. I didn't want to think about the blood debt. I had no intention of letting another vampire feed from me. Ever. "Thanks for the reminder." I gave him my 'drop-it' look.

He gave me his 'as if' right back. "What makes you think you're going to get out of this without more trouble?"

I clicked the end of my pen in and out. "It's a job. We go in, I solve the problem, end of story." More clicks. The rhythm seemed to go with the chant of *fat chance, fat chance, fat chance* in my head. I made myself put the pen down. "Simple," I added, trying to convince myself.

"That's what you said last time."

Right. Last time. When I'd agreed to help Dan track Tate's finances and come out of the job with a brand new ability to change into a wolf and in debt to a vampire. Not to mention in love with a werewolf who didn't seem so sure anymore that being in love with me was a good idea.

But this time wasn't going to be like that. Not if I could possibly help it. "And I'll tell you what I told Dan. Bambi ended up king of the fucking forest. So let's get to work."

After about three hours of stony silences, cool coffee and other behavior aimed at letting me know Jase disapproved of our newest client, the intercom buzzed.

"There's someone here to see you," Jase said. His voice sounded strange...distracted almost.

"Who is it?"

"He says his name is Nikolai."

This time Jase sounded dreamy rather than distracted. Crap. The last thing I needed was my PA falling for a minion of the dark side. And Niko was very much Jase's type.

Hell, he was everybody's type. Not that I had any idea which team he batted for, but he'd flirted with Dan as well as me, so I figured Jase could be fair game. Particularly if Esteban wanted to gain some sort of advantage by ordering his employee to seduce mine.

Fuck.

I practically sprinted into the foyer. Sure enough, Niko was perched on a corner of Jase's desk, smiling his depraved angel smile. Jase gazed back with an expression that reminded me of a Labrador who'd just seen five pounds of prime rib drop into his food bowl.

"Nikolai," I said, trying to figure out how to put myself between him and Jase—impossible unless I climbed onto the desk. I settled for staying on the far side of the desk so Niko would at least have to look at me. "What are you doing here?"

He turned the smile my way and the female part of me went almost as melty as Jase looked. But the wolf snarled. And when it came to vampires like Niko and Esteban, I'd trust the wolf's instincts over my hormones any day.

I folded my arms and waited. You can't exactly stare down a vampire—not when some of them can thrall you with a look —but I was learning a little about dominance games from my pack so I let the silence stretch between us while I waited.

Nothing.

"I asked a question." I let a little rumble underscore my tone. This was my office and I was the boss here, not Esteban or his errand boy. In fact, Niko didn't strike me as the type to be the boss anywhere.

Turns out my impression was right. Niko made an apologetic face, stood and actually performed a small bow in my direction. The action looked so natural for him I had to wonder exactly how old he was. I knew Marco was old—at least four hundred—but I had no idea about Esteban. Or anyone else in his lineage.

"My apologies, Ms. Keenan," Niko said. "I was distracted. So much beauty in one room."

"Cut the crap. Get to the point."

He leaned down and picked up a stainless steel briefcase. I hadn't noticed it before because I'd been too busy looking at his face.

"My lord requested that I bring this to you." Niko held the briefcase out.

I took it gingerly. Quite frankly I'd rather he'd handed me a box of live snakes. They'd be less problematic than the keys to Esteban's finances. "Thank you." I passed the case to Jase. "Jason, can you please get this data loaded into our system and secured?"

Niko frowned. "Lord Esteban said the information was for you."

"And Jason is my assistant. He assists. In fact, he'll be working with me on Lord Esteban's...matter."

Niko looked like he wanted to object again but then his face cleared and he trained another charm-angels-from-the-sky smile on Jason. "Then I shall look forward to furthering our acquaintance."

"We don't socialize with clients," I said, watching Jase's eyes glaze over with something like adoration. This *really* needed to be nipped in the bud. "Sorry."

That earned me a 'we'll see about that' sort of look from pretty boy and I let another low growl escape me. Niko shrugged, bowed again, and then turned and glided out of the office.

I waved a hand in front of Jase, who was gazing after Niko like a man who'd just had a close-up-and-personal encounter with a fantasy come to life. "Earth to Jase."

He focused on me slowly. "Who *was* that?"

"His name is Nikolai. He's Leah's brother. You remember Leah, don't you?" Jase had been at the meeting with Marco and Leah that had led to me incurring my stupid debt in the first place.

Jase wrinkled his nose, some of the worshipful look disappearing from his face. "Yes."

"Right. So stay away from this one. He works for Esteban and if he's anything like his sister, he's trouble."

Jase's expression seemed to indicate any amount of trouble might be worth it if it came in a package that looked like Niko.

I intended to change his mind. "Why don't you deal with what's in the briefcase and then we can talk about the best approach?"

"Sure. And while I'm doing that, you can tell me exactly what happened last night."

Now was the time to ask him about Esteban's powers but something made me hesitate. "Briefcase," I repeated. "Then work. Remember work? Pays the bills? Stops your paycheck from bouncing?"

"You're stalling."

"Boss's prerogative," I said with a grin, and then ducked back into my office before he could do any more interrogating.

About twenty minutes later, Jase wandered into my office and lowered himself into a chair with a low whistle. "Someone's ripping off Lord Esteban? All the data is transferred onto the secure server. Filed under 'Bad Idea.' I put the briefcase and the hard drive in the safe." He passed me a hardcopy file, already bulging with paper.

"Yeah, seems like a good way to commit suic—" I broke off as Jase winced. "Sorry. I meant it's pretty monumentally stupid. Can't imagine Esteban is big on leniency."

I opened the file and flipped through the first inch or so of paper, scanning the contents. Pretty standard stuff. A list of the clubs Esteban thought were involved, financial statements for each of them including budgets so I could see the discrepancies between actual and projected cash flows, and then the myriad financial details. Bank accounts. Employee lists. Creditors. Debtors. Inventory. On and on and on. "This is pretty comprehensive. Esteban obviously pays attention. Which makes our fraudster really stupid."

"Either stupid or smug," Jase muttered.

"What do you mean?"

"You either have to be very stupid or think you're completely safe from repercussions to pull something like this with an Old One."

Damn. My stomach lurched. Jase was right. If we weren't dealing with stupid and greedy then the likely perpetrator had to have protection. Or clout. Or both.

Great.

But I couldn't afford to let myself get distracted playing

what-ifs. I needed to get down to the business of identifying whoever was doing this. Then Esteban could do whatever the hell he wanted with them.

I stared at the list of club locations. It didn't add up to the number of clubs Esteban had mentioned last night. I'd have to ask Esteban for a list of all his properties. Just because he'd found anomalies at these clubs didn't mean there weren't any at the ones not on the list. I sighed. Another cozy chat with Esteban was high on my list of things I never wanted to do.

Unfortunately, I'd got myself into this mess and I was the only one who could get me out again. "So what do you think?" I handed Jase the list of clubs. "Where do I start?"

"Where do you want to start? Smallest club? Smallest discrepancies? Closest to home?" Jase squinted at the list. "None of these have anything much in common that I can see other than being owned by Esteban."

Actually, I wanted to start with not starting at all. Failing that, I wanted somewhere low on the freak factor.

"Maybe we could just sort of ease into it," Jase said.

I narrowed my eyes. "Are you reading my mind?"

He went still. Then relaxed. "No, I just know you too well. I've never been able to get you anywhere near a dark club."

"That's because I don't fancy being a snack."

"That's hardly your problem anymore. You've moved up the food chain."

"Ewww. That's so not true." Well, it was kind of. Vampires could drink shifter blood but it was generally a consensual arrangement. Most shifters, and particularly werewolves, were a pretty even match, strength-wise, for a vamp. But I didn't want to think of myself or anybody else in terms of food.

He grinned. "Well, you're higher than a human. How high depends on how alpha you want to be."

"Alpha isn't exactly a choice," I pointed out.

"Not pack-ruling Alpha, maybe, but the rest is up for grabs."

I grimaced. I didn't need *Werewolf Politics 101* on top of everything else. Besides, Jase wasn't exactly correct. Dominance in a werewolf wasn't purely choice. It was partly innate to the person. If it was a choice, Dan and I wouldn't be butting heads so often.

Maybe.

I made another mental note to talk to Ani. Soon. I'd hoped maybe today but there wasn't going to be time. Until I could, my plan for sorting out the issues Dan and I were having was to do the best I could. I had the same plan for dealing with Esteban. "We were talking about dark clubs."

Jase wiggled his eyebrows at me. "Coward."

"Paycheck."

"Invaluable personal assistant who could let you try and navigate these clubs alone."

I stuck my tongue out. "And what part of paycheck don't you understand?"

"The part where you can't live without me." He smiled smugly.

He had me.

"Here." He ran his finger down the list of clubs. "Infradark. It's small and it's mostly a wannabe club. You get a few feeders but the rest is death metal and people who are way too fond of black and who only think they're tough."

I didn't ask how he knew. He might think it was tame but anywhere that the feeders—vamps who drank live blood from willing victims—hung out wasn't tame. It was gross. And dangerous. "Infradark, huh?"

Jase nodded. "Tonight?"

I sighed. "You're going to make me wear leather again, aren't you?"

"No. Just black. That killer suit—the one with the lapels. That'll work."

I nodded and Jase left me to try and figure out logistics for the day. I pulled my calendar up and did some calculations. I still had real work for paying clients to do, plus I had to put in some time with the Taskforce.

Dark clubs didn't open early. So any way I looked at it, it would be close to ten or eleven before I even got to Infradark. Another long, long day. A chance to nap seemed unlikely. I was just going to do it the old-fashioned way. With gallons of coffee.

* * *

Dan's office door was closed when I reached the Taskforce about seven p.m. and his privacy screen had turned the glass wall opaque. I hesitated, wondering whether to disturb him. So far today we'd managed not to argue and right now I was feeling the effects of a twelve-hour day on way too little sleep and way too much coffee. And I still had Infradark to look forward to. It might just be easier to go straight to my cubicle.

But I wanted to know if he'd found out anything more about the suicide. And, if I was completely honest, I wanted to see Dan. It was crazy when we'd known each other so long but I still got the good kind of butterflies when we'd been apart, even for a day.

I knocked on the door.

"Hey," Dan said, sticking his head out.

Not exactly the warmest of welcomes but at least he wasn't scowling. "Hey, yourself."

"Did you just arrive?" He stepped back so I could come in.

"Yeah, busy day." I paused as I saw a man I didn't know occupying one of the visitors' chairs. I cocked my head at Dan.

"Ashley Keenan, Andy Ramirez," he said, waving me toward the chair next to the stranger's.

"Agent Ramirez." I assumed he was FBI. The Taskforce didn't use many civilian contractors. I was the odd one out.

Agent Ramirez ran a hand over closely cropped dark hair. "Ms. Keenan. Dan was just filling me in on what you've been doing with this case."

"You're an accountant?"

The lines bracketing his dark blue eyes deepened as he smiled, flashing very white teeth against olive skin. "No, but I've done a couple of stints with the organized crime guys so I know a bit about money laundering."

Well, that was a point in his favor. Extra help could only be a good thing. We'd hit dead end after dead end in the hunt for the source of Tate's funding. But even though my brain was pleased at the prospect of assistance, my heart couldn't help wondering if this meant Dan thought I wasn't good enough for the job.

I know. Pathetic.

"Welcome aboard," I said, trying not to study him too closely. Something about the way he was sitting—a kind of just-a-little-too-alert faux relaxed pose combined with the hair and the lines made me think he hadn't spent all his time in underground FBI offices. Military, perhaps? Or an ex-cop like Dan?

His background wasn't the only intriguing thing about him. His scent teased my nose, evoking warmth and dust and a contradictory hint of deep green places. It was almost familiar but I couldn't place it other than knowing it tagged him as some sort of shifter. Not a werewolf—I knew wolf scent—but something I should know. Asking was out. Shifters tend to operate on an 'I'll-tell-you-if-I-want-to' model. A hang-up, perhaps, from the times when human-supernatural relations weren't quite as friendly as they were now.

I gave up trying to identify the scent and focused back on Dan. He looked tired and smelled frustrated. Maybe his day hadn't been any better than mine.

"I'd like you and Andy to take another look at the Synotech records," he said.

"Fine with me." I'd gone through them so many times I could practically recite them from memory. I was more than happy to turn them over to Ramirez and watch his eyeballs start to bleed from staring at printouts and computer monitors.

Dan smiled. "Good."

"Did you find anything more about the suicide?"

The smile vanished. "No. Not yet."

I wanted to ask more but didn't want to push things with Dan. Not when it looked like we might actually make it through the day without an argument. I stood. "Okay. I'll take Agent—"

One of the other Taskforce agents stuck his head in the door. "Lord Marco has arrived."

Dan nodded and waved him away. I sat back down, knees suddenly wobbly. Old Ones made me nervous. "Marco? What's he doing here?"

"I want those tapes from Maelstrom last night. Marco is here to act as an intermediary."

He sounded calm but he wasn't happy about it. He practically bristled with tension.

Marco made me nervous because he was an Old One. He'd always been helpful to me even if he exacted a price. He was fair and probably as reasonable as it got when it came to powerful old vampires. But Dan didn't see it that way. Marco was a thorn in his side because of the debts I owed the vampire. Which meant this would probably be a good time for me to beat a retreat to my cubicle. Having me around wasn't going to help Dan negotiate.

"How about Agent Ramirez and I leave you to it?" I said a little too brightly.

Dan gave me a look but nodded. I hustled Ramirez out of the office before things could go downhill.

My cubicle was small for two people to share. When I'd been human I would've been hard-pressed to be so close to a shifter without getting shifter buzz. Now, all I had to worry about was the fact Ramirez was crowding my personal space. I'd gotten better over the last few months at putting up with the closeness of the pack but a strange shifter didn't get the same privileges.

I pushed my chair as far away from his as I could and set about giving him the background information he needed. It took a while to explain the tangled web of Synotech, the anti-vaccine and the contagious vamps, Doctor Smith and McCallister Tate. Fortunately, he seemed to be a quick study. He asked intelligent questions and generally applied himself to the problem at hand.

I wound down my spiel and picked up a stack of files. "Start with these, they're all the background Synotech stuff we've done already."

He looked at the files dubiously. "You said Synotech was proving to be a dead end."

"Yes, but you're a fresh pair of eyes. There has to be a new angle in there somewhere." My gut told me Smith had known my father. My father who had worked for Synotech doing immunology research. There had to have been a connection even though I hadn't found it.

"Have you looked outside Synotech?"

"We're tracking all of Tate's assets—"

He made a dismissive gesture. "I meant for Doctor Smith. Where else have you been looking for him?"

I sighed. Truth was, we couldn't really look anywhere else for Smith. We had no idea who he really was. My memory of his appearance didn't click with anyone on any of the government databases. Either he'd been a very good boy until he hooked up with Tate or he'd changed his appearance. Add in an obviously false name and looking for Doctor Smith without the connection to my father was another big dead end. "We still think Synotech is our best chance."

"There are other biotech companies."

"Well, gee, Ramirez, why didn't we think of that? We've looked at those too. So far nothing."

"What about your father?"

I steeled myself to stay professional. I hated talking about my dad at the best of times, let alone to someone I barely knew. "Synotech have given us access to his records or what's left of them. As has every other company he worked for and his alma mater. There's nothing there."

"Personal papers?"

"My aunt and I got rid of a lot of stuff when I went to college. There was nothing in them related to his work, that I remember."

Ramirez looked disappointed and I tapped the files again. "Trust me, start here. Maybe you'll get some inspiration. Now, I need to work, so go do your thing somewhere else."

Unfortunately, Ramirez didn't come running into my office yelling "Eureka" any time during the next few hours. I didn't get any sudden stunning insights into the case either. Which meant that, as I headed back to Dan's office to say goodbye, I was still cranky and sleep-deprived with the prospect of another four or five hours work looming ahead of me.

Still, I tried to push the frustration away as I knocked on Dan's door again. Making it through the day without fighting with Dan would be one small victory in a very average day.

"He's in the conference room," Esme Walsh said from behind me. "With Lord Marco."

"Still?" Dan and Marco locked up together for several hours was not a good thing. Esme, unusually, looked tired. "Should it be taking this long?"

She shrugged, her scent—heat and steamy green—edged with the same static annoyance I imagined must be spiking through mine. "Vampire politics are delicate right now."

O-kay. So perhaps I'd skip my goodbyes. Me blundering in and putting Dan on edge wasn't going to help matters. "Then can you tell Dan goodbye for me? I have to get back to the office."

Her mouth twisted a little but she nodded, smoothing a stray piece of hair back into her French twist with a jerk. Definitely not her usual calm collected self. Something was bothering our were jaguar.

"Everything okay?" I asked.

Violet-blue eyes met mine but then she shrugged again with her peculiar feline grace. "Everything's fine. I'll talk to you tomorrow."

From her tone I figured fine in this case meant the fucked up kind, not 'situation all good.' But I didn't have time for a girl talk. Something else to feel guilty about. I sighed as I headed for the exit. My path took me right past the conference room and the door swung open just as I got there.

Unfortunately, it was Marco who stepped out. "Ashley, *cara, buona sera.*" Green eyes smiled at me.

Perfect. To Marco, Italian good manners and charm were as natural as breathing. But to certain male werewolves—and, if I was honest, to my female instincts—his old world approach came off as flirting. "Lord Marco," I said warily, trying to see if Dan was behind him. "I hope your meeting went well."

"I could say the same to you."

I wasn't sure what he meant. My face must have showed my confusion.

He tilted his head. "Your meeting, with Lord Esteban last night? Was it productive?"

My eyes narrowed at a point between his eyebrows. Was this just politeness, was he digging or was there something else entirely going on? Dan's face appeared behind Marco and I decided now wasn't the time to find out.

"It was fine," I said. "I think I can help him with his, um, *issue.*"

"Excellent," Marco said with a smile. "A mutually beneficial conclusion." He inclined his head in a gesture more bow than nod and moved a little closer.

I moved back, pressing my lips together. I really wanted to tell him what he could do with his mutually beneficial conclusion but I wasn't up to picking a fight with an Old One tonight. Or ever, really. "I should be going."

"Wait," Dan said. "Going where, exactly?"

Something in his tone made me think he knew already. Damn. Jase had told on me. "Infradark. It's one of Esteban's clubs."

They both frowned, green eyes and silver ones registering identical levels of disapproval.

"Jase is going with me," I added defensively. "It will be fine."

"That's what you said last night," Dan said flatly.

Marco swung round to face Dan. "There was a problem last night?"

"No."

"Yes."

Dan and I spoke at the same time. He was louder.

Marco's attention remained fixed on him. "And?"

There was a lot of Old One in that tone. He expected the question to be answered.

"Esteban decided it would be fun to give Ashley a demonstration of his powers," Dan said.

That brought Marco's green eyes back to me. "You were not shielded, *cara*?"

Great, now I was going to be lectured by Marco on top of everything else. "I wasn't aware that there was anything to shield *from*," I pointed out. "Nobody *told* me."

"You were not hurt?" Marco said.

This time I beat Dan to the response. "No. Nothing physical."

Marco rolled his shoulders, the gesture a peculiarly fluid

demonstration of irritation. "I did not think Esteban would offer you any disrespect."

I really didn't want to be the cause of an argument between two Old Ones. "He was just showing me who was boss."

Marco's expression didn't change. "In this situation, I am the boss."

I swallowed, my throat suddenly dust-dry. It was going to be bad enough working for Esteban without having him angry at me for telling tales. "Of course, but I can handle him."

"I don't like you going there tonight," Dan said.

"I'm not going to Maelstrom, I'm going to Infradark. Jase says it's a wannabe club. I doubt Lord Esteban will be there." He wouldn't waste his powers on a bunch of posers, surely? He'd stay where the real action was. "Anyway, I'm not going alone, Jase is coming with me."

"Jason?" Marco and Dan exchanged a long look. "It would be better to take more than one."

"Esteban agreed to one assistant. And he expressly said no FBI." I stared at Dan, trying to will him to be reasonable.

Marco cocked his head at me. "I could accompany you."

"What?" This time Dan and I spoke in unison. I sounded surprised. Dan's tone was more a pissed off growl.

Green eyes warmed and my hands curled into tight balls. Marco was enjoying this. Or enjoying annoying Dan, at least.

"Lord Esteban cannot object to me," Marco said.

That was true. But Dan sure could. I looked at Dan, waited for him to protest. Instead he stayed silent while his scent grew smokier and smokier. Marco could probably read that anger as clearly as I could but it didn't seem to bother him.

"After what we have discussed this afternoon, Daniel Gibson, you do not want her unguarded," Marco prodded.

A growl rumbled in Dan's throat. "No."

Every muscle in my back tensed. Dan agreeing with

Marco? Not good. "What exactly did you discuss?" I demanded.

"Many things," Marco said smoothly. "But to cut to the chase, as you say, I agree with your wolf that this morning's incident is disquieting."

Shit. Marco was worried about me too? I folded my arms, more to make myself feel better than any defiance. "Did you get the tapes from Esteban?" I asked Dan.

He shook his head. "No. Not yet."

"Then what's changed?"

Marco cleared his throat softly. "Let us say that our instincts are in agreement, Ashley."

"You think there's a threat? To me?" I wanted to hear them say it.

Dan rubbed his wrist. "We think there's cause for concern."

"Do you think Esteban is involved?"

Marco shrugged and Dan frowned.

"There is no proof either way," Marco said. "Still, his clubs are not safe. They skirt the wrong side of the line."

"Off the grid. Easy to infiltrate if you're a skilled hacker," Dan added.

I fought a shiver. "Okay, I get it. So, Marco comes with me?" An Old One wasn't too shabby as bodyguards went.

Another growl rumbled from Dan.

"You can't have it both ways," I said. "You want me to have more backup. You can't come. Neither can anyone else from the Taskforce. Marco can."

"Fine," he said eventually. "But you're taking this." He held out a small black disc.

I took it. "What is it?" I rolled it in my fingers, peering at a circle of shiny black plastic about the size of a nickel, but fatter. The center had a small indent, making it look like a tiny black mutant donut.

"Panic button. Hit that and there'll be agents with you in five minutes max."

Five minutes was a long time if something went wrong in a dark club. Particularly anything that an Old One couldn't protect me from. The agents weren't likely to find anything but a very chewed-on Ashley corpse if I ran into that kind of trouble. But if carrying it made Dan feel better then I'd carry it. I closed my fingers around the disc. It was still warm from Dan's hand. That made my heart warm a little too.

"Thanks." I slipped the button into the pocket of my jacket.

"Use it," he said warningly. "For anything that makes you nervous. *Anything.*"

His eyes slid toward Marco and I fought the urge not to roll mine. Marco was not going to leap on me and try and have his wicked way with me. I didn't think for a moment he was actually interested in me in that way. His flirtatious manner was, as far as I could tell, part innate, part enjoying tweaking a werewolf's—Dan's—tail. Even if I was wrong about it, if Marco did try anything, I was hardly going to just stand there and let him.

"Perhaps I shall wait for you by the elevator, *cara*," Marco said diplomatically. "I have my car here."

Marco's limo was better than having to pay a taxi a bonus to take me to a dark club. I nodded and Marco glided away.

Dan stayed silent, the smell of smoke still rolling around him.

"I could say something about being hoist on your own petard," I said sweetly. "But I won't."

Another growl vibrated in his throat and I sighed. "I don't want to fight, Dan. You're the one who brought the subject up in front of Marco. I'm taking the protection. You should be happy."

"I'm never happy when you're with vampires," he said

softly, arms folded tightly enough that his biceps strained the fabric of his suit.

"Even Jase?" I tried to lighten the mood.

The corner of his mouth lifted slightly. "Jase gets a pass. Nobody else."

"I know this is hard," I said. "But we just have to get through it." I hoped we could get through it. The alternative didn't bear thinking about. I'd let Dan go once before and it had nearly killed me. I wasn't sure I could do it again.

After a moment, Dan uncrossed his arms, rolled his shoulders and nodded. "It will get better."

I wanted to believe him. But I couldn't see how it would unless he forgave me for going to Marco. Which, given the front and center position Marco had just taken in my life, seemed unlikely to happen any time soon. We were going to keep going round and round until one of us broke. I didn't want it to be me. Despite my doubts, I wasn't ready to let go of Dan. In fact, I didn't know if I *could* let go of him, even if I wanted to. So I lied. "Yes."

It earned me a proper smile. I couldn't tell whether it was 'thanks for trying to make me feel better' or 'I believe you.' I smiled back and reached out to straighten his tie. Or rather, to use my straightening his tie as an excuse to touch him. Things seemed to work better for us when we focused on the physical.

He bore my girly fussing without comment until I dropped my hands.

"Finished?" he asked dryly.

"Hardly." I grinned up at him, grabbed his tie again and yanked his head down to kiss him goodbye. Screw behaving well in the office, sometimes a girl needs a good pulse-pounding lip-lock to take her mind off all the crap.

Chapter 5

THE TRIP to Infradark was largely silent. As Marco's driver wound his way into one of the dodgier areas of town, cold tendrils of anxiety wound their way around my spine, making the skin on the back of my neck crawl.

Another dark club.

Too soon. My mind kept flashing back to Esteban and Maelstrom, the memories a confused blur of lust and panic and the smell of blood. The faint scent of vampire that filled the car, like a hint of acid beneath the expensive colognes that both Marco and Jase wore, didn't help.

The wolf interpreted that scent as a threat and put my senses on high alert. Even the small warm bump of the panic button in my pocket didn't relax me, no matter how often I told myself that Esteban wouldn't be at Infradark.

The limo headed down a narrow street, then pulled to a halt beneath the one operating streetlight that shed a yellowish pool of light over the entrance to an even narrower alley. The driver's voice came through the intercom. "This is as close as I can get, sir."

I fought the temptation to snarl. I didn't want to walk down a dark alley in this part of town even with a couple of vamps as bodyguards. For one thing, I was bound to get something disgusting on my shoes. But it wasn't as if we could change the laws of physics and make the limo suddenly skinny enough to navigate the alley.

Reluctantly, I climbed out of the car. The darkness beyond the thin light from the streetlight seemed to press around me and the smell of trash was overwhelming. Someone hadn't been emptying their dumpsters.

I wrinkled my nose and tried not to breathe. Wolf senses aren't always a good thing. The only thing that made me feel better was the matching expression of distaste on Marco's face. "So where is this place?"

Jase pointed toward the darkest end of the street. "Down the alley."

From where I stood, the mouth of the alley had a faint reddish glow as if there was a neon sign or something lighting it from within. About as inviting as the gates of hell. But I had no choice but to walk straight into them. "Let's get this over with."

"Stay close to me." Jase headed down the street and I took his advice, hugging his side like a puppy following its owner. As we neared the alley, the smell of trash was joined by an equally charming mix of stale alcohol, vomit and urine. I stopped, half-gagging. Stupid wolf nose.

Though you'd have to be a human without a nose not to notice the stink. Maybe Esteban was losing money because this place was a total dump.

"Gee, Jase," I said. "You take me to all the best places."

"Hey. You're the one taking me." He smiled down at me and offered an arm. "Shall we?"

"I guess." It had to smell better inside the club. At least, I hoped it did. We rounded the corner, Marco at our heels, into the dull glow of red neon spelling out Infradark over a nondescript doorway in an equally nondescript brick building. Spilling down the alley in the opposite direction from us was a long line of people dressed in black, black, and more black.

Maybe black cut off your sense of smell. If so, I was obviously wearing the wrong shade of black.

Marco ignored the line and headed for the bouncer. Happily for my nose, the bouncer seemed to know who he was. The threadbare black velvet rope barring the door was lifted at warp speed and before I had time to really think what I was about to do, I crossed the threshold.

The interior of the club wasn't any more appetizing than the exterior. Shabby was putting it nicely. The dim lighting wasn't dim enough to hide the dingy paint and battered looking tables and chairs. Each step I took, my shoes stuck to whatever the hell had soaked into the carpet. Whatever Esteban was spending his money on, it wasn't this club.

The place reeked of half-smoked cigarettes, sweat and stale beer. The stink wasn't as bad as the alley but still not pleasant. But it didn't reek of blood and fear like Maelstrom so maybe Jase was right, maybe this was a wannabe club. Fine by me. Maybe we'd get out of here all in one piece after all.

Marco scanned the room with one quick look and apparently he didn't see or sense anything that upset him because he gave me a small nod.

Permission to proceed, I assumed. "Jase, what was the name of the manager?"

"Arthur Dempsey."

"Okay, why don't you go to the bar and ask where we can find him?" No point trying to do it myself, Jase and Marco would both just protest.

Jase nodded and headed into the gloom.

Which left me alone with Marco. I tipped my head in the direction Jase had gone. "He won't be long."

"I do not mind."

I raised an eyebrow. "This is hardly the sort of place I'd expect you to enjoy." I tried to decipher his bland expression.

Despite the seemingly uninterested face, he seemed just a little too...satisfied, that was it...to be here. "Why did you insist on coming?"

"Like I said at the office of the FBI, I agree with Daniel Gibson. This place is somewhat *pericoloso*—dangerous."

It was a little too glib. He was making me nervous. "Why do you care what happens to me?"

Marco smiled at me, all Italian charm. "Let's just say I am protecting my investment, *cara*."

His investment? Me? I bristled a little. Sure I owed him but that didn't make me his property. "I thought this cleared things between us?"

He raised an eyebrow at me, gaze dropping to my throat. I looked away, trying not to think about the blood debt.

"Who says I am talking about only you?" His eyes flicked to Jase, threading his way through the crowd back to us.

Jase? "You're here to protect Jason?" I almost laughed. Then frowned. What the hell was Marco teaching Jase and what the hell kind of powers did Jase have if he was valuable enough for Marco to keep an eye on him? And who did he need protecting from here?

The answer appeared like magic. *Niko*. Looking better than ever in a body-hugging black T-shirt and jeans. "Good evening, Ms. Keenan, Mr. Trent." He bowed, slanting a gaze at Jase as he did so.

I didn't return the greeting. Instead I watched Marco who was looking at Niko with something close to distrust.

"Nikolai, I wasn't expecting you," I said.

"It is a night for surprises," Niko purred. He cocked his head at Lord Marco. "Always a pleasure to see you in one of our establishments, my lord Marco. Can I fetch you a...refreshment?"

I didn't want to know what a *refreshment* might mean in a dark club. Because, quite possibly, it would be a real live human rather than stored or manufactured blood.

Marco frowned at Niko. "I am fine, as I am. Why are you here?" His tone should've frozen Niko on the spot, which only confirmed my feelings where Niko was concerned. If Marco didn't like him, then he had to be very bad news.

"My lord Esteban thought I could assist Ms. Keenan and Mr. Trent." His eyes strayed again to Jason and he smiled. It made him look unnaturally beautiful, an effect only amplified by our grimy surroundings. Looking at Niko in this place was like finding the statue of David in a trailer park.

Jase returned the gaze. His expression didn't change but something about his posture made my heart sink. He was attracted to Niko, despite my warnings.

"I doubt Ms. Keenan has much use for a less than talented painter," Marco said. "Managing finances has never been your strong point."

There was a definite sting in his tone now and I wondered again about Niko's history. Maybe Marco would tell me if I asked nicely. I could use any help I could get to keep Jase from getting entangled.

Niko's face turned somewhat sulky. "I am here at my lord's command. I do what *he* tells me to do."

Marco took a step toward him and the hairs on the back of my neck sprang to attention as the atmosphere went super-charged.

"Your lord answers to *me*," Marco said with menace positively dripping from his voice.

We couldn't afford a scene. I couldn't risk giving away the real reason we were here. So I did something really dumb. I ignored every ounce of self-preservation I possessed and stepped between an Old One and the vamp he was pissed at. "What I need," I said in my best non confrontational voice, "is to do my job."

I looked from one to the other, my nerves screaming warnings from the tension vibrating from them both. "Lord Marco, please."

Marco stared at Niko a moment longer then the sense of danger evaporated. "This can wait."

I let out a breath. "Thank you. Nikolai, where's the manager?"

"He's not here."

I crossed my arms, wishing I'd let Marco take Niko out after all. "Excuse me?"

"He's detained," Niko said.

"Detained by who?" I demanded. "Esteban said to ask for Arthur Dempsey. He should be here."

Niko's smile would've been pretty if it hadn't been so smug. "I can show you what you need to know."

"You're a painter." Or at least, so Marco had said.

"I was a painter, now I'm a fixer."

"What's that?"

"Someone who wastes your time," Marco said curtly.

That earned us a shake of dark hair and an annoyed look. "I can show Ms. Keenan everything she needs to get started." Niko shot a sideways glance from me to Jase.

I got the feeling I wasn't the one he wanted to get started. The back of my neck tightened. The lack of a manager and Niko's appearance to replace him was too convenient. He was obviously flirting with Jase and I doubted Niko did anything without Esteban signing off. The whole situation smelled of game playing and subterfuge. Or perhaps a setup. What if Esteban was involved with Tate and Smith?

So the choices were retreat and come back when the manager was here or stay and risk walking into a trap of some kind. I gritted my teeth. There was no point leaving. If Esteban was involved then he could set me up whenever he chose. If he wasn't then I risked angering him if I delayed getting to work on his problem. Right now, that possibility worried me more than a threat that I had no real proof existed anywhere other than in my head.

I flipped a hand at Niko. "Let's get on with this."

Niko smiled happily while Marco's face went studiously blank. It didn't take long for us to be whisked upstairs to a suite of small rooms that were nearly as dingy as the rest of the place. The only difference was the carpet didn't have the same beer sodden stick to it and there were desks and filing cabinets and a couple of computers instead of a bar and ratty small tables.

Despite the manager's absence, there was one guy sitting at one of the desks, looking bored senseless, as his fingers flew over a keypad entering numbers. He leaped up when Niko ushered us into the room, eyes widening when he noticed Marco behind me. At least, I assumed it was Marco rather than me who brought the expression of shock to his face. I also figured from the reaction that he was a vampire.

"Lord Marco," he said with a bow. Then he straightened. "Nikolai." This time the bow was barely a bend. Apparently Esteban's pet wasn't terribly popular.

Nikolai curled his lip. "These are the systems people. You have created the account Lord Esteban required?"

The vampire nodded. "Yes, it will give them access to all the data. But I still don't understand why we need new—"

"Because our lord wishes it," Nikolai interrupted, voice chilly. "Do you think it's wise to question his decision?"

The vamp swallowed. "No. Of course, whatever Lord Esteban wants."

As a display of fawning, it was actually kind of pathetic. And said something about how Esteban ran his lineage. Iron fist all the way.

No more questions arose. The vamp gave us log-on details, sped us through a lightning speed tour of the systems and then scurried out when Niko suggested we wanted to work in private.

As the door closed behind him, Jason opened his briefcase

and started connecting a portable drive to the server. In the interests of spending as little time in the clubs as possible, we were going to dump all the data and analyze it in more detail back at the office. It would also leave less trace of an investigation for anyone who might be monitoring the system.

While Jase downloaded, I opened up the accounting package and skimmed through transactions, looking for anything that caught my eye, familiarizing myself with the common names and amounts flowing through the club's books.

It didn't take long to see that there was some creative accounting going on. Not large amounts, but there was definitely a mismatch between the bank balance and what sort of money the place should be making based on inventory turnover and door takings. If those figures were correct, of course.

Now all I needed to do was figure out where the money was going. But at least I'd be able to tell Esteban he definitely had a problem here. I wouldn't want to be in Arthur Dempsey's shoes when I told Esteban what was going on.

I worked steadily through some of the major account balances, skimming over recent entries, as Jase kept downloading then turned my attention to the bank accounts. The list in the system matched the list Esteban had provided but there could be others. Out of curiosity, I opened up a browser and clicked to the history. Amid a scary number of porn sites and a smattering of other sites with names that suggested that vampires were embracing the web in ways I didn't want to think about, there was an URL for a bank in the Cayman Islands.

Alarm bells clanged in my head. The manager of a tin-pot club like this one shouldn't need off-shore banking facilities personally and there was no Cayman account listed in the info on the club's accounts provided by Esteban.

I clicked on the link. Sure enough, it came up with a log-in page, requested my account details.

Someone had been a naughty boy. I beckoned to Niko. "I think you should get your manager in here. He's got some explaining to do."

Niko nodded and then crossed to the desk where Jase was working and picked up the phone. I noticed he took the opportunity to sit almost close enough to touch Jase. I also noticed that Jase made no effort to shoo him farther away.

Niko made a call—speaking so quickly I wasn't sure if it was Italian or Spanish or French he was spouting. Not English, anyway. Did he have something to hide?

He hung up the phone, smiling smugly. "It is done." He made no move to leave his position.

"The manager is coming here?" Marco asked.

I jumped. I'd forgotten he was in the room. He'd taken a seat in a corner when we'd first come in and kind of faded into the background as vampires do when they're being very still.

Niko nodded.

I tried to pretend I hadn't just spooked like a skittish horse. Queen of cool, that was me. "Where else would he—"

My cell rang. Probably Dan checking up on me. I found my earpiece, hooked it over my ear and pressed the button. "Look, I'm fine," I said in a teasing tone. "Stop worrying."

"But you insist on doing things that concern me," the voice on the other end said.

I froze. Not Dan. Dan's voice wasn't cold and dispassionate. It didn't make my mouth go dry. Dr. Smith. *Fuck.*

I broke out in a sweat, stomach churning as memories of Smith and what he'd helped Tate do to me flooded through me. A human, aiding a monster. Which made him worse than the monster in my books. In my nightmares it was just as often Smith hurting me as Tate.

I wanted to bolt. I wanted to throw up.

"Are you there, Ashley?" said the voice that I'd hoped never to hear again except in a courtroom or maybe standing outside a jail cell with him safely inside.

"I'm here." My voice shook and I struggled to breathe, bright lights dancing in front of my eyes. *Pull it together.* I couldn't faint or lose it. Not yet. I was safe, I reminded myself. Surrounded by vampires who were on my side. I sucked in a deep breath.

"You sound a little breathless. They told me you were looking tired this morning at that unfortunate incident."

He had someone watching me. This morning. At the suicide. Dan was right. This time I nearly did throw up, bending over as I fought not to retch. Jase and Marco were both by my side in an instant. I held onto Jase as I struggled for control, thoughts racing. Was he just watching or did he have someone here in the club?

Fear closed my lungs for a moment but then the wolf came to my rescue, anger and rage burning away the terror. Smith. We'd been tracking him for weeks and now the prey was in sight. Or hearing, at least.

I straightened, biting back a snarl. "I'm just fine." I needed to keep him talking. I had no idea whether the FBI were actively monitoring my calls or not. If they were, I could expect agents racing through the door any second. If not, well, this was about to be a very interesting conversation and I was pretty sure if the Taskforce weren't actually listening to my phone calls, they were, at least, recording them. "Where are you?" I demanded.

"That doesn't concern you. What should concern you is your own location. And what you think you're doing there."

Another wave of ice chilled me. He knew where we were *now*. I reached for a piece of paper. It fluttered as my hand shook. "I don't think what I do is of any interest to you at all," I said proud that my voice was steady.

"You disappoint me, Ashley. You're not nearly that naïve."

I scribbled frantically on the paper, underlining SMITH several times then held it up so Jase could see. He snatched the page, fury lighting his eyes.

"And you're not naïve enough to think you can just call me with no repercussions." I slipped my hand into my pocket, wrapped my fingers around the panic button. Should I push it? Was calling the FBI in on what was supposed to be an incognito exercise a smart idea? It boiled down to who did I least want pissed at me—Dan or Esteban? Or the lunatic talking on the other end of the phone?

I realized I hadn't heard the last thing Smith had said properly. Something about wolves and pride.

That decided me. The FBI arriving to save the day would only cause more trouble, angering Esteban and maybe triggering Smith into acting against those close to me—the way Tate had killed one of my Pack to draw me and Dan out. If Smith had anyone actually in the club, they would've tried something by now, surely? So we were probably okay. I wasn't quite ready to blow everything up and bring more pain raining down on everyone around me just for a threatening phone call.

Beside me, Jase was dialing his cell and I made frantic 'cut-it' gestures at him.

He scowled at me. "I'm calling Dan," he mouthed.

I shook my head and mouthed, "Dial and you're dead," as I tried to think. Jase lowered his cell and I took a deep breath. Keep Smith talking, that was the first step. "What do you want, Doctor?"

"I want you to stop poking your nose where it doesn't belong, Ms. Keenan. I would regret having to cut it off your pretty face."

I knew he wasn't making idle threats. Smith was ice cold. He would've killed me at Tate's without a second thought. Tate had stopped him. Who was going to save me this time? "I thought doctors were meant to do their best to protect human life?"

"I never said I'd kill you. Believe me, there are worse things than death."

Yes, there were. I'd met at least one of them. But Tate was dead and now the people who'd held his leash were warning me off again. Only a crazy person would bait them. Or someone who needed to keep one of them on the phone just in case the FBI were listening and could trace the call. "I don't tell the FBI what to do."

"I think you underestimate your influence with Special Agent Gibson. I have faith in your skills of persuasion, Ashley. I hope you put them to good use. Or I can guarantee you won't like the results."

The phone went dead and I snarled in frustration.

"I'm calling Dan." Jase was already hitting the button on his phone.

I grabbed it and hit the screen to disconnect the call. "Don't."

"He needs to know. He needs to know now."

Anger and menace roiled off Jase and I almost moved back. But I forced myself to stay still. "I'll tell him."

"When?" He reached for the phone, tugging it toward him.

I held on. Vamp versus wolf. A pretty even match though Jase was bigger than me. A muscle bulged in his jaw as he gritted his teeth and I held on tighter.

"When we leave," I snarled. "We don't need a busload of agents descending on this place. It's hardly going to keep what we're doing a secret."

Jase looked like he didn't much care about keeping Esteban happy. Niko, lounging against the desk, looked relieved for a brief moment then slipped back into his default 'I'm gorgeous' half-smile. Marco was doing a pretty good imitation of a statue again. I tried to match his level of casual.

Which was probably pointless in a room full of three vampires who could hear exactly how fast my heart was pounding.

"What did Smith want?" Jase's grip let up a little but he obviously wasn't going to let the subject slide.

"He wanted me to—" I realized Dan's displeasure would only be increased if I gave away details about an investigation in progress to outsiders and stopped talking. Maybe Marco and Niko had heard both sides of the conversation anyway, given vamp hearing but I would take that risk over being the one who actually gave them anything that might hint at the real situation with the anti-vaccines. I didn't know how much Dan had told Marco about what Tate had been up to but I knew for sure he wouldn't want Esteban to know any of it. I yanked the phone out of Jase's grip. "Let's talk about this later."

"You'll be talking about this with Dan later."

"Then I'll tell you after that."

Jase frowned, opened his mouth, and then closed it again. His face went kind of blank, as though whatever made him Jase wasn't behind his eyes anymore.

It was actually kind of spooky. "Jase?" He didn't respond, just kept staring at me. My head buzzed suddenly—an unpleasant sensation like static—and suspicion bloomed.

"Jase, what the hell are you doing?" It better not be what I thought it might be. I shoved him, rocking him back a few steps. "Jason!"

He winced and blinked, expression flowing back onto his face in a way that was only slightly less spooky than the blankness.

"Tell me you weren't just doing what I think you were doing."

He rubbed his chest, avoiding my gaze. "What do you think I was doing?"

"Trying to read my mind." Okay, now that I was saying it loud, it sounded kind of stupid. But I knew telepathy worked for werewolves and vampires had all sorts of psychic powers wolves couldn't even begin to imagine. Marco's interest in Jase wasn't because of his pretty red hair. I stared at Jase, hoping I was being dumb and that my best friend hadn't just tried the mental equivalent of mugging me.

A faint hint of pink hit his cheeks. Pretty red hair goes with pale skin and easy blushing—even if you're a vampire.

Fuck. I was right. My stomach heaved again and I had to sit down. "You were really trying to read my mind?" Jase knew how I felt about mental control. He knew Tate had thralled me. "How could you?" I whispered.

"I was—"

His guilty tone only confirmed it. I snarled at him, as a bitter taste rose in my mouth. My best friend had just betrayed me. "Do not even try to make excuses." I whipped my head around and nailed Marco with a glare. "You taught him how to do this?"

Marco shrugged. "Jason shows promise."

"Promise? What the hell does that mean?" How many more vamp tricks did Jason have in his bag? Was this even the first time he'd tried? Fuck. Fuck. Fuck. This was worse even than Esteban's sexual lure. That at least was mostly physical.

This was my mind. My privacy.

I'd vowed never to let someone into my head uninvited again. I'd let Tate in under duress and Marco only to get rid of Tate's influence. The telepathy I shared with the pack in wolf form was different. They never knew what I was thinking —well, apart from the fact most werewolves were pretty darn good with body language—they only heard what I wanted them to hear. "I said, what the hell does that mean?" I repeated when Marco didn't answer me.

"He has certain abilities."

Okay, so Marco wasn't going to tell me what the hell was going on. But I was sure as hell going to make Jason tell me.

Just as soon as we left. Which was going to be now. I was done for the night.

"You and I are going to talk," I said, turning back to Jase. "So pack all this up."

"You're leaving?" Niko said.

"Yes," I snapped.

"You are overreacting, *cara*," Marco said mildly. He moved from the chair he'd been lounging in to the desk I was using a little too quickly and I flinched.

Which made me madder and I surged to my feet, locking eyes with Marco. "Oh really? Anyone read your mind lately? Against your will?"

Jase flinched. I glared at him then turned my attention back to Marco. Keep your eyes on the biggest threat in the room. Jase had powers but he was no Old One.

Yet.

"Jason, why don't you go find Ashley a cab?" Marco said smoothly.

Hesitation, then resignation, flowed across Jase's face. He put down the cable he'd been winding and went to the door. Niko trailed behind him after a glare from Marco.

"Where do you get off ordering my employee around?" I snapped as I slammed my laptop shut.

"I am head of his lineage, I have as much right as you to order him around."

"I don't order him around."

"Don't you?" Marco looked politely disbelieving. "Then why does the idea of Jason coming into his powers upset you so?"

"It upsets me," I said, trying to stay calm, "because he tried to read my fucking mind. That's a violation."

"He cannot always help himself at the moment."

"You mean he wasn't trying to find out what Smith had said to me? Oops, sorry, just tripped and let my telepathy get away from me?"

Marco smiled suddenly, his deep green eyes lighting with humor. It was a disconcerting reminder that he was, in his way, attractive as Niko. More attractive really, because he didn't have Niko's smug self-satisfaction. But I wasn't going to let GQ charm sidetrack me.

"Why can't you leave him alone?" I shoved the laptop into its case and started piling everything else in the pockets. Cables. Mouse. Portable drive. Sanity. In some ways this was all Marco's fault. If he'd just left Jase alone I'd still have a best friend I could trust. I yanked the zipper on the case closed with enough force to tear the metal tab free. I tossed it to the floor.

"That would not be wise."

"Why not?"

The humor faded. "*Cara*, there are some things I do not need to discuss with you. In fact, I would remind you that I am here to help you as a kindness. I do not owe *you* anything."

"I didn't ask you to come," I snapped then sucked in a breath as the degree of aggression in my tone suddenly sank in. I was alone with an Old One. An Old One who'd just pointed out that I still owed him a debt. And I was yelling at him.

Unease cut through my anger like ice water. *Way to go, Keenan.*

I took another breath and picked up the laptop case. "I'm sorry, Lord Marco. That was rude."

"You are upset. But believe me, Jason was not trying to hurt you. Also, he was right about one thing."

"What's that?"

"You need to talk to your wolf about what happened here. Tell him his instincts were correct."

I hate it when people are right about something when I'm pissed off. So I didn't answer, just headed down to the club, wondering how much Marco had overhead of Smith's phone call. The crowd had picked up so that the smell of fresh sweat and too many five dollar aftershaves mingled with the stale beer-and-Marlboro smell.

I started to head for the door then spotted Jase at the bar.

Talking to Niko.

The hairs on the back of my neck stood up. Something in the angle of their heads or the just-a-fraction-too-close way they were standing made my stomach churn all over again. Surely Jase wasn't going to make things even worse by being stupid enough to fall for someone as blatantly bad news as Niko?

I pushed through the crowd and shoved in between them. "I thought Marco asked you to get a cab?"

Jase stared down at me. "I rang for one. It'll be a couple of minutes."

"Great, we can wait outside." I grabbed his arm and yanked. "Say goodnight, Niko."

Niko curled one corner of his mouth at me. "Goodnight, Ms. Keenan. Au revoir, Jason."

Yeah, well, there'd be no meeting again between these two if I had anything to do with it. I kept my fingers firmly around the expensive wool of Jase's jacket and headed for the exit.

* * *

It would've taken a chainsaw to cut through the furious silence in the cab. Probably self-preservation on Jase's part. On my part it was rage choking my throat.

I still couldn't believe Jase had tried to read my mind. Each time I pictured the weird expression on his face and the odd sensation in my head, fury boiled through me. I dug my fingers into the upholstery, the fabric shredding beneath my nails like Kleenex. I was going to have to tip the cabdriver like crazy.

I managed to make it all the way into the office before I started yelling. "Don't you *ever* try that again."

"Ash—"

"Do *not* 'Ash' me." I dumped my purse with a thump on the reception desk and clenched my hands so I wouldn't pick it up again and hurl it at Jase's head.

"I didn't mean to upset you."

"No, you just tried to read my *mind*."

He pulled off his jacket and tossed it toward the coat stand. "If it makes you feel any better, it didn't work."

I watched the jacket miss by a few inches. Jase never missed. "No, it doesn't make me feel any better. I have to be able to trust you, Jason, or this isn't going to work anymore."

"You can trust me." The hurt in his eyes almost made me believe him.

Almost.

"Can I?" Three hours ago I would've sworn on a sky-high stack of bibles that Jase would never hurt me. Now I wasn't so sure. Not when I had no idea what he was actually capable of psychically or while he seemed to be not entirely disinterested in Niko.

Jase tugged at the points of his collar. "I won't try it again."

"Unless Marco tells you to."

"No! Jesus, Ashley, who do you think I am?"

I didn't know, that was the problem. And if I couldn't have Jase as the one constant thing in my world, then everything seemed just a little too hard. My eyes started to burn and I blinked. I wasn't going to cry over this. I was mad. I had a right to be. Jase knew how I felt about this subject. And he'd done what he'd done anyway. "Why should I trust you? You can pick things out of my mind."

"No, I can't."

"Not yet." I was wearing a groove in the carpet in front of the desk, pacing up and down restlessly.

"I won't." He held up his hands in a what-do-I-have-to-do gesture.

I rubbed my forehead. We could go round and round on this for hours but I didn't have time. I still had to go home and go round and round with Dan about why I hadn't called him immediately to tell him about Smith. So I changed the subject. "Okay, why don't we talk about what the hell you were doing downstairs with Niko? I told you to stay away from him."

Jase scowled, baring his fangs. "I was just talking."

"That wasn't talking. That was flirting."

All expression drained from his face. "I don't think that's any of your business."

"When you start hanging out with the lord of the dark side's henchman and then suddenly you start losing your mind and trying to read mine, it becomes my business."

His lips pressed together. "I think I'm going home now."

"Fine. You do that. I'm late for Dan anyway."

"Make sure you tell him what happened." Jase stalked over and picked up his jacket from the floor, scowling at the wrinkled mess. He shook it straight with a vicious snap and tugged it on.

"Yeah because my night's been just a barrel of laughs so far."

He ignored me and reached for the door handle. Then stopped and turned back. "If it helps, I'm sorry."

"About Niko?"

Head shake. "About the mind thing. I just wanted to be able to tell Dan if you didn't."

"And that's supposed to improve my mood about you?"

"It's meant to be an apology."

I shrugged as my heart cracked a little. I wanted to forgive him but the anger burned too hot. Not yet. Not while the memories of what Tate had done to me was so fresh. Maybe not for a long time. "Okay. But we're not done with this." I looked at my watch. "Now, I have to go yell with someone else for awhile." I headed for my briefcase. I had to store the information we'd downloaded before I could go to Dan's.

"Well, actually, no you don't."

I swiveled back to Jase. "Excuse me?"

He smiled, more than a little grim satisfaction in the expression. "Dan just stepped out of the elevator. Good night, Ashley."

Chapter 6

I FOUGHT the urge to bolt into my office and lock the door as Jase walked out, turning sideways to let Dan come in. Running would be pointless. Dan could burst through a door in a nanosecond if he wanted. The look on his face made me think it wouldn't even take that long.

So much for keeping anything a secret. "Does this mean my calls are still monitored?" I said, moving behind the reception desk. I didn't think faux marble would be much protection against Dan either but it still made me feel a little better.

Dan halted on the other side of the desk. He looked rumpled, stubble shadowing his jaw. The darkness echoed the shadows under his eyes. And the fury on his face. "Marco called me. Right after the night team did." His voice was way too controlled.

"So that's a yes."

"Of course your calls are monitored," he snarled. "The case isn't closed."

My hands curled into fists. "Thanks for telling me."

"You really want to complain about me not telling you stuff? After what you just pulled?" His voice rumbled dangerously.

I inched backward as his scent overwhelmed me with smoky fury. "I was going to tell you."

"I gave you a panic button." He put one hand flat on the marble as if preparing to vault the desk if he had to. "You want to tell me why the fuck you didn't use it?"

I backed up a little farther but there wasn't far to go. My legs bumped into the cabinet that held our printer. "Because I wasn't in danger. And I didn't want the FBI raiding one of Esteban's clubs for no good reason."

"Not in danger?" The rumble in Dan's voice grew rougher. "You had one of the people who kidnapped and tortured you on the other end of the line and you think you weren't in danger?"

He was right but I wasn't going to tell him that. This was my life and I was going to live it my way. Too many people were trying to pull my strings at once. I was about to stage a marionette rebellion. "I was with Marco. In one of Esteban's clubs. They have pretty good security."

"What makes you think Esteban's on your side?"

"Well, he's trusting me to find out who's stealing millions of dollars from him, so he kind of has a vested interest in keeping me alive."

"There are other forensic accountants, you know."

"He wants the best." I picked up a pencil from Jase's neat little desk caddy. The tip was blunt. For a moment it was tempting to just stab myself with it. It would be the perfect end to the day.

Dan's hand circled his bad wrist, thumb rubbing the scar Tate's silver chains had left. "Come out from behind there."

I stayed where I was. If I went to him and let him hold me, I might just give in to the fear hearing Smith's voice had summoned and burst into tears. I was trying to prove I could handle all of this. I had to be strong. Tears weren't going to help. "I like it here."

Dan's arms tensed and I wondered whether he was going

to leap over the desk after all. "Ash, right now I don't know whether I want to kiss you or kick your ass. If I have to come round and get you, I might just lean toward the latter."

I wanted to go to him. I made myself stay. Told myself Smith wasn't going to win. But despite my best intentions, thinking of Smith made me shiver.

"What?" Dan's eyes sharpened.

"Nothing."

"You're shivering."

"No, I'm not."

Dan bounded over the desk and pulled me to him. "Come here, you idiot."

I let his warmth soak through me for a moment. He smelled like damp wool and tired man and the wild tang of wolf edged with anger. His arms tightened around me as I pressed my face against his shoulder, inhaling the scent of safety, and trying to believe I really was safe.

We breathed together for a few minutes, until the tension drained a little out of Dan's muscles as my fear ebbed away. Not one hundred percent gone but manageable again. Ever since Tate had reemerged, I'd been living with a certain level of fear. I'd gotten used to it.

"I really am okay," I said.

Dan's arms pulled me closer for a second. He dropped a kiss on the top of my head and then released me. "What did Smith say?"

"Not much. He warned me to back off." I eased sideways and picked up the laptop bag again so I could stash it.

He followed me as I walked into my office and started the complicated process of opening my safe.

"Or?"

I put on a fake dramatic voice as I entered the last passcode and the safe swung open. "Or I wouldn't like the consequences. He's all talk." Or so I hoped. The laptop just squeezed in with the other files I had in there. It would be safe enough until we could download the information we'd taken from Infradark but really if I was going to keep getting these ultrasensitive jobs, I needed a bigger safe.

"Ash, these people aren't the type to mess around. They think that vampires who turn everyone they bite are a good idea, remember?"

That made me shiver again. I covered it up by slamming the safe shut. I wasn't sure my body could handle another meltdown tonight. Adrenaline overload already had my muscles feeling like I'd been run over by something the size of Marco's limo. "Well, there hasn't been a rash of new vampires lately. Particularly not ones complaining about the fact they just got bitten and whoosh, vampire."

That actually raised a smile. "Whoosh, vampire?"

"You know." I waved a hand vaguely. I really had no idea what happened when a vampire turned other than it happened at sunrise the day after they were infected. "Instant vampire with none of the normal woo-woo stuff. That means their anti-vaccine doesn't work. It didn't work on me."

That wasn't strictly true. Because Dan had bitten me at the same time I'd received Tate's blood, none of the doctors had any idea whether I'd changed because of the anti-vaccine or my own vaccines failing as part of normal odds or something else altogether. The anti-vaccine could work perfectly for all we knew.

"I'm still increasing your protection," Dan said.

My jaw clenched. "Define increasing?" In the first few weeks after I'd killed Tate, Dan and I had had agents watching our house and following us everywhere. But when it seemed that there wasn't going to be any immediate retaliation by whoever the hell Tate was working with—or for—other than Dr. Smith, I'd been able to convince Dan to ease everything back.

I knew that the Taskforce kept an eye on my house and maybe even on me but I no longer saw them or had de facto bodyguards accompanying me to the office and the grocery store. I preferred life without an audience and besides the privacy issue, being surrounded by Taskforce agents on protection detail just made it harder for me to move on from what had happened. It's hard to forget with a constant reminder following you around.

"You have people watching over you now. It doesn't interfere with your life."

"Yes, but you're not talking about just watching, are you?" I said.

Dan looked wary. "No," he admitted. "Now that Smith has resurfaced, I want you to have a detail again."

A fresh batch of fear landed in my stomach with a thud. And it brought a side order of frustration with it. The combination made my stomach hurt. Was my life ever going to get back to normal? I didn't want it to be the same as it had been before Tate. After all, it couldn't be the same. I was a werewolf now. But I wanted to live without looking over my shoulder every second. Without weird-ass supernaturals playing games with me and Old Ones using me as pawns. Was that really so much to ask?

But apparently the universe wasn't quite done with screwing around with me just yet. And it was hard to argue with Dan. Tate's cronies had kidnapped me once. They'd taken my aunt and Dan too. I had no desire to let them get their hands on me again. "I can't take a protection detail into Esteban's clubs," I pointed out. Dan's expression turned grim and I held up a hand. "No, you don't get to tell me to give up Esteban's case. If I have to live with a protection detail, you have to live with me getting rid of my debt to Marco. The detail will have to wait outside. I'll take the panic button."

Dan's lips compressed but then he nodded. "All right. Though I'm going to speak to Marco and see if there are any of his people who can go with you to the clubs as well. You need more than just Jase if Smith tries something."

I couldn't argue with that. And other than Jase and the few vampires I'd met at the Taskforce, I wasn't friendly enough with any other vampire to ask for help. And it wasn't exactly the sort of favor I'd want to ask one of my clients. I didn't want any of them knowing what I was getting mixed up in again. It had taken some pretty swift talking to soothe tempers after I'd had to go AWOL for awhile after being changed by Dan and then again after Tate.

"Deal," I said. "I don't like it but okay."

Dan looked relieved as he sat on the edge of my desk. "My job is to keep you safe. You don't have to like it. I don't like it either. But I will keep you safe."

I really, really, hoped he was right about that.

* * *

I woke up the next morning, my stomach still churning and my nerves pulsing with adrenaline. The strange mix of fear and anger powered my racing heart. Giving into the fear wasn't going to get me anywhere so I chose to go with mad. Mad enough to need to burn off some of it if I was going to be able to function. If I went to the office in this mood I was going to end up fighting with Jase again. I hadn't forgiven him for the crap he'd tried to pull but I didn't want any more tension right now. I could go out back to the home gym I'd set up but lifting weights and pounding a heavy bag wasn't what I was in the mood for. So I decided to go to Hagan's.

Until I stepped out my front door and found Andy Ramirez and Esme on my porch, dressed in his-and-hers versions of blend-into-the-background gray suits. I knew a protection detail when I saw one. Damn. I'd forgotten I'd agreed to this. Dan had wasted no time getting things organized.

"How long have you two been here?" I asked.

Andy held up a hand. "We were trying to work out who

got to tell you. Dan said you were okay with a detail but Esme was skeptical. I voted for rock paper scissors but Essie here is scared I'll beat her."

Esme's lip curled. "In your dreams. And I told you not to call me that. We just got here," she added to me. "We're the day shift."

Day shift? "There's been someone out here all night?" Dan had been even faster than I'd thought.

"Yes. Plus the perimeter guys."

Muscles the length of my spine tightened, the familiar claustrophobic sense of being watched settling over me. All this because of one stupid phone call. I took a deep breath through my nose. I'd agreed to this. This was how I stayed safe. So I needed to suck it up. "Sorry you drew the short straw. I'm sure you have better things to do."

Neither of them looked like they disagreed with me. But neither of them replied. Agents on the job didn't generally complain about their orders.

"There's a team meeting later this morning," Andy said. "Dan asked us to tell you."

"I have something I need to do first." I couldn't quite keep the sharpness from my tone. "He'll just have to cope without us."

Esme started to protest. I shook my head.

"No arguing. If you want to protect me, fine. But you go where I go."

The disapproving silence as we walked to their car nearly made my ears ring.

* * *

"Well, well, look what the cat dragged in," Tommy Hagan said as I stomped through his door. He flashed me a smile that revealed the dimple in his cheek, eyes twinkling. "What brings you here, Ash, darlin'?"

I ignored his flirting. Half-Virginian, half-Irish, Tommy oozed charm like the rest of us breathed. His southern drawl combined with the dark hair and Newman blue eyes he'd inherited from his father, slayed women in the aisles. I wasn't in the mood to be slain. "I need to shoot something."

He cocked an eyebrow. "Who was dumb enough to piss you off?"

That made me smile. Tommy was the one who'd taught me to shoot when I'd decided that if I was going to take on supernatural clients, I needed to be able to protect myself.

"Thomas, the number of people dumb enough to piss me off these days never ceases to amaze me." I pulled out my membership card and slapped it down on the counter.

"Got any pictures?" He picked up the card and swiped it through the reader. "I can project them up on the targets and you can shoot their sorry behinds."

His eyes twinkled and I knew I'd made the right decision to come here. Tommy always cheered me up. Something about a cute guy treating you like a goddess even if you were only a friend was good for the female ego.

"No pictures. But thanks for the offer."

"And your friends?" He cocked an eyebrow as he handed me my card back.

"Can you give Esme a guest pass? Agent Ramirez—" I jerked my chin toward Andy "—will be staying out here."

"That's not a good idea," Esme said.

"Why not? You and I will be inside and armed. So it makes sense to have someone out here to stop anyone getting inside in the first place."

Esme scowled then turned her ice-queen expression on Tommy. "Are there any other entrances or exits?"

"Just the service door out back."

She looked torn. I knew I was putting her in a difficult position. I knew a little about how protectees should behave from my previous stint with a detail and I hadn't given them a chance to check out our destination at all but right now I just couldn't bring myself to care too much.

"I'm on it," Andy said, pulling out his phone.

"Get the perimeter guys to check it out," Esme warned. "You stay here."

He rolled his eyes at her as he backed away a little, talking low and fast into the cell.

"You got some ID, darlin'?" Tommy said as Esme watched Andy.

She turned and slapped her badge onto the desk. "Will that do? And the name is Agent Watson."

Tommy grinned unrepentantly. "Sure thing, Agent Watson. The FBI isn't playing fair though, hiring sweet things like you."

Esme's hands flexed briefly. If she'd been in cat form, Tommy's face might've wound up slightly less pretty. "Trust me, I'm not so sweet. Some might even say I have claws." The last word was almost a hiss and Tommy's eyes widened just a little.

"We'll need about an hour of range time," I said. "Put it on my account." I tried not to smile as Tommy kept a wary eye on Esme as he tapped in her details. It wasn't often I saw him knocked off his stride by a woman. Of course, he didn't usually date shifters. Just humans. Like I'd been.

We'd had a very brief–two weeks kind of brief–fling way back when Dan and I were over and I was in strict no-one-gets-my-heart-mode. Given that that was the way Tommy ran all his relationships, it had suited both of us until he got bored and I realized I'd rather keep his friendship than have him scratch my itches.

The computer finally beeped a clearance for Esme and Tommy passed her ID back. "You want to use your gun, Ash? Or try something different? I've got some new toys."

What Tommy didn't know about guns probably wasn't worth knowing. I'd always thought that was the reason he hadn't hooked up with someone permanently—his heart belonged to cold steel and gunpowder.

"What sort of toys?" My Glock could do some damage but I figured whatever Tommy was offering might be more fun. Just what the doctor ordered.

"Let me choose. I've got a couple of things that make nice big holes. That should blow the blues off your back."

"Perfect. How come you always know what I need?"

"Darlin', I live to serve, you know that. And for you, Agent Watson?"

"I'll use my gun," Esme said coolly.

"You're losing your touch, Tommy," I teased.

His grin faded as he stepped out from behind the front desk. "And now I'm hurt. As I should be. You haven't been around here for quite some time, sweetheart. And I hear things."

Shit. He was right. I hadn't been here since I'd changed. And he was letting me know he knew I was a werewolf. I raised my eyes and met his. "Do you have a problem with the things you hear?"

He grinned again. "You going to bite me or my customers?" He included Esme in the question as he looked from me to her.

I wrinkled my nose. "Hardly. I know where you've been."

This time he laughed out loud. "Then we're good. And I'm looking forward to seeing if your new reflexes can improve that tragic inclination of yours to pull to the left. You might even be able to handle something with a bit more kick now."

* * *

Turns out that shooting stuff was exactly what I needed. I blew holes in targets and holograms until my fingers started to cramp. As a bonus, Tommy was right. I was stronger now. No more being jolted backward by recoil.

"Feeling better?" Esme asked as I stepped away from the range, double checked the gun was clear of ammunition and then put it with the others waiting for cleaning.

Her tone made me look up. "Better than what?" I wriggled my fingers to ease them. I could handle more kick but that didn't mean the different grips and size of the guns I'd been trying hadn't stretched my hand in unfamiliar ways.

Esme met my gaze squarely. "Than whatever it is that has you so cranky lately."

Tommy shot me a look then gathered up his guns and left us alone in the empty range.

"Cranky?" I said.

"Angry. Aggravated. *Bitchy*," she clarified. "You've been giving everyone a hard time for weeks."

"No, I haven't," I said automatically.

Esme shook her head. "Yes, you have."

"Well, you're hardly sweetness and light yourself today," I pointed out. In fact, she'd blown away just as many targets as I had.

"We're not talking about me."

Her denial was a little too fast and I realized I was onto something. Esme was cranky and not just about me. I cocked my head, smelling the ozone tang of annoyed cat and suddenly it hit me. That's why Andy's scent was so familiar. He smelled like Esme. "Ramirez is a cat shifter," I said slowly.

There weren't that many big cat weres in America. Esme was the only jaguar in Seattle, and there were no other cats working for the Taskforce in Washington.

"So?" Esme said.

"So maybe that's why you're snapping at me."

"That man has no impact on my mood," she snapped.

I tried not to smile. I knew denial when I heard it. Maybe this was a territorial thing...or, I reconsidered, trying to work out what exactly could get Esme so annoyed, maybe an *attraction* thing. I tried not to smile. "Really? You're a cat, he's a cat...what sort of cat is he, by the way?"

She scowled. "If you think I'm interested in knowing what species that man is, then you're mistaken."

I could almost see a bristling tail lashing behind her. Push a cat too far and you wound up scratched. "Well, he's your partner now."

"And you're trying to change the subject," she said coolly. "What's going on? You and Dan are arguing all the time."

I winced. Damn. I hadn't realized the agents had noticed the tension between us. Jase knew but I hadn't talked about it with Esme. She'd known Dan a lot longer than she'd known me. I didn't want to put her in the middle.

"Are you still seeing your counselor?"

Color filled my cheeks. The Taskforce and the pack had provided counseling after I'd changed but I'd kind of stopped going.

"It might help. Something's obviously wrong." She looked me up and down. "And you've been through a lot." Sympathy softened her tone.

"I—"

"You have to do something, Ash. Like I said, the bitch thing is getting tired."

My whole body went hot. Guilt and embarrassment was not a pleasant combination. "I'm sorry, I don't mean to be."

"You could talk to me," Esme said gently which only made me feel worse. "What's the problem you and Dan are having? Is it the case?"

"Not completely," I admitted. "But that isn't helping. He's just being...overprotective."

"People *have* tried to kill you."

"I know," I said, hearing frustration rise in my voice. How could I explain it? "And I'm grateful to be protected but he never *asks*. He just lays down the law. And even when I agree to what he wants, he always wants that little bit more."

"He is a werewolf," Esme pointed out. "And he's an alpha."

I sighed. "That's half the problem. So am I."

Esme looked confused for a moment then understanding dawned. "Oh."

"I've tried to tell him but he doesn't listen. I just want to have a say in my own life." I ran my hands through my hair, straightening the bits mussed up by the ear protectors. "I don't know what else to do. You're pretty alpha, how do you handle it?"

She shook her head. "It's not quite the same for cats. We don't have packs. There's not as much hierarchy. And we don't bond the same way as wolves do." She looked a little wistful.

"Trust me, bonding isn't all it's cracked up to be. Not that I even know if we are bonded," I muttered the last bit but Esme heard me anyway.

"You need to talk to Ani about this."

I turned back to the range, staring at the rows of paper targets with their hearts blasted out. I knew how they felt. I wasn't sure I was up to letting Ani see my wounds. "I know."

"You should talk to her soon. We could go now."

"I thought you said there was a meeting this morning?"

Esme smoothed her hair, which hadn't even rumpled with the ear protectors. "Well, you can go to the meeting you're already late for and fight with Dan some more, or you can go talk to Ani and try and work out how to stop fighting. Your choice."

"Can I choose just staying here and shooting things?"

"Nope. Call Ani."

* * *

I knocked on Ani and Sam's front door then stepped back and waited. Now that I was here, I was nervous. What if Ani didn't have the answers I needed? If my Alpha couldn't help me figure out how to make Dan and I work, then I was in serious trouble. I took another step back and bumped into Esme standing behind me. I jumped forward again and she pointed at the door, looking stern. Crap. Even if I wanted to bail, she wouldn't have let me. She definitely came from the school of tough love. I swallowed and stared at the door. The sound of footsteps pounding down the hallway inside practically vibrated against my ears and the door flew open.

"Hi, Ms. Keenan. Mom's coming." Caleb, Ani's oldest son, grinned up at me then turned and bolted back down the hall, dodging around Ani as she walked toward me.

"He's feeling a little rambunctious," she said, smiling after Caleb. The sounds of a squeal then a peal of laughter sounded from the depths of the house.

"No school today?" I asked.

"No. Lucky me. I've got the whole horde home."

Ani sounded half-amused, half-frustrated. Her rust-colored shirt had a streak of flour on one sleeve and her red hair was escaping the green scarf she'd wrapped around it, short curls springing out in several directions.

I didn't know how she did it, running the pack, a web design business, and raising three kids. "If it's a bad time, I can come back."

She shot me a look. "I think it's about time we talked, don't you?"

The tone was Alpha-with-a-capital-A. Which I took to mean she'd been expecting me to turn up on her doorstep before now. I definitely wasn't getting out of this little chat. I followed her through the house to her office and parked myself on the overstuffed old sofa that took up half of one wall.

"You look tired," Ani said as she settled herself on the

other end, sitting cross-legged. Her dark jeans had flour streaks that matched her shirt.

I shrugged. "Long day yesterday." Tired had become kind of a default state of being for the last few months. I could go for longer on less sleep now that I was a werewolf but that didn't mean that I enjoyed it.

Another squeal of laughter broke the silence and Ani leaned across to close the door. Which only muted the noise to a dull roar.

"Caleb's birthday is coming up, isn't it?" I asked. His thirteenth birthday. Children born of werewolves usually underwent their first change around that age. Not all of them survived, though there hadn't been anyone lost in our pack for a long time. Still, I felt guilty that I was adding to Ani's problems at a time when she had more than enough on her plate.

"Next month," she agreed neutrally. "What can I do for you, Ashley? Are you here about Dan?"

I squirmed a little. "What makes you think it's Dan?"

"Ash, the day I can't read tension in my own pack members is the day Sam and I will hang up our Alpha hats and retire to Hawaii. You two have been avoiding us but, as the saying goes, you can run but you can't hide."

True enough. Running certainly hadn't been getting me anywhere anyway. "It's not just Dan," I said.

"Well, do you want to start with him or the other stuff?"

"The other stuff."

Ani made an encouraging sound and I tried to work out exactly how to ask the question without sounding clueless. As always, Ani's scent—a mix of deep green wilderness, the spice and home smell of the pack and a thread of fire that was hers alone—had a calming effect on me. I sank a little deeper in the sofa, hugging a cushion to me. "I need to know if I can shield from a vampire; from someone trying to read my mind or influence me."

"Nothing can protect you if you're thralled," Ani said slowly.

"I know that part." I wasn't planning on gazing into any vamp's eyes and letting them take me over any time soon. I needed to know how to deal with the other powers they could wield. "But some of them can do things without thralling you, can't they?"

"Uh-huh." She nodded, and then tilted her head, big green eyes darkening a little. "Anyone in particular been bothering you?"

Might as well go with the truth while I was here. "I'm doing a job for Lord Esteban. To pay off my debt to Marco," I added quickly when her mouth dropped open a little. "He pulled some sort of voodoo on me at his club."

"Define 'voodoo.'" There was a definite rumble underscoring the words. Mama Wolf didn't like anyone messing with her pack.

I looked away. "It's kind of embarrassing."

"From what I hear he's pretty good at turning people on," Ani said. "Would that be in the ballpark?"

I nodded then shivered, feeling cold all over again. "He didn't even *touch* me. At least Tate had to thrall me to make me do what he wanted."

"And you're worried that Esteban might not have to?"

"Dan said—" I broke off. I didn't want to think about the scenario Dan had outlined too hard. "Dan said that he wasn't as affected. That I could learn how to shield."

"You can. How well depends on your natural talent for it."

I leaned forward. "How exactly?"

"Shielding partly depends on the person's force of will." Ani grinned at me suddenly. "Somehow, I don't think you'll have a problem."

"Dan said I had to learn from an Alpha."

Ani nodded. "Plus it's usually better if a woman learns from a woman."

"Why?"

"I think it boils down to the fact that male and female brains don't work in quite the same way. Girls can explain how it works in a way that makes sense to girls."

"So Dan didn't teach me because he hasn't got ovaries?"

"I'd guess Dan didn't teach you or ask me if I had because he's running himself just as ragged as you are. And I doubt he was planning for you to be tangling with Esteban."

I scowled.

"What?" Ani asked.

"You asked what was going on with me and Dan. That's it in a nutshell. He's trying to run my life."

Ani leaned back against the couch, rubbing one jean-clad thigh thoughtfully. "He's used to being in charge."

"So am I. Jase says we're both alpha."

"He's right."

I blew out a breath. "So how do you make it work? How do you and Sam figure things out?"

"Well, for one thing we didn't fight the bonding process quite as hard as you two seem to be doing."

"Pardon?"

"Bonding isn't as simple as the chemical reaction. You have to make the emotional commitment. From what I can tell, you're both holding back."

"Because he keeps trying to run my life," I said. "I can't just lie down and surrender control. I want a partner, not a keeper. Which is why I'm here asking you how to fix this."

"The same way you fix anything, hard work and persistence and a little love," she said gently. "If you want each other then you'll both have to give a little. You want me to get Sam to talk to Dan?"

"Will it help?"

"At this point the question is more will it make things any worse? Sam and I have done this before. Sure, the two of you are more evenly matched dominance-wise than most couples in the pack but it can work. If you want it to. You called claim on him, so I have to assume you did at the point. Has that changed?"

I studied the row of framed children's drawings on the wall, the most basic proof of Sam and Ani's love for each other. Did I want that with Dan? Children? Marriage? Forever? It all felt overwhelming right now. Still, if I walked away from Dan, when we were partly bonded, I might be walking away from any sort of a future with another were-wolf. I couldn't see many humans wanting to take a werewolf on.

And, deep down, I didn't want to give up on Dan and me. Not while we still had a chance.

"Well?" Ani prompted.

"It hasn't changed. But I don't know if it can work if Dan won't let me be me."

"No alpha is ever going to be happy with his mate being at risk."

"I'm not asking him to be happy about it. I'm not happy about it either. But I want him to work with me, not against me."

"Have you told him that?"

"Yes. He doesn't listen."

"Keep trying. Sam and I used to butt heads too. See what happens after Sam has a chance to talk to him."

I wished I could have the same sort of quiet faith that Ani's voice held. "And if that doesn't work?"

"We'll cross that bridge when we get to it."

I shook my head. "That all I get?"

"No," she said, shuffling forward on the couch. "You also get this." She reached out and rested two fingers between my eyebrows.

"Whuh—" was all I had time to say before there was a confused blur of *shield-moon-glass-wall-think-protect* spin-ning through my head with hazy images and a rush of emotions. I rocked backward, breaking contact. "What the hell?"

"Shielding," she said with a grin. "At least the basics."

I shook my head, trying to ease the buzzing sensation in my brain. "I don't understand."

"Give it a day or so to settle and then we'll try it out."

"But—"

"Trust me, it's easier this way. If I sit here and talk you through it, you're just going to wind up confused and frustrated. Come over in a couple nights and I'll tell you some more."

"Why night?"

"It's easier in moonlight, at least at first."

"Why?"

She grinned. "We are tied to the moon. Makes sense that she gives us strength."

I was still trying to sort through the images and sensations floating through my mind. "I'm seeing myself in a glass box, moonlight reflecting everywhere. Is that right?"

"Close enough. Don't worry at it, it'll make more sense if you wait."

"Shielding is seeing myself in a magical moonlit glass box?" I couldn't help the incredulous tone.

"What did you expect? Secret mind exercises and mysteries passed down the generations?" Her grin grew wider. "Actually, that's kind of what you got. Just packaged up for speedier delivery."

"So a few days and I'll be able to do this?"

"No, a few days and you'll understand how to do it. It takes practice to get good."

"Great, I'll just avoid Esteban until I get good."

"Sounds like a plan to me." Her eyes suddenly focused on the door. "I think I smell trouble. I'd better go see what the brats are up to before they burn the house down." She stood and then bent down and pressed a kiss to my cheek. "Try to relax and give Dan a chance. And come see me in a few days."

* * *

"You're late," was Dan's only greeting when I finally arrived at the Taskforce.

"Actually, I'm early." It was just after one. Most days I didn't arrive at the Taskforce until after five. "I was busy."

Dan yanked open his desk drawer. "Doing what? Jase said you hadn't come into the office." He dropped a file into the drawer then closed it with a bang.

I lifted my chin. "I went to see Ani." I wasn't going to mention Tommy.

"You smell like gunpowder."

"I bought bullets," I lied. "I thought I should stock up."

Dan looked disbelieving. "You think you need more ammo but you won't use your panic button? You think if someone tries to take you that you're going to turn around and blast your way free?"

"You think they're going to stand around while I push a button?" I used my foot to push the door shut behind me.

Dan came around the desk. "No. But it doesn't take long and you might get a chance to at some point."

I blew out a breath. "Are you picking a fight for a reason? You know exactly where I was all morning because Esme and Ramirez were with me the whole time."

His face tightened. "I'm not picking a fight, I'm trying to protect you. You're putting yourself in danger. You didn't use the button last night."

"My choice."

"Don't I get a say?"

"Not if what you really mean is 'don't I get to choose for you?'"

"I mean—" He broke off and sat down with enough force that the chair creaked in protest. "I just want you to be safe."

"And I don't want to be in danger, but I have a job to do, several of them in fact. Esteban's my client, Dan. And I don't think he's the type to mess around if I piss him off. So I'm trying not to piss him off."

"I told you not to take that job."

"I need to discharge my debts—" His face darkened at the reference. "I mean, debt. I have no intention of doing anything about the other one."

"You could've asked Marco to give you something else to do for him."

"What makes you think that would be any better than this?"

He tugged at his tie as he stared up at me. "It couldn't be much worse."

I sighed and sat in the chair beside his. "I think this conversation is going around in circles. Can we try a different subject? What was the meeting about this morning?"

"Smith calling you. What else?"

"Well, then you didn't need me. I already know what he said. You have the transcripts, I'm sure."

He nodded. "And after listening, we all agree on one thing."

This couldn't be good. "What's that?"

"Whatever you're poking around in for Esteban has to be linked to this."

What? I sat down next to him as my knees went weak. "Are you kidding me?"

"Why else would Smith suddenly decide to threaten you? It's been over two months since you killed Tate."

Esteban and Smith in cahoots? Admittedly it had crossed my mind last night but nothing really bad had happened. If Esteban was trying to set me up for something then last night was a perfect opportunity. It didn't feel right to me. "I don't know...slow day at Psychos'R'Us, maybe? What makes you think Esteban has anything to do with this?"

"I didn't say he did. But whatever he's got you investigating pushed Smith's buttons."

"He couldn't just be warning me off the case?"

"You've been working on this case for weeks now, since Tate died. Why start threatening you now unless something has changed?"

"I don't know." I shrugged. "You've got to admit it's only the last few weeks we've gotten serious again. You were hurt and..." I trailed off. There were really no words for the total insanity of the first few weeks after Tate died. "Or maybe Ramirez triggered something and Smith thought it was me. Have you asked him?"

"He says he was only looking at stuff you'd already been over. Something set Smith off last night. The only new link in the chain is Esteban."

I didn't like the spiky scared feeling in my stomach that agreed with him. "But we'd hardly done anything," I objected. "Just downloaded some data and looked at a few accounts. How would Smith even know?"

"You're the forensic accountant, you tell me."

I tried to think about it objectively. "There could be some sort of tracking program—in the system or in one of the banks—or someone at the club tipped them off. Those are the most likely options."

"And if it's something in the system?"

"Could be anything." And really, how unlikely was it that we'd stumble into that particular club first off? So were all of Esteban's clubs being subverted somehow? Jase was right, whoever had the balls to embezzle from an Old One had to be pretty darn sure of themselves.

The sort of person who'd felt comfortable holding Tate's leash would seem to fit that description pretty well.

"Earth to Ash?" Dan prompted. "What are you thinking?"

I swallowed, trying to ease the sudden desert in my mouth. "I'm thinking I need to get back to the office and look at what we pulled from Infradark last night. Look for clues."

"Sounds like a plan. Why don't you take Andy with you?"

"Esteban agreed to Jase helping me, not the FBI."

He shook his head. "Don't worry, we'll deal with Esteban."

"How exactly?" The last thing I needed was Esteban after me as well as Smith. Dan wasn't exactly in a 'treat the vampire with kid gloves' kind of mood.

"If you find anything we'll get a warrant for the data from him. After all, he's a good, law-abiding businessman or so his lawyers always claim. He should want to cooperate with the FBI."

"He didn't show much sign of wanting to cooperate with you the other night. He's going to go nuts."

"That's my problem."

"I kind of think it will be mine. He wanted this to be a secret."

"You didn't tell us anything. Smith's call tipped us off."

"You know, someone warned me a little while ago that I was jumping from the frying pan into the fire. Maybe you should take your own advice." I rose. "I have to get back to the office, are you still coming to Caldwell with me tomorrow?"

"Of course."

The no-hesitation answer made me feel better about things. "Thank you."

* * *

By six a.m. I was up, packed, and pacing around my house, well before Dan was due to pick me up. He'd been called out to another case just past midnight so hadn't made it home.

By nine a.m., I'd had too much coffee, too little sleep, and there were too many elephant-sized butterflies tap-dancing in my stomach. The sight of Dan's big Jeep pulling into the driveway calmed them a little. Only a little. I carted my bags out onto the porch while he was still parking.

"You're keen," he said, easing himself out of the car. He walked over and picked up my case. "You okay?"

"Not really. But I'm going anyway."

He nodded. Then dropped the bag and pulled me toward him. "I'll be right there with you." He smoothed hair back from my face then lowered his mouth to mine.

His kiss was soothing rather than sexy, just a gentle press of lips moving softly over mine as if he could transfer some strength or vitality to me.

I was the one who pulled him closer and kissed him back frantically. I hoped that he might be able to make everything go away for a few moments.

And he did. Heat and Dan replaced everything else in my brain as his tongue touched mine. It reminded me that the full moon was coming next week. The waxing of the moon always stirs a werewolf's blood.

Which made it kind of bad timing that we were about to spend the night at my aunt's. A small bed and the knowledge of Bug just a few walls away tended to keep us behaving ourselves.

Then again, it was unlikely I'd be still in the mood once I got home.

Not with what I had to do tomorrow.

I pulled away after tasting Dan one last time. "We should get going."

He nodded and I saw the same combination of regret and hesitation and lust in his eyes that coursed through me. "Can't keep Bug waiting."

I didn't talk much on the way down. In fact, I stuck the earbuds of my iPod in my ears and focused on trying to find something in my music library that suited my mood.

Nothing seemed to help all that much. My mind kept returning to tomorrow.

To the memorial service.

To everything I didn't want to remember.

To pain.

The memorial service is held in two parts. A nondenominational service at the town hall and then laying wreaths and flowers at the graveyard.

Everyone walks to each of the victims' graves.

Everyone cries.

I know it's meant to help but it never makes me feel any better to look down and see three granite stones carved with the names of my parents and sister and to know they're gone forever.

In fact, I'd rather have a tooth in need of root canal.

That's the part that hurts, you know. The before. People say I'd rather have root canal but that bit doesn't hurt. Not if your dentist has the lovely needles. Sure it hurts a bit afterward, which is why God invented Codeine but it's the piercing, throbbing, ache beforehand when your tooth is trying to tell you it's dying that's the painful part.

That's what standing over those graves feels like to me each and every year.

Like being pierced by it all over again.

Like part of me dying all over again.

I wasn't looking forward to the experience. Worse, I couldn't help thinking about the reminder that had popped up on my calendar yesterday about my vaccinations.

Every year for twelve years I'd been to the memorial, and I'd done it with an arm that ached and burned from the vaccine boosters. It felt necessary somehow; like my suffering honored theirs and that my commitment to staying alive for them was renewed.

This year my arm wouldn't hurt at all.

This year, I wasn't human anymore. Werewolves didn't need the vaccinations.

Which was only going to make the pain worse than ever.

Dan had the sense to stay quiet for most of the trip down, only asking if I wanted anything when he stopped for gas. I shook my head, keeping my sunglasses on and the music loud as I stared out the window, not really seeing the familiar scenery whizzing by.

He held my hand as we walked up to Bug's front door.

Bug bustled us inside and started fussing.

It was almost more than I could bear and I ended up pleading a headache and escaping upstairs for a nap for a few hours. But I couldn't hide forever.

Chapter 7

THE NEXT MORNING dread churned my stomach, making me refuse Bug's breakfast. And turning down Bug's pancakes and bacon with homemade syrup is a crime. Dan and Bug both frowned when I turned down coffee as well. I told them to stop fussing. Bug made me peppermint tea then left me alone.

I retreated to the front room, staring out at the sunny day. The memorial started at noon. I guess they picked the time as a statement about humans and daylight and survival. Though sunshine wasn't guaranteed on any day in Caldwell.

When it came time to get ready, my stomach was worse than ever. I wondered whether I'd make it through the ceremony without puking. But I told myself I felt like this every year and I'd be fine once it was over. I was lying. It didn't feel this bad every year. This year I was upset and anxious, not just upset. I couldn't shake the feeling something bad was going to happen.

Apparently Smith had spooked me more than I'd realized.

"You're sure it's okay that I'm here?" I asked Bug for the twentieth time as we descended the stairs.

"You're one of us," Bug said to me, tugging at the top

button of the collar of her bright purple dress. They'd introduced a 'no black' rule after the first year, on the theory that the service should be a celebration of the lives of the victims. We all obediently wore cheerful colors but it still didn't feel like a celebration. My suit was dark green. Jase had said that was cheating so I'd added a vivid raspberry scarf. He'd approved the combo. I wasn't sure it didn't just make me *look* like a raspberry.

I watched Bug fussing with her collar then reached out to do it for her. "But how many of them know I'm a werewolf now?" I smoothed the collar into place.

Bug shrugged, twitching at her skirt. "It doesn't matter."

It was a nice lie but a lie all the same. Some of Caldwell's population would have huge issues with a werewolf being at the memorial if they knew. Today they were getting two of us.

When we reached the town hall, I tried to get inside quickly but it seemed everyone wanted to talk to me and congratulate me on killing Tate. Which only made me feel sicker and sicker. I was about to bolt for the bathroom when I spied someone I did want to talk to.

"Rhianna!" I yelled across the room and saw her turn with her characteristic mile-wide smile. The same smile her sister Julie, my best friend, had had.

I wriggled through the crowd and wrapped my arms around her. "Look at you," I said when we finally let go of each other. Rhianna had just turned twenty-one. And somewhere in the year or so since I'd seen her last—other than via emailed photos of her college exploits—she'd grown up.

She didn't look like a teenager anymore. Apart from the fact her hair was shorter and a lighter blond than Julie's, she looked pretty much like her sister might have looked if she'd gotten the chance to reach Rhi's age. The sight made me laugh and cry at the same time.

Rhianna handed me a handkerchief. It was hot pink, like

the flippy sundress she wore. "No crying," she said. "You'll never make it through if you start crying now."

Her matter-of-fact tone made me laugh again. And chased away the tears so I could grill her about college and her life.

She was pre-med and enjoying herself as much as a girl intent on getting into one of the top med schools could. Her tales of college life were hilarious. She had the same sharp sense of humor as Julie too and I felt another pang. I'd never really had another female best friend since Julie died. Rhi was more like a little sister.

Jase was pretty much my best friend now and had been for a few years. Before that it had been Dan while we'd been together. Right now I wasn't sure if you could call us best friends. Or even friends at all sometimes.

Though today he was doing a pretty good job. I looked for him in the crowd, found his dark head close to Bug's silver one and smiled.

"That your guy?" Rhianna asked.

"Yes. Dan." I couldn't remember if they'd ever met when we'd first been going out.

Rhianna squealed. "Oh my God! You two are back together? That's great!" She suddenly looked sixteen again as she bounced on her heels. Then she stopped abruptly. "Didn't something happen to him?"

"Sort of, he got hurt when we went after Tate," I hedged. I was hoping that was what she was referring to, and not the reason why Dan and I had broken up originally. A.k.a. him being a werewolf. I didn't know where Rhianna fell on the whole supernatural issue. "But he's fine now."

"Oh." Her face cleared but not completely.

Time for a distraction. "I think it's time to go in. Let's talk afterward." Which meant I couldn't just escape back home to Seattle after all. I'd have to go to the post-service potluck. Me and my big mouth.

The service, as expected, was excruciating. We had sermons from Father Schmidt and Reverend Flannery and Rabbi Sara. People sang. People talked about the ones they'd lost. All of it grated on my nerves but I steeled myself to keep my eyes front and pay attention. I owed the victims that much.

Then the worst bit of all happened. Mayor Lockridge got up and made a speech about me.

Oh God, they were going to make some sort of presentation.

I dug my elbow into Bug's side when I realized what was going on. "You didn't say anything about this," I whispered trying not to move my mouth.

She looked smug. "You wouldn't have come."

Gah. Suckered.

I should've seen this coming. Caldwell loved a celebration. The town did all the major holidays in a big way. Trick or treating at Halloween, lighting the huge tree in the town square at Christmas, a Fourth of July parade, a leaf turning festival, homecoming parades and too many other events to count. They were always awarding some poor schmuck with something. Only this time the schmuck was me.

I gritted my teeth through the speech and rose obediently when the mayor called my name, trying not to let the cursing running through my head show on my face.

I let the mayor give me the key to the town and smiled for the cameras. As Lockridge stepped back from the mike and gazed at me expectantly, I realized that everyone was expecting me to say something in return.

Fuck.

I stepped up to the lectern, trying to think of something to say. As I reached to adjust the mic—Mayor Lockridge being half a foot shorter than me—I froze.

Because I was sure I'd just seen Marco at the back of the hall. Just for a second before he'd ducked out of my line of sight.

What the hell was Marco doing here?

This was the last place anyone wanted to see a vampire. It couldn't have been him, could it? Maybe it was just some new resident of Caldwell with Italian heritage.

And green, green eyes.

Mayor Lockridge cleared his throat. Whoops. Five hundred or so people were waiting for me to speak.

I didn't know what the hell to say. I didn't want to be thanked for killing Tate. I didn't want to think about Tate at all. Heat swept into my face, combining with my lack of food to make me feel dizzy and borderline nauseated.

But all the faces in the audience were waiting. They smiled at me proudly, like I had done something amazing. They didn't know what it had cost me to do it.

Swallowing hard, I leaned closer to the mic. "Thank you," I said, and then stopped, because I really couldn't think what to say next. When in doubt, stick to the tried and true. "I'm honestly speechless."

Short and sweet but it won me a round of applause. Which only made me feel guilty all over again. "I don't think I deserve an award, but it does mean a lot to me, if what I've done has helped some of you. I know McCallister Tate hurt a lot of people in this town. I'm one of them. I also know he won't be hurting anyone else ever again."

"No more than he deserves," someone yelled from the crowd. There was a swell of muttered agreement and nerves crept up my spine. The mood in the hall suddenly felt ugly.

Someone-could-end-up-getting-hurt kind of ugly. My eyes strayed again to the back of the hall but I couldn't see the man who'd reminded me of Marco. I hoped if Marco was here, that he'd been sensible enough to leave already.

"This town has suffered," I said, as the crowd got noisier. They quieted a little at my words. "We've suffered but we've survived. We live. And in doing so, we honor those who are no longer with us. By doing good, by each small act we take in the world, we remember them."

"Yeah, like killing vampires."

I couldn't see who had spoken but he got a round of applause all of his own.

Once upon a time I would've joined in. But my world wasn't black and white anymore. I wasn't enough of a hypocrite to let the murmurs of 'death to vampires' go unanswered. Even though defending them might mean Caldwell deciding to change its locks when it came to me.

I took another deep breath and gripped the sides of the lectern. "Not all vampires are evil," I said firmly. "Not all weres are. Just like not all humans are good."

Silence rippled across the room. The weight of five hundred pairs of disbelieving eyes pressed in on me. "I'm not defending Tate. He was a monster. But if we want revenge, if we hurt others to ease our own pain then what's the difference between him and us?"

The muttering in the crowd increased.

"I killed McCallister Tate," I said. "I did it because he was trying to kill me. But killing isn't the answer. Hatred isn't the answer. The only possible answer when the world turns dark is to shine our light."

I had a horrible feeling I was sounding like a Hallmark ad but I couldn't think of a different way to say it, that the only way to move on was to let go of some of the hatred.

I hadn't wanted to. I understood exactly where some of the crowd were now. Angry, bitter, looking for someone to blame. I'd been there myself. I'd done my best to fight against those feelings and then I'd had to change.

I hoped some of them might be able to without such a drastic reason as mine.

Silence flowed across the hall and for a moment I wondered whether they were going to storm the podium and tar and feather me.

But then Rhianna got to her feet and started applauding, tears standing in her eyes. Bug joined her, then Dan, then in ones and twos, others stood. Not everyone but it was a start. And it eased the tension back to an acceptable level.

It was getting close to three by the time the service wound up. It took another fifteen minutes or so before the hall emptied and everyone headed for the cemetery.

I walked with Dan and Bug, bracing myself for what was to come. I gripped the bouquet of coral-colored roses I was carrying too tightly. Thorns bit into my hand.

"Ow," I muttered.

"Do you want me to carry those?" Dan said.

I shook my head. He already carried an identical bunch, as did Bug. The scent of the flowers mingled with the complicated scents of the crowd. Sorrow. Grief. Too many perfumes and powders and soap. Nervous sweat. The scents of life.

For a moment the coral roses blurred. I blinked back tears. I was *not* going to cry.

The roses came back into focus. My mom's favorites. The flowers she carried on her wedding day. After twelve years of memorials, I hated coral roses. I had an extra bunch of lavender and irises for Julie.

With every step, the crowd grew a little quieter until we walked in near silence. The quiet was eerie when you thought about just how many people there were in the crowd.

It took almost forty minutes for everyone to file into the cemetery. There were so many people, we broke into smaller groups to make the rounds.

I started with Julie's grave, along with her family. Her headstone had her photo reproduced on a plaque hung over the white marble.

Julie grinning up at us with braces and her favorite sparkly lip gloss. I let her family go first, Rhianna stony-faced and her parents crying, then I laid my flowers as well, touching the photo briefly, whispering in my mind to her as I always did, telling her about what had been happening to me, about Dan, about my newest boots and the latest showbiz gossip, all the things we used to giggle about until all hours of the night.

Telling her how much I missed her.

But I didn't cry. No, I managed to hold it together as I straightened and moved back from the grave.

One of the worst down, three to go.

I left my family until last, looping between the other victims' graves, stopping at each to listen to the families and friends tell their familiar stories.

After all this time, I knew most of them. How Tom Hardiger had almost missed his own wedding because of a faulty alarm clock, how Sunita Gillis was a champion brownie maker.

Each family had stories they held onto like cherished toys, repeating the memories that kept the lost alive for them one after the other.

But finally I'd done everyone else and I couldn't put off the hardest part any longer. I headed to where my family sheltered, beneath the branches of a huge oak tree. As I walked up the small hill to where the graves lay in dappled light, I saw a limousine parked on the road that ran along the edge of the cemetery. Somehow I knew Marco was inside, watching me do this thing. Marco, who was partly responsible for the fact we were all here. After all, one of his lineage sired Tate.

My hands clenched, squeezing Dan's arm tightly enough that he stopped walking.

"What's wrong?"

I couldn't tell him about Marco. He'd probably go over there and put his fist through the windshield. So I shook my head. "Nothing. I just want to get this over with."

He pulled me a little closer, kissed the top of my head. For just a moment I let myself lean into his strength, closing my eyes and pretending none of it was real.

Then I knelt by the graves of my family and placed the

flowers I'd brought them, splitting the bouquet between the three of them, fussing with the blooms in an effort to try not to think about how much it hurt just to be there.

How much I missed them.

As usual I couldn't really think of what I wanted to say.

Instead I rose and let Bug take her turn, holding Dan's hand as she followed my example and separated the flowers between the graves.

I stayed silent as Bug told stories about my family, knowing that I couldn't trust myself to talk. She seemed to find comfort in it. Me, I just hurt.

Hurt like every cell in my body was on fire.

Seeing everyone standing around, laughing softly or smiling at what Bug was saying only made the fires burn hotter.

Eventually I'd had enough.

"Get me out of here," I said to Dan.

"Sure." He squeezed my hand then stepped over to Bug and whispered something in her ear. She nodded and made a little shooing gesture.

I blew her a kiss then walked with Dan toward the cemetery gate. I couldn't see the limo.

I hoped Marco had left.

Old One or not, I wasn't sure I could bring myself to be courteous to a vampire right now.

Bug caught us up a little way outside the gate. She looked tired. I figured she'd reached her limit too.

Her presence made me doubly glad Marco had gone.

I might have to deal with Marco but I didn't want Bug or anybody else to meet him.

Not today.

Surely he'd left?

No such luck, it seemed.

As we approached the hall, I saw the limo again, pulled into a side street. In the rapidly falling dark it might have been inconspicuous, apart from the fact that Caldwell isn't a limo kind of town.

Marco was skating on some very, very, thin ice. I let go of Dan's arm. "I'll meet you inside. I left something in the car."

He nodded absently, his attention on Bug, who'd caught us up, and the story she was relating about something my dad had done when I was about ten. Rhi followed the two of them as they continued on to the hall. I watched until I was sure they'd all made it inside then hurried back the way we'd come.

The limo hadn't moved and I felt a little stupid as I raised a hand to knock on the darkened glass. What if it wasn't Marco?

Part of me knew it was.

The rap of my knuckles against the glass echoed loudly in the twilight and I looked around guiltily, hoping no one was watching. The window didn't roll down. It still wasn't completely dark, so I guess Marco was being cautious. Instead, the driver's door opened and the driver came over to me. He was short and bald and dressed in an expensive dark suit.

"I want to speak with Lord Marco," I said before he had a chance to speak.

To my surprise he just nodded and opened the door for me. Which kind of threw me—maybe it was dark enough after all.

I climbed into the limo and the door gently closed behind me. Instead of Marco, I faced a matte black divider—the kind that usually appears in a limo between the driver and passengers. For a moment I freaked out, wondering if I'd just climbed into a car with someone I shouldn't have but then the glass slid back to reveal Marco smiling at me. The divider, I realized, must be UV treated—protection against any lingering sunlight that might have hit the inside of the car when the driver let me in. Nifty.

"Ashley, *cara*, how nice to see you." Marco nodded at me as if it were perfectly normal that he was here.

"Don't 'cara' me," I said. "What are you doing here? This isn't a vamp friendly environment."

"They do not seem to mind werewolves."

"Most of them don't know I'm a wolf."

"Truly?"

I nodded. "Believe me, Caldwell is not pro-supernaturals. I'm surprised you're here." I studied his face for a moment but it was an unreadable blank mask. "Why are you here, exactly?"

"Jason had some concerns."

He did? He hadn't raised them with me. Not that I'd given him much of a chance. "What sort of concerns? And why wouldn't he come himself?"

"I presume, because he knows Caldwell's attitude to our kind."

"That didn't stop you from coming."

"I can take care of myself." He tilted his head toward the driver. "I have resources."

One vampire and one bodyguard might not be much good against an angry mob. But it wasn't my job to look after Marco.

It was my job to look after my friends and family.

"What sort of concerns?" I asked again. Was Jase worried about me? Having another premonition? He wouldn't bother Marco if he was just worried about how I'd cope with the memorial.

Also Jase would know that if Dan found out Marco was around, there'd be trouble. So it had to be something more serious. My hands curled in my lap as I waited for Marco's reply.

"He wasn't specific, he just said he thought there might be a problem."

"Why tell you? He should have told Dan, we could have brought some agents."

He looked out the window. "You should get back to your gathering. Your wolf will be wondering where you are."

There was a distinct lack of answer to my question in that statement. But he was right. And getting out of the limo before this conversation got any weirder sounded like a plan to me.

I found Dan inside the hall, clutching a take-out coffee cup and looking nervous, surrounded by Aunt Bug and a gaggle of her friends. If I knew my aunt, he was probably being grilled about when he was going to make an honest woman out of me.

I caught his eyes and smiled. He grinned back and extricated himself from the group.

It didn't take him long to reach my side. Our fingers snaked together. "How much longer do we need to stay?" he asked softly. He glanced back over to Bug and her cronies, looking faintly worried.

They'd definitely been grilling him about us. "Not long, I just want to say hi to a few people, then we can go back to Bug's." I knew he wanted to be back in Seattle, working. The full moon was approaching and we'd lose a couple of days going to the Retreat. We needed all the time we could get right now.

He nodded, looking resigned. "Want some coffee?" He held out the cup. "There's no booze in it but it's hot."

"Were you expecting booze?"

A head shake. "Next year remind me to bring a hip flask."

Yeah, that would go down well. My stomach didn't like the thought of alcohol much but I desperately needed caffeine. "I'll go make my own. I know the coffee here. It needs help."

So I was a coffee snob, sue me. Caldwell was your basic white or black, cream or sugar type of town. There was no place in town to get a good espresso or a caramel latte. And the town hall coffee, from memory, was not even good basic coffee.

"Grab me a brownie," Dan said with a grin. He dropped a kiss on my cheek then settled into one of the seats lining the walls.

I didn't know how he could eat. I still felt like live eels were occupying my stomach. But I made my way across to the tables that held piles of muffins and cakes and brownies and sandwiches supplied by the good women of Caldwell. Homemade, delicious and full of calories. It made me regret my lack of appetite.

I snagged Dan a couple of brownies and made myself a coffee with triple sugar and extra milk. I figured that would see me through to Bug's where a hot bath, some Advil and a nap might render me into a suitable state to actually eat something.

When I turned to grab a paper napkin for Dan, I almost bumped into Rhianna.

She looked less bubbly than earlier, her smile strained around the edges.

"How you holding up, kiddo?"

She grimaced. "Ask me tomorrow. And remind me next year to wear sensible shoes."

I laughed. "You won't listen."

Her lips curved. "Maybe not. Well, at least remind me to wear cheap shoes that dirt won't ruin." She stared down at her feet, smile vanishing.

I looked down. She was right. The high spiked heels on her candy colored sandals were a dirt-colored mess and splotches of mud made them look like the leather had come from some sort of mutant pink and brown cow. "Ouch."

Her blue eyes were rueful as we both straightened. "Ouch in more ways than one. I paid retail for these." She sipped her coffee. "Are you going back to Seattle tomorrow?"

I nodded. "Dan needs to get back." Using him as a scapegoat was easier than admitting that I could hardly wait to get away. I always needed a break from Caldwell after the memorial. Bug could come to town for our next girly bonding session.

"Mom says he works for the FBI? Doesn't that worry you?"

For once I wished that I knew exactly who in Caldwell knew the truth about me and Dan.

Was Rhianna fishing for information about Dan being a werewolf or was she just asking? My brain was too tired to figure it out from her expression.

"Less than when he was a cop," I said honestly. He spent less time in the field, for one thing. And he was a werewolf now. Harder to kill.

She shivered. "I couldn't do it. I'd worry too much."

I frowned. "I don't think about it. After all, any of us could—" I cut myself off. Idiot. This was not the time or place to be talking about accidental deaths. "So is there a guy worshipping at your feet, as usual?"

To my surprise, she blushed. Rhi was the men fawning at her feet type. But she never took them that seriously.

I grinned at her and raised an eyebrow. "Don't tell me you're in luuuurve."

Her gaze dropped back down to the mutant cow shoes. When she looked back up, her face was a similar pink to the unsplotched parts of the leather. A grin spread across her face making her look like her sister all over again. "Maybe."

My eyebrows shot up. "Maybe? You're blushing over but *maybe*? Okay, dish the dirt."

She glanced over her shoulder and I saw her parents standing a few feet away. "Not here. Mom and Dad don't know yet."

I wasn't letting her get off that easily. A little big sis-little sis gossip was just what I needed to take my mind off the day we'd just had. Something *normal*. "Rhianna Anders, you are not going anywhere until I'm fully informed. Let's go outside. It's getting hot in here anyway."

She giggled then nodded. I dropped Dan's plate of calories off to him and then caught up to Rhianna. We ended up sitting on the front steps of the hall.

We weren't the only ones finding it a little close indoors; Aunt Bug and her friends had taken up position on the double row of park benches outside the hall. The sun had set now but the lights from the hall shed plenty of light across the lawn. I smiled to myself when I saw Stanley Douglas, who, Bug insisted was just a bridge partner, hovering around her.

"So," I said, turning my attention back to Rhianna. "Tell me about this guy."

She started to reply but stopped as a big black van suddenly squealed to a halt just near the hall's front gate.

"Who's that?" I said, frowning. Most of the town's population was inside. And I didn't think it was the sort of night that kids would be joyriding. Reporters maybe? The van's side door slid backward and several men piled out. Something about the way they moved—a little too quick and fluid—made my heart stop. Vamps. Shit.

I jumped up. "Rhi, go get Dan. And Sheriff Kenny."

"What?" She looked confused.

I yanked her to her feet. "Go *now*."

The vamps were scanning the street, heads turning and seeking like a pack of dogs scenting the air. One of them looked straight at me. A nasty grin spread across his face. I stood my ground.

The group of vamps started to flow toward the hall.

I saw Stanley step into their path, saw one of them push him hard enough for him to hit the grass. Saw the looks of horror growing on the faces of the ladies around him. Including Bug's.

I was down the steps and between her and the vamps before I could stop to think what I was doing.

"Get out of here." A growl underlined my words. I heard Bug murmuring something behind me. "Stay back," I said without turning around. "In fact, go inside. Now."

"What makes you think inside will help?" The tallest of the vampires sneered.

"I told you to leave," I said, trying to ignore the fact my heart was hammering and that the vamps would be able to hear it, clear as day. Where was Dan? And the Sheriff and his nice guns? Come to think of it, where the fuck was Marco?

"We'll leave. But you're coming with us."

"I don't think so." *Hurry up, Dan.*

Hurry *the fuck* up.

I could hear noises coming from the hall—footsteps—but I didn't know if Bug and her friends had retreated or whether someone was coming to help. I wasn't turning my back on four vampires to check.

"You come quietly or things will get messy." The vamp snarled.

My skin went cold. Another vampire attack might just break the town for good. On the other hand, being held by vampires again was very likely to break me for good. I needed to stall. "Who sent you?"

"Who said anyone sent us?"

"Get away from her."

Dan's voice. Relief weakened my knees.

The vamp slanted dark eyes past me, pale skin almost glowing in the dim light, lip curling to reveal his fangs. "Going to make me?"

"Yes, we are." This time it was Sheriff Kenny speaking.

I risked a glance over my shoulder. Dan stood just behind me, Kenny and another guy I assumed was one of the deputies with him. Both the cops had their guns out. About time. I turned back to the vamp. "I suggest you leave."

Something like fear flashed in his eyes. Obviously the

thought of going back empty-handed to whoever was pulling the strings here didn't appeal. "I don't think so."

He lunged for me, hands closing over my forearm. I snarled and tried to pull free.

"Ash!" Dan yelled my name and the vamp reeled back as a fist connected with his face. He and Dan tumbled to the grass, rolling and punching. I sucked in a breath, trying to work out where the other three had gone. Kenny had pulled a gun and I saw one vamp frozen in place but that left two unaccounted for. Two vamps loose in the crowd.

I whirled back to face the hall, trying to remember what the vamps had looked like. Dark hair, dark clothes. There was nothing distinctive. Then my brain kicked in. Dark clothes. Most people were wearing color. Look for black.

A shriek came from the steps. Bug's voice. I broke into a run, saw her lifted off her feet by one of the vamps. "Bug!" I shrieked, speeding up. "Get away from her."

Another vamp loomed up in my path. I hit him full force, striking blindly with one fist. It connected with his head hard enough to send pain screaming up my arm but he went down and I leapt over him and closed in on Bug.

The vamp swung around just before I reached him, holding Bug in front of him like a shield. "I'll kill her." He snarled at me. "You stay where you are."

I froze as the color drained out of Bug's face. "Let her go. I'll come with you—"

"No," Bug said, struggling. "You stay where you are."

"Let her go," I repeated.

The vamp just smiled and leaned his face closer into her neck. "I don't think so."

I tried to calculate how quickly I could close the gap between us and how badly he might be able to hurt Bug in the time it took me. Too badly seemed to be the answer but I had to try anyway. I got ready to leap for him but then Rhianna loomed up behind the vampire and smashed a chair over his

head. He crumpled and I leaped for Bug, hitting the lawn
before she did, so I cushioned her fall. She landed on top of
me with a grunt and half-winded me.

"Are you—" I started to ask but a snarling sound interrupted me. The vamp. I turned my head in time to see him
spring to his feet, face twisted with rage and fly at Rhianna.
He grabbed her and buried his fangs in her throat before I
could move.

Chapter 8

RAGE roared through me and the wolf blazed to life. I changed and rolled to my feet, snarling.

Screams echoed around me, people stumbling backward at the sudden appearance of a huge wolf in their midst. I ignored them, focusing on the vamp. He didn't lift his head from Rhi's throat. I didn't have time to lose. He could drain her or hurt her fatally in another few seconds.

I sprang, snapping at his arm. My fangs sank through the cotton of his black shirt and buried themselves in muscle and flesh. The rank taste of vamp blood boiled into my mouth but I held on and twisted, using my body weight to force him away from Rhianna.

He screamed with fury and pain. His free arm connected with my ribs with a thud. Vamps pack quite a punch. Agony bloomed along my side and I let go, retreating with another snarling growl, trying to get him to follow me. Rhianna lay on the ground behind him and the scent of human blood flooded the air, almost as strong as the vamp's.

Someone needed to help her.

"*Dan,*" I screamed in my head but then the vamp came at me again and I had to concentrate on staying alive.

Pain and fury blurred my ability to think about anything but the threat in front of me. The vampire moved almost too fast for me to follow, leaping through the air to come at me with bared fangs. I twisted frantically, trying to dodge. He had the advantage of legs and arms. But I was heavier and maybe even stronger in wolf form—if I could connect with teeth or claws. I swiped at his leg as he sailed over me and my claws tore through flesh.

The vamp shrieked as he hit the dirt. I snarled back, circling to face him. Behind him, people knelt by Rhi, faces stricken. Some guy I didn't know was holding a red stained cloth to her neck but she wasn't moving and the salt-metal-warm stink of blood was way too strong.

But I couldn't think about Rhi. I had to think about survival. The vamp flowed to his feet, blood staining the flesh on his thigh. He hissed at me, bloody fangs exposed. I growled, daring him to try me again. His eyes flicked to the side and I suddenly realized he was searching for another human shield. Something to distract me.

Not going to happen. Not if I had anything to do about it. My last vestiges of control over the wolf slid away and I let the vast anger of a werewolf protecting her pack surge through me. He wasn't going to hurt anyone *ever* again.

Once more I sprang, bowling him over. We rolled together, his hands reaching for my neck and fangs raking my side as we tumbled. The pain only increased my fury and I redoubled my efforts. The need to conquer the enemy, to destroy my prey, burned away all other thought. My teeth snapped, missed, and then found purchase. And for the second time in my life, I rejoiced as I snapped my jaws closed and tore out a throat.

As the vamp dropped limply to the ground, I spat blood and flesh, shaking my head in disgust. The taste of vamp wasn't any more pleasant the second time round; my stomach recoiled, even in wolf form.

When I looked up, it was to a sea of horrified faces.

Shit. So much for keeping the 'I'm a werewolf' thing under wraps. I'd well and truly outed myself.

By killing someone in front of my whole supernatural-hating hometown.

Even if my victim was a vamp, his blood still spattered my face and mouth, gumming my fur, sticky and bitter. No doubt I looked pretty terrifying to the humans watching.

Well, I could worry about that later. Right now, I needed to help Rhianna.

I took a step forward and someone in the crowd gasped. It sounded way too loud in the shocked silence. Silence that meant the fight was over. My lip curled a little in reaction to the noise but I kept walking. As I reached Rhi, the scent of human blood once more overpowered the vamp's.

Which meant there was a whole lot of it spilled around.

Too much.

Rhianna lay pale and still. Too pale and still but I could just hear a struggling heartbeat.

She needed help fast.

Someone stepped into my path. I didn't recognize the scent and I didn't have any time to waste. I growled warningly and they jumped away even as more startled noises blossomed through the crowd.

Movement flicked at my left side and I turned my head to see Aunt Bug coming down the front stairs.

Safe. For a moment that's all I could think. She hadn't been hurt. My pulse eased back a few beats.

"Ashley, is that you?" She looked a little wild-eyed as she approached me, so I dropped to my haunches and thumped my tail a few times. It was the closest I could come to a wag while I was this tense and there was no way I was changing back and winding up naked in front of the entire population of Caldwell.

Aunt Bug smiled shakily then reached out and touched my head. I stayed still, not wanting to get blood on her. Then her gaze turned from me to Rhianna and she paled. "Rhianna," she said brokenly. "Somebody call 911."

"I already have." Dan's voice cut through the nervous babble that had broken out. To the assembled humans, he would sound cool and calm. But I could hear the thump thump thump of his heart racing almost as fast as mine. I didn't know if it was from worry over me or the fight.

He stopped between me and the crowd and just stood there, all tall and commanding. The fact that he'd pulled back his jacket to reveal his gun didn't hurt either. The way the tension in the air eased back would've been annoying if it hadn't been to my benefit.

The blare of an ambulance siren suddenly cut through the crowd noise, turning the focus away from me for a moment as everyone stopped to watch it pull up. Dan moved closer to me.

"You should go home and change," he said as I inched nearer to his legs. When in doubt, stand by the guy with the gun. At least when you know he's on your side.

I tilted my head at him in the wolf equivalent of 'are you kidding me?' The telepathy werewolves used didn't work when one was in human form. At least not between Dan and me. But wolves are pretty good at reading body language whether on two legs or four. I glanced back to Rhianna, whining softly.

A red-headed paramedic knelt beside her, frantically applying bandages and sliding needles into flesh as her partner readied a gurney.

Rhianna.

For a moment I wondered whether anyone had worked on Julie like this after Tate. I'd never asked her parents for details —I'd been too busy grieving my own losses and trying to wipe the images of blood and death from my mind to want to add to them. I whined again. I could still hear Rhianna's heart beating but I didn't like the way it sounded.

And it was all my fault.

The vamps had been after *me*.

Rhi was hurt because of *me*.

And Caldwell was traumatized all over again.

"They won't let you in the hospital like that," Dan pointed out. "There's nothing more you can do here." He frowned a little and I read the 'except get yourself in a whole lot of trouble' he wasn't adding loud and clear.

I nudged his leg with my nose trying to breathe in the smell of Dan instead of vamp and blood and fear.

He touched my head, just for a moment. "Everything's under control. Go home."

But I'd missed my chance to slip away. As the paramedics loaded Rhianna onto the gurney, the crowd turned back to me.

"She can't leave. She's a werewolf," someone muttered, a little too loudly.

Dan's head whipped around and I heard the near silent growl that rumbled in his throat, even if no one else did. "Yes, she is. And she just saved several people's lives. You got a problem?" His hand strayed down to his gun again.

"Wolf lover," someone yelled and I winced. This could go downhill, fast. I hoped Marco had had the sense to leave town already. I'd probably get out of this but I didn't like the chances of any vampire caught within city limits just now.

He must have left. Otherwise, wouldn't he have warned me? Surely an Old One could sense other vampires in his vicinity?

I leaned a little closer to Dan as Aunt Bug stepped up beside him. She glared out at the crowd and I swear half of them shrank back. Amazing what a lasting effect being a schoolteacher has on people. Aunt Bug had ruled the local high school campus with a steely glare and a quick tongue for nearly thirty years before she retired.

"Yes? Does anyone have a problem with my *niece*?" She put her hand down on my head, rubbing my ear absently, like you would a Labrador. Normally I would've pulled away but this wasn't the time to act like anything but a lapdog.

No one spoke up but the vibes spilling from the crowd weren't friendly. Rhi's parents were being shepherded into the back of the ambulance, leaving me short another couple of potential allies. But maybe that was assuming too much. They had just as much reason to hate supernaturals as anyone else in this town.

Actually even more reason now.

I wanted to go with them but Dan was right. No one would let a giant wolf into a hospital. So I had to go change and get clothes first.

"Why don't you take Ash home?" Dan said quietly to Aunt Bug. "I have to stay with the Sheriff until my team gets here."

He'd called in the Taskforce already? Damn. I hadn't expected that. Just what the town needed, even more vamps and weres arriving.

Dan crouched down in front of me, silver eyes searching mine as if reassuring himself I was okay. I swiped his cheek quickly with my tongue. Wrong move. The streak I left was faintly pink, my saliva still tinged with blood.

My stomach turned queasy on me at the sight and the acrid stink of the vamp's blood drying on my fur hit me like a blow. I needed to shower. Fast. Or I was going to be the were-wolf famous for puking in public as well as killing vamps.

I stood shakily and nudged Aunt Bug's hip with my nose. She took the hint and put her hand on my head as we walked away from the crowd. My shoulder blades itched the whole time, expecting some sort of attack. As we walked through the gate I saw Marco standing across the street, half hidden in the shadows of one of the elms lining the road.

He inclined his head slightly as our eyes met. I wasn't sure if his expression was apologetic or concerned but neither helped me feel any better. In fact, the sight of him made me furious all over again. If he'd helped, maybe Rhi wouldn't be bleeding on her way to a hospital right now.

"*Get out of here while you can*," I thought at him, on the off chance he could hear wolf telepathy. "*If they spot you things will get ugly.*"

Our gazes held a second longer and then he nodded. I didn't know if it meant 'message received' or something else entirely but it would have to do. If I watched him any longer I might just draw attention to him.

I turned away and trotted at Aunt Bug's side all the way back to her house. I showered and changed in record time, only slowing to use about half a bottle of mouthwash as I scrubbed my gums till they nearly bled. It didn't help. Through the reek of mint and alcohol I could still smell the stink of vampire and taste acid blood in the back of my throat.

Aunt Bug was waiting for me in the kitchen when I came back downstairs, her hands wrapped around a mug of tea. Which said something about her frazzled state of mind. Tea in Bug's house came served in fine china cups with matching saucers. Mugs were for coffee, or cocoa.

"Are you okay?" I asked, sliding into the chair across from hers and resting my elbows on the table. Damp hair flicked into my face and I pulled it back into a ponytail without thinking.

"Don't do that, you'll catch cold."

"Aunty, wet hair does not cause colds." Plus werewolves couldn't catch colds.

She stared down at her tea. I was tempted to tell her she'd have to drink it if she wanted to know the future. But I didn't push. She'd just had quite a scare. And she'd just seen me as a wolf for the first time.

She'd never asked to see me that way since my change and I hadn't offered—mostly because I'd only wanted to change when I had to—at full moon. Humans weren't allowed at the Packs' Retreat when we gathered.

"Are you okay?" I repeated when she stayed silent. "I didn't mean for you to see anything like that." What did you say when your closest relative had just seen you kill someone?

"I'm fine," she said. The slight shake in her voice suggested otherwise. "I was just thinking about Rhianna."

"The doctors will be able to save her." I wanted to believe it. I couldn't bear the thought of having to stand over Rhianna's grave.

"Why did those vampires come here?" Bug asked, stirring more sugar into her tea absently.

I played with a stray strand of hair, watching as I wound it round my finger. "I don't know." I made myself look back up at Bug.

"Were they after you?" Her pale blue eyes turned sharp. "Are you in trouble again?"

Again. I heard the fear underlying that question, even though Bug was trying to hide it. I didn't know what to say. How to make her feel better. It wasn't like I'd asked for any of this and I definitely didn't go looking for trouble. Tate had found Caldwell and my family, not the other way around. Now Smith was taking the same approach.

"I don't know," I said helplessly. "I'm trying not to be." Bug might be scared for me but she deserved to know the truth. "But Dan will find out what's going on. The Taskforce will be all over this."

She looked away and I wondered what she was trying not to say. She was the one who'd pushed me all these years to give Dan a second chance. But perhaps the reality of me being tangled up so closely with the supernatural world wasn't quite what she'd expected.

It wasn't exactly what I had expected either. But there was no way to go back. I had to keep trying to move forward.

Starting with looking after Rhi. "I'm going to the hospital. Do you want to come with me?"

"I think I'll stay here."

"Okay." I rose, came around the table and dropped a kiss on her gray hair. "I'm still me, Bug. It's okay."

"I know." She sounded tired. I felt guilty. I'd be going back to Seattle, where vamps and weres weren't such a novelty. Where they were mostly accepted. Aunt Bug had to stay here in Caldwell, surrounded by friends and neighbors she'd known all her life and cope with the fact they all knew her niece was a werewolf now.

One of the monsters.

It wasn't going to be easy for her. I could well imagine the outrage of the community. Once upon a time I'd felt the same fear and distrust of supernaturals. I'd overcome it to a point, before I'd changed, determined not to let Tate's legacy turn me into a bigot but I'd still struggled.

Until Jase.

And then Dan.

And now nothing was simple. No black and white. "You're welcome to come and stay with me for a bit," I offered. "We could see a couple of shows, you could go to the museums."

Her shoulders straightened. "I'm not running away."

So much for me trying to be subtle. "I didn't mean—"

"Yes, you did. And I appreciate the offer. But it's about time this town learned to move along with the world. Or everyone's going to be stuck in what Tate did forever. So I'll stay."

She was tough, I had to give her that. I wasn't so sure I'd be willing to stay in her position. Then again, I was completely sure that if Bug set her mind to changing the current flavor of public opinion in Caldwell that she'd find away to do it given enough time.

Time was one thing I didn't have right now, though. I

squeezed Bug's shoulder, grabbed my purse from the chair and headed out the door.

I spent most of the drive to the hospital trying to get my Bluetooth headset to work. When I finally did, Dan's phone went straight to voicemail. Jase didn't pick up either.

Knowing he was back in Seattle alone with Niko sniffing at his heels made me nervous. I wanted to give him the heads up to be extra careful. If Smith was coming after me, who knew what tactics he'd use? I left Jase a tense message explaining what had happened and then wondered if I should call Marco.

* * *

I reached the hospital parking lot before I'd made up my mind. Turns out I didn't need to make the call. Marco appeared out of the darkness as soon as I'd parked. My heart leaped into overdrive and I stifled the urge to scream.

"Not a good idea to sneak up on me right now," I said, slamming the door of Bug's Honda. I'd retrieved my gun and it was safely tucked in a holster hidden by my jacket. If Marco wasn't more careful he was going to end up with a hole or two.

Marco didn't come any closer, hovering a few feet away where he seemed to blend into the pools of darkness between the arcs of the lamps lighting the parking lot. "My apologies. I didn't mean to scare you."

"You should be apologizing for what happened earlier at the hall," I snapped.

His eyes widened, then he frowned. "That was not my fault."

"You could've helped out." I started toward the emergency department entrance.

"I didn't think that another vampire appearing in the midst of that crowd would be helpful."

I couldn't fault that logic but couldn't help wondering if he could have prevented what had happened to Rhi. Was that why he'd been waiting for me? Because he felt guilty? I couldn't quite summon the courage to question an Old One about his motives, so I just kept walking toward the hospital entrance.

Marco kept pace with me, but still moved no closer. Was he keeping his distance because he thought I might be jumpy or for some other reason? Trying to keep him in my peripheral vision made my head ache.

"But I was watching in case things got too bad," he added as we neared the hospital entrance.

I stopped, turning to face him. The lights were brighter here but he still seemed to be part shadow, darkness wreathing around him. Which might explain why I hadn't noticed him during the attack. "Gee, that makes me feel better. Were you watching when one of my friends got her neck chewed on?" Or when I'd killed someone?

"I am sorry for your friend. I came here to offer you any help you may require."

Perhaps there was some guilt there after all. "Rhi's the one in hospital, not me."

He nodded a particularly fluid gesture. "I am just offering my services if you should need anything."

I could just imagine Dan's face if I told him Marco wanted to help me out. "Thanks, but I'm good."

"I shall wait here as long as possible. Perhaps you could let me know how your friend is?"

My eyebrows shot up. Marco was being a little too nice. But I couldn't read anything on his face other than concern. "I don't want to leave her family alone in there. Do you have a cell phone?"

He nodded and a card appeared in his hand. Unlike Esteban's this one said "Lord Marco Sebastiani" in flowing black script on a pale cream background. And then gave a single contact number.

I slipped it into my jacket pocket. "I'll keep you posted," I said and turned to leave.

"There is one more thing, *cara*," Marco said.

I swiveled back. "What? I'm in kind of a hurry."

He reached into his pocket again. This time his hand came out bearing a bundle of fabric. Black fabric. He held it out to me.

"What's this?"

"I believe it is yours."

I took it. The fabric was smooth and slippery, warm under my fingers. Silk. I unfolded it and found my cross.

My hand flew to my throat. I hadn't even noticed it was missing in all the excitement. The chain must have broken when I'd changed. My cross. My fingers curled around it. The platinum cross Bug had given me. I could've lost it.

And Marco had been the one to stop and find it for me.

"How did you know I'd lost it?"

"You were wearing it. At the graveside."

Which meant I'd also stepped into his car wearing it. A cross generally had to touch a vampire to hurt them but Marco tolerating one anywhere near him said something about him trusting me.

Problem was I didn't know exactly what.

Something else to worry about later. I was running out of time. I slipped the cross into the pocket of my jacket. "Thank you. This is important to me."

Marco made a small bow. "I know. *Buonanotte, cara.*"

"I'll let you know if I hear anything." I nodded to him—it wasn't as if he and I had the sort of relationship where we'd shake hands or hug or anything—and stepped from the shadows into the bright lights of the emergency department.

To my surprise, no one gave me any trouble when I asked

where Rhianna was. I found her parents waiting in chairs beside an empty bed.

"What's happening?" I asked, hovering in the doorway.

Mrs. Anders looked at me, her face shell-shocked and drawn. Her complexion looked gray against the pretty lemon dress she wore. She'd looked like that in the days and weeks and months following Julie's death. My throat tightened. Was Rhi...?

"She's in surgery," she said quietly. "They're repairing the damage to her neck. The doctors are hopeful. Why don't you come in here and sit with us?"

I hesitated. Was she just being polite?

Mrs. Anders watched me for a moment with the big blue eyes she'd given to each of her daughters then she patted the seat next to her. "Ashley, you saved Rhianna's life, you're always welcome with us, you know that."

I didn't know what to say, so I just smiled and sat, taking her hand as if it could make a difference. When the truth was, if Rhi didn't survive then nothing on Earth would help.

The minutes ticked by so slowly I began to wonder if the clock on the wall was even working. Unfortunately my watch said it was. An hour passed, then another. There were a few fumbled attempts at conversation but it was hard to think of anything to talk about that didn't seem like either an attempt to avoid the topics of werewolves and vampires or clichéd 'everything will be okay' platitudes so we kept subsiding back into silence.

When the door to the room opened again, we all looked up expectantly but it was Dan who stepped through rather than a doctor. My heart bumped at the sight of him. He was all in one piece. Obviously things had stayed under control at the hall.

"Mr. and Mrs. Anders," he said politely before turning to me. "Ashley, can I talk to you a moment?"

I blinked at him. "Here?"

"In the hall."

"What's up?" I said once we'd left the room and walked a few yards away from Rhi's room. "Has the team arrived?"

He reached out, ran two fingers down my cheek. "Are you all right?"

Something in the sound of his voice made the back of my neck tingle. And not in a good way. I took a deep breath. He smelled agitated. Maybe it was just a holdover from what had happened at the hall but the tingle told me it wasn't. "I'm fine. Just a few bruises."

I didn't want to admit my ribs still hurt like hell where the vamp had socked me. They must have been cracked by the force of his blow. Changing back to human form had helped but it would take another change or two to heal completely. Dan would just want to haul me in front of a doctor to get checked out and I didn't think there was a lot that a doctor could do for bruised ribs.

Dan stared at me, as if he was trying to decide if I was telling the truth, then blew out a breath.

"What's wrong?" I asked. "You're making me nervous."

"It's Rhianna," he said and my knees buckled.

Dan grabbed me, pulling me upright. "Ash, it's okay, she's still alive."

I sagged against him. "Don't scare me like that," I mumbled into his chest. Then I realized he hadn't actually told me what was wrong yet. I lifted my head. "What about Rhianna?"

"There's something screwy going on with her blood work."

My heart took the express elevator to my feet. "Screwy? What sort of screwy?"

Dan swallowed then took my shoulders and pushed me back a little so I was nearly leaning against the wall. "Ash, they think she's going to be a vampire."

What? How? For a few seconds my mind whirled crazily.

And then it landed on the only possible explanation. The vaccine. Tate's goddamn anti-vaccine. If the vamp who'd bitten Rhi had been made that way...

"*No.*" The denial was automatic. "They must have gotten the tests wrong. I'd never heard of a false positive on the vamp virus but it had to be possible, right?

He shook his head, eyes sad. "They've rerun the tests. In fact, they're doing them again right now. But they're pretty sure they're right."

God. "But how?"

"You know how," he said. "The vaccine..." He stopped talking and looked around. No one was standing nearby but that didn't mean nobody could hear us. Quick as a flash he bundled us into an empty room, closing the door carefully. I stood near the bed, gripping the metal rail at its foot, hoping he wasn't about to say what I thought he was.

"The vaccine," he continued in a soft voice. "Tate's vaccine."

I shook my head, trying to deny what I was hearing. But I couldn't. If Dan was right...the consequences were plain. And too terrible to think about. "But that means that Rhi will be like that too, if Tate was telling the truth. Anyone she bites will be turned."

His face grew grim. "Which makes her a danger to anyone she comes into contact with."

My palms went damp. "What are you saying?"

"Ash, we can't let her run around free. And we can't let anybody know why we're holding her. If word got out that there are vampires who can turn people without having to exchange blood—who can turn people who are vaccinated, we'll have a panic on our hands. That's why the fact that the anti-vaccine exists was classified in the first place."

I understood the argument. I just didn't understand what the government thought the alternative was. Surely they wouldn't...they *couldn't*..."Dan, you can't just let her die. It will kill her parents."

Let alone the firestorm it was likely to start in Caldwell. Another death from a vamp attack would devastate the town. I sank onto the bed, not sure my knees were going to hold me up much longer.

"I know," Dan said. He tugged distractedly at his tie. "But this is out of my hands. As soon as the doctors got the test results, I had to report in. This is coming from very high up. Nosebleed high."

"You can't let her die," I repeated. My head swam. This couldn't be happening. Not to *Rhi*. She was so young.

She'd never want to live as a vampire. I knew that for sure. Not after what had happened to her sister. I knew how I'd felt when I'd been faced with the possibility. And Rhi had been through the same things as me. Tate had taken from her, just like he'd taken from me. She'd never want to be one of the monsters.

Maybe letting her die would be kinder.

All the air slammed out of my lungs at the thought, my chest tightening with a wrench that left me breathless. Kind or not, I couldn't do it. Couldn't open my mouth and tell Dan what I was thinking. I couldn't lose anyone else. He had to save her. *We* had to save her or all the pain that came afterward would be my fault.

Something maybe I wouldn't be able to live with.

I sucked in a breath. "You can't let her die," I repeated. Tears stung my eyes and I wiped them away with the back of my hand. "She has to live."

The mattress dipped as Dan sat beside me. Breath whooshed out of him in a sigh. "Ash, the doctors will do everything they can. But if she survives then she'll have to be quarantined."

"What does that mean?"

"She'll be taken to a secure facility, held where she can't infect anyone else."

Where she'd be poked and prodded and hidden away from the world. "Treated like a prisoner and a guinea pig? She hasn't done anything wrong."

Dan's eyes had gone opaque. "No, she hasn't. But neither have any of the people who could become her victims if she's free."

"What if she can be controlled?" I was clutching at straws. The thought of Rhi locked up—studied like an amoeba—was unbearable.

"Controlled how?" Dan said. "The vamp who sired her is dead. And we have no idea of his lineage." Meaning there was no way of knowing who was next up the chain of command so to speak and therefore who might be able to control Rhi. Newly turned vampires sometimes went a little wild for a time. Just like new werewolves, their control was shaky and the bloodlust could lead to them killing without meaning to.

Werewolves weren't quite as risky unless they were separated from their pack somehow. Their control can be shaky sometimes—which Dan had learned to his cost and mine—but the only time a new wolf has the uncontrollable need to change is under the full moon. And a full wolf pack can take care of most problems that arise. A vampire, on the other hand, needs to feed to survive—and young vampires have to feed more often than the older ones. Daily, usually.

I pressed the heel of my hand into my forehead, trying to think. If Rhi couldn't be controlled, then there was no way the authorities would let her go free. But without a vamp from her lineage to take charge of her, she really was a danger. So the question was, could she be controlled any other way? "What about Marco?" I said suddenly.

"What about him?" Dan's lips pressed together. The smell of agitation intensified. He obviously didn't like my suggestion.

"Tate was his lineage. Isn't it likely that Tate sired the vamps who've been given the vaccine? So Marco could maybe control her."

Dan grimaced. "Maybe. But we don't have much time."

Dawn was only hours away. If the doctors were right, if Rhi was infected, that's when she'd turn. I bit my lip. "Marco can be here pretty fast." I knew Dan was going to flip when he heard Marco was in town and worse, that I'd seen him earlier and hadn't mentioned it, but Rhi was more important than Dan's feelings right now.

Dan stepped toward me. "What do you mean pretty fast?"

I dug into my pocket for the card. "He's here in Caldwell. Call him."

The look Dan directed at the card had me surprised it didn't burst into flames.

"You have his number?"

"Yes, I have his number. He gave it to me. I didn't ask for it."

"You have his number," Dan repeated, voice low.

If I didn't know better, I'd think he was jealous of Marco. But that would be just dumb. Sure, I was in debt to the guy but that didn't mean I wanted to do the nasty with him. I was having enough trouble with the man I was sleeping with without adding another one to the mix. "Don't be an idiot, Dan. We don't have time. Call him. He might be able to help."

He shook his head. "I don't think they're going to let her go free, no matter whether she's under control or not. They want me to tell her parents she died."

"What? I surged to my feet. "You want to lock her up and not even let her family know? Dan, you can't do that. It's beyond cruel."

"They can't know why she's being held," he said, shaking his head as he got to his feet. "They might tell people."

"Get them to sign something." The FBI had wrapped me

up pretty good in nondisclosure agreements and other legal bonds after Tate. Why couldn't they do the same to Mr. and Mrs. Anders?

"Ash, they're from Caldwell. You really think if they find out there's a new breed of supervamps out there, they're going to keep their mouths shut?"

My stomach turned over. No. I didn't. He was right. They'd talk. But telling them their daughter was dead? That was torture. "If they think she's dead, there'll be a whole lot of trouble in town."

"What's the alternative?"

He'd moved closer to the door. If he left, would he do what the government wanted? I had to convince him there was another way.

"Can't you say she needs to be transferred to another hospital; a military hospital or something for specialist surgery? You can control her there." And buy us some more time to solve the problem.

"Maybe." He didn't look very hopeful.

"Won't you try? Please, Dan. For me?"

He rubbed his wrist. "Okay. I'll ask. But I'm not promising anything." His body language relaxed a little and he reached for the door handle.

"Thank you," I said. And then, because I'm an idiot who doesn't know when to stop, I added, "You should still call Marco."

Dan's hand jerked away from the handle. He turned back to me. "*Why?*"

"It will be easier on Rhi if she has somebody there to control her."

"I've asked a couple of the Taskforce vamps to come here."

"None of them will be Seattle lineages," I pointed out. Taskforce vamps were generally assigned outside their home cities. I think the government figured it lessened the chance of conflicting loyalties. Good policy but really not helping in this case. "And none of whom is an Old One."

"The vamp who bit her might not be of Tate's lineage," Dan objected.

"Marco's an Old One. Maybe he can do something anyway. He's the best chance she's got." I held out the card again. "You know it's true. Call him."

Dan snarled. "Maybe you should call him; you're such good friends with him."

Pain started throbbing behind my right eye. Lord save me from idiot men. "You really want me to ask for another favor from Marco?" I watched a wave of frustration and anger break across Dan's face as he figured out what I was getting at.

He snatched the card out of my fingers with another snarl and yanked his cell phone from his jacket pocket, stabbing the numbers onto the keypad with such force that I was surprised the phone survived.

"Lord Marco," he said after a few moments, voice tight. "This is Special Agent Gibson."

Chapter 9

THE CONVERSATION DIDN'T TAKE LONG. Dan's sentences got shorter and his voice sharper as he made his request. Finally he shoved the phone back in his pocket, scowling. "I'm going to escort him here. I don't want the locals freaking out. I'll meet you at the secure ward."

"You're doing the right thing," I said as he opened the door.

"We'll see."

I took a few minutes to compose myself and wash my face. Then I went back to the room where Rhi's parents waited and lied to them about Dan needing me for a statement and Rhi's surgery going well so far, guilt slicing through my stomach like shards of glass the entire time. But I wasn't going to be the one who took their hope away. Maybe Rhi could be controlled. Maybe there was a way to cure her—not of vampirism but of the ability to infect with a single bite—if it turned out she really was that kind of vampire.

Yeah and maybe there was a pot of gold at the end of the rainbow.

I escaped from Rhi's room, feeling like her parents had

been able to tell I was lying but telling myself that was just a hangover from them knowing me when I was a teenager. These days I had a pretty good poker face.

Finding the secure ward was a little more difficult. Most hospitals have one these days; a reinforced, no windows ward where vampire or were bites can be treated. Wards designed to contain a monster.

They'd never put me in one but I'd been surrounded by pack from the get go. Ani and Sam weren't the type to let rogues run around their city. I hoped Marco had the same philosophy.

And that he and Dan wouldn't kill each other over the next few days.

Two guards stood outside the door to the ward. Well, I assumed they were guards. They weren't wearing uniforms but something about the subdued cut of their black suits and the flat stares I received as I stepped out of the elevator screamed military, or, at least, FBI to me.

I held up my FBI ID. "I'm Ashley Keenan. I work with Special Agent Gibson."

"Agent Gibson isn't here right now, ma'am."

"I know. He asked me to meet him here." The suits looked at each other then back at me. One of them touched his earpiece, murmuring something I couldn't quite make out.

My hands clenched as I waited. Dan hadn't been kidding about how seriously the government was taking this. Up until now my Taskforce ID had been enough to get me admitted wherever I wanted to go.

The guard stopped talking then swiped a passcard through the reader at the side of the door. "You can wait inside. Please don't go into the ward itself."

I nodded but didn't speak. I wasn't going to leave Rhi

alone in a ward if I could get to her. But she might still be in surgery.

The heavy steel door slid shut behind me. The room looked like just about every other hospital waiting room I'd ever been in. Vinyl seats, prints from the blander than bland school of art, and pastel walls. An ancient-looking coffee machine blinked and gurgled in the corner. Old magazines and papers littered the table in front of one bank of chairs. The air smelled like disinfectant, slightly stale air, worry and fear. All perfectly normal for a hospital. If you didn't count the massive steel door—even bigger and more imposing looking than the one I'd just entered through—that took up most of the far wall.

No windows broke the expanse of metal, so I had no way of telling whether or not Rhi was inside without buzzing to be let through the door. I got the feeling if I did that, the two guys outside might just march in and throw me out.

It seemed I was going to have to wait for Dan and Marco after all. I carefully eased myself onto one of the seats, trying to find a position where my ribs didn't ache.

I didn't have to wait too long. Ten minutes later the outer door opened and Dan stalked through, annoyance radiating from him. Behind him, looking so perfectly at ease, I knew it had to be an act, came Marco.

I pushed up from the seat, doing my best to ignore the protesting throb in my ribs.

"Lord Marco," I said. "Thank you for coming."

"It is always a pleasure to see you, Ashley," Marco said as if we hadn't spoken just ninety minutes ago. Apparently he was practicing discretion. A fact I was devoutly thankful for. "I wish the circumstances could be more pleasant."

His green eyes glinted at me and I realized he was, once again, enjoying himself. Which meant I couldn't completely rely on his discretion.

I looked at Dan who was leaning against the back of one of the chairs. "Is there any news on Rhianna?"

He straightened, rubbing a hand over the back of his neck as he nodded. "She's in recovery. We can go through and wait in her room."

We filed through the main door—once Dan had used a swipe card and palm scan to open it—and found ourselves inside a hospital ward that looked almost as normal as the waiting room. A nurses' station guarded the entrance to a short corridor with five or six doors. Only in normal hospital wards, the station wasn't surrounded by reinforced steel and the doors to the rooms weren't foot-thick steel.

The sterile scent of antiseptic seemed stronger here, maybe because the air had taken on the bland tinge of recycling. A closed system.

I recognized the smell from my trips to my dad's lab as a kid. There the closed air circulation system was to prevent and contain leaks of any viruses or pathogens. I wasn't entirely sure why they needed one here. Unless they used this ward for quarantine or something when they weren't housing supernaturals. Which, come to think of it, if I knew Caldwell, was probably most of the time.

Still, the government funding that had been provided to all hospitals to upgrade facilities a few years back when they were trying to prove how inclusive they were being of the supernatural community, had been put to good use.

The nurse on duty inspected Dan's ID and mine and ran them through a scanner. Marco she studiously ignored. After her scanner had beeped approvals, she led us down the corridor to the only one of the doors that was shut and typed a long code into the keypad.

The room we stepped into had no windows. A long strip of fluorescent lamps flooded the room with harsh white light that blasted every corner and left nowhere to hide from the fact that this was a hospital room. I took one of the two visitors' chairs and tried not to picture Rhianna lying in the big empty hospital bed. Marco stayed near the door.

"It shouldn't be much longer," Dan said. He'd taken up position between me and the bed. Between Marco and me as well. "They'll bring her in as soon as she's cleared from recovery."

I knew how hospitals worked. I'd spent too much time in them. Dan knew that too. So he was just filling in time. Trying to distract me. I decided to play along. "What's her prognosis?"

"They've confirmed she's carrying the Stoker Variation. A mutated strain."

"She's a vampire." My hand slipped down to my jacket pocket, curled around my cross.

"She will be by dawn." Marco's voice sounded almost...sad. But that couldn't be right.

"Can you help her?" I asked him, blinking back tears. A vampire. Julie's beautiful little sister was going to be a vampire. Worse than that. A vampire who couldn't be let loose in the world. Who couldn't have any semblance of a normal life at all.

"That remains to be seen, *cara*," Marco said after a wary look at Dan. "If she has been sired by someone in my lineage then I should be able to ease the transition. If not, we shall have to see."

"Has Dan told you what's going on?" I didn't care if I was breaking five kinds of rules. Anything I could do from this point to make life—unlife—easier for Rhi, I would do.

"He said it is a new strain of the virus. One that can infect without the exchange of blood." His face was grave. "This is not a good thing."

"No shit." A bitter laugh tore itself from my throat.

"I would've thought you'd be happy," Dan said. "An easy way to increase your population."

"An easy way to increase fear and prejudice," Marco

retorted. "We have worked hard to get to where we are now. This is an act of—" he muttered something nasty sounding under his breath in Italian "—it can bring no good things."

"Maybe we're wrong," I said. "Maybe it's just a random mutation."

"*Cara*, apart from the small variations in powers bestowed, the source of our power has operated in the same way for millennia. To become a vampire, one must give and receive. It is a gift."

Some gift. About as welcome as the Spanish Inquisition from where I stood. Still, some did choose to turn voluntarily, lured by the promise of near immortality or power or whatever else it was they saw in vampires. Something I'd never understand.

Jase had made that choice. To live as a vampire rather than die a human. But it had, at least, been his choice. Rhianna had been denied that.

I rubbed my arms. "What happens when they bring her here?"

"Marco will try to control her while she changes. If everything is okay—" Dan meant if she survived"—then we'll take her to a military hospital.

"I want to go with her."

"Ash, that's not—"

"I want to go." I glared at him. "I'm not letting her be locked up alone. Surrounded by strangers."

"What about the case? And your practice?"

"They can both survive without me for a few more days."

"It will be full moon in a couple of days. What about that?"

"I'll worry about that when the time comes. Surely Ani and Sam will understand if I can't go to the retreat."

"It's not that simple."

"I'm staying with Rhi."

Dan made a humphing noise, his gaze sliding to Marco. I

knew he didn't want to make a scene in front of the vampire. It would be a sign of weakness or something.

"How will you help her?" I asked Marco, more from the desire to turn the conversation to something that wasn't an argument, than from any burning desire to know the ins and outs of how a vampire becomes a vampire.

I knew the general process but had never paid attention to the finer details.

Lycanthropy is different to vampirism. It takes hold in your body, changing you and doing whatever it is—the part the scientists haven't yet figured out—that lets werewolves change shape. It ramps up your immunity and sharpens your senses but there are no outward physical signs until the first time a werewolf changes. For me, it had felt like going through a second puberty on ultrafast forward. Aches and pains and mood swings like you wouldn't believe. And waves of the overwhelming need for sex the waxing moon ignites in adults.

Vampires however, change physically. They grow fangs. They get fatally sensitive to ultraviolet light. They grow cold and pale. They start to drink blood, to *need* blood to live. There were other changes too. Did it all happen at once? Or gradually? I wrapped my arms around myself. I didn't want to know the answer to my question.

"Ashley?"

Marco's voice was quiet and I realized I was staring off into space. "I'm sorry. I was thinking."

"You asked a question."

"Yes. Yes, I did."

"Do you wish for an answer?"

I nodded slowly. If nothing else, I wasn't sure how many more surprises or shocks I could take today. Better to know exactly what the next few hours might hold.

"*Bene.* Very well. When the doctors bring Signorina Anders here, I will attempt to establish a bond with her."

"How?"

"It is something like a thrall. But not exactly. If she is my lineage then her mind will—I cannot explain it exactly—her mind will recognize mine. Recognize my authority over her blood."

"And if she isn't?"

"Then it will depend. If things go well my age will give me the advantage and I will establish a link anyway."

I assumed that meant by force if necessary. "What if that doesn't work?"

"I will try to bind her to me another way."

"How?"

"I will give her my blood. If I am stronger than the vampire who sired her then it should let me take temporary control. Enough to prevent her from hurting herself or anybody else during the transition."

A thought struck me. "Is that safe for you?"

Marco shrugged. "I am already a vampire. I can't be reinfected."

I hugged myself harder. None of it sounded good. "Does it hurt?" Changing to a wolf for the first time had hurt like a son of a bitch, no pun intended. But only for a short time and then it had felt good.

"There is some pain," Marco admitted. His hand rubbed his chest above his heart as if remembering a sensation. "The body fights the changes."

So now Rhi had to suffer as well as be a vampire?

"I still don't even know how this has happened," I muttered.

"You were there," Dan said.

No point muttering with a vampire and a werewolf in the room, they'll both hear you just fine. "I mean, I don't understand how the bite had this effect. Rhianna must've been vaccinated. Tate fed me that anti-vaccine for three days before he tried turning me. So why has this worked?"

"The doctors will try and look at that but we don't know."

"It could just be bad luck," Marco said. "The vaccines do not always work."

"Bad luck?" My voice was high and shaky. Bad luck was losing your purse or breaking your favorite coffee mug. Not being bitten by some freak vampire and having your vaccine fail. Had Smith perfected his plague vamps so their bite could always overcome the vaccine? "It's not bad luck. She didn't drink that vamp's blood, so it can't just be a vaccine failure. And she's going to be a vampire. And the government wants to—

Dan's phone rang. "Gibson." He listened for a moment then hung up. "They're bringing Rhianna down now."

A shiver ran through me. This was all about to become real. "Did they say anything about how she is?"

"No. The surgeon is coming with her."

"The surgeon will not matter if she's going to turn," Marco said.

I blinked at him. "What?"

"Changing will heal any physical issues."

I hadn't thought of that. But, much like werewolves, in fact much faster than a werewolf, a vampire's body was healed of wounds and illnesses during the transition. Healed permanently of any number of things.

Including the ageing process and fertility and the need to eat and drink anything but blood.

My mouth tasted sour. "I need a glass of water," I said faintly, sinking back down into the chair. I wasn't sure I was ready for what was about to happen. I'd barely eaten all day and fatigue and adrenaline were combining to make everything seem unreal and slightly fuzzy around the edges.

"I will speak to the nurse. This could be a long night," Marco said.

"It can't be that long," I said, as he left the room. "It's four a.m. already." A few more hours to sunrise. That was all the time Rhianna had left. Tears rose in my eyes and I blinked them back. "Dan, you have to let her parents see her."

"I'm sorry, Ash," he said. "I can't do that." He came over to me, hunkered down by the chair. "It's not what I want. But I have to follow orders."

I looked down into his eyes. Saw the regret in them. But feeling bad about it didn't change what he was doing. "Screw your orders; you can't just take their daughter away from them. What are you going to tell them? That she's dead? That their only surviving daughter is dead? They'll want to see the body."

"For the moment, we're telling them that she's being transferred to a military facility for more specialized treatment and that we're working on clearance so they can visit."

"Are you?"

He closed his eyes briefly. "I don't know what the final decision will be."

"It's wrong." I stared at him, wishing there was some way to make him understand. He'd never been through what I'd—what the Anders had—been through with Tate. He didn't know what losing someone violently did to you.

"We have to think of the greater good."

I laughed. "The greater good? Christ, what is that?"

He laid a hand on my cheek and I flinched away, I didn't want comfort, didn't want to feel better. I didn't deserve it.

Voices in the corridor brought Dan to his feet again. The door swung open and a woman in blue scrubs came through, propping the door open. Then an orderly wheeled Rhianna into the room on a gurney.

Her eyes were closed, her neck was bandaged and, to my eyes, she looked far too pale and still. The woman helped the orderly shift Rhi onto the bed, then started fussing with tubes and IVs, hooking Rhi up to several different monitors. I wondered why they were bothering. If she changed, then there was nothing in any IV that could do her any good. Unless it was a bag of O positive.

"She's still a little in and out," the woman said when she caught me watching. "The surgeon will be in to speak to you soon." Her expression, as she smoothed a last piece of tape over the IV needle in Rhi's hand, was pitying. The last shred of hope I'd been holding onto shriveled up and blew away.

I gripped the armrest, needing to hold on to something so I wouldn't start screaming.

"Water, *cara*."

I flinched. Once again, Marco had managed to sneak up on me. He held out a plastic cup. I took it and sipped, hoping my stomach wouldn't rebel.

"They will bring some coffee and sandwiches," he said.

"What about you?"

"I am fine."

I took another sip. The water eased the sourness in my mouth but wasn't helping with the tight burning feeling in my throat. My head and ribs seemed to throb in unison. I should've asked Marco to score me a shot of something while he was out. Valium. Oxycontin. Morphine. Unconsciousness seemed pretty inviting right about now.

I closed my eyes for a moment, willing the pain away. Neither my body nor my mind paid any attention.

"Agent Gibson?"

A male voice. The doctor, I hoped. I wondered whether if I just sat here with my eyes shut, would everything go away? Then told myself to suck it up and opened them.

Dan was shaking hands with a man in scrubs, just like the nurse's. The doctor looked tired, stubble darkening his jaw line

"Ashley, this is Dr. Samuels."

My legs didn't want to cooperate when I tried to stand. I gritted my teeth and told my body to do what the hell it was told. "Doctor." I took a few shaky steps. "How is she?"

He came toward me, a frown pulling bushy eyebrows together. "Are you in pain, Ms. Keenan? I understand you were involved in the same...attack as Ms. Anders?"

I waved a hand, careful not to wince as my ribs twinged again. "I'm fine. Tell me about Rhianna."

He sighed. "We've managed to repair the damage to the arteries in her neck. In one way, it's lucky—"

"Lucky?"

"Agent Gibson has told you that she's positive for Stokers?"

I nodded.

"It's helping her. She might not have made it otherwise."

I couldn't help feeling that might have been better for her. "I don't consider becoming—"

Rhianna moaned. I twisted toward her. Bruised-looking blue eyes stared at me.

"Rhi? Can you hear me?"

She nodded slowly. "Ashley? What are you doing here?" She turned her head, eyes widening as she spotted Dan and the doctor. "I'm in a hospital?"

I took her hand, curling my fingers around hers. She didn't react, her fingers stayed limp under mine. "Do you remember what happened?"

Her eyes closed. "No. Was there an accident?"

"It's fairly common not to remember much straight after surgery," the doctor offered. "The anesthesia. And shock."

I tightened my fingers around Rhi's. Her skin felt hot. Too hot. Weren't vampires supposed to be cool? The burning in my throat doubled and I had to swallow hard before I could speak. "Not an accident, Rhi. You don't remember the hall?"

"We had coffee."

"After that?"

Her head moved from side to side. Her hair fell across her face, limp and bedraggled. I smoothed it back.

"I don't remember." Her mouth trembled a little and suddenly she looked very much like Julie at sixteen.

I glanced up at Dan, hoping he'd jump in. I didn't want to be the one to tell Rhianna what had happened. But Dan's expression didn't look like he'd be letting me off the hook.

"Ashley?" Rhianna said. "Is something wrong?"

I swallowed hard. "Sweetie, something happened at the hall. There was an attack. You got hurt."

"An attack? What sort of—" Her hand drifted upward to her neck, touching the dressing with shaking fingers. "Why does my throat—oh God. *No*." Her eyes filled with horror.

"I'm sorry, Rhi. It was a vampire."

It didn't seem possible that she could turn paler but she did. "But I'm okay, right? I mean I'm vaccinated, so I'm *okay*."

Dr. Samuels cleared his throat. "We've repaired the damage to your neck, Rhianna."

"Why do I get the feeling there's a big 'but' in that sentence?" Rhi pushed herself up on the bed, wincing as she moved. "Somebody tell me what's going on."

"Rhi, the vamp who bit you, he was—" I stopped, no idea what to say next. How did you tell someone who is only twenty-one that life as she knew it was over?

"He was carrying a mutated strain of the virus," Dan said into the quiet. "I'm sorry, Rhianna, but the test results show that you're infected."

I held my breath, expecting her to start screaming or something. Instead, she broke into laughter. The sound rang round the room as she grinned and giggled. Even when she covered her mouth with her hand, snorts and chuckles escaped and her face grew pink.

The rest of us looked at each other, not entirely sure how to react. "Is she hysterical?" I asked the doctor.

"I'm not hysterical," Rhianna said. I saw dimples flash in and out of her cheeks as she tried to sound serious. "I just figured this out. It's a joke, right? How can I be infected? I didn't drink any vampire blood. And I'm vaccinated."

"Sweetie, no." I reached for her hand again. "Listen to me. It's not a joke, I'm serious. The virus was mutated. You're infected. By sunrise you're going to be a vampire."

The smile on her face froze. "You're wrong. You have to be wrong."

Marco stepped forward. "She is not wrong. You are changing."

"Who are you?" She stared at him and the scent of fear suddenly filled the room.

He bowed and I knew he was trying hard to make the move look human rather than unnaturally graceful. He was only partly successful. His bow was like a dance.

"My name is Marco. I'm here to assist you in your transition."

Rhianna shrank back. "You're a vampire."

"Rhi, he's okay," I said. "He won't hurt you." Her racing heart sounded like drums. Jungle drums. Warning of impending doom.

"He wants to turn me into a vampire!" The pounding of her heartbeat grew louder.

I touched her face, trying to calm her. "He's here to help you."

"No." Her voice was shrill. "No. No. *NO!*" She ripped her hand out of my grip, wrapping her arms around herself.

I looked at the doctor. "Can you give her something?"

He shook his head. "No, her system won't respond to most sedatives at this point. We were lucky she stayed under for the surgery."

"Maybe I can help," Marco said.

I shot him an incredulous look as Rhi's protests redoubled. "Maybe not right now."

He ignored me and walked to the end of the bed. "Rhianna."

She shut her eyes, curling into a ball.

"Rhianna, look at me." Marco's voice dropped to a silky, commanding tone. He moved up to her side, reached out and touched her head. "Open your eyes."

Her eyes opened reluctantly. "Go away." She tried to shake off his touch but his hand didn't move.

"I'm not going to hurt you. Let me help you relax. It's easier if you don't fight."

She shivered. "You'll thrall me."

Her voice broke and I felt my heart break with it. I wanted to reach out and hold her but I didn't dare in case it interfered with whatever Marco was trying to do.

"No." His voice dropped lower, until it was almost hypnotic. "No, I'll just help you. Just listen to my voice."

Rhi panted, the fear scent rolling off her until it filled the room. It made me want to retch. The wolf liked fear but the human remembered that smell.

Remembered stinking of it herself when Tate had held her.

When he'd taken her blood and her mind.

"Rhianna, just breathe. In and out," Marco said softly.

Her face twisted. I watched as she struggled to slow her gasps, wincing with each sucked in breath, each hitch and pound in her pulse. Breathing this hard had to be hurting her.

But I knew the fear was hurting her worse.

"Slower." Marco's voice seemed to come from nowhere and everywhere, floating on the air like a song playing on an unseen radio. "Just breathe. Easy. You're safe here."

Gradually Rhi's breath grew calmer and her heart slowed. When her pulse was almost normal, Marco nodded. "Good. That's good. Now, Rhianna, I want you to listen to me."

She nodded. "I'm listening."

"I need to tell you what's happening."

I saw his eyes flick to the clock on the wall above the bed. Four thirty. Sunrise would come all too soon.

"O-okay." Her heart rate had bumped up a little again but her voice was mostly calm.

"The virus is changing you. You're going to feel hot."

"I'm hot now."

Her face was flushed. I'd assumed it was from panic but now the pink staining her face—making her look healthy and normal instead of sick—was ominous.

"All right. So you will feel warm. And then you will get cold."

"I'm going to die?" It sounded like a child's voice in the dark.

"Not die, Rhianna, change."

Marco lied too easily. I didn't care what the arguments were. Becoming a vampire was death.

"Will it hurt?"

"There will be some pain, *bella*. But only for a little while."

I didn't know if that was another pretty lie.

"Can't you give me something?"

"No. The drugs won't work on you now. But you will be all right, I promise."

Rhianna swallowed. "Can I see my parents?"

I looked at Dan, hoping he might relent.

But he shook his head. "I'm sorry, Rhianna. We have to contain this virus. Until we can control it, we can't risk your parents coming in here."

"But it's blood-borne, isn't it? How would they catch it? Why can't they be here if you can?"

"Ashley and I are werewolves," Dan said. "We can't get the vamp virus too."

That was what we were telling ourselves anyway. Because if Smith and friends had finally made a better version of their mutated vamp virus, perhaps one day it could affect weres. I didn't want to think about what a vampire shifter might be like.

"It's not safe for your parents, Rhi," I said, taking her hand again. Her skin burned against mine. Her eyes were bright with fever, her cheeks pink. She didn't look like someone about to die. "Vampires can be unpredictable when they change. The three of us are stronger than...your parents."

I wondered whether we should tell her the whole truth— that Marco was here to control her if needed—but he shook his head at me slightly when I met his gaze across the bed.

"I just want to see my mom," Rhianna said. Tears leaked under her eyes. "Just one last time."

"You can see them after," I lied. "Once we know every- thing is okay."

"My parents hate vampires," she said. "They're not going to want to see me."

"They love you. They'll adjust to this."

"I don't think so." She closed her eyes again. "How much longer?"

"Sunrise is about two hours away," Dan said softly.

More tears. I left Marco still crooning something soft and Italian to Rhianna and went to Dan, huddling into him. His arm closed around me, strong and comforting. I wished I could stay there forever.

"I'm going to leave you to it," the doctor said. "Hit the buzzer if you need help."

I couldn't really blame him for fleeing the scene. I didn't want to stay either. I looked back at Rhianna. The color had faded from her cheeks.

Fear flared. I went over and put my hand on her forehead. She was cooler. Much cooler.

"Is it supposed to happen this fast?" I asked Marco.

He frowned. "Everyone is slightly different." He kept his

voice low, staring down at Rhianna. Her eyes were still closed, the fine blood vessels in her eyelids standing out against the too white skin. Marco looked back at me and shook his head.

"Too fast?" I mouthed.

He nodded.

"Is something wrong?"

A very Italian shrug which I took to mean, 'let's wait and see.'

Chapter 10

So we waited. The hands on the clock kept moving forward and Rhianna kept growing colder and colder. When she started shivering we piled on blankets.

It didn't seem to help.

I went in search of more. As I came back with another couple of blankets the nurse had warmed, my cell rang.

I ignored it and started tucking the blankets around Rhi. It didn't stop the shivers running through her body but her teeth stopped chattering.

The phone went silent then shrilled into life again.

"You should answer that," Dan said.

I shook my head. "They'll call back. I'm surprised it even works down here."

"It could be Bug."

"She'll be asleep." The ringing cut off again and I relaxed. "See, nothing important."

"Check the number."

"Look, nothing is more important than Rhi right now. Your team would call you if something big had happened, right?"

His pager had already buzzed once. They were keeping

him posted but so far the Taskforce agents had found no sign
of the vampires who'd attacked us. Not that I'd expected there
would be.

I went over to my purse and dug around for the phone. If
I switched it off, then I wouldn't have Dan nagging me to
answer it.

Just as I picked it up, it shrilled to life again, making me
jump half a foot. I flushed and answered the call. "Ashley
Keenan."

"Ms. Keenan. I hope you enjoyed our little message this
afternoon."

Smith. Fuck. "Not as much as I enjoyed killing one of
your freaks."

Dan's head snapped around at the snarl in my voice.

"What do you want, Smith?" I figured I might as well let
Dan know who was on the line.

"I called to see how the girl is doing."

"She's just fine," I said.

"Really? Somehow I doubt that."

"Listen to me, you sick bastard. Leave me alone, leave my
family and friends alone or I swear you're going to regret it."

"Why are you so angry if your friend is fine? She's not, is
she? Let me think. I'd suspect that right now she's feeling a
little under the weather. Cold perhaps?"

I snarled again, this time a full growl, the sort of wolf
sound you shouldn't try in human form. It hurts your throat.
Dan's fingers blurred as he tapped out a text message on his
phone and he made a 'keep it going' gesture at me."

"Tut, tut, Ashley. That is not polite."

"Fuck you."

"Don't speak to me that way. I told you to stop what you
were doing. I told you there would be consequences."

"And now I'm telling you to expect some consequences
yourself. I'm going to nail your ass to the wall, Smith. I will
hurt you. Tate got off easily. You're going to pay."

"I don't think so."

"I—" Rhianna suddenly let out a piercing scream, her body bowing up off the bed like all her muscles had suddenly cramped.

"Sounds to me like your friend is not feeling so well after all," Smith said. "Perhaps I'll leave you to it. Though I'll be interested to hear how things turn out. I've made some improvements to the formula since last we met."

Rhianna screamed again, her back arching upward as her body spasmed. I hurled the phone across the room. It smashed against the door, raining splintered metal and plastic down on the floor.

"Help her," I yelled at Marco.

"She can't hear me right now," he replied calmly. "We have to wait this part out."

Rhi screamed again, an agonizing sound that went on and on until I felt like someone was carving the noise into my brain with a blunt blade. Then it cut off abruptly and Rhi collapsed back on the bed.

"Rhi! Shit." I bolted to her side. I couldn't see whether she was breathing. My fingers pressed into the uninjured side of her neck. There. A pulse. Weak and thready and way too slow, but a pulse. It stammered and jerked, like a car struggling to start on a cold morning. "Marco, now what?"

"Now the change really begins and we see if she will listen to me."

"What do you want us to do?"

"Just stay where you are. You might need to hold her down if..."

"If you can't establish whatever link it is you have with your lineage?"

He nodded. "Yes, if I have to give her my blood, she will most likely fight it."

"What do we do then?"

"Contain her, make her drink. If we have to, we knock her out."

"The doctor said drugs wouldn't work on her."

"There are other ways to knock someone out."

I shivered at his matter of fact tone. "I don't want to hurt her."

"We may not have a choice. If we can't control her, she may hurt herself worse than anything we can do to her."

I looked at Dan. "What do you think?"

Dan had agent face again. "I think we have to listen to Marco. He's the expert."

"Don't they teach you this stuff in the FBI?"

"Yes, but I've never witnessed it. And they never taught us about handling a vampire who's infected with a mutated virus and whose sire is dead and not around to help."

Uncharted territory. Even for Marco if I thought about it. "Okay." I nodded at Marco. "Where do you want us?"

We positioned ourselves around the bed, Marco on her right, me on the other side, Dan beside me. Minutes ticked by while Rhianna's breathing grew labored and her pulse shimmered and skipped.

I reached for Dan's hand, squeezing hard and we watched as shudders wracked her body, each one punctuated with hoarse moans.

Marco watched her, his expression strangely distant, as if he was watching a half-forgotten memory. His eyes seemed very green, the green of forests, of life. A strange color in the face of the undead.

"Do you remember?" I asked him. "Do you remember what it felt like?"

"A little..." He made a gesture. "It is like an *incubo*. A nightmare long past."

"Did it hurt? Do you remember pain?"

"No one remembers pain," he said softly. "We remember it hurt, we do not remember the sensation itself."

"But still a nightmare," I said.

"What do you remember from your first change?" he asked. "The pain or the sensation afterward?"

"Both."

He raised an eyebrow at me.

"But mostly the feeling afterward."

"So it is for us."

I wanted to believe him. But it was hard to believe that dying wouldn't hurt.

The sounds of Rhianna's breathing grew too loud in my ears, the pause between each breath a little too long.

I was about to ask Marco how much longer when Rhi started screaming again, writhing on the bed as if she was trying to turn herself inside out. The dressing on her neck turned suddenly red.

"Should she be bleeding?" I said, looking around for something to help. "Get the doctor."

"Let me try to calm her again." Marco put his hand on Rhi's head but she twisted away from him with another shriek, as if his very touch had burned her.

I moved without thinking, shoving at him. "You're hurting her."

Marco fell back.

"Ash, he's just trying to help," Dan said.

I scrubbed a hand across my face, trying to hold back the tears rising again. If Dan was defending Marco then there was definitely something wrong with the situation. "He's *hurting* her."

Rhi screamed again, her voice scratched and ragged.

"She's hurting regardless," Dan said. "Let him do what you brought him here to do."

I stepped back. Dan was right. I had to let Marco try. Marco leaned closer to Rhianna, put his hand on her arm. Her screams redoubled, so agonized I expected to see the skin on her arm blistering where his fingers lay.

But it remained pale. Unmarked.

Unlike the bandage, which was almost soaked through, adding the sharp scent of blood to the other smells flooding the room. Though her blood didn't smell entirely normal to me. There was an edge to it...not the soured acid of vamp blood, not quite, but no longer purely human. It was another reminder that what was happening was inescapable.

I glanced at the clock. Sunrise was still an hour away. I didn't think I could take another hour of Rhianna screaming.

"Is it going to be like this until...." I didn't want to finish the sentence.

Another infuriating shrug from Marco. "It is not an exact science. Some succumb a while before and rise again with the sun. Some have less of a delay." He looked down at Rhi gravely and I realized he was listening to her heart, the same as me. "I do not think Rhianna will be much longer."

"Until she succumbs?" I said bitterly. Such a pretty word for dying.

"Let us hope. It will be easier for her."

"None of this passes any definition of easy."

"I know," he said. "I am sorry for this, Ashley."

A sizzling tide of blame rose in me but I choked it back. Me screaming at Marco wasn't going to change anything. And I needed him for Rhianna.

She screamed again, though this time it was shorter, softer. She gasped at the end then went quiet.

I focused on her, straining to hear the next breath. I heard her heart beat, once, twice, a struggling third, and then there was silence.

My knees buckled. Marco caught my arm and I yanked myself free of his grip, turning blindly toward the chair I could no longer see through the tears suddenly bathing my face.

"She's dead," I said.

"Only for a little while," Marco offered.

"No." I shook my head, as if I could shake myself free of the sudden all-consuming grief. "No. The Rhianna I knew is dead." Sobs choked my throat and I hid my face against my knees, bent double with the weight of the sadness. How was I going to face her parents?

I felt arms go around me, lifting me. I didn't resist, just turned myself into the warmth Dan offered and cried.

The tears felt endless, I tried to stop myself but every time I managed to struggle to some semblance of control, I'd take a breath and then start over again. Dan just murmured in my ear and stroked my hair. Thankfully his scent did a pretty good job of masking the fact that Rhianna's human smell was fading.

Finally I heard footsteps approaching.

"Ashley, the time is nearing," Marco said quietly. "I will need your help."

I burrowed harder against Dan's chest, not wanting to lift my head and see Rhianna lying on the bed. Or to see what happened next.

Dan's arms loosened around me. "Ash."

I shook my head. "I can't."

"Yes, you can. Ash, Rhi needs you now."

My eyes felt like I'd been crying acid and my throat wasn't much better. "I can't help her."

"Yes, you can. You can help her with her life now. Help her through this change. She'll need you."

Yeah and if she had the same reaction I'd had initially to becoming a wolf then the kindest thing I could do for her would be to help her find a patch of sunshine to walk into. Not that Dan was going to allow me to do any such thing.

Still, if I could help Rhi then I had to. I owed her.

I peeled myself away from Dan, brushing my cheeks with my hands and blinking as the light hit my swollen eyes.

First order of the day was to splash something on my face. The cool water didn't take away the taste of tears in my mouth or the sting of salt in my eyes but it did make me feel slightly more alive.

I came back to the bed, forcing myself to look at Rhi.

She was dead.

There was no two ways about it. She didn't look like she was asleep; she looked dead. I'd seen enough bodies in my life to know the difference.

At least Rhi wasn't broken or maimed, if you discounted the stained bandage still wrapped around her neck. Dr. Samuels came through the door, joining Marco by the bed, his expression grave.

"What now?" I said to Marco.

"We have a few more minutes," he said. "She'll wake with the sun."

I'd never understood that. Vampires were creatures of the night, the sun was their enemy. It seemed ridiculous that their change was tied to the one thing guaranteed to kill them.

But no one had ever said this had to make sense. The viruses weren't simple diseases. No other disease did what these did. Changed you completely. There was something more at work than the physical, something deeper. I'd never been comfortable with the word magic but it was beyond natural. How else was it that the light of the full moon called me to be a wolf and the rising sun would seal the change in Rhianna that would doom her to darkness?

"Do not look so sad, *cara*," Marco said. "She will adjust."

"Her family has suffered enough. *She's* suffered enough."

"Some would say her suffering is about to end forever."

"I think we'll just have to agree to differ." I smoothed Rhianna's hair into place. The ticking of the clock seemed to fill the room.

I met Marco's gaze. "Once she wakes, you'll try and make the link with her?"

Marco nodded, beckoning Dan to stand on the opposite side of the bed to me. "Be ready, she may resist." He took up position again near Rhi's head, standing close to Dan. "Doctor, it would be safest if you left now."

Samuels nodded and left us alone after reminding Marco that there was blood in the small bar fridge in the corner of the room.

The clock ticked on and we waited. My stomach rolled and twisted with each breath. Only willpower kept me standing—kept me in the room. Every part of me wanted to flee.

Then, as the waiting seemed to fill the room like a weight, pressing down on us all, Rhi's eyes snapped open.

I flinched backward, unnerved despite myself. Then leaned forward. "Rhi?"

Blue eyes stared up at me with a blank expression. Then slowly they filled with rage.

"Rhi?"

With a snarl, she sprang, hands groping for my throat. Dan managed to grab her as I stumbled backward. I crashed into the wall behind me, unable to stop the momentum of the instinctive leap I'd taken to avoid the attack. The impact knocked the wind from me. I slid to the floor trying to suck in air with lungs that wouldn't obey.

"Do your thing, Marco." Dan snarled. "Fast." His arms tightened around the furiously struggling Rhianna.

"Turn her to me," Marco said. Dan twisted and Rhianna made a hissing sound of fury as Marco came into her view.

"Blood of my line, heed me."

Marco's voice was low and intense as I hauled myself to my feet, still wincing as I tried to breathe deep.

Rhianna hissed again and Marco spoke. "Heed me."

His only answer was a shriek of fury. Rhianna lashed out with one hand, her nails scoring down his face.

"I take it that means she's not of your lineage?" I said, leaning on the bed as Marco retreated a few steps.

"*Si*," he snapped, eyes still on Rhianna. "Hold her still, Agent Gibson."

"Easier said than done." Dan said through gritted teeth. He shifted his grip, trying to pin Rhianna's hands to her body. She snapped her head back and only his lightning reflexes saved her from connecting with his nose. He winced as he tightened his grip and changed position.

I felt a rumble in the back of my throat as I reacted to the threat to Dan. "Perhaps it would be easier if we got her back on the bed," I said. "You and I can hold her, Dan. Then Marco can try whatever it is he needs to try next."

"Actually, it will be easier this way," Marco said. He had removed his jacket and was calmly rolling back the cuff of his right sleeve. There was blood on his face and drops splattered onto the snowy expanse of cotton of his shirt like shredded rose petals. His eyes stayed on Rhianna, assessing.

I moved nearer, eliciting another shriek as Rhianna tried to twist toward me. The rage boiling from her eyes was shocking.

This wasn't Rhianna. There was nothing of the girl I'd known behind the snarl of hate. It was all animal, intent on inflicting harm. She hissed, a wordless sound of enmity that made the hairs on the back of my neck rise. Not least because for the first time, I could see the fangs that hadn't been there when she'd taken her last breath.

"Come around behind me, Ashley," Marco said softly.

"What are you going to do?"

"Provoke her."

That didn't sound like such a good plan to me, but he was the expert.

I did as he asked, moving warily, ready to help Dan if he needed it. Sweat beaded Dan's forehead—holding a newly risen vampire down by sheer force couldn't be easy.

Marco muttered something in Italian, something curt and brutal sounding. Then he stepped close, holding out his wrist.

"You want to hurt something?" he said to Rhianna. "Hurt me."

Another hissing, snarling wordless protest rose from Rhianna, but then she struck, lightning fast, burying those newly minted fangs deep into the flesh of Marco's wrist. So deep, pain twisted his face.

Rhi's throat worked as she swallowed greedily, sucking down Marco's blood like she was starving for it. Drops splashed down her chin, the deep red looking unreal in the fluorescent lights. As she drank, color started to fill her cheeks but the ferocious look in her eyes didn't change.

She still looked wild. Feral.

Predatory.

After a minute or so Marco said, "Enough."

Rhianna took another defiant swallow. This time it was Marco who hissed in pain. Then he wrenched his wrist free with a wet tearing sound that made me want to throw up.

"Now what?" I asked as he clutched his wrist to his chest, blood spilling down his shirt.

"Now we see whose blood is stronger."

I looked at his arm in concern. "Do you need something for that?"

He shook his head. "No, it will heal soon enough." His gaze was fastened on Rhianna's face. I wasn't sure what he was looking for but after a few moments he smiled. "Now we shall try this again."

He stepped closer to her, dropping his arm so I got a fleeting glimpse of his wrist and saw the wound had already scabbed over like it had been there for days.

Wolves heal fast too but not that fast. We have to change forms. More than once for most things.

"Blood of my blood," Marco said softly. "Look at me."

The snarl on Rhianna's face disappeared and her blue eyes locked with his.

"*Si*." His voice was a soft croon. "*Si*, look at me. Let me in."

Let me in? I flinched. What exactly was he trying to do? I looked at Dan and saw the same wariness in his eyes as he turned his head away from Marco, not wanting to get caught in whatever the hell it was that Marco was weaving.

"*Si*. Look at me." The croon sounded a little strained but Marco didn't move from his stance. "See me. Good. Come to me."

There was a sudden sensation of electricity in the air—a snap like lightning striking in the distance—and then just as suddenly, it disappeared and Rhianna went limp in Dan's arms.

"I have her now," Marco said. "Put her back on the bed."

Dan obeyed with a look of relief, laying Rhi down carefully. Her eyes were open but peaceful, the rage and fury gone.

"What did you do to her?" I said quietly to Marco.

"I established a bond. I think."

"You think?" I looked from him back to Rhianna. "What if you're wrong?"

"She is quiet for now, yes? So I am probably right."

He sounded confident but I noticed he was watching Rhianna not me.

"Can all Old Ones do that?"

"It is something that comes with age, but it does not always work."

"Now you tell us."

"It had to be tried. She would have hurt herself. And perhaps us."

"How long can you keep her like that?" Dan said from the other side of the bed where he stood, one hand rubbing at his neck and shoulders. He looked wrecked.

"She needs to feed, then she will come back to herself over the next day or so," Marco said. "I think I can keep her calm until then."

"So she belongs to you now?" I didn't understand exactly what he'd done. Something like a thrall or something that meant the bond a vampire had with their sire—and through them—the head of their lineage had been transferred to Marco?

"I am not entirely sure," Marco said. "She feels...different. Whatever they have done to the virus made it difficult. I'm not sure what would happen if someone of her lineage tried to take her from me."

Oh, wonderful. But then again, given the government wanted to lock Rhianna up, it was unlikely anyone would be challenging Marco's control any time soon.

"Should we feed her?" My eyes strayed to the fridge in the corner of the room where the doctor had put the blood packs hours ago.

"*Sì.*" Marco went to the fridge and opened it, looking at the contents. "This is manufactured," he said, holding up a pack to the light with a frown.

"It's what a lot of vamps drink," Dan said. "Given her circumstances, I don't think it's wise to let her get a taste for real human blood."

"Real blood is best for the young ones."

"She'll just have to make do," Dan said. He crossed to Marco and took the pack out of his hands, laying it on top of the fridge as he opened the long cardboard box the doctor had also left. He withdrew a fleshy color tube that looked like it was made of rubber or foam.

"What's that?"

"Feeding tube," Dan said.

"Can't she just drink it from a glass or something?"

"It is easiest for the young ones to bite," Marco said. "It calms them."

"Just like a wolf's first hunt," Dan said as he slid the blood pack into the tube with an ease that spoke of experience.

"This warms the blood and gives them something to bite into."

It looked ridiculous. Like someone had chopped the arm off a flesh-colored store dummy and rubberized it. Surely biting rubber couldn't be satisfying? But what did I know?

Dan passed the pack to Marco. "You can do the honors."

"How do you know about feeding new vampires?" I said as I watched Marco approach Rhianna and coax her to sit up.

Dan came over to sit beside me. "They teach us in the Taskforce. We come across new vamps every so often. Easier to use one of these than have someone get bitten."

"I guess." The conversation was making me feel vaguely nauseated. Which was dumb, given that I'd eaten fresh raw deer my first night as a werewolf and bitten the throats out of two vampires since then.

Rhianna's hands closed around the feeding tube. I turned away as she sank her fangs into it, sucking greedily.

"I'll go get Dr. Samuels," Dan said. "See if he can clear her for transport."

"What about her parents? Can we tell them Rhi will be okay?"

He shook his head. "Not yet."

"When?"

"I can't promise anything."

He was halfway to the door when Rhianna suddenly gagged and dropped the feeding tube, clawing at her throat.

I turned to glare at Marco. "What the hell?"

"Get the doctor. She is not reacting well to the blood," Marco snapped.

Understatement of the year. Rhianna gasped frantically, sounding half-choked. Raw red blisters bloomed around her mouth. If the outside looked like that, what the hell was happening inside her throat?

I heard Dan calling down the hallway for help as if he was speaking through a fog. Everything sounded wobbly and far away as I stared at the sores breaking out and marring the whiteness of Rhi's skin.

"Help her," I said to Marco.

"There's nothing I can do," he said. "Her body needs to process this. It will heal."

"How do you know?" Rhianna wasn't a normal vampire...that much was clear. Marco couldn't predict what was going to happen with any certainty, even if he liked to think he was in control of the situation.

"Can't you tell her to go to sleep or something?" I added desperately as Rhi's sounds of pains redoubled. She retched violently and started vomiting blood. The thick sticky redness splashed over the pale blue hospital covers. Some of it splashed on my hands. It looked like someone had been slaughtered on the bed. Too much blood.

More than she'd drunk.

Marco lunged toward her, grabbing her shoulders. I froze, not knowing whether to help him or go find the doctor. Before I could decide, footsteps pounded down the hallway and the door flew open.

"Keep her under control we don't need anyone else getting bitten." I said to Marco before someone hustled me out of the room and slammed the door behind me.

I stood there, shell-shocked at the sudden silence. There was no sound from Rhi's room. Good soundproofing I guess but the sudden transition made it feel as though I'd gone deaf.

I leaned against the wall, trying to breathe, trying not to think about all that blood spilling over Rhi and the bed. Trying not to smell the blood splashed on me. I ached to help but what could I do? I wasn't needed inside, that much was plain. And I could hardly go back upstairs to Rhianna's parents looking like I did.

My stomach clenched as I thought about them sitting upstairs, waiting for news, not knowing whether Rhi was dead or alive.

Even worse, not having any idea she was now a vampire; a monster out of their worst nightmares. The same kind of creature who'd killed their other daughter.

I wondered if they'd been told anything at all. Or maybe the government had gone ahead and told them Rhi was dead.

Dan had said he'd try to stop that from happening, but he hadn't been able to promise anything.

How would the Anders cope if they thought Rhi was dead?

How would they cope if they found out the truth?

I eyed the doors to the waiting room. Would anyone notice if I snuck out and told them?

They deserved the truth.

No one who hadn't been through what we'd been through with Tate had the right to take that away from them.

I took two steps then stopped as the doors swung inward and Dan walked through. He had a take-out coffee cup in one hand and the other held his cell to his ear.

When he saw me, he said something I couldn't quite make out then put the phone away.

When he reached me, he held out the coffee. "Thought you might need this."

The warm rich smell made my stomach growl then lurch queasily. As much as my brain ached for some caffeine to burn away some of the foggy confusion that came with too much stress and too little sleep, I knew I'd just make myself sick.

I shook my head. Dan shrugged and took a mouthful himself. He'd always had a cast iron stomach—a useful trait for a cop.

One I envied right now.

He reached into his pocket again and pulled out a candy bar. "How about this?"

Chocolate? It wasn't exactly what I wanted but it was at least something to keep me upright.

I took the bar from him, opened it, and took a cautious

nibble. My stomach didn't feel any worse so I took a bigger bite, letting the chocolate melt on my tongue, the sweetness masking some of the stale taste of fear and fatigue.

"What's happening in there?" Dan nodded towardRhi's room.

I shook my head. "Your guess is as good as mine. Who were you talking to?"

"Esme. She's coordinating with the army."

"So you're going ahead with it?" Locking Rhi away. The taste of chocolate turned sour as my throat tightened. Rhi loved people. Loved connections. She wanted to be a doctor for God's sake. And they wanted to lock her away somewhere where she'd hardly have any contact with anyone.

Dan took another gulp of coffee, pulling a face. "We don't have a choice, Ash. She can't be let loose until the doctors figure out exactly what we're dealing with. Right now, she'll get better care at the base than she will here."

"She'd get better care somewhere like Seattle Northern," I said. Northern was the main hospital used by Seattle's supernatural population. Not that we suffered from many illnesses but some injuries still required assistance.

"We take her there and news about the mutated virus takes about three seconds to hit the street. The base is secure."

He was right, I knew he was right. That didn't mean I had to like it. I finished the candy bar with several vicious bites.

"I want to go with her," I said, holding up a hand as he opened his mouth to argue. "No, scrap that. I am going with her. I'm not letting you lock her away surrounded by strangers."

"Okay," Dan said.

I eyed him with suspicion. That was way too easy. I'd expected an argument. "Marco needs to go with her too. He's the only one who has some influence over her."

"If Lord Marco wishes to assist us, then the government will be grateful," Dan said carefully.

I took that to mean he thought it was a terrible idea but someone higher up had had the same thought as me.

"And her parents."

Dan shook his head, crumpling the empty coffee cup in his hand. "No. They're not going to be allowed to see her."

"But they know she's alive?"

"They've been told she's in isolation."

"What for?"

He shrugged. "I'm sure they've come up with something good."

"When are they going to move her?" If I was going too, it would be nice to at least have time to go back to Bug's and get my things.

Then I realized that was actually a terrible idea. Because I'd have to see Bug. Who always knew when I was lying. I wouldn't be able to fool her if she asked about Rhianna.

"As soon as the doctors say it's okay."

We both looked at the door. There was still no sound from inside, which explained why we'd been left alone when Rhianna had been screaming the place down. It took pretty good soundproofing to fool werewolf ears. Whoever had designed the room had known what they were doing.

Right now, I wanted to kill them for their competence. I wanted to know what was going on, if Rhianna was okay.

Instead there was only the door. And it wasn't talking.

"What time is it?" I asked.

"A little after seven."

Meaning I'd been awake more than twenty-four hours. The most sensible thing to do right now would be to lie right down on the floor and try to sleep for as long as I could until the doctors finished.

"Maybe we should wait in the lounge."

Good idea. There'd been chairs in the lounge. It seemed like several lifetimes ago that I'd arrived at the hospital.

I nodded my agreement and pushed away from the wall.

But we'd barely walked ten feet when the door opened behind us. Dr. Samuels came out peeling surgical gloves from his hands as he came. Blood stained his scrubs. Several nurses and another doctor trailed after him, but they continued down the hall past us.

Dr. Samuels came over to Dan and me. He looked as tired as I felt and I wondered how long he'd been on duty.

"Is she okay?" I asked.

He nodded. "Yes. We've controlled the allergic reaction. Your friend is trying to get her to feed again. Real blood this time."

I didn't know whether to be relieved or worried. I had to be glad that Rhianna was okay. Surely I was? But Dan hadn't wanted to give her human blood.

Now it seemed she had to drink it.

And she was a vampire who could never be allowed to feed directly from a human if she was one of Smith's plague vamps.

"Is it safe to move her?" Dan asked.

I shot him a glare. Was that all he cared about? Getting Rhi to her dungeon so she could be studied and controlled?

"Yes, as long as she doesn't react to the blood this time. Give it an hour or so."

"Great," Dan said. He pulled out his phone and punched in a number. "Esme, it's me."

I couldn't believe he was being so calm.

"I'll be in helping Marco." I snapped and left the pair of them to it.

Chapter 11

"So how are we going to move her?" I asked an hour later. Rhi had drunk the fresh blood with no adverse reactions and Dr. Samuels had cleared her for transfer.

She still seemed kind of dazed and she hadn't spoken to me at all while I'd helped her shower and put on a set of scrubs the nurse provided. Hadn't spoken when Marco had explained what had happened to her again.

"I think I can keep her calm," Marco said.

Dan rolled his neck, stretching up from the chair beside me. "We'll use restraints all the same."

I frowned. "Is that really necessary?"

"You want to try fighting a crazed vampire in a helo?"

I didn't want to fight another vampire anywhere. And as much as I wanted to treat Rhianna like nothing had changed, the fact was, she had changed.

I had to stop pretending she hadn't.

I didn't know who Rhianna was as a vampire. Whether she'd stay the same, like Jase or embrace the darkness like Esteban and Niko.

The mutated virus burning in her blood made her even more of an unknown quantity.

So I shrugged my assent at Dan and tried to stay out of the way until we were ready to leave.

Esme arrived eventually, escorting two army doctors and several burly enlisted guys. I didn't know enough about army ranks to read the insignia on any of the uniforms but if I had to guess, one of the doctors was definitely at least a major. He had the same air of used-to-giving orders that Dan and Marco projected.

All too soon, we were loaded into the chopper and headed toward Fort Lyman.

The chopper—big enough for all of us and then some— had been modified to transport vamps. Its rear passenger compartment was completely sealed off so no hint of sunlight would get through once inside. They'd erected a tunnel-like canopy that stretched from the exit door on the hospital roof to the helicopter that let us walk Rhi and Marco safely through the early morning light.

"This better be completely safe," I muttered to Dan as we climbed aboard, taking our places opposite Marco and Rhi in the compartment. Esme slid into place on my left. Three weres, an Old One and the restraints around Rhi's wrists and ankles should be enough to keep Rhi under control if she panicked.

I didn't want to think about what would happen if it wasn't.

"It's safe," Dan said. "Stop worrying."

"I just don't want to have to explain to the vampire community how we fried the head of the city."

"Nor would you appreciate the power struggle that would follow," Marco quipped from the darkness as Dan slid the door shut.

Right. I suppressed a shiver as I snapped my harness shut. I hadn't even thought about that. A major vampire turf war was definitely not something we needed. Now or ever.

The line of lights on the roof only gave off a low light. Guess they figured vamps and werewolves could see well enough in the dark. With no windows, no line of sight to orientate myself, the lurch of the chopper lifting off made my stomach roll. I swallowed hard. There would be no throwing up.

Rhianna huddled in the seat next to Marco. She still hadn't spoken. The restraints looked too heavy for her wrists, the black metal—I had no idea what they were made of—making her bones look fragile. She stared blankly at the wall, not looking at any of us.

"Is this normal?" I asked Marco, to distract myself from the queasiness in my stomach. The last time I'd been in a heli-copter, I'd been flying to confront Tate. The memory didn't help my motion sickness.

Hopefully this time there would be an ending that didn't involve multiple deaths.

Marco looked at Rhianna for a long moment. "Everyone is different. She will talk when she's ready." His voice sounded tinny over the headsets we all wore—all of us except the silent Rhianna.

We hadn't figured she'd need one.

I hadn't been exactly Little Miss Sunshine myself when I'd found out I was going to be a werewolf. But Rhianna was different. It wasn't despair written on her face. It wasn't really anything. Instead there was a strange kind of absence, as if everything that made her Rhianna had packed up and fled.

I had no idea how to fix that.

Silence descended over the headsets, everyone engrossed in their own thoughts as the roar of the engines and rotors surrounded us.

The flight took about thirty minutes. We landed with a

gentle bump and the engine noise cut off. I started to unbuckle my seat belt but the pilot's voice came over the radio, asking us to stay where we were.

There was another series of bumps and thuds and metal grating against metal as the chopper lurched around alarmingly.

I gripped Dan's arm. "What's going on?"

"I think they're taking the chopper in somewhere under cover, so everyone can get out safely."

"Oh." I swallowed again, my stomach not liking this movement any more than the flight.

Mercifully, it didn't take very long. The pilot's voice eventually gave us the all clear and the compartment door slid back. I followed Esme out, leaving Dan with Marco and Rhi. We were in some sort of windowless hanger. A few other choppers sat around with crews swarming over them in harsh artificial light. Our chopper had been placed well away from them though and we had a welcoming committee. Another medical team—all dressed in army green scrubs and white coats—waited for us with a gurney. Behind them was a squad of soldiers with nasty looking guns.

My wolf bristled at the sight.

"Easy," Dan murmured, moving closer to me and putting a hand on my back. "It's just a precaution."

I wished I could believe him but I couldn't make myself relax until Marco led Rhianna down from the chopper. She put up no protest as they helped her onto the gurney and fastened yet another set of restraints across her chest.

As one of the doctors moved his arm, the sleeve of his coat fell back slight revealing black fabric padding his arm.

I nudged Dan. "Body armor?"

He nodded. "I'd imagine they're trying to limit the risk of anyone getting bitten."

If that was the aim, they'd be better off wearing good old-fashioned metal armor. Though that would probably make it hard to do any doctoring. If I was in their place, I wasn't sure that I'd be happy treating a vamp whose one bite could turn me.

But they were doing what they'd been told to do. Just as well I had never enlisted.

Following orders had never been my strong point.

Marco walked beside the team as they led us across the hanger and into an elevator, the squad of soldiers surrounding us in a square. We went down, not up. Still more time in rooms with no windows, no fresh air, no sunlight. The full moon was only a few days away and I was starting to itch for the feel of wind on my skin and dirt under my feet. It had only been twelve hours or so since I'd been outside...how was Rhi going to cope if this was the rest of her life?

The elevator doors opened into a long passageway, a tunnel really, that took us into the hospital. The scent of anti-septic and the weird sterilized feel to the air made me feel sick all over again. I'd really had my fill of hospitals.

We reached a junction in the corridor and the doctor I'd picked as in-charge held up his hand. Everyone came to a halt.

The doctor gestured to his right. "This is where we part company." The team started wheeling Rhi away from us.

"Wait, where are you taking her?" I protested.

The doctor gave me a quick nod. "We're going to do some more tests and see what we're dealing with. If, uh, Lord Marco could come with us, someone will be along to see to the rest of you."

"What are we supposed to do? Just twiddle our thumbs?" I snapped.

His expression suggested he really didn't care. "Rest. Get some sleep. Our tests will take most of the day. There's nothing more you can do right now."

I felt a growl rise in my throat, suppressed it as Dan's hand tightened on my arm. "How are you going to control her if she resists?"

"We have our ways."

I didn't see what they could be. As far as I knew the government actively discouraged weres from joining up and vampires were excluded on the basis of their inability to function in daylight. Though there were rumors about elite covert ops teams involving supernaturals, none of the soldiers with us were shifters. No human would be able to subdue a maddened vampire short of doing something that would probably kill her. I hoped that wasn't their plan.

Maybe they did have drugs that worked on vamps. Or maybe the rumors were true and there was a squad of supernaturals somewhere in the building waiting to take charge.

"The Taskforce needs to be kept informed of your progress, Major." Apparently Dan had no trouble with military insignia.

"Someone will update you regularly. Now, if you will excuse me, I have to attend the patient." The steely shuttered look on the major's face suggested he wouldn't be answering any more questions. He turned on his heel and marched after the team.

"Can't you do something?" I asked Dan. "You're Taskforce."

"The doctors need to do their thing, Ash. You can see her after that."

"I just want to see where they're taking her."

He put a hand on my shoulder, rubbing it gently. "I know. But right now, you have to let them work. I'm sure she's getting excellent care."

I wasn't. I didn't trust anyone in this place as far as I could throw them. Probably even less than that. If I made myself think like a human—which wasn't that hard since I hadn't really gotten used to the fact I wasn't anymore—then Rhianna not surviving this was the best possible outcome for the human population.

If she was dead, they could study the virus without risk to themselves. And come up with an antidote. I gritted my teeth. Fighting with Dan at this point wasn't going to help. Luckily, a nervous-looking private came around the corner of the corridor before I had time to change my mind around that and told us he'd been sent to show us to our quarters.

* * *

The room they showed me to wasn't any more inviting than the rest of the hospital. Obviously the army wasn't in the business of lifting the spirits of anyone who stayed here. The walls were a dull shade of cream and the sole chair was gray-painted metal with black vinyl padding on the seats and arms. The blankets on the narrow single bed were gray too.

The only good thing about the room was that it didn't smell like a hospital.

It let me pretend I was just in a really cheap and nasty hotel on a backpacking tour of some backwater European ex-communist country, maybe, and that just outside was rolling scenery and good beer. It was a nice fantasy for the thirty seconds or so it lasted. Then reality came back with a vengeance, rolling me in a wave of guilt and exhaustion.

It was an effort to stay on my feet. Thankfully the room had a small bathroom. I stumbled into the shower and tried not to fall asleep while I stripped, tossed my clothes out of the cubicle without looking where they fell and wrenched the taps on full. The pounding water—at least the place had decent water pressure—eased some of the tension from my body. Just enough to let me realize how truly awful I felt.

I dried myself off in a half-daze. I just wanted to sleep. Maybe even never wake up again.

I shucked off my towel and climbed into the sweats that had been left in a neat pile on the bed for me. Gray, of course.

Gray seemed appropriate. The color of bureaucracy. Of hopelessness.

A fitting end to this endless day and night that had started off in color but ended in pain.

I sat on the edge of the bed, drawing my knees up and wrapping my arms around them, the mattress barely dipping under my weight. Even though every part of me was crying for sleep, I couldn't quite bring myself to lie down. Not when Rhianna's face still danced in front of my eyes even when I pressed my face into my knees. Not when much worse than that might visit me in my dreams.

A soft knock made me lift my head just in time to see Dan slipping through the door.

"I wanted to see how you were." He shut the door behind him. He wore sweat pants that matched mine and a white T-shirt with "ARMY" stenciled across the chest in more gray. His damp hair smelled like soap and water and Dan.

"I'm—" I stopped. Actually I had no idea how I was. Except that suddenly I didn't want to be alone. "Better now that you're here," I finished with a half-smile that was the best I could summon right now. "You?"

He rubbed at the stubble scruffing his jaw. "Not my favorite day ever."

"I'm not sure I even know what day means right now." I closed my eyes, trying to ease the gritty, what's-sleep-again feeling.

Somewhere along the line I'd passed through fatigue to that weird over-adrenalized but near collapse twilight zone that feels half-foggy, half-surreal. The state where you know you won't sleep if you try, even when you'd kill to be unconscious. The state where your mouth tastes sour and tension lights your nerves to fever pitch even when you can't move another inch.

The state where only someone's arms around you can make any difference to how you feel.

I patted the bed. "Come over here."

His eyes were cautious. "Is that such a good idea?"

"Right now, it's the only one I've got. And, no, I don't want to hear anything you might come up with."

One side of his mouth quirked. "Ah."

I closed my eyes again to wait, heard the click as he locked the door.

Another click and I knew he'd turned off the light. Then I heard him walk across the room, smelled him coming closer.

"Can you do me a favor?" I said as he lowered himself to sit beside me.

"Of course." His voice was quiet and low, floating on the air like a drift of velvet.

I opened my eyes. There was enough light coming under the door for me to be able to just see his outline. I reached a hand out and ran my own fingers down the line of his jaw, feeling the prickle of his stubble against my fingertips. "Help me stop thinking."

He sucked in a breath. "What did you have in mind?" That voice had dropped lower now, deeper. It curled through the air, sank through my skin and lit a spark low in my belly. The first good thing I'd felt for hours. Days, maybe.

"You," I said softly. "Just you."

"Ah," he said again, bending his head into my palm. I pushed my fingers into his hair, feeling the heat of his skin under the cool of damp hair, slid them around the back of his head and pulled him toward me.

I wanted to taste him. Wanted the flash-fire I knew he could evoke. Wanted the flood of desire to drive away the rational thinking. Wanted hot and fast and NOW.

Dan, it seemed, had other ideas.

His kiss was slow. Gentle. Like he wanted to sink his lips

through mine one fraction of an inch at a time until we melted into each other.

Every time I tried to answer him with more speed, more heat, he pulled back a little, until I decided to let him take the lead and surrender to the slow burn.

He eased me backward, covering my body with his, sending warmth floating through me, easing the small twinges and hurts in my body even as he started a whole new set of aches. Each kiss was slow and deep and true; an offering of pleasure to chase away the pain. The taste of him and the touch of his mouth and tongue as he kissed me sent me floating until I stretched from sheer pleasure, lifting my arms above my head in surrender.

Somehow my sweatshirt drifted off above my head.

Dan's hands skimmed my bare skin softly like warm air caressing me. I sighed and settled into being stroked, letting him coax my muscles into relaxing one inch at a time with fingertips and mouth.

I let myself float in the bubble of sensation. Felt the need build in me. When Dan's mouth finally closed over a nipple, I arched off the bed, pulling his head closer.

His answering chuckle shivered against my flesh, sending all sorts of wicked vibrations along my nerve endings.

My hands slipped from his hair to his shoulders, stopping when they hit thin cotton.

"Too many clothes," I muttered, tugging at the T-shirt.

Dan laughed again but lifted his head and yanked it off.

That set us both off and slow and easy became a mad rush to divest ourselves of the barriers of cloth between us. In about a minute flat we were both naked and pressed face to face, breathing rapidly, his weight pressing me into the mattress in that way that made me shiver with pleasure. I couldn't see the color of his eyes in the darkness but I knew they'd be hot silver if I could. The color they always were when the heat rose between us.

"Darn," Dan muttered softly, skimming a hand over my shoulder and down my arm. "I'd just gotten you all relaxed."

I giggled and hooked a leg over his thigh. "I'll be relaxed again in a few minutes."

"Minutes?" He sounded insulted and I giggled again.

"I'll give you minutes." His head drifted down to mine and his lips feathered my ear, making me shiver again as the nerves sighed under his touch. "Lots of long, slow minutes. So slow you'll want to scream."

"I'm counting on it," I said and drew his mouth to mine.

Great sex is meant to mean you wake up feeling on top of the world. I woke up feeling like I'd descended to the underworld. The hard way. Possibly hitting every rock on the way down. My ribs throbbed, my eyes burned as I peeled them open and every inch of me seemed to have a protest to register.

My mouth was drier than Death Valley. I sculled water from the glass on the bedside table and squinted through the darkness, trying to orient myself.

All too soon it all came back to me. Military base. Vampires. Rhianna. No wonder I felt terrible.

Sleep beckoned me back into oblivion. I fought the urge, yawning until my jaw cracked. I had no idea how long we'd been out already. I wanted to see Rhianna.

Dan's warmth stirred sleepily behind me as I reached for the lamp. He muttered a squawk of protest as the yellowish light filled the room, his arm tightening around my waist to pull me back down to him.

I resisted. "Dan, wake up."

"Ugh. Why?" He sounded like he wasn't feeling any better than me but he let me go when I pushed against his arm.

His watch sat on top of the bedside table, next to a jug of water. I poured myself another glass, swirling the water around in my mouth in an attempt to wash away the gunk coating every surface before swallowing. I downed two glasses then reached for the watch.

Five p.m.

We'd slept for quite some time.

Exactly how long, I wasn't sure. I'd lost track of exactly what time it had been when we'd reached the base but it had been barely midmorning.

Apparently even great sex and six or seven hours sleep wasn't enough to make me feel better after the events of yesterday.

Which was slightly worrying. The full moon was just over a day away. I should be buzzing with energy. The fact I felt like a wet dishrag meant I'd pushed myself almost beyond even werewolf tolerances.

"C'm back here," Dan mumbled.

I shook my head, poured another glass of water and twisted around to pass it to him. "Drink this. I'm going to have a shower. I want to see Rhi."

"The doctors would come and get us if there was anything happening." He cracked one eye open and held out a hand to beckon me back to bed.

I pushed the water into it. "No offense, but I don't trust the doctors here. Their loyalty is to the government."

"They take the same oath as every other doctor."

"Yeah, and they can be ordered to break it."

"You're being paranoid."

I shrugged. "Well, you know what they say about paranoia."

He blinked at me, looking sleepy and scruffy. And pretty darn good. "It's not paranoia if they're really out to get you?"

"Exactly." I slid from the bed, pausing when all my aches flared back to life as I straightened. I sucked in a deep breath, waited for the sensations to settle back to a dull roar. The sensible thing would be to change and see if that helped but I wasn't sure I'd have enough energy to change back again and

I didn't think having to come up with twenty or thirty pounds of steak to refuel an overtaxed werewolf would endear me to the base staff.

"Rhianna's here for her own protection," Dan said. "We just want to help her."

It was a little more complicated than that but I didn't want to get into it until I'd showered, had some coffee and hopefully some food. Lots of food. For the first time in several days I was feeling hungry. Ravenous even. Maybe that was the pull of the moon kicking in. If so, I was grateful. I needed fuel. I got the feeling it might just be another very long night.

* * *

The female soldier on duty at the first office we found didn't look particularly happy to see us. I couldn't blame her. I looked like something Esme might have dragged in after one of her jaunts in jaguar form. Or, more likely, Andy; Esme was way too fastidious to bother with something as bedraggled looking as me.

But Dan looked and sounded commanding even in borrowed gray sweats. We were promptly escorted to another, larger office where we found Esme. She looked perfectly composed as usual, blond hair smooth, black suit unwrinkled, shoes gleaming black patent leather. Of course she hadn't been through what I'd been through. She raised an eyebrow toward me as she took in my outfit.

"They haven't given me back my clothes," I said defensively. I was kind of happy about that. I don't think I ever wanted to put the stuff I'd been wearing at the hospital on again. It would just remind me of what had happened to Rhi. Still, Esme made me feel even more frumpy. I folded myself into the closest chair, crossing my arms over my chest.

Dan stayed standing. "Esme will get someone to get some of your stuff from Bug's. Or get Jase to go to your house."

"And what are you going to tell them?"

By now Bug would be frantic to know what was going on. And Jase wouldn't be happy if he was left to juggle my appointments and fob off clients yet again.

Neither would my clients for that matter. I had pushed my existing goodwill with them almost to breaking point during the Tate fiasco but they'd stuck around. If I disappeared again so soon, I might not have the same luck.

"That something's come up on the case and you're needed for a few days."

"Jase knows we need to be at the Retreat later today. I assume we're going?" I didn't want to leave Rhi but at the same time, I was itching for the outdoors. The hundreds of acres of forest that surrounded the Retreat sounded heavenly. Yesterday I'd told Dan I wouldn't go but I'd changed my mind. I would go crazy cooped up here and I wasn't comfortable with the thought of changing forms around so many humans who didn't exactly seem friendly to supernaturals. Surely Rhi would be all right for twenty-four hours? I ignored the guilty twinge.

"I'll take care of it," Esme said before Dan could respond. I got the feeling she was trying to stop us from arguing.

"Yes, we're going," Dan said as though Esme hadn't spoken. He took a seat next to me, giving me a 'don't argue' look. "Ani *and* Sam would skin me if I kept you away. You're still practically a cu-newborn."

I ignored the fact he'd almost called me a cub. "I'm only going if Rhi's okay."

He leaned closer, gearing up to convince me. "You're going regardless, even if—" His teeth snapped shut when the door to the office opened.

The officer who walked in looked like he'd stepped out of a recruitment poster—if they had recruitment posters for forty-year-olds. The chest of his jacket was a multicolored declaration that he'd seen the world and shot at stuff. Lots of stuff. His pants had razor edged creases that made me even more acutely aware of my scruffy state and the shine on his shoes put Esme's to shame.

He put the file he was carrying down on the desk and then stood looking at us, his posture screaming command.

He wasn't an alpha wolf but he was just about the closest thing to it I'd seen in a human. Dan rose from his chair and Esme and I followed suit.

The man nodded acknowledgment. "I'm Colonel Morgan."

"Sir." Dan nodded back. "I'm Special Agent Gibson, this is Agent Walsh and Ashley Keenan. Ms. Keenan's a contractor with the Taskforce."

"I know who you all are." His tone was neutral. Too neutral. If I knew anything about undercurrents, I'd say that he wasn't too happy about having Rhianna or us on his base.

Tough.

"Sir, can you tell me how Rhianna is?" I said. Screw protocol or whatever.

"Ms. Anders is currently resting. The other vampire is with her. My team is still carrying out tests."

"Can we see her?"

"The Taskforce has requested that I extend you every courtesy. But I want to make sure you all understand the ground rules."

He could screw his ground rules. I listened with half an ear as he talked on, trying to look like I was paying attention but all I wanted was to see Rhi. Finally he stopped talking containment and approach protocol and procedures and summoned another enlisted guy to escort us down to the hospital wing.

The sting of disinfectant and old blood and all those hospital smells made my stomach lurch as we passed through the entry point after having our identification inspected. Three checkpoints later, each one taking longer than the one before, we were ushered into an elevator and descended down into the bowels of the hospital.

* * *

Marco looked up when we entered the room but Rhi didn't. Her gaze stayed fastened on the picture hanging on the wall— a vista showing open country leading up to mountains— where the window in most hospital rooms would be. This room had no windows. Just that one small picture.Which might be the closest that Rhi got to the outside world for a very long time.

Her head didn't move when Marco stood to greet us. His suit was a little rumpled but otherwise his appearance gave no indication that anything was out of the ordinary.

"How is she?" I asked softly. I wasn't sure if it was the fluorescent lights but Rhi's face looked shadowed, gray somehow. All vampires are pale, except when they've just fed, but they look healthy—energized—even when they're hungry. Rhi looked ill.

I took her hand and she flinched away, tugging free of my touch, eyes still glued on the picture.

"Rhi? It's me. Ashley."

Not even a flicker of recognition.

"Rhi, it's okay. You're safe here."

She squeezed her eyes shut. "No."

I reached for her hand again. "Yes, you are. It's okay."

Her eyes flew open, finally looking at me. Fear colored her expression. "Speak softly. They'll hear you."

"Who will? It's okay, sweetie, we're looking after you. I'm here. And Dan. Do you remember Dan?"

"You can't stop them." Her eyes squinched shut again and she curled into a ball. "You can't stop them." Her voice was almost a wail, high and eerie.

"Stop who, sweetie?" I looked at Marco hoping he could

shed some light on what she was so afraid of. He shrugged. Highly helpful. I tried again. "Rhi? Stop who?"

She didn't answer, just curled tighter, shivers running through her body. This couldn't be normal. Sure, being turned had to be a little confusing, I hadn't exactly handled the knowledge that I was going to be a werewolf gracefully myself but Rhi had been rational before the change. "Why is she so scared?" I asked Marco. "Did the doctors do something to her?"

"Not the doctors," Rhi whispered. Her eyes half opened and I could see her pupils wide and black. Too wide. She looked stoned.

"Did they give her something?"

"No, *cara*. They took some samples but nothing else. She had been like this since she woke."

"This isn't normal?"

He pursed his lips. "Normal is hard to define. We are not dealing with a normal transition."

"She's terrified," I said.

"She's been through a lot," Dan offered. "Maybe she just needs some time."

"No more time," Rhi whispered.

My head snapped back to her. "Rhi?"

"No more time," she crooned. Her eyes were shut. "All out of time."

"Dan, maybe you should get the doctor." He nodded and left. I squeezed Rhi's hand. "Rhi, it's Ash. Do you remember where you are?"

Blazing blue hit me as she suddenly looked at me. "I'm with the monsters," she said quite clearly. "Careful. They'll hear you." Tears started to run down her face.

I reached for a tissue. "There are no monsters here, Rhi. There's just us. We're at the hospital."

She shook her head, ducking away as I tried to wipe her face. "No," she said. "There are monsters." She held out her hands, looked at me beseechingly, "Monsters everywhere. Fangs and claws."

Her fingers curved inward and I caught her hands before she could hurt herself with hard vamp nails.

"You're remembering the attack," I said. "It's okay now."

"No. Fangs and claws." She bared her teeth at me and I flinched at the sight of the two sharp fangs in her mouth.

"Monsters everywhere," she repeated. "Monsters in *me*."

I squeezed her hands, blinking back tears. "You are *not* a monster."

"Monsters in me. Blood and fear. Can't run. Nowhere to run." Her voice rose a few notches, high and thin.

"Rhi, it's me. It's Ashley. You're safe." I felt stupid, repeating the obvious but I didn't know how to reach her. How to get through the layers of fear and stress to the girl I knew was in there somewhere.

Rhi blinked at me then looked down, pale hair falling over her face. It was lank and greasy-looking. I'd never seen Rhi with dirty hair. She was the type of girl who practically carried a flat-iron in her handbag, even as a teenager. Maybe if I could coax her into a shower, she might feel better. She smelled like blood, sweat, fear, and the faint acid smell I associated with vampires. If I could smell all of that on her, she could too. Which had to be confusing as well as unpleasant.

Everything had to be confusing. Everything would be too loud, too bright, too hard. Until she adjusted to her new senses, it would be like being a newborn all over again.

A newborn who could kill a man in seconds.

I eased my grip on her hands, worried I might be hurting her. "Honey, do you want to take a shower?"

She didn't change position. Didn't indicate she'd heard me at all. "Blood and fear," she sing-songed. "So much blood. Sweet and salt. I never knew it was sweet." She smiled at me suddenly, eyes wide. "Did you know that?"

I swallowed hard, trying not to remember what the blood

had felt like running down my throat the first time I'd eaten a freshly killed deer with the pack. It had been sweet. Too sweet. Too good. Not like the acid filth of Tate in my mouth. "I know."

Rhi blinked at me. "You know the monsters." Her smile vanished. "You've got the monsters in your head too."

She wasn't really making any sense and I wondered how long the doctor would be. I worried that she was having some sort of breakdown.

"There's nothing in my head but me." I summoned a smile. "Nothing in your head but you."

"No. No, there are monsters. And voices." She peered at me. "And secrets all hidden away." Her eyes lit with something I couldn't name. Curiosity? Glee?

I no longer knew if she was talking about herself or me, but whichever it was, it was creeping me out. I looked back at Marco. "What's going on?" I mouthed.

"So many dark twisty places." Rhi's sing-song tone broke in before Marco could say anything. "They think they have hidden it well. But I can see. A tiny light."

"See what, Rhi?" I asked. "What do you see?" I glanced over at Marco, wanting reassurance.

Marco came up beside me, staring down at Rhi with pursed lips. Then he shook his head. "I did not think of it before but it's possible she has some psychic ability now."

I stared at him. Rhi winding up with vamp powers other than the normal stuff hadn't crossed my mind.

"Psychic? She's reading our minds?" I moved backward, I couldn't help it.

Rhi still crooned to herself, nonsense syllables interspersed with 'dark' and 'blood' and 'no'.

"Can't you do something to help her?" I asked Marco.

"If I try and control her now, it might do more harm than good," he said. He moved closer to the bed and Rhi's head twisted toward him.

"Monster. There's one." She laughed. "Pretty monsters. They try and fool us. Pretty like secrets. All tucked away. They all want it. No one knows where it is. All ashes and dust. He was clever."

"Who was clever?" I hoped she was just babbling but if Marco was right, then she might not be.

Rhi looked at me. "Your father," she said. And then she started screaming.

Chapter 12

SHE DIDN'T STOP until they sedated her. And even when they had her unconscious and strapped back to the bed, the memory of her cries still rang in my ears. I sat there for half a day while the doctors came and went.

Dan dragged me away to sleep eventually but I was back at her bedside as soon as possible. There was a doctor there, pumping something into her IV.

"Can't you let her wake up?"

He shook his head at me. "We tried a little while ago. She started screaming again. Then she hit one of the nurses."

I had a vision of a nurse flying across the room to smash against the wall. "Is she okay?"

"He'll be fine," the doctor said. "A couple of cracked ribs and bruises. No thanks to her."

The look he directed at Rhi made me nervous. He didn't want to help her. He wanted her out of the picture.

"Isn't keeping her asleep bad for her? New vampires need to feed, don't they?"

"We'll put in a nasogastric tube. That will keep her nour-ished for now." He met my eyes, had the grace to look slightly sheepish. "Sleeping might be what she needs. Sometimes the mind just needs time."

I couldn't see how sleeping would help Rhi. When she woke up she'd still be a vampire. An outcast in her town. Quite likely an outcast in her family as well.

The door opened behind me and I turned.

Marco.

He looked tired. And troubled. I didn't know what to say to him.

"She is still sleeping?" he asked.

"The doctors are still sedating her."

"Ah." He looked down at the floor then back at Rhi.

"Do you think she'll be okay?"

He started one of his very Italian shrugs and I held up a hand.

"Tell me the truth."

"The truth is that I do not know. This is not how it is supposed to be." He came closer to the bed and something close to anger passed across his face. "The change should be a gift. Not a violation. This new thing. It is *male*."

Mah-lay. I didn't know what *male* meant but his tone made it clear it was bad. Very bad. "Vampires have been changing people forever. You can't tell me it's all voluntary."

"No. But I like to think that we have changed too. We can be better."

I pictured Maelstrom and Tate and Esteban. "Not everyone agrees with you."

"Maybe not. But I doubt many would agree with this." He straightened the blanket at the end of Rhianna's bed as she moved restlessly despite the drugs.

"Can you tell anything from your bond?"

He sighed. "Her mind is not easy. She is...confused."

Confused being the polite term for crazy perhaps? I'd seen very little of Rhi in the creature she had become.

I tugged at the blanket covering Rhi, pulling it up over her shoulder. It fell back again almost immediately when she twitched. "Will she become less confused?"

Silence.

"The truth, Marco."

"She may."

My heart grabbed onto that 'may' like a lifeline. "Then she could be okay?"

"Apart from the mutation she carries? Apart from not being able to live the life most of us live? Perhaps. But I have been a vampire a long time. I have seen many become our kind. Most do not react this way. Even those who did not choose it. They adjust."

"Rhi's different. Her virus is different. Maybe her body needs more time."

"Perhaps. But she also needs to want to adjust."

"What are you saying?"

Green eyes met mine and they seemed deep and endless. I wanted to look away but I told myself I could trust Marco. He wouldn't try for my mind. He was on my side.

"Those who take the change this way—those who are it to this extent—"

I licked my lips and swallowed against a mouth dry as grave dust. "Yes? Just tell me."

"Those ones. Most often they choose the sunrise."

Choose the sunrise. The words echoed through my head on constant replay. Marco thought Rhianna would kill herself. Would walk out into the sun and let it burn her away rather than live. Would become a pile of stinking acid ash like the vampire outside my office.

Not on my watch.

Not while there was any chance I could get hold of Smith and find a way to fix what had been done to her. Not change her back—I knew that wasn't possible—but make her a normal noncontagious vampire. So she could feed and be free.

I made them bring her out of the sedation before we left for the Retreat. Just enough so her eyes flickered open slowly.

"Rhi, it's Ash." I held my breath, wondering if she'd respond. Or whether we'd get screams or violence.

"Ash?" She sounded tired. "I'm sleepy."

"You're in hospital. It's the medicine."

"Medicine?"

Shit. She didn't remember. Well, maybe that was a good thing. I wasn't going to tell her. "Everything's fine. They're taking good care of you."

"Okay." Her eyes started to drift close again.

I squeezed her hand before she could fall back asleep. "I have to go away for a while. But I'll be back. We can talk then."

She smiled at me. "I dreamed strange things. There was blood."

Surely it couldn't hurt to let her think it was all a nightmare just for a little while. "Bad dreams. It's the medicine. I'll see you soon, okay?"

"Uh-huh."

I started to rise but she shot out a hand and grabbed my arm. "Careful," she said. "There are monsters in the dark. Don't go into the woods today."

My pulse sped into overdrive. The woods? Did she mean the Retreat or was she just dreaming? With no way of knowing, I nodded at the doctor. "I'm fine, Rhi. Go back to sleep." The doctor pushed the plunger on the syringe, sending another dose of whatever the heck they used to sedate vampires into her system.

"Cutting it close, aren't you?" Ani asked as we reached the front porch of the Retreat's main building.

I glanced back over my shoulder to where the sun was burning its way down the sky. "Moonrise isn't for another forty-five minutes."

"You're meant to be here at least two hours before, you're new." Ani's eyes narrowed at me.

"Dan's old." Old and currently humping our luggage into our guesthouse.

She shook her head, making her red curls bounce around her face, like a pissed off Raggedy Ann doll. "Old won't help if you leave it too long."

"I'd be okay with Dan with me."

"Neither of you will be okay if you suddenly change into wolves while driving a car." Ani leaned back against the porch post, crossing her arms. She looked at me pointedly as I tried not to flinch. That had happened to Dan and me once, back when he'd been new. In fact it had been the thing that had made me realize I couldn't be with him and stay human.

That had made me break up with him.

Not my favorite memory. Obviously Ani thought I needed the reminder of how wrong things could go. I sighed. I didn't want to fight with my Alpha on top of everything else. "Okay, you're right. I'm sorry. Rough weekend."

"I heard." Her eyes were a deep, deep green in the growing twilight. "Are you okay?"

I shrugged. There was no way to answer that question. Not in the time left before the moon came up.

"Go change," Ani said, smiling at last. "We can talk after."

It was pretty much full dark when Dan and I walked toward the stand of woods nearest the buildings. The pull of the moon tingled through me, like being washed in waves of warm, wild energy. But there was a thread of nerves under the anticipation. I hadn't done this often enough to be blasé.

"Ready?" Dan said as we reached the trees. He smiled at me, and I knew he felt the same thrum of the moon's invitation.

I smiled back, knowing that for the next nine hours or so I could let the wolf rule and not have to worry or think about everything that waited for us back in Seattle. "Last one to change is a rotten egg."

Dan's laughter turned into a liquid howl as the moon broke over the trees and hit us. Wolves don't laugh so I had to content myself with yipping at him, to let him know how ridiculous he sounded.

He waggled his ears at me then came over and bumped shoulders with me. "*Wanna run?*"

I leaned into him for a moment, breathing in his scent. But the moon surged in my blood, calling me to move. The wolf wanted action and I wanted to give her free rein.

Rhi's 'don't go into the woods today' echoed through my head. I ignored it. I was surrounded by the Pack. Dan was here. The Retreat was safe.

I ran with Dan, dodging and winding through the forest trails, drinking in the night scents as we played, nipping at each other's heels and staging mock ambushes in a puppyish fit of silliness that reflected the need to let the tension of the last few weeks go.

When we crossed the trail of a larger group, led by Sam, we turned and followed it until we caught up with the group of wolves pelting through the night for no better reason than the sheer joy of movement. I lost track of Dan in the darkness and the flickering bodies of wolves flowing around me.

When someone howled, signaling that a scent had been found, I pulled back.

I didn't want to hunt. Not tonight.

I stopped on the side of the path until everyone had run past, ears flicking backward and forward as I tried to figure out exactly where I was. We'd run for miles and nothing around me looked familiar. I hadn't been a wolf long enough to know every twist and turn of the woods that covered hundreds of acres of the Retreat.

I could tell I was higher up than I'd started. That probably meant the main house lay down and to the west of where I stood. I could either go north on the tail of the pack I'd just left or continue upward on a faint trail I could see leading east.

Up sounded good. If for no other reason than it should let me get my bearings if I could find a clearing with a view.

I headed up, following my nose, which promised rock and grass up ahead rather than leaf mold and the damper scent of trees that surrounded me now.

Twigs cracked under my paws and I amused myself pouncing on shadows as the trail grew steeper. The tension riding me started to melt away. Until I stepped out into the clearing at the trailhead and smelled a scent that didn't belong anywhere in the Retreat.

Vampire.

I froze, half in and out of the tree line, trying to listen and smell and look.

Nothing.

Nothing but for the distinctive scent of vampire hanging on the breeze.

"Don't hide in the trees, little doggy."

The voice came from my right, soft and eerie. Sexless somehow. I turned my head, scanning the shadows, trying to decide whether to retreat or just stay where I was. There might be more than one. If I ran, I might just be running into trouble.

"*Dan,*" I thought urgently.

"I don't think he can hear you from so far away, doggy."

The fur on my neck stood on end. The vamp had heard my thoughts?

"I'll come out if you do," the voice said. This time it held a coaxing note that made me think female.

"*Fat chance,*" I thought and took a step backward. "*Dan, hurry.*"

"Don't do that," the voice said sharply. "Play nice or the other little doggies will be in trouble. *Come here.*"

The last two words cracked like a whip.

I fought the urge to move forward. *"You come out first."*

Leaves rustled and suddenly a woman appeared in the clearing. A woman where I'd swear no one had been a few seconds ago. She wore a long dark dress but where her skin was visible it glowed like the moon. So how the hell hadn't I seen her?

A growl rumbled in my throat. *"Who are you?"*

"Oh no, puppy. No names. Not yet. All you need to know is that I'm the beginning and the end. Alpha and Omega."

She smiled at me and I moved uneasily, bracing myself for an attack. There was nothing particularly sane in the expression. It made me glad I couldn't see her eyes. But crazy or not, there was something horribly familiar about her face. She moved her head a little and a shadow fell across her mouth, turning her lips dark and suddenly I realized who she was. The woman from the club. The one with the muzzled vamp.

Fuck.

"I said, come here," she repeated and the urge to move blossomed within me.

More vamp powers. Double fuck. I needed to shield. I reached for the knowledge Ani had implanted in my head but it was still a mostly confused jumble of impressions and feelings. So I went with the glass cage image, trying to imagine the moonlight solidified around me. For a moment, the need to walk toward her lessened and I thought I'd succeeded.

Then she just laughed. "Don't be rude, puppy. You don't want to annoy me. Come *here.*"

I couldn't resist the words this time. The glass in my head shattered and my paws moved without me willing them to. One step. Two. Three. Then I sank my claws into the dirt and held on for grim life, snarling at her. *"I'm not a pet."*

"He said you would be difficult." She sighed theatrically. "I had hoped he would be wrong."

He? Who was he? Smith? Tate? Esteban?

"Difficult? You don't know the meaning of the word. But you will once the pack gets your scent."

"I think your pack may be otherwise occupied."

As she spoke the crack of a gunshot echoed through the night. It was far away, but a barrage of furious protesting howls rose immediately.

Furious but not anguished. I strained my ears, trying to catch every nuance of the sound. I heard only anger, not distress. There'd be more than anger if the bullet had found a target. I had to believe no one was hurt. Which meant my most immediate problem was making sure I didn't get hurt either. I turned all my attention back to the vampire. *"What do you want?"*

"You have something of mine. Several things."

"I really don't."

"I want her."

"I have no idea who you're talking about."

Anger twisted her face. "She is mine. We made her. You have no right to keep her from me."

Made her? Was she talking about Rhianna? No way was I handing Rhi over to some lunatic vamp. I tried to lunge at her but my paws were suddenly rooted to the grass.

The vamp leaned toward me and her breath—old blood and something that made my hackles rise even more stiffly—blew across my face.

"My child. I want the child."

Child? Well, I guess Rhianna was a child to a vampire. A growl rumbled through me. *"If you're talking about my friend then sorry, I know both her parents and neither of them is called alpha or omega."*

"They will be called dead if you cross me."

"Try it." I snapped my teeth, straining forward, though I got nowhere. She danced backward, the skirt of her dress

swirling around her. Fabric brushed my mouth and I snapped again, felt teeth engage as the smell of vampire and violets and soap flowed into my nose. A piece of the skirt pulled free and I spat it onto the grass. "*Just set one foot across Caldwell's border—*"

"Give me the child," she shrieked. Then, as the sound of howls rose again, closer this time, her face suddenly wiped clean of expression. "Last warning, puppy."

"*Bite me.*"

She smiled, teeth gleaming almost as white as her skin in the moonlight. "Oh, I will. Eventually. The taste of your blood will be sweet."

Another snarl boiled out of my throat. "*The last vamp who thought that found the price a little too high.*"

"I am not McCallister Tate."

"*You're doing a pretty good impression of being as batshit crazy as him.*"

"Do not presume, puppy," she snapped. "I told you last warning."

"*I heard you the first time.*"

The howls were closer still and she looked behind me at the tree where I'd been standing.

"I have to go," she said.

"*Really? So soon? But I wanted you to stay and meet the family.*" I bared my teeth at her, wanting to throw my head back and howl like my packmates but still not able to move.

"You need to learn respect," she said softly. "Consider this a lesson."

Her hand slashed toward me, there was a searing pain in my head and then everything went dark.

I woke to the sensation of something warm and wet brushing the fur on my face. Dan's scent surrounded me, sharpened by anxiety. I cracked open an eye just as his tongue swiped my face again.

"*Ew,*" I thought, protesting. "*What are you doing?*" I was lying in the clearing, pretty much where I'd been when the vamp had put the whammy on me. I could smell other wolves. Sam and Ani. They stood behind Dan, watching me, ears flicking backward and forward between me and the noise of the pack howling in the distance.

Dan nosed my ear. "*You were unconscious.*"

"*And you thought doggy breath would wake me up?*" I tried to lift my head and fire shot through my skull. I lay back down.

"*I don't have doggy breath.*" His nose nudged me again, sniffing my fur. "*What happened?*"

In truth, he didn't have doggy breath, he smelled like Dan.

"*Vampire,*" I said.

"*I can smell that,*" he said impatiently. "*What happened to you?*"

"*I don't quite know. One minute she was making threats, the next minute I was knocked out.*" I remembered the gunshot. "*Is anyone hurt?*"

Ani padded closer. "*No. No one.*" Anger thrummed though her mental tone. "*Apart from the guy with the gun,*" she added with vicious satisfaction.

I decided I didn't want to know any more about that just at the moment.

I braced myself and tried lifting my head more slowly. It hurt but not quite as much as my first attempt so I risked rolling to my stomach.

"*I can't see any wounds,*" Dan said. "*What did she do to you?*"

"*I said I don't know. She waved her hand then wham.*"

"*Someone hit you?*"

"*I don't* know." I snarled then whimpered as my head throbbed a protest. Dan nosed my ear and I closed my eyes and pushed to my feet, swaying a little as the world spun around me.

Sam moved around to my other side, pressing into me to keep me upright. "*Did you recognize her?*"

"Yes. She was the one with that muzzled vamp at Maelstrom."

A rumbling growl broke from Dan's throat. *"I knew that suicide was too close for comfort."*

"Did she say what she wanted?" Ani asked.

"As far as I could tell through the crazy talk, she wants Rhianna."

Dan's ears went flat. *"I don't think so."*

"That's what I told her." I took a deep breath and caught the lingering smell of violets and vampire. The dress. I looked around me but I couldn't see anything lying in the grass. *"I tore her dress. Can you see a piece anywhere?"*

"No." The thought came from all three of them.

Ani twitched her tail. *"There was nothing here in the clearing but you. Dan heard you call him and we came pretty fast but it must've been at least thirty minutes before we got here. We've got people following the scent trail out of here but it will probably dead end at the nearest road."*

Damn. The fabric might've been able to tell us something; might've even held a trace of DNA. Now we had yet another mystery. I stifled the whine that rose in my throat.

Dan's nose rubbed my cheek again. *"So this woman and our suicide vamp are mixed up with Smith?"*

The hairs on my neck rose again at the mention of Smith. *"I guess. Rhi was bitten by one of Smith's vamps and she wanted Rhi."* I looked at the sky, trying to judge the time. The clouds were starting to turn that deep blue predawn shade. *"Shouldn't we head back before sunrise?"*

Sam cocked his head. *"Are you up to it?"*

"There isn't much choice. It's not like you can piggyback me." Werewolves are bigger than normal wolves but we still can't do most things wolves can do. And none of us can change back to human form under a full moon.

Dan sat. *"We can wait. You might feel better if you changed."*

I shook my head. *"I'm not walking miles with no shoes, no hat and, oh yeah, no clothes. Let's go."*

It was a long and painful trek back. My head pounded with each step and I felt like I hadn't eaten for days. By the time I limped from the tree line near the Retreat, just as the sun was threatening to break above the horizon, I was ready to drop.

I reached the cabin Dan and I were using as the moon set and shimmered into human form gratefully. The pain in my head eased but didn't vanish completely. Which told me whatever had caused it wasn't completely physical.

Perfect. Because what I really needed was another vamp with bonus psychic whammy powers pursuing me. I was getting very tired of being chased. Not to mention knocked out.

Dan left me alone while I showered. When I came out wrapped in my towel, the table was laden with enough food for about five people. Or two hungry werewolves as it turned out.

We ate in silence, shoveling eggs, bacon, steak and toast down as fast as we could. The food eased my head a little more but pain still niggled, biting hard if I turned my head too fast.

"What's wrong?" Dan asked after I'd winced reaching for the platter of bacon.

"My head hurts."

"Since before you changed?" His voice sharpened and I nodded.

"Because of what that vamp did?"

I shrugged while I chewed and swallowed. "You're the expert on supernaturals."

Dan pushed back his chair. "We should get you checked out."

"I just want to go to sleep," I said. "I'm tired and I want to get back to Rhi." I gave him a pleading look. "I promise, if my head still hurts when I wake up, I'll let the doctors at the base take a look at me."

"But she might have—" he broke off as I shot him a look.

"She knocked me out. She didn't thrall me. I know what

being thralled feels like, remember?" At least I didn't think she had. She'd made me come to her but she hadn't controlled me totally.

Dan's eyes darkened. "I could hardly forget."

I sighed, swigged the last of my orange juice and wiped my mouth. "Let it go. Just for a little while. Please, Dan? I'm going to bed. Are you coming?"

I woke up alone. I vaguely remembered Dan crawling in beside me at some point but he'd obviously left again. The clock on the bedside table told me it was almost midday. Five hours sleep wasn't exactly enough but it would have to do.

After my run-in my new least favorite vampire I was uneasy about leaving Rhi alone, even on a heavily guarded military base. Smith seemed to have a long reach and I didn't want him to get his hands on anybody else I knew. Especially not Rhi.

By the time I'd taken another shower to wake myself up and made coffee, Dan reappeared. He tucked his cell phone into the pocket of his suit jacket as he joined me near the coffeemaker.

"News?" I asked.

"No." He poured himself a cup. "But I need to check in with the office before we go back to the base. So we're going to Seattle first."

I stiffened. A little consultation might have been nice. "How about you go back to town and I'll go back to Lyman? Someone here will lend me a car."

Dan shook his head. "Marco will watch out for her."

"She doesn't *know* Marco. And she didn't really seem that keen on vampires generally. She's all alone there."

"Something she'll have to get over."

I almost choked on my coffee and shot him a death glare. "Gee, Dan, your empathy is making me cry."

"Ash, I know she's your friend but the sooner Rhi adjusts to reality, the better off she'll be. You know that."

At least he sounded as though he thought she might adjust to reality. I hadn't told him about Marco's assessment. It was easier to try and believe Dan was right. "Not everyone can just snap their fingers and be overjoyed their whole life has changed," I pointed out. "Rhi's only had a few days. And she's been unconscious for most of that time."

"I know." He rinsed out his mug and set it on the sink to dry. "But I'm not letting you drive back there alone. Not if Smith and his crazies are planning on making another move. Going back to the city won't take too long. I'll see if I can scam a helo to take us back to the base afterward."

"You could get someone from the team to escort me."

"Ash, they're all busy right now. Besides, I need you to see if you can ID your vampire from Esteban's tapes."

Right. Busy with what had happened in Caldwell. And here at the Retreat, presumably. "How many dark-haired women leading muzzled vamps do you think were there that night?"

Dan shrugged. "It's a dark club. Who the hell knows?"

He had a point. Besides, if I could ID our lunatic vamp, maybe we'd find her image in one of the criminal databases. Maybe we'd finally have a lead.

Or maybe not.

"What if she's not on the tapes? We need to keep looking for Smith too." How the hell could we get at Smith? What was the chink in his armor? When in doubt, stick to what you know best. In my case, that's money. Money equals leverage. "Maybe we should try and encourage him to make a move."

We weren't having much luck tracking Smith down following the paper trail. If we could smoke him out and capture him then we'd solve all our problems. Stop the anti-vaccine. Cure Rhi. Kill Smith and all his cohorts slowly and painfully.

Dan looked as if he thought I'd gone mad. "That's a bad idea."

"Why? We're hitting nothing but dead ends."

His frown deepened. "I suppose you think you should be the bait?"

Hardly. I wasn't planning on putting myself back in the not-so-good doctor's hands any time soon. But Dan had a point. I was the most obvious thing to use to provoke Smith. Apart from Rhi. And that wasn't going to happen.

Neither was staking me out like a goat. So, next idea required. We needed to hit him where he lived. Stop him. "No. I think we should try cutting off his funding."

"Don't we need to find his funding to do that?"

I rubbed my temples, trying to work out what my instincts were telling me. Putting together puzzle pieces. "He rang me at Esteban's. He knew what I was doing there. So something —or someone—warned him that we were looking into Esteban's problem. Maybe we should freeze Esteban's accounts, see what happens."

"You want me to try and get a court order to freeze Lord Esteban's accounts?" Dan leaned down, staring at my eyes. "Is this the same Ashley who freaked when I wanted to get his security tapes? Are you sure you don't have a concussion?" He held up three fingers. "How many fingers?"

I batted his hand away. "I'm serious. Making vaccines, doing high-tech biological research and all that stuff doesn't come cheap. He needs a facility and staff and all sorts of supplies and equipment. Cut off the money and Smith will be in trouble."

"I thought you didn't want to piss Esteban off," Dan said slowly.

"Maybe we can just ask him to go along with it. Give him a chance to move enough cash to keep him afloat for a week or so to a brand new account that we can watch. Freeze the rest." Even as I spoke, it sounded like a terrible idea. Esteban wasn't exactly the kind of guy to help the FBI out of the goodness of his heart. Maybe Dan was right; maybe I *did* have a concussion. Or maybe I just needed to find the right way to sell the idea to Esteban.

"What if he's helping Smith?"

I shook my head. "I don't think he is." I didn't know why I felt so sure. Esteban had a nice little thing going on with his clubs. Not so little really. He made his money from humans and vamps. He didn't need an army of infectious vampires causing trouble with humans. Besides, Tate had been Marco's lineage...something told me, Marco would've gone after Esteban already if he had any suspicion Esteban was in any way involved in creating a blot on Marco's bloodline.

"It's a big risk to take if you're not sure."

"Do you have a better idea?"

He shook his head. "Other than seeing if we can identify your mystery vamp, no."

"Who says we can't do both?" I put my mug beside his on the sink. "I'm sick of waiting around for Smith to jump out at me. Let's make him jump."

He hesitated.

"Look, they knew about Rhianna. They're three steps ahead of us. We need to do something unexpected. Will you think about it, at least? Smith might be Rhi's only chance."

"What do you mean?"

"I mean, Smith might be able to fix her—no, not change her back," I said as Dan's eyebrows shot up"—make her noncontagious. I—" My throat closed for a second.

"What?"

"I don't think she'll survive the way she is. Marco said he thought she'd choose the sunrise."

Dan went still. "Suicide?"

"Yes. Dan, I can't lose Rhi too. Please, we have to try something." I held my breath, waiting for an answer.

Eventually he nodded. "I'll think about it."

"Well, well, look who's here," Jase said when I arrived at the office after a long drive which had featured a heavy rotation of Dan trying to dissuade me from asking Esteban to cooperate with us. Apparently 'thinking about it' meant 'try to come up with every possible reason why it's a bad idea and tell me about them.'

But despite his misgivings, my theories seemed to have gone some way to convincing him that there was some merit in trying to cut off Smith's funding. He currently seemed to be leaning toward getting a court order to freeze Esteban's assets.

I don't know what Jase thought he had to feel snippy about but I wasn't in the mood. "Last time I looked, I owned the place," I said shortly. The few parts of the trip that hadn't involved me arguing with Dan had been spent trying to understand more about shielding. I'd only had time for a few minutes discussion with Ani before Dan had wanted to leave and really, I was none the wiser. She'd suggested more practice but that would mean finding a vamp to try and voodoo me. Not an experience I was keen to have.

Jase passed me a stack of mail. "I thought you were at the Retreat." His tone was more polite this time. Which was almost worse. Jase and I didn't do polite.

"I was. But I'm heading back to—" I paused "—Caldwell." I wasn't allowed to tell Jase where Rhi was. I wasn't allowed to tell anyone.

"Caldwell isn't Lake Stewart."

Lake Stewart was the town nearest the base. I hoped my surprise didn't show on my face. How did Jase know about Fort Lyman? Was he...?" Get out of my head." I slapped the mail back down on the desk.

His lips went thin. "I'm not in your head."

"Then how do you know about Lake Stewart?"

"That's where all your cell calls have been originating from." He looked insulted. Insulted and upset.

Just like I felt. I hated the fact that my mind had leapt straight to 'Jase is reading my mind.' I wanted to trust him again. I rubbed my temples, feeling the first twinges of yet another headache. "Oh. Right. Sorry."

Jase nodded, as if accepting my apology. "What's in Lake Stewart?"

"Would you believe a romantic getaway with Dan?"

Jase picked up a pile of message slips from the desk. "On a weekend between your memorial and full moon? Hardly. Try again."

"It's something to do with the Tate case. Something I can't tell you." I held out my hand.

The message slips hit it with a slap. "Several of these are from Esteban. He's not happy."

"I'm surprised he didn't send his pet to deliver them."

Jase's hand strayed up toward his throat, faint color staining his cheeks.

Shit. What had Jase been up to with Niko? Whatever it was, it couldn't be good but I had bigger problems right now. Like convincing Esteban to go along with my plan. I could just imagine the conversation. "So, Lord Esteban, wanna give me all your money for a few weeks to help me?" Followed by Esteban laughing wildly and squashing me like a bug. I needed a backup plan. But the only one I could think of was Marco. He could pull rank on Esteban.

Asking Marco for yet another favor would cause Dan to squash me like a bug instead.

Maybe I should let Dan go after a legal solution after all.

But that could take days. Or weeks. Not to mention the fact that a judge would want something more than my gut instinct to tie Smith and Esteban together. It would take too much time. Time I didn't want to give to Smith.

"Where is Lord Esteban likely to be at this time of day?"

"How should I know?" Jase snapped.

"I thought you might be familiar with his routine seeing as you've been hanging out with one of his...minions." I didn't know what the correct term for Niko was.

"Niko is not Esteban. And he's not a minion."

"Employee then. He works for Esteban, yes? I'm in a hurry here, Jase. Do you know or not?"

"Most likely Maelstrom or his house."

I had no idea where Esteban lived so I guess that meant I was going to Maelstrom. Wonderful.

Chapter 13

EVEN AT FOUR p.m. the music pounded at me as I walked through the doors of Maelstrom. I couldn't help looking toward the stage. Luckily it was empty. The dance floor wasn't. It wasn't as packed as it had been last time but it seemed like the freaks of Seattle had plenty of time to party all day long. As I headed for the stairs, the tall black vamp who'd hassled us last time stepped into my path.

I moved around him. "I'm here to see Lord Esteban. He's expecting me."

Maybe expecting was overstating it. I'd left a message on his voicemail that I was coming to see him. He hadn't responded. I was taking silence as consent.

"He didn't mention you," the vamp said, blocking me again. Vampire speed is annoying when you're in a hurry.

"Does he discuss everything with you?"

Silence.

"Fine. Then let me through." I spotted Leah standing on the balcony. I doubted she'd go out of her way to make this easier for me but I was feeling desperate. I wanted Smith and Esteban was my best chance at smoking him out. "Ask Leah. She'll vouch for me."

"Leah doesn't like werewolves."

"I didn't say she was my best friend, I said she'd vouch for me. Get out of the way." I put my hand on my hip. The gun I usually carried in my purse was on my belt today. With no one to back me up, I wasn't walking into Maelstrom unarmed. The bullets were silver hollow points. According to Tommy, they'd blow a big hole in either a vamp or a were. I'd never had to test out their effectiveness for real.

It didn't look like today would be the day either. Leah came halfway downstairs and beckoned. The vamp moved out of my way.

"Ms. Keenan," Leah said when I reached her. "Lord Esteban has been expecting your call. For several days now."

Something about Leah always made my spine creep. The hairs on the back of my neck rose as the scent of vampire mixed with the spiced amber perfume she wore hit my nose. If I hadn't come to ask a favor I might've been inclined to try those bullets after all. "I was out of town. Family emergency. Which is why I've come to see Lord Esteban in person today."

"He is not a patient man." Her tone suggested that she was looking forward to the dressing down I was about to receive.

"Then why are you keeping him waiting now?" I asked sweetly.

It earned me a glare that sent an even stronger prickle crawling across my nape. Note to self: do not ever be alone with Leah in a dark alley without an even bigger gun than the one I was carrying. Maybe even two. But hey, pissing her off was worth something. I raised my eyebrows as she held her ground. She broke first, whirling with a sound close to a snarl and heading up the stairs.

I followed, concentrating on keeping my balance so I wouldn't accidentally brush the silvered banisters. I wasn't going to give Leah the satisfaction of seeing me hurt.

Instead of taking the corridor I thought led to Esteban's

office, she turned right at the top of the stairs heading toward another wall of black-mirrored glass. A door slid open as she approached and she stepped through. I stopped. The air coming out of the door smelled like blood and pain and fear. With a heavy side of lust. Not a combination I wanted to become any more familiar with. But if Esteban was inside, then I had no choice. I steeled myself and stepped through the door.

The blood scent hit me like a blow. Old, old blood mixed with new. Beneath the blood was sweat and suffering. And sex. I wrinkled my nose, tried to breathe through my mouth as my eyes adjusted to the lack of light.

The long narrow space I'd stepped into was lit by dim bulbs in lanterns hanging high on the walls. The lights flickered like flames, giving off a reddish-orange glow but I didn't smell smoke. It reflected off the mirrored walls, setting up weird flickering shadows and infinite reflections of flames in the walls. I put my hand back on my gun.

"Welcome to the dark side," Leah said with a smirk.

She stood about ten feet beyond me. In the strange light, her hair and eyes seemed to glow red.

"Charming," I said. "What's with the lighting? You guys forget to pay the electric bill this month?"

"Our guests like the dark."

I just bet they did. I suppressed a shiver. I didn't want to think about what it was that people did to each other behind those glass walls. "I appreciate the tour but I'd really like to see Lord Esteban."

"Are you sure? You might find it educational. You might even like it." She waved a hand to her left and a panel of glass in the wall from floor to ceiling turned transparent.

Which gave me a bird's-eye view of what the occupants of the room beyond the wall were doing. A naked man hung from chains suspended from the ceiling, his arms stretched painfully above his head. There was a woman dressed in strips of black something kneeling in front of him, her face buried in his crotch.

At first I thought she was blowing him but then I noticed the blood running down his legs and the angle of her face. She was *biting*, not sucking. My stomach rolled and heaved. But I wasn't going to show my distress to Leah. Instead I kept my face blank and watched as the man bucked against her. A door opened in the wall behind him and another woman stepped into the room. Her strips of whatever were red, not black. In her hand she carried a long blade that glinted red in the light.

I looked back at Leah, not wanting to know what happened next. "Lord Esteban?"

She grinned at me, not in a good way. "This way."

As we walked down the room, she kept gesturing at the wall, revealing one room after another of twisted sex and pain. I tried to focus on her back but the reflections and the lights made it hard to miss what was happening in those rooms. In fifty feet I saw more bodies and blood and leather and live sex acts than I ever wanted to. Sweat started to trickle down my neck as one tableau after another brought back the scent and feel of Tate to me.

I gritted my teeth, determined not to faint. At least I couldn't hear anything even though the scents grew stronger the farther we walked. When we reached yet another blank wall, I braced myself for what would be revealed by another wave of Leah's hand.

But the wall didn't turn transparent. Instead a door, like the first slid open, revealing yet another room. Esteban stood by a long low padded leather bench. As we entered he was buttoning the top button of his shirt. The smell of blood was stronger than ever. But he was alone and I was just glad that I hadn't witnessed whatever it was he'd just been doing. I wasn't sure my stomach could take it.

His eyebrows lifted as we appeared. "I thought I wasn't supposed to be interrupted?"

Leah made a half-bow. "Ms. Keenan insisted, my Lord."

Gee, thanks for blaming me. As Esteban turned his blue gaze on me and I felt the squirming of my stomach change from nauseated to something more pleasant but equally unwelcome, I tried to resist the urge to throw Leah across the room. "Lord Esteban, I didn't want to keep you waiting any longer." I told myself to ignore the desire creeping over me. Not real. Just vampire mind games. Pity it felt so real.

"That hasn't seemed to bother you the last few days." His voice was cool but still managed to warm my skin.

I flushed and then gritted my teeth, breathing through my nose. Maybe the smell of blood would remind me that the vampire was not something desirable. "I was detained on other business. I apologize." Now would be a good time to practice that shielding, I realized and tried to conjure up the image of the moonlit glass again. It shimmered a few times then seemed to stick. To my relief, the warmth in the pit of my stomach retreated.

"Your other business costs me more money each day. The thief is still at large."

"These investigations take time. I didn't promise instant results."

"You didn't tell me you would be leaving town either." His eyes turned a brighter shade of blue. "You should have told me, Ashley. Do I need to remind you that I could make you wish to never leave?" He lifted a hand and for a moment, I thought the shield had held when nothing happened. Then, once again, glass shattered in my head and desire suddenly roared through me. My nipples went hard and I took a half step toward him, toward the source of the pleasure that suddenly seemed like all I needed.

All I had ever wanted.

The weight of the butt of my gun digging into my palm as

my hand clenched brought me back to myself. Just a little. Just enough for me to stay where I was.

My breath came faster. It was an effort to speak. "If you do that, then your case won't get solved either."

He smiled. "Do you think so? I think you'd do whatever I asked."

I squeezed harder on the gun. "Yeah, but it's so hard to read spreadsheets when you're having multiple orgasms."

His shout of laughter startled me. Like a tap turning off, the need for him vanished, leaving only a vague sense of frustration and a pounding heart. He gestured to Leah, who bowed slightly then left the room.

"I can see why Lord Marco likes you," Esteban said, settling back onto the bench. "You are entertaining for a wolf."

My mind blanked on a suitable response to that. I still wasn't comfortable with the thought of Marco being on my side. And I really didn't want to think about Esteban taking an interest in me either. No, not that kind of interest. I had no illusions about that. Esteban didn't want *me*; I doubt he really wanted many people.

He liked what he could make them do.

He liked being in control and watching others lose it. Which might just be how to get him to agree to my proposal. "I have been doing some work on your case, my Lord. I have a theory. How much do you know about McCallister Tate?"

"The vampire you killed? I know that he was crazy and Lord Marco thinks you did us a favor by ridding us of him." He paused as if expecting me to jump in.

I didn't. I was trying to work out whether he knew anything else and wasn't telling me. And if he didn't know anything else, how much could I actually tell him without getting myself in trouble? The Taskforce had gone to a lot of trouble to keep the news of the anti-vaccine quiet. I didn't want to be responsible for letting it slip to a vampire with questionable ethics.

"Is there more to the story?" Esteban asked.

"There is." I chewed my lip. "I can't tell you too much. But Tate wasn't working alone. He was involved in...in a conspiracy."

"To do what?"

I still didn't know if he was testing me or in the dark. "Let's just say something that wouldn't be great for either the supernatural population or the humans. Something that required him to have access to quite a bit of money. Money we haven't been able to trace. Tate wasn't running things. A human was." At least Smith seemed to be running things. There might still be someone—or some*thing*—else pulling strings somewhere higher up. Like my freaky friend from the woods.

"Does this human have a name?"

I shook my head. "We don't know his name. I met him but he was using an alias. And, as I said, we haven't been able to make much progress in this investigation."

"What did he call himself?"

"Smith."

Esteban's mouth quirked. "Original."

"Effective."

He nodded. "Continue."

"I think Smith might be the one who's stealing from you."

Leather creaked as Esteban shifted on the bench, expression thoughtful. "You think or you would like to think?"

I shrugged. "Call it accountant's intuition. I don't think it's a coincidence that someone has started stealing from you at the same time that Smith and Tate and their cronies surfaced. Tate is dead but Smith isn't. He needs money to keep doing whatever it is they're doing. If they don't have it themselves then—" I paused, trying to think of a diplomatic way to say what I wanted to say.

"Yes?"

"Sometimes it's easier to steal from those who don't do everything by the book."

"Are you suggesting I am such a person?"

I smiled cautiously. "*I* would never suggest such a thing. Let's just say you're someone whom others might perceive that way."

"So you think these conspirators are stealing from me?"

"I think it's likely. You and maybe others."

"And what do you propose we do about it?"

Deep breath, Ash. "I think you should let me freeze your accounts. Cut off their funding and see if that forces their hand."

His eyes narrowed. "You want me to hand over my money to you?"

"Not hand it over. Just make it so no one can access it without all sorts of issues. For a limited time only. Say a week." From what I'd seen at Infradark, money was being siphoned off daily. It wouldn't take Smith long to catch on to what we'd done. Then he'd have to make a move. And we'd be waiting.

Esteban pulled at his cuff, smoothing the black silk. "How do you propose that I run my business in the meantime?"

"We can transfer some money to a clean account for your immediate expenses. And secure the cash flow in your clubs."

"How?"

"Either we use agents—"

"Not acceptable."

"Well, then we can use staff you know are not thieves. People you trust. Or perhaps Lord Marco could assist?"

His upper lip curled. "My business is my business. I do not need those of Marco's lineage poking their noses around here anymore than I need the FBI."

"There's no point freezing just the accounts. They might be siphoning cash rather than accessing your funds."

"Shouldn't you be able to work out which it is?"

"Not in the next day or so."

He rose, looming over me. "What's the rush?"

I dropped my gaze. I couldn't tell him about Rhianna. "I have reason to believe they're getting ready to try something again."

"Try or have tried?"

"Try." That was true. Rhianna was an accident. A feint at me. But they wanted her, accident or no. She was proof their anti-vaccine worked—if they didn't know already—and with that knowledge I didn't think they'd hold off much longer from trying whatever it was they intended to do.

Esteban shook his head. "But you have no evidence at all? Why should I agree?"

"Because if I'm right, then your problems are solved."

He eased back onto the bench, shaking his head. "And if you're wrong, I will still be losing money and my business will be in chaos. It is hardly an appealing proposition, Ms. Keenan." He tapped his fingers on his knee. "Would you advise a client to make such a bad business decision?"

"You are my client, and in these circumstances, yes, I would."

"But you are acting out of self-interest. You wish to catch this man. He hurt you."

My fingernails bit into my palm. Smith had done more than hurt me. He'd hurt those I loved. He'd killed. He'd turned my world inside out and upside down over and over. "I would say our interests are aligned. It would be unethical of me to give you advice that isn't to your benefit."

"Some people are not overly troubled by ethics. Not when the things they hold dear are at stake."

"I'm not one of those people."

"No?" His finger crooked at me. "Come here, Ashley."

I stayed where I was. "Why?"

Another curl of his finger and in its wake a slide of heat

passed through me like hot golden honey slipping under my skin. "If you don't come, I will not agree to what you say."

I fought the snarl burning in my throat. And stepped forward.

"Closer."

Another few steps until my feet were a foot or so from his knees. I looked down at Esteban even as I struggled to keep myself from moving closer. My brain was foggy. The wolf thought being above him was a position of power but my human mind knew better. I was nowhere close to being in control of this situation. And I didn't like that feeling one little bit. My hand flexed toward my gun.

"I don't think so."

Esteban's hand closed over mine, tightening to the point of pain. I swayed as my nerves swamped with a dizzying mix of pleasure, pain and fear. Contact, it seemed, strengthened the effect he had on people.

"Kneel."

I wanted to do what he said. Oh, yes. It would be so easy. So right.

But the last time a vampire had made me feel this way, it had been Tate thralling me. I'd had no choice and ever since then I'd had to live with the consequences of what I'd let him do to me in the name of self-preservation and to save Bug. But I wasn't thralled now and I had a choice. I reached again for the image of moonlight and glass, tried to imagine the silver caress of the moon against my skin. Suddenly I could see Dan's reflection in that shimmering glass, silver eyes gleaming at me. *Dan.* For a moment I smelled his scent and it gave me enough strength to twist free of Esteban's mental grip. "*No.*" It was almost a shout.

Esteban surged to his feet. "You refuse me?"

Dan's image wavered then shattered with the glass. Another wave of desire wracked me, and I shuddered, my body wanting the release the sensations were promising even as my mind refused it. "Yes."

"Even if it costs you my cooperation?" His finger stroked my lip. "Such a little thing to give for what you want so badly?"

Maybe before Tate I would've chosen differently. I hoped not. I'd like to think I'd never been the sort to kneel at the feet of a monster and do whatever it was they wanted. But the last few months had shown me things about myself that made reality less black and white. It's harder to choose between shades of gray but in my mind, this particular choice was clear. I would not submit.

Not again.

I bared my teeth. "No. Not even for this."

Esteban frowned and the fire eased a little. "Isn't catching this man your heart's desire?"

"It's one of them." Not bowing to Esteban was another right now.

"And if I insist?"

This time my hand did close on my gun. "Then we'll both just have to be disappointed."

The lines between his eyebrows deepened and his eyes glinted dangerous blue. "You think you can get out of here if I choose to keep you?"

"I think you'd have to kill me to stop me." My voice shook but I didn't care. He could tell from my heartbeat and my scent that I was scared. What mattered to me was that I was scared and still able to defy him.

"A woman of convictions." To my relief, he stepped back.

"I like to think so," I said. My voice didn't shake quite so much this time. I couldn't quite make my hand let go of the gun though.

Esteban studied me with an expression I couldn't decipher. "Perhaps you've convinced me after all."

I stared at him. Did he mean what I thought he meant? I

opened my mouth but before I could ask the question my cell rang, the noise shrilling into the silence like a fire alarm. I winced and jumped. "Sorry," I said, rummaging in my bag. "I'll turn it off." I didn't want to ruin everything, now that I was so close. "So do we have an agreement?" I switched the phone to vibrate, dropped it back into the bag.

He nodded. Relief swept through me. "Thank you." I inclined my head, which was as close as I came to bowing. "How long do you need to set up a new account and transfer enough money to keep you going?"

"A few hours. I'll use one of my personal accounts. Nothing's gone missing from them."

It didn't surprise me that Esteban had accounts ready to go. In my experience, vampires believed in liquid assets and they embraced the ease and freedom of access to international finance provided by the internet. "And the list of accounts I have now for the clubs is complete?"

A nod.

"Then we'll freeze them tonight." I figured Dan should be able to pull that off if Esteban was cooperating. "Then we just need to secure the cash."

"I can do that.

He sounded certain. I believed him. Cash fraud happens when people think the boss isn't watching. Having Esteban or some of his nastier lieutenants prowling around each club and counting money would probably put an end to any delusions his employees might have that the money was easy pickings.

"Yes. You have one week. And I expect you to keep me informed of any progress," Esteban said as I finally managed to make myself let go of my gun.

I nodded, mentally crossing my fingers that it would be enough time and that my crazy theory might be right. "One —" My phone buzzed to life. "I'm sorry," I apologized again. "I have to take this."

To my relief Esteban nodded and gestured. The door slid

open. I stepped back into the corridor, hoping I hadn't just ruined everything. The walls were all dark again, which improved the view, though the dim light didn't make my cell any easy to find in my purse. I followed the vibrations and closed my fingers around it. "What's so important?" I snapped as I moved down the corridor.

"We have a problem," Esme said. "Rhianna went nuts again."

My throat tightened. "Shit. What happened?"

"I'm not sure but she almost tore someone's arm off before they got her under control."

Not good. In fact, very, very far from good. And I didn't think Esme was telling me the worst of it. "Will he survive?"

"I think so. But that's not why I'm calling. They've kicked me and Marco out but I think they're going to transfer her. That colonel went ballistic. Said they couldn't keep her secure."

Did the army even have the right to kick the FBI out when they were involved in a case? "Transfer her where?"

"I'm not sure, I'm trying to find out but someone mentioned Grayson."

My heart nosedived. Grayson Prison. One of the government's nastier innovations. Supermax for supernaturals. No. No. No. It would kill Rhianna to be locked up by herself twenty-three hours a day. "She hasn't done anything wrong, how can they send her to jail?"

"It's the military. I guess they can do what they want if they can convince someone national security is at stake. They've got her on assault at a minimum and I'm sure they can come up with more charges if they choose."

I tried to think. "She's not competent at the moment."

"I don't think they care."

"Does Dan know?"

"Yes, he's trying to pull strings right now."

"Do you know when they're going to move her?"

"No. But they were really pissed, Ash. They want her out of here. Marco and I are going to come back to Seattle." Esme sounded pretty pissed herself. I wondered exactly what the army guys had done to her.

"No. Stay there. You can't leave her."

"Ashley, I'm not with her now. I'm sitting in a jeep outside the base. They won't let us back in."

In a jeep?"Where's Marco?" He couldn't be in a jeep. My mental image of army jeeps involved a distinct lack of roof. Even if the army was pissed off, I doubted they wanted to take responsibility for flambéing an Old One.

"They let him call a car. He left already."

Leaving Rhianna alone with a bunch of soldiers who had less reason than ever to treat her well. "Can't you stall and see if you can keep an eye on the place?"

"I'm looking at about eight guys with automatic weapons pointed at my jeep and my driver has one too. I don't think they're going to let me just sit here. Dan told me to come in."

Damn. I had no say in that chain of command as far as Esme was concerned. She would follow Dan's orders. So I needed to get to him.

Chapter 14

As soon as I hit the street outside Maelstrom, I started shaking. Adrenaline overload is never a good thing. I staggered over to a handy bench and sat with a thump, breathing deep and trying to will away the feeling I was about to lose my lunch. Not that I'd actually eaten lunch.

The bouncers standing outside the doors watched me curiously but they were the least of my problems. So what if they told Esteban I fell to pieces when I'd gotten outside? The main thing was I'd actually made it out of there in one piece in the first place.

"Need a ride?"

My head shot up. Agent Ramirez stood next to the bench, looking unhappy.

"What are you doing here?" I asked.

"Dan sent me to fetch you. We missed you at your office. Your assistant told us where you'd gone."

Dan had sent a protection detail. I guess I should've expected it and, to be honest, right now, I was happy to have a few armed men around me. Plus it would save me cab fare back to the Taskforce.

I had to tell Dan that Esteban had agreed to my plan. Dan

probably wouldn't like it but he wasn't going to turn down a chance to catch Smith. I'd deal with any fallout I had to in order to keep Rhi safe. She wasn't going to prison if I could help it. Particularly not Grayson.

She hadn't done anything except be in the wrong place at the wrong time. She didn't deserve to be locked up with crazy vamps and rogue weres.

In fact, I couldn't wait until I got back to the Taskforce. I needed to know what was happening now. As Andy ushered me to the waiting SUV, I called Dan.

He answered the phone after just one ring. "Is Ramirez with you? You know it's not safe for you to be out on your own. You should have waited for a detail." He sounded exasperated.

"I had my panic button," I said. Which was true but I hadn't actually remembered it was somewhere in my purse until this very moment.

"I'd prefer it if you didn't go places where you'll need it."

"Me too. But that doesn't seem to be working out right now. And, before you start yelling, I got Esteban to agree to let us freeze his accounts."

"I hope the next words out of your mouth are 'thanks to the power of vid-conferencing'."

"No."

"You went to see Esteban alone?" His voice dropped low.

Andy's head swiveled to look at me from his position, riding shotgun. Clearly he could hear both sides of the conversation. Damn weres.

I ignored Andy's half-amused, half-interested expression and focused on soothing the cranky werewolf on the other end of the line. "It was fine. No big deal."

"Then why do you sound so nervous?"

"I'm worried about Rhi."

"I'm worried about *you*."

"Don't be. How long will the paperwork take? Esteban says he can be organized by early tonight. Seven."

"Something tells me he's thought about this possibility before."

"Maybe. But that's not important. How long?"

"Seven is fine. I'll get the team on it. There's no issue if Esteban is consenting."

"And what about Rhi? You can't let them put her in that place."

"Ash, I'm trying but it's out of my hands."

"She hasn't—"

"She almost killed someone. There are laws."

"She hasn't had a trial."

"No judge would grant her bail right now, so a trial wouldn't change much."

"I don't believe you."

"That doesn't change anything. And before you go nuts, I said, I'm trying. I didn't say I agreed with what they'd done."

Fury boiled through me but aiming it at Dan would be misdirected. I should save it for the man who deserved it. Smith. And his bitch of a vampirella sidekick. "Fine. I'll be there in fifteen minutes. You can give me an update then."

When I got to the Taskforce, Dan was closeted in his office with the head of the Seattle branch. Not the sort of meeting I could just barge into, particularly not when I wanted to stay in the Taskforce's good graces to get help for Rhi.

Instead I parked myself at my cubicle and then helped Andy fill out the seventy gazillion forms involved in getting the banking system to cut off someone's funds.

By the time Dan got out of the meeting I was starting to go cross-eyed. When he appeared at my desk, bearing coffee, I shook my head. "No more caffeine. I'll never get to sleep."

"That would be the idea."

"What does that mean? Do you have news about Rhi?"

He shook his head. "So far we haven't been able to get any traction. She's still scheduled for transfer to Grayson."

"When?"

"Soon."

"Tonight?"

"Probably."

"Then we should go. We could meet her there." I started to gather my things.

"They're not going to let us see her straight away. New inmates are meant to be cutoff for the first few days. Help them adjust."

"New inmates? Rhi's not an *inmate*. She's a twenty-one-year-old girl, who's probably terrified, not to mention traumatized. She needs me."

"I'm trying to get you permission but you just turning up there isn't going to help persuade them. Play by the rules, Ash. It's quicker in the long run."

The problem with the long run was that Rhi might not survive it. She hadn't exactly been holding on to sanity with both hands when we'd left her. I'd been unable to do anything to save Julie or my sister from Tate. Damned if I was letting Rhi go without a fight. Rules or no rules.

"I'm sorry, Dan, but no. This isn't as simple as that. This is personal. Rhi's the closest thing I've had to a little sister since I lost Julie and my family. I have to help her."

"I'm your family too," he said. "Don't you trust me to help you?"

He put his hand on mine and for a breath I let myself just be still. Everything seemed better just because skin met skin. But, just like the desire Esteban had evoked, I couldn't let the physical reaction I had to Dan sway me. Lust didn't outweigh my ties of loyalty to Rhi. Neither did love. I loved them both. But right now, Dan could take care of himself so my choice was simple.

Rhi needed me.

Dan would forgive me—I hoped.

"I'll give you a couple more hours," I said finally. I owed Dan that much. "But then I'm going to Grayson."

He moved his hand and, as the warmth faded from my skin, I watched his eyes turn silver glass. "Don't do anything stupid, Ash."

"I'm not going to. It's not like I can attack Grayson with a revolver and break her out of there. I'm just going to see her. I'll camp out on the damned doorstep if I have to."

"Give me until midnight," he asked.

That was six hours away. Six hours Rhi would be alone and scared and out of control. "We'll see," I said. "Now, let me get back to work."

"There's something I need you to do first."

"What?"

"May I?" He gestured at my keyboard and I rolled my chair back so he could get in.

With a few quick keystrokes he pulled up some sort of photo database.

"What's this?"

"These are all the images of dark-haired women from Maelstrom's security cameras that night. See if you can find your mystery vamp."

I scrolled through the images. They were grainy and the lighting was weird. After a couple of minutes of nothing that rang any bells, I started to wonder if every woman who went to Maelstrom had dark hair. It felt like I'd looked at hundreds of pictures already. "How many of these are there?"

"About three hundred."

Seems Seattle wasn't lacking in vampire freaks. I started scrolling the pictures again. Nothing. Nothing. Nothing. Wait. Dark lips smiled out of the screen. "*Her.*"

"Are you sure?"

I leaned closer, stared at the eyes in the photo. Even in yanked-from-security-camera grainy resolution they were creepy. Dark. Empty. Soulless. Yep. That was her all right. "Positive."

Dan smiled. "Great. We'll run her through the FBI and police databases and I'll get the guys to redo the search on the tapes, see if they got an image of the guy with her. Remember, don't do anything stupid."

I didn't watch Dan leave. Despite my success at identifying the woman's picture, I couldn't shake a sense of foreboding. Finding her picture meant we'd hopefully find the name of the crazy vampire out to get us this time. Knowing the name didn't make the fact there was a crazy vampire out to get us any easier to deal with. It seemed the harder I tried to hold onto normality, the quicker it fell to pieces.

So maybe I needed to stop trying. Embrace being different. Maybe the only thing that would let me stop these people would be to play the game the way they did.

Only thing was, in Dan's world, even being different had rules. Lines you didn't cross. Black and white. If I started coloring outside those lines, I wasn't sure he would follow me bond or no bond.

With a sigh, I turned back to my computer and the paperwork on Esteban's accounts. At seven, I tried to log-on to the accounts, only to be rewarded with a very satisfying 'Access denied' message. Hopefully Smith would have the same experience if he tried siphoning out more funds.

Esme arrived back from the base around nine. She let me interrogate her about Rhi but she didn't have much more to add to what I already knew. Marco's phone, when I tried all the numbers I had for him, was diverted to a very polite answering service that didn't offer anything more than "Yes, ma'am, I'll pass on that message and all your others."

Finally I reached frustration overload. Exhaustion kicked in with a vengeance. "I'm going home to get some sleep and grab some stuff," I said to Esme. "Tell Dan I'll check in at midnight." He hadn't come to speak to me again so I had to assume so far the picture of our mystery vampire hadn't resulted in any hits on the database searches.

"Are you sure you don't want to talk to him yourself?"

I glanced down the line of cubicles to Dan's office. I could just see his head bent over something on his desk. He was wearing a headset and talking to someone. Hopefully about Rhi. I didn't want to interrupt him or, if I was really honest, let myself in for another argument. "No. He can call me when he's done."

Esme's perfectly glossed lips pressed together. She was worried. About me? About Dan and me? About the case? I couldn't face getting into it with her just now.

"Look, I'm going straight home, I promise." I held up two fingers. "And I'm telling Andy, so he and his guys can follow me. Scout's honor and everything."

She raised an eyebrow at me. "Were you a scout?"

"No, I was a mathlete. But mathletes don't have cool salutes." I smiled, trying to convince her everything was fine. "Now, I'm wrecked and you must be too. I'll see you later."

I spent most of the cab ride home in a semi-daze, jolting in and out of a half-asleep state that made everything seem distant and floaty. I had one hand in the pocket of my jacket, fingers rubbing over the little black panic button without really registering it. In my more awake moments, I checked that Andy was following me and his black SUV was there every time.

As the cab pulled up in front of my house, I spotted the second SUV—the rest of the detail Andy had sent ahead— parked half a block down. I resisted the temptation to wave at them out of the window.

My cell rang as I paid the driver and I fumbled for it with my left hand. I'd stashed it in my jacket pocket too, wanting to be able to get to it fast if Dan called. I looked at the display. Dan.

Maybe with news of Rhi. But even as I went to hit receive,

another wave of exhaustion washed over me and I changed my mind. I desperately needed some sleep. Werewolf energy only took you so far. Whatever Dan wanted could wait an hour.

Andy opened the door for me and I climbed out of the cab and followed him up my front path. I stumbled up the porch steps, searching for my keys before I realized Andy had a set and was already at the door. The phone rang again as the door swung open.

I reached for it as Andy went inside. I knew enough to wait for his all clear at least. But before I could answer, there was a strange muffled sound followed by a thump.

"Andy!" I yelled, and dropped the phone as I went for my gun with one hand and the panic button with the other. Something shoved me from behind hard and I was three feet inside the house before the smell registered.

Vampires. And blood. A lot of blood.

I jerked my gun up but a light blazed to life and the vampire from the woods stepped forward and suddenly I was frozen again.

"Hello, puppy," she said. "So nice of you to join us." I just had time to catch sight of Andy sprawled on the floor behind her but then she pointed a finger at me, pain seared through my head, and the world blacked out.

My brains felt like they'd been scrambled. With something sharp and pointy. Every part of me voted for staying still and going back to sleep until the stabbing sensations went away.

It took a few seconds to work out why I felt so strange but then I remembered the vampires. And registered that I was sitting up, not lying down. Worse, whatever I was sitting on was moving. My head rested on something thin and soft but behind that metal vibrated. I cracked my eyes open, just a little.

I was in the back of some sort of vehicle. Something big. I smelled diesel, not gasoline. My hands and feet were bound with leather lined metal cuffs and chains. Another chain ran round my waist then disappeared from view. I guess it was attached to the wall of the truck or whatever it was that I was inside.

"You're awake then."

I squinted harder through the gloom, vision blurry. Weres have good night vision but the pounding of my head made me reluctant to open my eyes wide enough to use it. One of these days I was going to have to stop getting myself knocked out. I was getting really tired of it. Waking up with a pounding headache should be the result of tequila not terror. Didn't any vampires ever kidnap someone awake?

I blinked, trying to clear my vision but it stayed blurry. I could just make out a dark figure sitting near the opposite wall to me. A vampire. Violets and acid hit my nose. Not just any vampire but my friend from the woods. Perfect.

I peered harder at the vamp. As my vision slowly refocused, her pale skin and dark hair became clearer. She sat on a bench seat, looking serenely composed. Someone else was lying on the seat too, their head in the vamp's lap. I couldn't see the sleeping—I hoped they were sleeping not unconscious —person's face, just the outline of them, covered by some sort of blanket.

My kidnapper stroked their hair with one hand in a way that made the hairs on the back of my neck stand on end.

Creepily possessive.

And, I realized, as my nose sorted through the conflicting stinks of vampire, violets, hot engine, fuel and metal, there was another familiar smell in the mix.

Rhianna.

I surged forward only to be brought up sharp by the chain around my waist. I fell back against the wall with a thump that rattled my teeth and jarred my back.

"Careful, those are silver."

I ignored her jibe. The cuffs on my wrists weren't burning me so obviously they weren't silver, even if the chains attached to them were. The vamp was trying to distract me. "What have you done to Rhi?"

The vamp smiled.

At least I thought it was a smile. It involved a flash of very white fangs and an expression of smugness.

"I rescued her."

Rescued? From what? Comprehension dawned. "You boosted her from the hospital?"

"No, we waited until they were moving her."

My skin crawled. How had they known Rhianna was going to be moved and what sort of force could they muster if they could take on a military transport and successfully steal their prisoner? "What did you do?"

"Stupid humans moved her in a van with a single escort vehicle. It wasn't that hard."

Stupid dead humans I imagined. What sort of trouble did that mean Rhianna was now in? Would they think that she'd organized this?

I hoped not. After all, she'd been under tight security for days. How would she get herself rescued without help? Which, I realized with a sudden flash of horror, made the other most likely suspect *me*. Fuck.

I put that less than welcome thought out of my head. The Taskforce would stick up for me against the army. I had a bigger issue right now. If I didn't survive it didn't really matter what the army or anyone else thought I'd done.

I took a deep breath. The other likely outcome of a hijacked transport and a vanished prisoner was that a lot of people would be looking for Rhianna. Which could only be a good thing. I couldn't feel the hard bump of the panic button in my pocket, so really, our only hope of being found quickly was a massive manhunt for Rhianna.

Another deep breath revealed no hint of Andy's steamy green scent in the truck. God. Was he still alive? Had they killed him back there at my house? I shoved the thought aside. If he wasn't here then I'd have to worry about him later. He couldn't help me and I couldn't help him.

It was just me and Rhi.

So I needed to keep both of us alive until we were found. I looked down at my wrist. No watch. Damn.

No way of knowing how long I'd been unconscious or how long it had been since they'd taken Rhi. I didn't even know what the protocol was for a prisoner transfer. How regularly did the drivers check in with their destination? Or, put another way, how long until the army and Grayson would notice the transport had gone AWOL?

"Is Rhianna okay?"

"She's just sleeping," the vamp crooned, softly. "She'll be fine. Now that she's with me."

"She needs to be with her family." Stall, Ashley, stall. Try and figure out what had happened and where we might be headed. They had to have taken Rhianna on an isolated stretch of road. These vamps were organized. They planned. I wasn't dealing with Tate, though whoever the vamp across from me was, I didn't think she had a much stronger grip on reality than he'd had. But even if she was nuts, she seemed to be capable of going after what she wanted with great success.

"I am her family now."

"Like hell you are."

She snarled, fangs glinting white in the dim light. "Watch yourself. You're in no position to piss me off."

Piss me off. Interesting. In my experience, older vamps didn't tend to use modern slang quite so easily. I slotted the information away. Younger usually meant weaker but she had already demonstrated impressive psychic powers. Then again Jase was strong in that department too. But pinpointing her age would be useful information if I got out of this. It would help identify her, for a start. "Well, I'm still alive so far. You must want me for something."

"You'll find out soon enough."

Wonderful. I settled back against the wall, tried to find a comfortable angle for my head and shut my eyes. I couldn't do anything in my current position and Rhi didn't seem to be in immediate danger. Insanity wasn't catching, after all. Might as well try and conserve energy. I had a feeling I was going to need it when we reached our destination.

"Oh no, puppy. You go to sleep when I say so."

"Sorry, but I just don't find egomaniacal vampires all that interesting. Besides, I've had kind of a long day."

Color flared against my eyelids. The vamp had turned on a light. A torch or a lamp, maybe. I squeezed my eyes tighter together and let out a snoring sound.

"I wouldn't sleep if I were you. After all, I might get hungry."

Cold spiked through me and my eyes flew open.

The vamp grinned at me nastily. "That woke you up."

I summoned my best 'try it and you die' expression. "Like I told you in the woods, the last vamp who drank from me paid a high price."

"Tate was an idiot. And weak."

Well, that was something we agreed on. "I suggest you learn from his mistakes then. Don't mess with me."

"I'm not going to mess with you. I'm going to use you and then get rid of you."

I felt the hairs on the back of my neck stiffen. "Use me for what?"

She shook her head and raised her hand. "You're boring me. Maybe you should go back to sleep after all."

I didn't even try to fight it; just let the pain flaring through my skull carry me into darkness.

When I forced my eyes open for the second time, I was lying on a mattress shoved in one corner of a small room with bare walls painted an industrial shade of beige. There was no sign of Rhianna or the vampire. A bottle of Gatorade sat on the floor within reach.

The sight of it, combined with the renewed throb of my head made me want to gag. I couldn't stand the taste of Gatorade since Tate. But my mouth felt like I'd been breathing sand all night and I was starving. I held my nose, chugged the bottle as fast as I dared and then forced myself to my feet. I wanted to change, to see if that might help the headache but weak as I felt, I wasn't sure I'd have enough energy to change back or just how much weaker I'd be if I did manage it.

The door was shiny silver metal. I pressed a tentative fingertip to the surface then pulled it back as the skin started to sting and burn. Unlikely that the door itself was silver but whatever it was painted with obviously contained at least some silver. If the paint covered wood, it would be worth the effort to cover my hands and try and break it but there was no way I could rip a metal door off its hinges in my present state. The walls had no windows so there was no other way out. I retreated back to the mattress, sitting with my back to the wall and my eyes on the door.

They'd come for me soon enough.

While the minutes ticked by, I sucked absently at my fingertip, trying to ease the sting. Someone had once told me that some weres eventually gained enough control to change just one part of their bodies to heal a wound. I didn't know if it was even true but right now I wished I knew how.

What I really needed was my panic button. Whether I was anywhere within range of Dan's monitors was anyone's guess. I could be still in Seattle or half a country away.

But he had to be looking for me. I'd smelled blood in my house. More than just Andy's. I was guessing they'd taken out the second detail before Andy and I had even arrived. As soon as they missed a check-in call, Dan would have raised the alarm. But still, I didn't know how long I'd been unconscious or whether I'd been in any other sort of transport before the truck.

The only one who was likely to get me out of this mess was me. Unless Jase could hear me. I spent a few minutes concentrating on him and yelling '*come get me*' in my head before my headache worsened to the extent that I had to stop.

I was just about to curl back up and try to go back to sleep when the door swung inward. The fact I hadn't heard any footsteps outside told me something else unwelcome. My cell was probably soundproofed.

I expected my favorite nutty vampire again.

Instead it was Smith.

Chapter 15

I SCRAMBLED TO MY FEET, backing into the wall.

"You're awake. Good." He looked at me coolly. "That makes things easier."

I didn't really see how. My heart was jackhammering like someone had just dropped a sack full of rattlesnakes into the room. But Smith was human. He couldn't hear how scared I was. So I didn't intend to show him. "Did you miss me?" I asked, proud of myself when my voice didn't shake.

He looked at me with icy blue eyes. Cold. That's what I remembered about him. From the silver rims of his glasses to the snow white lab coat to the gray hair and emotionless voice, the man was ice. "Still a smartass then? You must be a slow learner."

"I guess we're both slow learners," I quipped. "You keep trying the same old shit even though it gets you into hot water every time."

He smiled slowly, and somehow that was worse than his default 'you are a bug and I will study you' expression. "I'm doing just fine. You're the one back in chains."

I pressed harder against the wall as my knees went a little

weak. I would not show fear. "You're the one about to have the full force of the law back on your ass."

"They'll be scrambling around trying to work out what happened. By the time I have what I need from you, they'll still be looking in the wrong place."

"What is it that you need from me?"

"Information."

"Trust me, doc. Anything I know, I'm not telling you. I don't talk to people who play with insane vampires. Where do you find them, by the way?"

He regarded me for a long moment and something almost like an emotion swam in his eyes. Then it disappeared. "Oh, I think you will." He turned and gestured behind him. Four vamps stepped into the room. "Now, Ms. Keenan. This can be painless or painful. It's entirely your choice."

I looked at the vampires. Four of them. Not good odds. Though it was tempting to start a fight just to piss off Smith, I wasn't the only one I had to worry about. Rhi was probably somewhere nearby. I wasn't leaving her to Smith and his gal pal. In some ways, Smith was scarier than Tate had ever been. Tate, at least, had insanity as an excuse. Smith was completely sane. And completely amoral from what I could tell. "I'll behave."

"Very sensible of you." He nodded at the vamps and two of them came over and grabbed an arm each.

They hustled me out of the cell and down a corridor, past several other doors. It seemed to be some sort of office building rather than a house but I didn't have time to form much more of an impression than that before we arrived at our destination.

Smith opened the door and the vamps hauled me inside and strapped me down to something that my brain insisted on labeling a dentist's chair, though it wasn't quite the same.

"What are you doing?" I said to Smith. "Your anti-vaccine won't work on me now, I'm a werewolf." God, I hoped I was right. The last thing anyone needed was Smith coming up with something that could create some sort of weird were-vampire hybrid. That would really have the humans up in arms.

"Relax, I'm not trying to turn you."

"Forgive me if I don't find being tied down relaxing," I snapped, tugging my arm against one of the ties, fear churning in my belly. This was all too familiar, and panic was starting to eat into my control.

"I thought you said you wanted to do this painlessly?" Smith said. "Do let me know if you've changed your mind."

The lack of emotion in his voice chilled me and I stopped moving. "What do you want with me then?"

"Information, puppy." The vamp from the woods appeared in the doorway. Smith smiled at her. I reconsidered trying to snap the bonds. She was wearing another long flowing dress like the ones Leah favored. I wondered whether there was a crazy vampire boutique somewhere. Leah usually wore dark colors though. Mystery vamp's was a soft silky fabric in a gentle peachy shade. Against the dead white of her skin, it looked horrible.

She strolled into the room and hooked an arm through Smith's. The look she gave me wasn't friendly. "Is the puppy behaving herself?"

Smith patted her hand and disengaged his arm smoothly. I wondered whether she creeped him out too or whether he was just eager to get down to business. He took a syringe off the tray beside the chair. "Cilla, I thought we agreed you'd let me do this?"

Cilla? So much for Alpha and Omega. But knowing her name didn't make her any less creepy. She had that same nothing-home-behind-the-eyes look as Tate.

"I changed my mind." She bared her fangs. "I want to watch."

He shrugged and busied himself filling the syringe from a

glass bottle that looked all too familiar. "It's not going to be very interesting. I'm just going to ask a lot of questions."

"Questions about what?" I couldn't help interrupting. I didn't trust Smith in the slightest and the anti-vaccine he'd pumped me full of at Tate's had come in exactly that sort of little bottle.

"We want what's in your head, puppy."

"In my head?" Now I was truly confused. "About the investigation?"

"No," Smith said. He picked up a scalpel and sliced open my sleeve, baring the crook of my elbow. "About your father."

I clenched my teeth, biting back a hiss of pain as he slid the needle under my skin none too gently. "What's my father got to do with it? He's dead." Panic surged again. I didn't know anything about my father's work. I'd been sixteen when he died. What happened when they asked questions I couldn't answer?

"True. But he left something behind before he died."

"He hid it," Cilla said, moving closer.

I blinked at her, feeling tiny prickles of heat breaking out across my skin as I sucked in a breath. My vision blurred slightly. "Hid?" I shook my head, trying to clear it. "What did you give me?"

"Just something to make you cooperative," Smith said. He picked up my wrist, pressed his fingers over my pulse. "A little fast but nothing to worry about."

Easy for him to say. He wasn't the one feeling as though the room had decided to turn into a carousel. A carousel in overdrive. I closed my eyes as the walls blurred and shimmied and whirled. I tasted bile in the back of my throat and swallowed, hard. "I don't know anything about my dad that you would be interested in," I managed.

"You might know more than you think," Smith said.

"Your father was working on an important project," Cilla's voice was too close to my ear. Hair brushed my face and I jerked my head. "Maybe he told you over a nice family dinner. He was always boring us with stories of your family dinners."

"You knew my father?" I forced my eyes open, swallowing against the nausea again.

"We worked together for a while."

Fuck. It wasn't Smith we should have been looking for. It was Cilla. I tried to remember a name like Cilla or Priscilla from the long lists of Synotech employees I'd read over and over. But everything was foggy, sliding away from me like the remnants of a dream. My heart pounded. "I don't feel so good."

"Just relax," Smith said. "Tell me about your father. What did you know about his work?"

Despite myself, I started talking. About how my daddy was an immunologist. About the vaccines he'd researched. About how he was helping people whose systems attacked them. How he smelled. How he came to watch me play basketball and to my dance recitals. A stream of memories came flooding out of my mouth. Unfortunately none of them seemed to be what Smith and Cilla wanted.

Cilla's hand grabbed my jaw, her fingernails biting into my face. "Stop babbling."

"Can't." I started to laugh, then to cough. I couldn't catch my breath.

Smith grabbed my wrist again, his fingers curling to take my pulse. "Too fast. I'm going to bring her out of this."

"Why bother?" Cilla said. "She doesn't know anything."

"We don't know that. We were barely getting started. And we have other things still to try."

Another needle bit into me and an icy sensation flooded my veins. Better than feeling like someone was choking me. Just.

Smith watched me for a few moments, and then nodded. "Looks like we're going to have to do this the painful way after all."

* * *

I didn't like the sound of that and braced myself when the four vamps came back into the room. But they just dragged me back to my cell and dumped me there, next to yet more Gatorade and a tray of sandwiches. I choked it all down because I had to keep my strength up. Whatever was coming next wasn't going to be fun.

Of course, eating was also a distraction. Except that it led to the more pressing need for a bathroom. I spent a few minutes pounding on the door then settled back down to wait with tightly crossed legs. To take my mind off my immediate dilemma, I tried to focus on what Cilla had told me.

She knew my father.

Had I ever met her?

Her face wasn't familiar and her being a vampire made things tricky. She might have been younger when she worked with my dad or around the same age she appeared now.

She might have already been a vampire. Dad hadn't said anything at the time but the Taskforce had discovered that Synotech did have a couple of supernatural employees and, of course, it had to trial its drugs on live subjects. The vast majority of drugs were for humans of course but testing vaccines required supplies of vamp and were blood and shifters—and to a lesser extent vamps—still needed things like anesthetics and painkillers that worked on them.

Had Cilla been a guinea pig? Was that what this was about?

I didn't think so but that was, like much of the rest of what I was working with, just a feeling.

For someone who likes figures and cold hard facts, this case was turning into torture.

I dropped my head to my knees, banging it gently.

Think, Ashley.

What had my dad been working on?

Something about auto-immune diseases. I'd never been really interested—what teen paid much attention to their father's work when said work was something distinctly uncool like being a scientist geek?

Plus Dad wasn't really allowed to talk about what he was working on much. I had nothing. Just infuriating scraps of information that refused to join up and form any sort of useful pattern in my head.

When the combination of frustration and fear got too much, I got up and pounded on the door again. This time Smith came and slid open a hatch in the door to peer through.

"Bathroom," I snapped.

He nodded. "Of course. We wouldn't like you to be uncomfortable."

"Heck no, I could tell that by the luxury suite you've got me in."

"If I were you, Ms. Keenan, I'd hold that tongue of yours and save your energy for later."

I stared him down even as my stomach turned over. "I want to see Rhianna."

"I don't think so."

"She needs a friend."

"Cilla is taking care of her." A couple of the vamps appeared behind Smith and he started doing something to the door.

"Great, that makes me feel so much better." I stood quietly while the door opened. "You know, you sure have a knack for picking the crazy ones."

He looked at me with cold eyes. "Careful. You're trying my patience."

Heat flared along my cheek, a memory of Smith's hand connecting hard with my face. I had to remind myself that he wasn't the middle-aged GP he resembled. He was someone not afraid to hurt people to get to what he wanted. But I still couldn't resist baiting him. I might learn something useful. "Tate, I can understand. He was muscle. What's she?"

Smith nodded at the vamps and they grabbed me. "Someone you'd be wise not to annoy." For a moment his expression almost seemed...sad. But that couldn't be right?

"If you didn't like Tate, then I suggest you don't cross Cilla," he added.

I had a hard time believing that someone who liked floaty peach dresses was scarier than a serial killer but if Cilla had Smith cowed, then I wasn't going to underestimate her. "Why are you doing this?" I asked as one of the vamps tugged me toward the door.

This time he definitely looked sad. "I made a mistake once."

I didn't get a chance to ask anything else before the vamps dragged me off. A mistake? What did that mean? A mistake answering my questions? A mistake getting involved with Cilla, whoever she was?

Just another puzzle piece that didn't fit.

I ground my teeth as the vamps hauled me down the corridor. They weren't grabby like Rio and Kyra—Tate's flunkies—had been but they weren't exactly gentle. Plus they smelled like old blood and vampire, which was rapidly becoming a combination that turned my stomach.

They pushed me into a bathroom and locked the door behind me. It was another windowless room, so I did what I had to do, then washed up, trying to make myself feel semi-alive with cheap smelling soap and cold water.

I took advantage of the change of scenery to try yelling for Jase in my head again.

When the door crashed open, I jumped, my thoughts cutting off guiltily.

Cilla stood in the doorway watching me with a grin. "Bad dog," she said. "No calling for help."

"I wasn't doing anything."

"Lying isn't going to help." She stepped into the bathroom and I moved backward until I hit the wall with a thump. "I could hear you."

Dumb. I'd forgotten about the Retreat. She used telepathy on me then too. Crap. Did that mean she could hear me now? Or only when she was trying to? Or only when I was trying to talk to someone?

The look on her face as she stood there, head cocked to one side didn't give me any clue. Then she reached out and squeezed one hand around my throat. Pain seared up my neck. Like Esteban, Cilla liked silver. Rings around every finger.

"No calling for help," she said as I struggled to breathe. "There's no point. And you'll upset the children."

Children? Who? Rhi? Did that mean Rhi could hear me too?

"Do you understand?" Cilla asked, squeezing tighter.

I nodded, unable to speak. Even nodding was difficult.

"Good," she said, releasing me. My knees sagged and I slid down the wall, trying to suck air back into my lungs. My throat burned, my skin felt like it was blistering. Only changing would help ease the pain and the predatory look on Cilla's face made me certain I wasn't going to be allowed to do that any time soon.

I closed my eyes, trying to sense whether it was night or day, trying to see if there was any lingering trace of the moon but either it was daytime or I was too tired to feel anything.

"C'mon, puppy," Cilla said, hauling me up with one hand. "It's time for the hard way."

* * *

The hard way apparently involved me being dragged off to yet another room. I figured Cilla had to be the decorator. The walls were painted black and there were heavy black curtains everywhere. It would've been funny—the clichéd vampire lair — but the bare bulbs in the ceiling combined with all that black to starkly spotlight the other main features of the room.

A large rack filled with a variety of nasty-looking implements and a whipping post that stood taller than my head. This post wasn't black like the others it had been my misfortune to see at Maelstrom. No, this one gleamed silver. Somehow I doubted it was chrome plated.

My stomach churned at the thought of being pressed against that much silver. It would be like being dipped in acid.

New goal. Avoid the post.

"I already told you," I said, turning a nervous circle, trying to keep Cilla and the other vampires in sight as they ringed around me. "I don't know anything about my father's work."

"I think you know more than you think you know." Cilla's voice seemed to bounce off the walls, reverberating weirdly in the small room so it came from all around me. More vampire mind games perhaps. The vamps continued to flow around me, the shadows they cast adding to the disorienting effects of Cilla's voice. Cilla, though, stopped by the rack, one hand trailing over the whips and knives.

She also had a knife in a sheath at her waist. A long sheath. The knife had to be ten inches long.

I shook my head, swallowed as the muscles in my throat tightened and my stomach dropped. "No, I don't."

"Yes, you do. Secrets are sometimes hidden." She ran a hand along the top of the rack, her fingers drifting over the hooks that held each whip and blade like she was pleased by the feel of them.

"I was sixteen when my father died. He didn't exactly tell me the nitty-gritty about his research."

"Maybe not that you remember. Maybe you just need encouragement." She lifted a bullwhip, shook the long length of it free until half its thong coiled on the floor like a snake. "This one is leather." She tapped the handle up the row of whips, coming to rest against one that was little more than a length of barbed chain. "This one is silver. Trust me, you won't like it if we play with this one."

My stomach heaved. I believed her. I'd seen what silver chains had done to Dan's wrists—damage that still hadn't completely healed several months later. And that was just from being bound in the chains. He hadn't been beaten with silver. "I don't know anything." This time it came out shaky and one of the vamps laughed. "Please, you have to believe me."

Cilla wrinkled her nose. "Believing you is no fun. And it doesn't get me the information I need." She began to coil the leather whip up into loops. Like someone preparing to use it. I stepped backward but one of the vamps grabbed me. Think, Ashley. *Think.*

The only thought I had was that it would be less painful to be beaten up by vamps than tied to that post and flogged by Cilla. I should fight.

Or I could stall. "What is it you think I know? Maybe if you gave me a clue, I could remember."

Cilla pursed her lips. "Maybe you could, maybe you couldn't."

"What does that mean? How can I tell you something if you don't think I can remember it?"

"Maybe it's something you don't know you know."

I laughed, I couldn't help it. "What, you think my father hypnotized me and hid some secret formula in my head?"

Cilla's face went still and I knew I'd hit home.

"Oh my God. I'm right. Are you crazy? My dad would never do anything like that."

"Your father was a cautious man, working on a project that would've been a major breakthrough in his field. All scientists protect their data." She tapped the handle of the whip against her thigh, studying me.

"How do you know what my father was working on?"

The whip flicked toward me, its tip whistling past my cheek with a hiss. "I'm asking the questions, not you."

"You are crazy," I repeated. "My dad might have encrypted his data or something but I think I'd remember being hypnotized." My mind whirled as I tried to work out what it was she wanted. It had to be something to do with the anti-vaccine. Something Dad had been researching. But I really had no memory of him ever telling me anything remotely connected to the vamp and were vaccines. Other than insisting we were vaccinated. I definitely didn't remember being hypnotized.

"It's possible to remove memories," Cilla snarled. "And your father wasn't trustworthy. He *lied*."

"No, he didn't."

The whip sang again and this time it didn't miss. My cheek went briefly numb then exploded with pain. Wetness trickled down my face as tears of pain flooded my eyes. The smell of blood told me it wasn't only tears. My knees buckled, only the vamps' hands bruising into my arms kept me upright.

"Your father was a liar. And others paid the price for his lies. I will find what he hid."

"You'll have to kill me before I'll tell you anything," I spat back. The wolf inside me snarled, anger burning away some of the pain.

"Oh, I'm not going to kill you," Cilla said calmly. "I'm just going to make you wish I would."

"You're going to wish you had, if you don't."

"Brave words, little puppy." She considered me coolly for a moment then nodded. "Strip her."

I exploded upward as they moved toward me, wrenching my arms free of the vamp holding me and using the momentum of the move to spin me and power a blow to the head of the next closest one. An answering blow slammed into my back and I spun again, moving on instinct to punch and kick as four assailants moved against me. But one against four isn't good odds. Especially when the one is barefoot, half blind from a swollen face and recovering from being drugged. Enough of their blows landed to hurt me. Hurt me a lot and finally a fist to the side of my head made me see stars as I hurtled toward the floor.

Four vamps piled on top of me and by the time I had managed to ride out the pain driving through me in sickening waves, my hands and feet were tied with several layers of rope and leather. They dragged me upright and hung my hands over a hook in one of the walls, so my toes barely scraped the floor.

"That was stupid," Cilla said as she approached me. She drew a knife out of the sheath and proceeded to cut the clothes from my body. She wasn't too careful about it either, the blade scoring along my ribs in the process. The burn of silver nearly made me black out. When my vision cleared, Cilla was watching me with the vamps ranged behind her. Hunger shone in their eyes.

"Now, let's try this again," Cilla said. She ran the back of her hand along my uncut cheek, touching me just hard enough for the metal of her rings to sting my face like salt water poured on a cut. "You're going to talk one way or another."

"I. Don't. Remember."

"I know that. So here's my proposal. I need what's in your head and you're going to give it to me. So you can let me thrall you now or the boys and I can hurt you until you're too weak to resist me. Your choice."

And after she got whatever it was she was after, I'd be dead. That much was clear. Some choice. The thought of letting Cilla rummage through my head made me want to puke but survival had to be my priority.

"Don't think too long, puppy," Cilla said. Her hand slid down my body, her ring lighting little fires under my skin everywhere they touched. She paused when she reached my pubic hair and I twisted away from her. "There's more than one way to hurt someone," she said looking pleased. "I could let the boys here fuck you. They like it rough. And we have some lovely silver toys."

This time, I did retch but apparently there was nothing left in my stomach to come up. God. I wanted to be strong, wanted to tell her to go to hell, but my body overrode my mind, the fear growing and growing until it overwhelmed me. I was shaking now, trembling and ice cold. No one wants to find out they're a coward. Everyone likes to think they'd be the one to withstand the pain, not give up the information but it's not so easy when your body is all too familiar with how much it will hurt. The survival instinct runs deep. Deeper than almost everything else.

"I'll let you see Rhianna, after," Cilla whispered in my ear. "She's been asking for you."

Rhi. How could I have forgotten Rhi? "Will it help her? What you're looking for?" I hated the way my voice shook, how small it sounded but I had to know.

Cilla smiled, fangs gleaming. "Yes. Yes, I hope it will."

God. I could save Rhi. If what was in my head meant that she wouldn't be so dangerous, wouldn't turn people with a single bite, then she could have a life. And there wouldn't be any more like her to put human-supernatural relations at risk. It could stop so much pain. Even if it cost me everything.

I opened my eyes. "All right."

Chapter 16

CILLA CROONED IN DELIGHT, "GOOD GIRL." She pulled the rings from her fingers one by one then pressed her hands to each side of my face. My vision swam again as she bumped the cut on my cheek and she made a soothing noise and bent and pressed her lips to the wound. I shuddered at the touch of her flesh against mine and the ache of my face grew worse.

I blinked back tears as Cilla straightened, her dark eyes huge in her pale face. "Look at me," she said softly. "Look right here."

I obeyed, even though every instinct I had screamed not to. But then, just as I felt myself start to fall into the darkness, I heard Ani's voice in my head. One single word.

Shield.

I couldn't help it. Suddenly the picture of me bathed in the moon's glow zapped into life in my head, the white light brightening until it formed a solid sphere around me. This time the mental image wasn't just me. There was a wolf curled at my feet.

Cilla pulled back with a snarl of frustration. "No wolf tricks now. Stop that."

I tried to obey but the light refused to dim and the wolf

just looked up at me with a doggy grin. I laughed stupidly. "I can't."

Cilla's hand grabbed my chin, fingernails digging into me. "I said *stop*." She pulled back and held out a hand. One of the vamps passed her a whip and pain sliced across my stomach as she struck me, once, twice, three times in rapid succession.

The shield didn't falter.

"I'm sorry," I said, trying to control the mix of elation and hysteria bubbling through me. "I didn't mean it." My stomach burned as the muscle tensed. I didn't want to look down and see what she'd done to me.

The whip slashed my face again, lighting a line of fire just below the existing cut.

Cilla's eyes narrowed. "Shields can be broken, puppy. You wouldn't enjoy it though." She drew back the whip again.

That didn't sound good and I tried again to dissolve the image in my head. No good. Another slash, this time the other side. I screamed and tears started pouring from my eyes. The salt water sliding down my face made the pain even worse.

"Cilla!" Smith's voice snapped through the room.

Cilla turned with a snarl. Smith crossed the room and put a hand on the whip.

"She won't be able to help if you kill her."

For some reason Smith intervening made the tears flow harder. I gulped and tried to blink my eyes clear while the wolf in my head prowled around, lips curled back in a soundless snarl.

Cilla drew back as though she could see the picture as clearly as I could. "Fine. We'll try this again later. In the meantime, I'll let the boys here give you some encouragement toward being more cooperative." She tossed the whip to the nearest vamp and spun on her heels, heading for the door.

As it closed behind her with a slam, Smith started to untie me. I stayed upright until his hand brushed my stomach and then my body finally cooperated by letting me pass out.

When I woke up, I was lying on the floor back in my cell and I hurt.

A lot.

Everywhere.

I swallowed and tried to open my eyes. That hurt too.

"You need to change," Smith's voice said from somewhere above me. "I've done what I can but you need to change."

I doubted I could summon the energy. "Can't," I mumbled.

"Try," he said. "Cilla's losing patience. You need to heal. And you need food. You can eat more as a wolf."

The thought of food made my stomach cramp. Which was just another sort of pain. Pain that changing might stop. I gritted my teeth, and focused inward. It hurt. Hurt more than the first time I'd changed. Which I didn't think was right and probably meant I was injured worse than I thought.

But the pain dissipated slowly, leaving me merely aching, and I managed to roll onto my stomach and push myself upward until I was sitting on my haunches. My side burned worst of all and I whined softly, fighting the urge to bend and lick the wound where Cilla had cut me with the silver knife.

"Good," Smith said.

My hackles rose at the sound of his voice. I looked upward. To wolf eyes, he looked tall—like all humans—but he also looked vulnerable. I knew I could crush his throat with a bite and a growl rumbled through me.

Without blinking, Smith pulled out a gun and aimed it at me. "Silver bullets," he said calmly. "So don't do anything stupid, Ms. Keenan." He nudged something with his foot and I realized there was another smell in the room beside human and antiseptic and fear.

Meat. Steak. And lots of it.

Smith's foot nudged the tray again and he stepped backward as I walked cautiously forward. The steak smelled divine.

It was even cooked, if you want to call rare and still oozing blood, cooked.

My stomach rumbled loudly and I couldn't stop myself, I devoured the contents of the tray in about one minute flat, gulping down pieces of meat like I hadn't eaten in days.

Which, for all I knew, I hadn't.

When I'd finished, I sat back, keeping my eyes on Smith.

"Change back," he said.

That made sense. Another change meant more healing. And I was far more comfortable dealing with Smith in human form. For one thing, I could talk.

I shimmered back to human form and ended up lying on the floor, breathing heavily. The aches—even the cut along my side—had eased back another few notches in the pain stakes. I was, amazingly, still hungry. I started to stand but Smith lifted his gun and I froze.

Smith tossed me a robe with his free hand and I put it on carefully, trying to avoid my sore spots.

"There are more clothes on the bed when you're ready," he said.

I pulled the robe tighter, wincing a little as my side stung. "Happy?" I asked.

"You should have done what she asked you to," he said, holstering his gun. He looked troubled.

Was he actually feeling sorry for me? It was hard to believe but I didn't want to waste the chance if he was. "Believe me, I tried," I said. "Can I ask you something?"

He shrugged.

"What is it you're looking for?"

"A piece of your father's research."

I nodded, I'd worked that much out. I considered Smith for a moment. I doubted he was going to tell me much more but it was worth a try. "Why are you doing this? Helping her? Why would you want to create a vampire that can turn people with a bite? Can't you see what it will do to us? You're human.

Why would you want to create something that could wipe out your own race?"

"That's why I need your father's research," he said.

"I don't understand. Why do this at all?"

His mouth twisted.

"Look, Cilla is going to kill me, we both know that. So at least tell me what I'm dying for."

"I can't." Again actual emotion showed in his eyes. This time I could even tell what it was. Pain. And regret. "I owe her."

Can't? That could mean won't. Or it could mean something I hadn't actually considered before. Smith might just be under Cilla's control. Just because he walked and talked didn't mean he hadn't been thralled. I shook my head. "What could you have done to owe her this much?"

He shook his head. "You wouldn't understand." He turned and reached for the door handle. "I'll get them to bring more food. But you should do what Cilla wants."

"Just tell me," I yelled as he closed the door.

And maybe he'd forgotten about werewolf hearing, or maybe he didn't care but before he walked away, I heard him say, "I killed her daughter."

* * *

Smith's words were still ringing in my head when they came for me again. He'd killed Cilla's daughter? How? When? And what did killing a child have to do with creating vampires who were infectious?

None of it made any sense.

The vamps that opened the door to my cell looked disappointed to find me dressed and standing. I was beginning to assign them names in my head. Butch was the blond one who had the good right hook and his darker buddy was the one who liked the whip. I called him Frank. Because it was easier to act tough around a guy called Frank than a vamp with a taste for leather.

Both of them were going to wish they'd never had names at all if I ever got some time alone with them.

"Hello, boys," I said with more bravado than I felt. "Where's crazy Cilla?"

"Waiting for you," Butch said with a sneer. "Come here."

I walked over obediently. I knew all too well that the two of them could beat me to a pulp and laugh while they did it. I was saving myself for another round of Ashley versus the crazy lady, and trying to figure out a way to get out of that alive.

We made the familiar trek through the hallways and then I was shoved through another doorway.

I'd expected Cilla and she was there. But she wasn't alone. Rhianna stood beside her, dressed in a floral sundress with her hair tied back in a ponytail. She looked completely normal. I just stared at her for a moment, happiness sweeping through me.

"Rhi," I said stupidly. "You're okay."

Cilla smirked at me and I came back down to earth with a thump. Whatever I was here for, it wasn't going to be fun.

Rhianna looked pale, her eyes too bright against the lack of color in her face. "Ashley. What are you doing here?" She looked from me to Cilla, frowning.

"Ashley is helping us with our project, dearest. Remember I told you about the project?"

Rhi's face cleared. "I remember. It will make us all better."

Fuck. What had Cilla been filling her head with?

"That's right, so you have to help me, remember what I explained?" Cilla gestured to the vampire holding me. "Bring her over here."

He pushed me forward then forced me into a seat, strapping my arms down.

Rhi was biting her lip, looking from me to Cilla. "I don't

understand," she said. "Why is she tied up? Ashley's my friend."

I smiled at Cilla, figuring she wasn't about to beat me up in front of Rhi, and then focused on Rhianna. "Rhi, you need to listen to me. Whatever she's asking you to do, don't. She's not a good person. Your parents wouldn't want you to do this."

Rhi's face crumpled and she rubbed her head, as if trying to remember something. "My parents. My parents are dead. Cilla is taking care of me. I've been sick, you know."

My heart sank. I don't know what Cilla and Smith had done to Rhianna but they'd clouded her memory somehow. Or maybe that was the effect of the change. Either way it wasn't good news for me.

"Your parents are alive," I said. Cilla stared at me, her expression carefully neutral but fury clear in her eyes. The vamp behind me shifted slightly and I tensed. Cilla's eyes burned but she didn't act. She was holding back. Which meant I was right. She wasn't ready to do anything to me in front of Rhi. Not yet. So Cilla couldn't be certain she had Rhi completely under control.

Rhi looked from me to Cilla, biting her lip. "My head hurts," she whispered. "I don't remember."

Cilla put an arm around her. "That's okay, Rhianna. You're probably just hungry. Why don't we get you something to eat?" She looked at me, fury turning to triumph. "Nice fresh blood, that's what you need."

I swallowed hard as Rhianna's expression grew avid. She licked her lips. "Fresh?" she said hopefully.

"Oh yes," Cilla said. "It tastes much nicer than that nasty stuff they gave you in the hospital."

"They hurt my mouth," Rhi said. She turned to me, frowning. "Ash, you let them hurt me."

I gritted my teeth, bit back the instinct to curse Cilla and forced myself to sound calm. "Sweetie, no. We didn't know you were allergic to the manufactured blood. It was an accident."

Cilla grinned at me. It was clear she thought she'd won this round. I heard the door open behind me, and footsteps approached from behind. I twisted my body around as far as I could with my arms strapped to the chair. The new vamp had his hand around a chain, leading the man at the other end— though man might be a stretch, the guy looked like he was maybe seventeen or eighteen. He still had that lanky not quite filled out look about him. He wore nothing but black boxer briefs and a dreamy expression.

Like he'd been *thralled*.

"You can't do this," I said as I realized what Cilla was about to do. It was beyond cruel to give Rhianna a taste for feeding from a human. Not when her bite was unsafe. Of course, if they intended for her to kill her prey, that wasn't such an issue. Nausea burned up my throat. If she killed someone, there was no turning back. Even if I got her out of there, she'd have to live with the consequences. "Rhi, listen to me. Don't drink from him. It's not right."

Rhi looked at me and, just for a second, her eyes swam with terror, as though the real Rhianna had surfaced for a moment. Then she blinked and her eyes burned bright with nothing more than need. "I'm hungry."

She turned, watching Cilla as the vampires fastened the man's hands into cuffs bolted to the wall. He didn't struggle at all. Definitely thralled. Or drugged, maybe. And while vampires fed from humans all the time—humans who volunteered and consented—I doubted that he'd agreed to what was happening here.

"No!" This time it was a yell. "Rhi, no. Listen to me. Think about it. You don't want to do this. Remember Julie. Remember Tate. This is what he did."

Rhi's head twisted back toward me. "J-Julie?"

"Your sister. Remember Julie. She was killed. By a vampire."

"Shut her up," Cilla snapped and the vamp behind me, clamped a hand over my mouth. I struggled and tried to bite him but all that earned me was a choking trickle of vamp blood in my mouth, making me want to retch. His hand didn't move.

Rhi, if anything, had turned paler. "Julie," she said softly. "Julie died."

Cilla scowled. "Don't think about that, dear." She gestured at Rhi. "You are hungry, aren't you?"

Rhi swallowed hard. The tip of her tongue brushed her lips as she looked from Cilla to the man hanging from the wall. When she made no move, I thought maybe I'd gotten through to her but then her head turned toward me. Her eyes had gone cold and expressionless like Cilla's.

"I'm very hungry," she said.

Cilla smiled and walked over to the man. "Of course, you are." She pulled out her knife and gripped one of his arms. One quick slash and blood started dripping from his wrist. I could smell it, strong and warm. I knew Rhi could too.

Cilla dipped a finger in the red, brought it to her lips. "Mmmm. Tasty."

Rhi took a step toward her.

I wrenched my head free of the vamp's grip. "No." One last try. "Rhi, don't do this."

Her head turned back and she smiled, for a moment looking just like her sister. Then she flowed toward Cilla in one of those too-fast-to-follow vamp moves. One second she was near me, the next she was standing by the chained man. As she reached for his arm, I closed my eyes. I didn't want to watch. But then almost immediately, I knew I had to. I had to bear witness.

Cilla's eyes met mine and she raised an eyebrow, as if daring me to do something. Not that I could.

Rhi sucked avidly at her victim's wrist, heedless of the blood spattering her face. Cilla watched her with an expression close to pride. When Rhi's gulps slowed, Cilla flicked the knife again and another cut opened on the guy's chest above his heart. Rhi plunged her face against his chest.

"That's right," Cilla crooned. "Isn't that good?"

I swallowed hard, fighting bile and tears as I watched the wild thing my friend had become feeding. Her victim's skin grew paler, his breathing coming in gasps. The fact that he didn't move or struggle—that he seemed to enjoy what was being done—made watching even harder.

Because I knew better. I'd been thralled. I knew that, even though he might be enjoying what was happening, might even find it pleasurable, there was some part of him, deep inside that was still free and knew what was happening. Some part that knew he was going to die. Some part screaming for help.

Help I couldn't give. My eyes filled with tears and I blinked them back furiously, curling my hands into fists as sorrow and rage burned in my stomach.

"Not so fast," Cilla said. "You don't want to miss the best part."

Rhi pulled her head back, frowning. Blood stained her mouth and her eyes blazed savage blue. Nothing like the Rhi I knew.

Cilla dragged the knife up the pale flesh of the man's chest, using it to carve a trail through his skin, moving up between his collarbones and around to his neck. "The neck dear—" The knife, hovered where his carotid beat too slowly against his skin"—it's always sweetest from the neck."

"You'll kill him," I gasped as Rhi's hand traced the same path as the knife. "Rhi, don't."

But she didn't hear me. Or didn't care if she did. Her gaze stayed locked on Cilla, like a snake charmed by a flute. Only this was more like the snake doing the charming.

As Rhi bent to drink, I struggled against the vamp holding

me. The man's pulse was fading, harder to hear over the rapid beat of Rhi's heart and the roar of horror in my head. If Rhi drank much longer he'd die. Of course, if she stopped, he'd become a vampire. One as dangerous as she was to the human population.

I didn't really know which was worse. But I didn't have to choose because suddenly there was no sound from his heart at all and he slumped in the chains.

Dead.

Rhianna straightened with a smile, wiping her mouth with the back of her hand. "Any more?" she asked.

I leaned to the side and vomited all over the floor.

Cilla laughed as I heaved. "Such a squeamish wolf," she said. "I'm sure you've killed before. In fact, I *know* you have."

"Not people," I managed between retches. "I'm not a murderer."

"Really?" Cilla asked. "So you don't consider killing a vampire to be murder?"

Rhi sucked in a breath and Cilla's smile widened. "Because you have killed vampires, haven't you?" She put an arm around Rhi's shoulders. "Rhianna, dear. Are you sure Ashley's your friend? After all, she doesn't think vampires are people. That it doesn't matter if you kill them."

"I never said that!" But it was too late. I watched Rhi's face shut down as she looked at me and huddled closer into Cilla.

"Monsters," she whispered and Cilla's laugh rang around the room, slicing into my skull like the sound of a thousand mirrors shattering.

Cilla held Rhianna close, stroking her hair. "It's okay," she crooned softly, making my bile rise all over again. "Ashley needs your help. It's what's in her head that makes her do these things. Remember what I told you? How you could help her? Remember what you did before?"

Rhi glanced at the corpse hanging from the wall. "I made him happy."

My stomach heaved again. Rhi had thralled him? I stared at her, wondering if there was anything left of Rhi inside that I could get to. If I could bring her back to herself, then maybe I could still save her.

Cilla nodded and drew Rhi back to face me. She shot a glance at Butch and he came around from behind me and busied himself taking down the body.

"Burn that," she said when he picked up the corpse and hoisted it over one shoulder.

I guess Cilla didn't want a body hanging around. It might give Rhi a chance to think about what she'd done. Right now, she'd done things the way Cilla wanted, but I wasn't convinced that she hadn't just been pushed right off the edge altogether. A mind—even a vampire's mind, I figured—can only take so much trauma before it shatters.

Rhianna had been balanced over the abyss before Cilla came along.

I tried not to shudder as Butch walked past me and one of the man's dangling arms brushed my shoulder. I couldn't afford to lose it. Not with my life and Rhi's at stake. I kept my eyes on Cilla and Rhi, waiting for whatever was going to happen next.

"Now, Rhi. Ashley's going to let you make her happy. Aren't you, Ashley?" Cilla's hand rested on the knife hilt for a moment. I got the message. Play along.

Easier said than done.

Being thralled by Rhi wasn't any more appealing a prospect than being thralled by any other vampire. Particularly not the Rhi standing next to Cilla, staring vacantly at me. The one who'd just drained the life out of someone without the slightest speck of remorse.

My skin crawled at the memory.

Maybe it would be like Marco, I told myself. When he'd been in my head, I'd felt safe.

Safer than anybody else other than Dan had ever made me feel.

Dan.

No.

I couldn't afford to think about him. Couldn't wonder if the Taskforce agents were riding to my rescue.

Couldn't rely on them.

All I could do was deal with what was in front of me. Wishing for Dan would only make me weaker.

I had to be strong.

"How will I know what I'm looking for?" Rhianna asked.

"You will," Cilla said confidently. "Remember, you told me Ashley had something in her head. Something hidden. Remember how you heard it?"

My head jerked up at the words. Rhi had been the one to tell Cilla about this thing in my head.

I closed my eyes, wishing I could just make everything around me disappear through sheer force of will. Where was a portable black hole when you needed one? Somehow knowing Rhi was helping Cilla and Smith was worse than everything else they had done to me.

"I can't hear it now," Rhi said, sounding puzzled.

"Just be patient," Cilla said. She moved toward me and tangled her fingers in my hair, forcing my head back.

"Look at me," she said quietly.

I did what she wanted, wondering why she was bothering to whisper. Vamp hearing being what it was, Rhianna would hear regardless.

Cilla's eyes were deep pools of malice. "Don't mess with me this time, puppy. What I did before was just a taste. No wolf tricks. You let the girl look."

I nodded, or rather moved my head the inch or so up and down I could without yanking the hair from my head. I didn't know if I could do what she was demanding. Raising my shields had been beyond my control last time. I didn't know how to stop myself, to let myself open to mind-rape.

The one thing I did know was that I couldn't not shield when I was so scared.

I took in a deep breath then another. "I need a minute," I said, hoping Cilla would believe me. Her grip on my hair loosened and she stepped back.

"One minute. Don't try anything."

I nodded and focused on breathing. In. Out. Slow. Nothing but the breath. When my heartbeat started to settle, I tried to think of something to keep the fear at bay.

Slowly Bug's face formed in my head, blue eyes smiling at me. My heart clenched. Aunt Bug. God, what I'd give to feel her arms around me right now.

My pulse started to speed again and I had to let go of the longing to be with Bug, to be safe, and focus on the memories. I let my mind linger on each line of Bug's face, summoning the scents I associated with her. Lavender. Roses. Hot, steaming tea. Olives and gin and vermouth.

Rich dark brownies.

My mouth curved upward. The scents of home and images of Bug ran through my head and I wrapped them around me like a blanket.

Rhi was part of that. Part of Caldwell. She'd grown up there just like me. The same places and people formed the bedrock of her memories. It would be okay. I could let her in. I opened my eyes, focused on Rhi's face, on my memories of her as a small girl, tagging along behind Julie and me.

"Okay," I said. "I'm ready.

Chapter 17

"RHIANNA, GO TO ASHLEY," Cilla said.

I tried to block out her voice. I wanted to think of Rhi and no one else. Rhi and home. I kept my eyes on Rhi, trying to lose myself in the sunny happy colors of the flowers on her dress.

Rhi came toward me, biting her lip again. "I still can't hear her."

"Put your hands on her head."

Rhi's hands were light, her touch gentle, unlike Cilla's. It was a struggle not to jerk away, to stay still and breathe. I breathed in the familiar smell of Rhi's. Drank in flowers and soap. Ignored the blood and fear.

"There's too much noise," Rhi said fretfully. "I can hear everyone."

Cilla sighed. "Focus on Ashley."

"Doesn't she need to be able to see my eyes?" I asked. Rhi stood to one side of me. With my hands strapped to the table, it was about the only place she could stand. "If you untie my hands, she can stand in front of me."

"Do you think I'm stupid?" Cilla said. "If I let you go, you'll try something."

"No." I mentally crossed my fingers behind my back. Thinking of home had given me the faintest glimmer of an idea. A way to reach Rhi. "No, I'll let Rhi do this, I promise."

And if it didn't work, then all bets were off. I'd do my damnedest to rip Cilla's head from her body, and to hell with the consequences.

"Untie her," Rhi said. Her voice was commanding and Cilla and I both blinked at her. "She'll be good. I can tell."

That seemed to convince Cilla. I tried to think obedient thoughts as she untied my hands and shoved the table back so Rhi could stand in front of me.

I summoned the images of home again as Rhi's hands cupped my face. Her eyes were gentle sunny blue, just like Julie's had been. I focused in on them until it felt like the whole world melted away into an endless summer sky.

Blue surrounded me, flowed through me, around me. It wasn't warm or cold, just blue. I let myself float in it and nothing stirred in my brain, no glow of white light or black wolf appearing to fight Rhianna off.

Blue started to steal through my brain, sliding gently. I felt myself slip deeper and fought to hold on. If my plan was going to work I had to try now.

"Rhi?" I thought. "Can you hear me?"

"Yes." Rhi's voice echoed through the blue. "Ash, where are we?"

"It's okay," I said. "I want to show you something."

"Ssh. I'm looking for something. I can feel it. It's just a little farther."

The blue grew a little darker, closing around me.

I dug my imaginary fingers into it, holding on. "I'll show you that, too. But there's something else you need to see."

"What?" She sounded curious. Hope pulsed through me. This just might work.

I summoned the image of a mirror in my head. "Can you see yourself?" I filled the image with the Rhianna I'd just seen in the room with Cilla. Looking confused and uncertain. One with drops of blood staining her dress.

"I see. Ash, is that me?" Her voice shook a little. She sounded lost.

It was up to me to help her find the way home. "It's one side of you. Can I show you what I see?"

"O-okay."

I let the mirror clear and started pulling memories to mind as fast as I could. All my memories of Rhianna, from the first moment I'd seen her as a newborn to the way she looked standing on the steps of the town hall before the memorial service. Happy. Smiling. Laughing.

I heard her gasp in my head and redoubled my efforts. "This is you, Rhi. This is your life. Remember this." I shoved memories at her. Julie and me playing in the yard, having a tea party with Rhi and her dolls even though we thought it was lame, her mother baking cookies, her room in their house with its pictures of boy bands and gymnastics trophies. The flowers in the Anders' front yard. The flag flying over the portico of Caldwell High.

"Remember," I begged her. "Rhi, don't you remember?"

Suddenly the memories stopped as if someone had slammed a door on them. Instead, an image of Rhi in her pink dress appeared in my mind.

"I remember," she said. Her face filled with horror. "Oh, Ash, I remember. What did I do?"

"Rhi, listen to me. We can get out of this if you help me. You have to find what Cilla is looking for. You have to give it to her. But then you have to remember who you are. And you have to help me. I can get you out if you trust me."

Tears ran down her face and around me the blue darkened further until I was surrounded by swirling indigo. "I killed him. I killed that guy."

"It wasn't you," I said soothingly. "It will be okay."

"I killed him."

"Rhi!" It was a shout in the stillness. "*Concentrate.* Cilla will kill us both if we screw this up. I need you to trust me."

"I trust you."

"Then listen to me. Can you find what she wants? The thing you saw in my head at the hospital?"

She cocked her head to one side, like she was listening. "I think so."

"Okay, that's good. Because whatever it is, I think it can help you. But you can't let Cilla know you have it yet."

"She'll know."

"She won't know. You're stronger than her. She couldn't get into my head. You can. So you can keep her out too."

Rhi took a breath. I felt it shudder through me like a wave breaking. "Okay, I'll try," she said. "But if I find the information, then what?"

"We need to get out of here. Dan and the FBI will be looking for us but we can't wait for them. And we can't get away with so many vampires around. I need you to get Cilla to get rid of them."

"How?" The blue lightened a little but it still swirled in agitation. I tried to think soothing thoughts at it until the swirls eased back. Which was good because they were making me seasick.

I outlined my plan quickly, knowing if we took much longer—though it was hard to tell exactly how much time had passed—that Cilla might just get suspicious.

When Rhi said she understood, I tried not to sigh with relief, not knowing what my body would do if I did. Cilla couldn't know what had just happened.

"Okay, then we have a plan. Now, let's find whatever the hell is in my head and you can get out of here."

Rhi's image wavered then solidified again. "Ash?" She sounded sad.

"Yeah?"

"Are we really going to get out of here?"

"I'll do my best," I promised. "And don't forget, the cavalry are coming too. Hey—there's a thought—do you think you could reach Jase?"

"Jase?"

"My assistant, do you remember him?" Rhi had visited me a few times in Seattle. I pictured Jase in one of his suits; trying to remember the last time Rhi would've seen him.

"I can try," Rhi said. "I don't know..." She hesitated.

"What is it?"

"Ash, will it really be okay?"

"Cross my heart and hope to—" I cut off the thought. "I mean, of course it will."

"I don't want to be a vampire," Rhi said softly.

The blue pulsed and sadness rolled over me. Rhi's sadness. I felt in my bones her revulsion at what she'd become. At what she'd done. And I shivered because, deep down, I didn't know if everything would be okay.

Because nothing could change what she'd become. Or what had happened. She had to choose to live with it.

Or make another choice.

No. I thrust the thought away. We'd both survive and Rhi would adjust. No other outcome was acceptable.

"Everything is going to be okay. Remember I love you and so do lots of other people," I repeated, doing my best to hug her mentally. "Let's get on with it."

For just a moment, I felt ghostly arms go around me. "I love you too, Ash," Rhi said gently and then the blue surrounded me completely and sucked me under.

* * *

When I came back to myself, Rhi was screaming. My heart leaped into my throat before I remembered the plan. At least, I hoped this was the plan.

"What did you do?" Cilla hissed at me as she reached for Rhi.

I shook my head, trying to clear the fog from my brain. "I didn't do anything. I remember Rhi holding my head and then there was floating and then—"

"Idiot." Cilla gathered Rhi closer as the screams redoubled. I had to hand it to Rhi, she could give any horror movie heroine you cared to name a run for her money.

"What is it?" Cilla said anxiously. "Rhianna, what's wrong?"

"My head," Rhi moaned. "It's so noisy." She pressed her hands to her ears. "Too many voices. Make them stop."

"Make who stop?" Cilla said.

Rhi glared. "I can hear you all. Spinning in my head. Monsters. They drown out the secrets."

"You didn't find it?" Cilla's tone sharpened and I fought not to smile.

Rhi screamed again, twisting in Cilla's arms. "Make them stop. It hurts."

Cilla nodded. "Of course. Hush now. I'll send them away and you can try again."

"Monsters. They're hurting me."

"Get out," Cilla snapped. I realized she was talking to the other vampires. "Take the wolf with you."

Shit. I hadn't planned on this. I needed to stick with Rhi if we were going to get free. But I couldn't protest or I might just give us away. I let the vamps steer me toward the door and tried not to be too obvious about catching Rhi's eye.

Cilla was focused on Rhi, rubbing her back like a mother soothing a fretful child. Rhi's eyes met mine but there was no hint of recognition. No hint that this was all an act.

But I had to pray it was and trust that she was just making sure Cilla believed her. I just had time to mouth 'remember' at her before I was hustled out of the room and back to my cell.

* * *

I'd barely had time to sit down when the door to the cell slammed open and Cilla stormed in. I scrambled to my feet but she was on me before I could get my balance. She backhanded me savagely and I crashed back onto the bed.

"What did you do to her?" she screamed.

I coughed and spat blood as I pushed myself up to a sitting position. "I told you I didn't do anything."

"Don't lie to me, bitch." With one yank she flipped the bed upward and over. I hit the floor hard. The bed came crashing down on me. I heard something snap and screamed as pain flashed down my side.

Change.

I did it without thinking. In a blink I was in wolf form and scrabbling free of the bed. Cilla paused for a moment, looking surprised. I sprang for her but she moved too fast and I missed, sliding into the wall as my nails found no purchase on the tiled floor.

Cilla picked up a piece of the splintered bed. "Try that again." Her face twisted in fury.

I watched her, warily, growling a warning. She still had the silver knife in her belt. That was the biggest danger. I could survive being hit by anything else. Hopefully.

Behind me the door stood open. I couldn't hear anyone else outside but vampires could be pretty quiet and the scent of Cilla's rage made it hard to smell anything else.

Tension stretched as we stared at each other, and then Cilla shrieked and leaped at me again. I could only see a blur moving toward me, she was moving at full vamp speed now; not the smartest idea in such a small room. I launched myself in the other direction, not wanting to be between her and the wall when she hit.

Plaster buckled and smashed as she did but it didn't seem

to stop her. She whirled back to face me, brushing plaster dust from her clothes. "If you've—"

"Cilla, what are you doing?" Smith's voice came from the doorway.

"She did something." Cilla hissed. "Rhianna was fine and now she's screaming."

Smith looked at me then back to her. I heard his heart beating. Fast. Almost too fast for a human to bear. But his face stayed calm. "She's a werewolf. She doesn't have the sort of psychic powers vampires do. What could she do?"

"Rhianna is screaming!" Cilla's voice was near to a shriek again. "She hurt her."

"Sssssh," Smith said. "Calm down. Maybe Rhianna just wasn't ready to do what you asked. She's only a baby, you know."

I stared at him, wondering what the hell was going on.

"She's mine," Cilla said. "I made her."

"I know," Smith said. "Your baby. And nothing's going to happen to her."

Cilla's face twisted. "I can't lose another one." She snarled at me again. "She already killed Henry in Caldwell. And poor Tony. Look what happened to him." She reached for another piece of the splintered bed. "She's going to ruin everything. Let me kill her."

I hunched back into the corner.

Smith moved a little closer. He was brave, I had to give him that. If I'd been human there was no way I'd be walking toward the crazed vampire. "Cilla, love. Calm down. We still need Robert's formula, remember? Did Rhi get it?"

"No. I told you. This stupid wolf did something."

"Then we need to try again." He kept his voice low, soothing.

"But Rhi's hurt. She says her head hurts." Cilla bit her lip, looking torn.

"She's not used to being telepathic, maybe it does hurt. She needs time to learn control," Smith said. "Maybe——"

"There's no time," Cilla said. "You know they'll be looking for her." She jerked her head at me. "We can't have another setback." She dropped the piece of wood and I relaxed, just slightly. "We need to do this now."

"Do what?" Smith said, still in that low soothe-the-spooked-animal voice.

"Get Rhi to try again. You need to get everyone else out of here. Clear the building."

"I'm not leaving you alone with them," Smith said. "It's too risky."

"You'll do whatever the fuck I tell you to." This time Cilla's fury was directed at Smith. She came forward in a rush. In a second she had him bailed up against the wall, one hand squeezing his throat. "This is all your fault, Ned. *All of it*. You owe me. And you *will* do what I say. Hear me?"

Smith nodded, face purple.

"Good." She let go of him and he gasped then started coughing. I winced in sympathy. "Clear the building. You have an hour." She turned back to me. "Give me any trouble and I'll skin you," she said coolly.

Something in her tone made me certain she wasn't kidding.

She stalked out of the room, dragging Smith with her. I heard the door lock behind them and changed back to human form with a shiver, trembling from surplus adrenaline. I was starving again but somehow I doubted Cilla would be feeding me anytime soon.

So I focused on finding what shreds of clothing I could in the wreckage of the room, and waited for her to come back.

* * *

I waited for what felt like hours. And in the time I had to think, I could only come up with one conclusion. I had to kill Cilla.

She was the one driving this whole insane business, the one who was going to try and kill me.

The one who wanted to turn Rhi into a monster just like her.

By the time Cilla came for me, I'd made up my mind.

Her or me.

But when she finally flung the door open, she was carrying Smith's gun. For a moment she regarded me, eyes gleaming dark pools of nothing. Then the gun lifted, pointing straight at my head.

My heart went into overdrive. She was going to kill me. God. Dan. Rhi. God.

Then she moved her hand slightly to the right and fired. A chunk of wall exploded next to my face and the noise nearly deafened me.

I stared at her, too stunned to react as my ears roared and rang and she just smiled. "Just in case you think I'm not a good shot," she said. Then she motioned with the gun. "Now, come with me."

We marched down the hall, the still warm gun pressed into my back right at the point where it would blow my heart out if she fired.

Needless to say I didn't try anything.

"Stop."

I stopped.

Cilla opened a door and then pushed me through. It was the same room I'd been in before with Rhianna.

The scent of fear and blood and death filled the room, making my throat close.

Rhi sat in a chair, hands bound to its narrow metal arms. Her face was tearstained and she didn't look at me as Cilla and I entered. Another chair stood opposite hers.

"Sit down," Cilla said, poking the gun harder into my back.

I sat. Cilla slammed the door shut, dark hair wild around her head. She swiped a card at a reader pad on the wall and there was a thunking noise as the locks clicked home. Ice swirled around my stomach and arrowed up my spine.

Locked up all alone with a pissed off psycho vamp. Not my favorite situation.

But fortunately—or unfortunately—one I'd been in before.

"Are you okay?" I asked Rhi as I tried to think. We needed a plan. Time was running out.

The room was small and mostly bare. Dark industrial carpet lined the floor and a row of empty glass and wood cabinets stood along one wall. The window was covered with the same wooden shutters sealed with rubber as the room Smith had interrogated me in. The sort of cheap sun protection places that don't have many vamp visitors use. After all, why pay megabucks for the UV proof glass when wood and rubber do a good enough job for occasional use?

I strained my ears and nose but apart from the three of us, I couldn't hear or smell anybody else. Which meant maybe, just maybe, I might be able to make a move if I got a chance. I had no illusions about surviving. I doubted Smith and his guards had retreated too far but at this point I didn't really care. Freeing Rhi and taking Cilla down were all that mattered.

Rhi's eyes flickered to me briefly but she stayed silent.

"So, are you ready to cooperate?" Cilla asked. The hilt of her silver knife hung at her waist. My side burned in remembrance.

"I already cooperated," I said, stalling. My head throbbed in unison with my side, a combination of the leftover pain of Cilla throwing me across a room and the strain of screaming in my head for Jase whenever they left me alone. "I did what you asked."

"That's too bad for you." Cilla aimed the gun at me again.

I shivered. There was no point in hiding my fear from Cilla. I reeked of it as badly as the room and my heart was pounding so hard I was half surprised I hadn't passed out.

Cilla moved to Rhianna. She shoved the gun into the belt at her waist then put one hand on the knife hilt and the other on Rhi's head, stroking her hair. "Maybe I can find an incentive for you to try harder." The knife slid free with a hiss of leather.

I stared at it, trying to focus. Tired. I was so tired. Tired of fear and violence. Tired of loss and pain and sacrifice. I tried reaching for the energy of the moon but got nothing but a faint buzz. Which meant, only a few days past full, that it must be daylight. Otherwise I'd be able to feel the moon. I glanced at the shutters. If Rhi wasn't here, I could try and break them and fry Cilla where she stood. Screw letting her be brought in alive. I wanted her dead.

Cilla laughed. "So close and yet so far." She traced the blade down Rhi's cheek. Rhi stayed still, but her eyes met mine. There was no fight in the expression. No hope.

Nothing to indicate she remembered our plan or cared about it.

I looked again at the tears on her face and wondered if Cilla had tried some 'persuasion' on her as well.

I hoped not. Cilla appeared to have left sanity—at least anything I recognized as sanity—behind a long time but she did seem to be fixated on no one hurting her 'children.' Rhi fell into that category, if children meant vamps made with the assistance of Smith's drugs.

Still, I didn't like the way the knife pressed just a little too hard into Rhi's skin. After all, push a psycho too far and they snap. Then anything or anyone in their way was fair game. Tate had taught me that. My mouth tasted like dust, drier than ever. I swallowed painfully. "If you hurt her, you won't be able to get what you want."

"Maybe not. But I don't think she's really tried to find out." The knife paused, then pricked deeper. The sharp sour smell of vamp blood joined the other odors in the room. Rhi jerked her head, blood trickling down her cheek.

My hands curled tight, a growl rising in my throat. "I'm happy to let Rhianna try again, you don't have to hurt her."

Cilla's eyes narrowed then she smiled. "I knew you'd see sense." She beckoned me, black painted nails looking like razor blades. I edged my chair closer to Rhianna's. This close, Cilla's violet scent filled my nose. It felt cloying and sticky, like it was trying to climb down my throat and steal my breath. My stomach heaved.

"Kneel down, puppy," Cilla said. "Rhianna needs to look into your eyes."

I slid off the chair and knelt. The floor was hard under my knees, the cheap carpeting doing little to pad the concrete beneath. Cold seeped upward, exacerbating the tiny tremors in my legs.

"Good. Now, Rhianna. Let's try this again. No one else is here. It's nice and quiet, just the way you wanted."

Rhianna looked at me. Still nothing in her eyes to indicate she was working with me rather than with Cilla. Fingers of ice gripped my spine. Either Rhi deserved an Oscar or I was in trouble.

Rhianna's hands trembled as she put them on either side of my head, leaning forward so our faces were only inches apart. Her breath brushed my skin, cool and still carrying the faint scent of blood.

Another reminder that everything had changed.

Once again, I tried to relax, tried to think of something to keep me calm enough to let Rhianna in.

"Hurry up," Cilla said.

Her voice broke my concentration. I glanced upward to

find her staring down at us. The knife was back in its sheath, the gun tucked beside it. So close. It would only take a second to make a play for the gun. But I couldn't make a move. Not yet.

I needed Cilla to be relaxed and off guard. Right now, tension practically vibrated through her.

"Look at me," Rhi said softly.

I flicked my eyes back to hers, forced myself to let that summer sky color in and breathe as the world flowed away.

"Ash?" Rhianna's voice was quiet in my head and as I watched, she appeared in my mind. But not dressed in pink. This time she wore black. Severe, unrelieved black. Pants and shirt and shoes in a black so dark and dense it seemed to absorb the light around her. Her hair was scraped back from her face and black ringed her eyes as well like she'd been on a three day bender with a kohl pencil.

"You going goth?" I asked nervously.

She shook her head. "I want you to listen to me."

A chill stole over me. "I'm listening."

"I've been thinking about what you said. About how it's all going to be okay."

"It will be. Just trust me."

Another headshake. "No. No, it won't. And I don't want it to be. Ash, I don't want to live like this."

The ice spread out from my spine, enveloping every inch of me. My chest ached with the cold, pain numbing me. "What are you saying?"

"I don't want to be a vampire. So, if there's a way to take Cilla out, then take it. Don't worry about me."

Was it possible to be colder than freezing? I couldn't feel my body. Couldn't think either but I had to. Had to convince Rhi that she was wrong. "I'm not leaving you behind."

"I'm not asking you to leave me behind. I'm saying don't worry about me."

"Rhi, don't do this. My father's research, whatever's in my head, maybe it can fix you."

"Turn me back?"

I couldn't lie to her. Nothing was going to change her back into a human. "No. But they could make you a normal vampire. You'd be able to live. Lots of vamps are happy." That much was true, most vampires seemed content enough. Of course, those who weren't, at least the ones I'd met, fell more into the rabidly insane category.

"I can't drink the manufactured blood."

"Lots of vamps drink human blood without killing."

"I know." She sounded so lost. "But, Ash, you don't understand. I liked it. I liked killing that man, draining his blood. I'm a monster now."

Chapter 18

My heart twisted, cracked, and shattered. "No! No, that's not true. You're still you. You can control what you do."

"But I can't control what I am. I'm sorry, Ash. I know this isn't your fault. You have to try and get out of here."

"Not without you."

"Any way you can."

The blue surrounding me turned paler, the color of a glacier's heart, cold as the razored shards of pain and fear slicing through me.

"Promise me." Rhi's voice was fierce.

I hesitated and that icy blue tightened around me like a net of glass wrapping around my brain so I couldn't think, couldn't argue.

"*Promise me.*"

I had to do what she said. "I promise."

"Thank you." This time her voice sounded happy.

I was frozen. Numb. I had no idea what to say to her. How to convince her she was wrong. To show her she was loved. Or rather, I had a thousand words but my tongue was as frozen as the rest of me, stilled by Rhi's will. The blue dissipated like fog but the constraint and the cold remained. I opened my eyes.

Cilla was hovering next to us. "Did it work? Did it work?"

I shook my head, still trying to shake off the feeling of icy command from Rhi, to speak, to reach her. But I couldn't. "Ask Rhianna."

Rhi's eyes were closed. She looked like she was sleeping peacefully.

But when her eyes opened I knew she wasn't at peace. She looked sad. Beyond sad.

"Did you get it?" Cilla asked.

Slowly, Rhi nodded. "I think so. There's lots of numbers and words I don't understand."

Was she telling the truth? Had she actually found something in my head? Something that might help us figure out how Smith had done what he'd done?

Cilla grinned, then pulled the gun out of her belt. She aimed it at me yet again. The urge to run exploded through me but something held me in place. "Then we don't need her anymore, do we?"

Rhi's face went white. "What do you mean? How do you know I got everything?"

"I'll take the risk," Cilla said. Her finger started to tighten on the trigger and I tensed. Now or never. A silver bullet—and I didn't doubt that the gun was loaded with silver—at such close range would kill me if she hit my head or heart.

"No!" Rhianna screamed and lashed out at Cilla, knocking the gun from her hand. It flew across the room landing God-knows-where. I lurched sideways, free to move but unable to think what to do next.

Cilla wasn't so slow. The knife slid free of the scabbard with a hiss and she whirled on Rhi. "What are you doing?"

Rhi backed up but only a little. "Stopping you," she spat.

Cilla's shriek of rage almost deafened me. She lunged with the knife, aiming for Rhi's heart. Rhi's hand shot out, grasping Cilla's wrist, stopping the blade's plunge. The two vamps stood locked, muscles straining against each other. Evenly matched despite the differences in size. I hesitated, unsure how to help without risking Rhi.

"Ash, the window," Rhi cried.

"What?" Cilla and I spoke together.

"The *shutters*."

Cilla gasped. I surged to my feet, fighting the compulsion to do as Rhi said. "No!"

Rhi's voice sounded in my head. "Ash, this is my choice. And your chance. You know what you have to do."

I shook my head frantically. "I won't, I *won't*."

Cilla started to laugh and, as I watched, the blade descended a fraction closer to Rhi's throat. Rhi was weakening. If she lost, Cilla would kill us both, if I didn't kill her first.

"Never put your faith in a dog, Rhianna," Cilla said mockingly. "They always bite the hand that feeds them."

I twisted my head looking for the gun. But I couldn't see it. It must've slid under one of the cabinets lining the far wall.

I turned back to Rhi and made the mistake of looking into her eyes.

Blue ice blew through me like a blizzard and wrapped steel fingers into my mind. "Open the shutters," Rhi's voice roared. "Do it *now*."

I fought her, I tried. Tried to summon the wolf and the moonlight to cut off her terrible command. It didn't work. Even as I screamed in my head for her to let me go, my body moved to obey, heading for the window. "Rhi, no," I begged. "Don't make me do this."

Her grip didn't falter and her mental voice was calm. "It's either you or the sunrise, Ash. I'd rather it was you. If you love me, you'll do this."

Tears rolled down my face, half blinding me. My arms reached for the shutter release as I heard Rhi scream behind me and motion blurred in my peripheral vision.

"NOW, Ash!" Rhi screamed and I watched myself in

horror as I pulled the release and flooded the room with
sunlight.

Cilla wailed behind me as I fell to my knees by the
window. Rhi's voice said "Goodbye, Ash," in my head as her
hold on my mind released. I felt a blaze of heat like something had exploded and pushed myself to my feet, twisting to
face the vampires. Maybe, if I could just shield Rhi,
somehow—

But even as I turned, I saw the flames engulf them, saw
Rhi's face smile then twist in agony. Then the fire went white-
hot and there was a whomping noise as all the air was sucked
out of my lungs. I flew backward and hit the wall with a crash
of plaster.

Then all at once the flames vanished and there was
nothing but fine gray dust raining around me as I lay there,
sobbing like a baby.

* * *

Gray ash coated everything. It covered my skin, filled my nose
and mixed to sludge on my cheeks where my tears mingled
with my friend. I lay there and let it fall, unable to move as it
floated down on me.

An alarm started to sound in the distance and suddenly
water poured from the sprinklers in the ceiling.

I let it soak me. Unwilling to move or think or react.

Rhianna was dead.

And I had killed her.

My eyes burned as tears flowed without stopping. Rhi was
dead. Another loss.

I didn't want to get up. Was half-willing to let Smith come
back and do his worst but somewhere—after minutes or
hours, I couldn't tell—my survival instinct kicked back in.

"Move," I told myself. "Don't think, just move."

Smith would be back. If they hadn't seen the flames or

heard the alarm then they'd be back after however much time they'd agreed with Cilla.

I pushed to my feet, feeling a thousand years old. I skirted the charred patch of floor in the middle of the room, the twisted metal that was all that remained of the two chairs and ran for the door.

Locked.

And, I remembered suddenly, Cilla had had the keycard. The plastic keycard that no doubt had been vaporized when the two vampires burned. I was trapped.

Fuck and double fuck.

Think.

Okay. Don't panic. There was a gun here somewhere and a window. I scrabbled around in the wreckage of the room and the gods must've decided I deserved a break because my hand closed over the smooth metal of the gun.

"Move," I repeated, and forced myself back to the window. To my surprise, it looked out onto some sort of office park. There didn't seem to be anyone around but it definitely wasn't the middle of nowhere.

On the downside, I was on the second floor. And there was no fire escape. I looked down at the pavement, calculated the distance. Survivable for a werewolf.

It was getting through the glass that was going to hurt like a bitch. I just hoped it wasn't reinforced. It would just be my luck if the people who owned the building were too cheap to pay for UV glass but had sprung for double glazing.

Only one way to find out.

And that way was going to bring some attention to my location even if the fire hadn't.

I retreated to the far side of the room, aimed the gun and fired three times.

The bullets left three neat holes in the window, surrounded by a spider web of cracks. Not exactly the result I'd hoped for but it should've weakened the glass enough that what I was about to do would hurt a lot less. I didn't want to waste any more bullets.

"Don't think," I repeated one last time and then pushed away from the wall, picking up speed as I leaped and hurled myself through the window.

I'd been right.

It hurt like a son of a bitch. Glass sliced into my arms and legs but I barely had time to register the pain before the cement hurtled up to meet me.

My landing knocked the wind out of me and I wasted a minute or so trying to convince my lungs to remember how to breathe and my back that it hadn't snapped in two.

As soon as the air started flowing back into my body I forced myself to change. Wolf then back in rapid succession. I could run faster as the wolf but I couldn't carry a gun.

Changing helped the pain and stopped the bleeding but left me shaky.

I gritted my teeth and hauled myself up anyway, taking a moment to get my bearings.

The fire alarms still shrieked in the distance. Hopefully that meant there'd be emergency crews on their way. But Smith and his vamps could well beat them back. It was daylight but from the position of the sun, late afternoon. Once darkness hit, any advantage I had over the vamps was lost. I needed to move.

I scented the air, trying to pick a direction. I mostly got a dizzying rush of city air, full of tar and sun and rubbish and the weird air-conditioned smell of office buildings. But to the west, I got just the faintest hint of food. Something was cooking. Cooking meant people.

Who would no doubt be thrilled to be visited by a naked blood and ash-stained woman waving a gun but so be it. I forced myself into a run, feeling like every step was taken over by broken glass and burning metal as my muscles protested the effort.

My lungs were screaming by the time I rounded a corner and saw a burger joint. Thank God for junk food.

I burst into the restaurant, ignoring the startled screams and vaulted over the counter.

"*Phone*," I snarled at the pimply clerk staring at me in terror. "Phone," I repeated as she started to cry but then I heard someone behind me saying, "I have an emergency." I whirled and saw another clerk with a cell in his hand.

"Is that 911?" I waved the gun at his phone.

He nodded, face pale.

"Good. Give me the phone."

He held it out without protest and I snatched it. "This is Ashley Keenan. I'm with the FBI." I babbled out the identification code Dan had drilled into my brain to use if I ever had to call the emergency line as the operator squawked in protest. But her objections turned to professionalism just as quickly. Obviously the code thingy did its job. The next thing I knew, I was speaking to Esme.

"Ashley, thank God. Where are you?"

"I don't know." I pointed the gun at the clerk. "Where are we, kid?"

"M-m-m, Cedar Park," he stammered.

Well, what do you know? Seattle. "Thanks. Okay, I'm in a Burger Heaven in Cedar Park. Somewhere near an office park. But listen, I'm not staying here. Smith might be coming back and I'm not risking all these people getting caught in any crossfire. I'll be heading west. Hurry."

I handed the cell back to the kid and handed him the gun. "Call the police again. Lock the doors until they get here," I said. "Don't let anyone in until they show you a badge. Especially not any men with gray hair and glasses. Possibly driving a black van. Got it?"

He nodded again; staring at the gun like it might just go off in his hand.

"Don't use that unless you have to," I said. "Just stay inside. And I'm sorry if I scared you."

Then I started running again, bursting through the back door. West. I told Esme west. And this time, the wolf was going to be faster and safer. I changed and started running, taking a side street to stay out of view. I felt the hairs on the back of my neck tingling. Somehow I knew Smith wasn't far away. Even though his vamps were limited by the sunlight, I couldn't afford to let them catch me.

I bolted a couple more blocks, then slowed, springing over someone's front fence to get some cover as I got my bearings. I could feel the sun starting to sink, feel the moon growing stronger. God knows what time it really was. Somewhere behind me I heard sirens. Not just fire trucks but police cars.

The sound of safety.

If I could get to them.

Dan would be there. The need to see him suddenly outweighed everything else.

I leaped the fence again then started running back the way I'd come.

I almost made it. I could even see the police cars surrounding the Burger Heaven in the distance. One more block. But as I started to cross the road, I heard a car scream to a halt behind me. I glanced back over my shoulder.

A black van.

Just like the one the vamps had used in Caldwell.

Smith sat in the driver's seat.

His eyes met mine and I saw the exact moment when he realized the truth. That if I was free, then Cilla was probably dead. His face twisted into a snarl of rage and loss and hate.

The van's engine revved suddenly and I looked back to the restaurant. Between it and me was a street of small stores and office. All closed. No cover there. No yards to dodge into.

All I could do was run.

I sprang into motion, running for my life. The van's tires squealed as it came after me.

In the distance I saw a dark-haired man step in front of one of the police cars, saw him turn toward me and freeze.

Dan.

I ran faster, the road stinging my paws with each bound but I could hear the van gaining on me, the roar of its engine drawing closer, the hot stink of gasoline and metal sharper in my nose and mouth as I strained for each breath, each stride. Surely Smith wasn't crazy enough to drive into a wall of police? It was my only hope for rescue.

Even a werewolf can't outrun a car.

Or maybe they could.

I was halfway down the block and they hadn't caught me.

My lungs burned, each breath like acid. I heard Dan yell my name as he raised his gun.

And then a bullet scraped my shoulder from behind. I stumbled and rolled across the road and back to my feet, fire blooming along the bullet's path, the bite of it nearly as bad as the pain in my lungs. I willed myself into motion, stretching like a leopard, praying for speed, angling down the road headed for Dan.

The sound of the van had faded but the sound of gunfire didn't.

"Ash, no!" I heard Dan scream even as bullets lit sparks on the road around me.

"*Dan*," I thought, just as something tore through my side like a lightning bolt and tumbled me into darkness.

* * *

I woke up in hospital. Dan was holding my hand.

"We have to stop meeting like this," I croaked. Then I didn't get to say anything else for several minutes. I was too busy having the life kissed out of me.

"Easy," I joked when he finally let us come up for air. "You'll give me a relapse."

He turned pale and I hugged him tighter. "Hey, joking."

"Don't joke," he said hoarsely. "I thought I'd lost you."

I stroked his face. "Nah. I'm tough."

His eyes gleamed silver. Damp silver. Shit, I'd made him cry.

"Ash, I'm serious. I can't keep going through this."

"Well, you won't have to. That crazy vamp bitch is dead." I wasn't quite ready to explain how.

"We didn't get Smith," he said.

I bolted upright. "Excuse me?"

"Everyone was busy with you. He got away."

I fell back against my pillows. "Shit." But somehow part of me wasn't disappointed. Because, this way, I got to hunt the son of a bitch down myself.

"It's okay. I'll get him," Dan said.

I forced myself to sit up a little, wincing as my side stabbed with pain. "What's this 'I' business?"

"It's my job."

"I'm on the Taskforce too, you know."

His face turned grim. "You're not putting yourself in danger again."

"Excuse me?" Outrage turned my voice even rougher.

Dan heard it too. But his expression didn't change. He just nailed me with a 'don't push me on this' look. "I mean it, Ash. You're staying in the office from now on."

"Like hell I am. He killed Rhianna."

"Rhi's dead?"

I looked down; grief and rage roiling through me like a blow. *Rhi.* One more loss to chalk up to the vampires and Smith.

One loss too many.

"Yes. And if you think I'm not getting the bastard who caused all this, then you need to think again."

"I'm the Agent in Charge, I get to say who is on the case."

"And who says I need the Taskforce?" I flared.

Dan went still. "What's that supposed to mean?"

"I mean, I'm getting Smith." I folded my arms and glared at him.

"There are rules, Ashley."

"Screw the rules. Smith doesn't play by the rules."

"You don't want to be like him."

I stared at him, not knowing how to make him understand. Not without telling him the truth about Rhianna and the knot of guilt and grief tearing me apart. Not sure, even if I did tell him, that he could understand. Dan saw the world in black and white. Right and wrong.

But I'd learned a lot in the last few months. I didn't care so much about right and wrong and legalities. I cared about good and bad. About surviving. And there were all sorts of shades of gray involved in that.

And, as I stared into my favorite shade of gray—the silver of Dan's eyes—I wasn't sure that he'd be able to forgive me if I learned any more.

I closed my eyes. "I don't want to fight. I'm tired." I held out my hand to him. "Just be here when I wake up, okay?"

His fingers curled around mine. "I'm not going anywhere."

* * *

They released me from the hospital the next day. I had a new scar on my ribs from Cilla's silver knife but that was the only visible wound. The invisible wounds were something I didn't want to talk about.

Though, over the next week, it seemed like I wasn't getting much of what I wanted. Every man and his dog wanted to debrief me about what had happened. The Taskforce, Dan, the police, other random FBI personnel and even Ani and Sam.

And, even though I was sure there should be something in the relationship rules about nearly getting killed bringing two people closer together, my desire not to fight with Dan wasn't working either.

He kept trying to wrap me in cotton wool. Hardly let me out of the house. All we did was fight and make-up with frantic sex. But each time, the gap between the fight and the making up part seemed to get bigger.

Just like the gap I felt growing between us.

We fought about the Taskforce.

We fought about Smith.

We fought about Marco when I said I wanted him to be the one to try to relocate whatever it was that my father had stashed in my head. Dan flipped. I stood my ground. I trusted Marco. And I wasn't letting anyone else—not even a Taskforce vamp, rummage around in my head. In fact, I was particularly keen for it not to be a Taskforce vamp. Because then they'd find out all the things I didn't want Dan to know; about what happened to me and to Rhi.

Fighting about Marco brought us right back to our starting point and we fought about my blood debt.

"Christ, you won't cut me a break at all," I yelled as Dan started on another 'you trust a vampire more than me' rant. Really, living with an alpha wolf was a bitch. And I'm sure Dan thought the same about me.

"How can I cut you a break when you keep running to him for help?"

"I went to him to save your life." I was so sick of this argument. I was never going to win.

"And now you want to go to him again."

"He's not going to do anything to me. I want him to help us."

"Maybe you just want him period."

That did it. I grabbed the nearest object and hurled it at Dan. "That's the stupidest thing I've ever heard you say." He ducked but the plate smashed into the wall beside him and a chip flicked into his face, cutting it.

"Really?" He wiped his cheek. "Well, I guess you'd recognize stupid when you saw it."

"Get out." It was a scream. I couldn't stand this anymore and if he didn't leave then one of us was going to do something irreversible.

"Don't worry, I'm going."

Dan slammed out of the house, leaving me staring at the wall and the shards of china littering my floor as fury churned in my stomach.

I turned over and over in my head but I couldn't see a way to resolve things. Dan wanted me to live my life his way and I wanted to live it mine.

All I could think was that there was one way I could reduce the number of things for us to fight about.

So I cleaned the floor carefully then headed for my bedroom.

* * *

Forty minutes later, I stepped through the door to Marco's office, wearing a strapless top and my favorite jeans.

Marco looked up from his desk, started to smile then froze as I held up a hand and pulled the door shut.

"I thought you might be thirsty," I said.

THE END

Ash and Dan's adventures continue in
Bring On The Night
Out now!

Want more Ash and Dan?

Did you read Book 1 The Wolf Within?

Bring On The Night (Book 3) is out now.
Find out more on my website www.mjscott.net
To keep up to date with new releases, sign up to my newsletter
at www.mjscott.net.

A Note from M.J.

THE DARK SIDE continues the adventures of Ash and Dan and I hope you're enjoying reading about them. Their story is wrapped up in BRING ON THE NIGHT.

As an indie author, it really helps me when readers get the word out about my books, so if you enjoyed the book, please consider leaving a review at the store where you purchased it and tell your friends!

If you want to stay up to date with all my news, find out about new releases and sales, then please sign up to my newsletter. by using the QR code below.

About the Author

M.J. Scott is an unrepentant bookworm who grew up in a family that fed her a properly varied diet of books. This cemented her story addiction and love of fantasy and romance. So it's not surprising she grew up to write books with both. When not wrestling with the magical worlds in her head, she can generally be found reading, doing something crafty, binge watching, and avoiding housework. She lives in Melbourne, Australia in a small house packed with books, cats, and craft supplies. She also writes romance as Melanie Scott. Her website is www.mjscott.net.

Also by M.J. Scott

Urban fantasy

The TechWitch series

Wicked Games

Wicked Words

Wicked Nights

Wicked Dreams

Wicked Ways

Wicked Deeds

Wicked Lies

The Wild Side series

The Wolf Within

The Dark Side

Bring On The Night

Romantic fantasy

The Four Arts series

The Shattered Court

The Forbidden Heir

The Unbound Queen

Courting The Witch (Prequel novella)

The Daughter of Ravens series

The Exile's Curse

The Traitor's Game

The Rebel's Prize

The Half-Light City series

Shadow Kin

Blood Kin

Iron Kin

Fire Kin

Romance (writing as Melanie Scott)

The Cloud Bay series

Don't Blame Me

Right Where You Left Me

You Belong With Me

The New York Saints series

The Devil in Denim

Angel in Armani

Lawless in Leather

Playing Hard

Playing Fast

Acknowledgments

Thanks to Sarah for beta reading, Sharon for being a web-goddess extraordinaire, the lovely Lulus for writer sanity maintenance, Miriam who is always awesome, and everyone else who has been there for me during this crazy year.

www.ingramcontent.com/pod-product-compliance
Lightning Source LLC
Chambersburg PA
CBHW030659120726
47905CB00001B/286